Godiva and the Golden Dragon

To Kathy,

Steven James

August 12, 2001

#56

Godiva and the Golden Dragon

▼

Steven James

Writer's Showcase
San Jose New York Lincoln Shanghai

Godiva and the Golden Dragon

Writer's Showcase
an imprint of iUniverse.com, Inc.

For information address:
iUniverse.com, Inc.
5220 S 16th, Ste. 200
Lincoln, NE 68512
www.iuniverse.com

ISBN: 0-595-17779-4

Printed in the United States of America

To mom and dad.

Contents

▼

Scotland

North Sea

Northumberland

Stamford
Bridge
York
Beverley

Chester
Mercia
Shrewsbury
England
East
Anglia
Coventry

Wales

Gloucester
London
Kent
Sandwich

Wessex
Bosham
Hastings

England's five major earldoms in the eleventh century

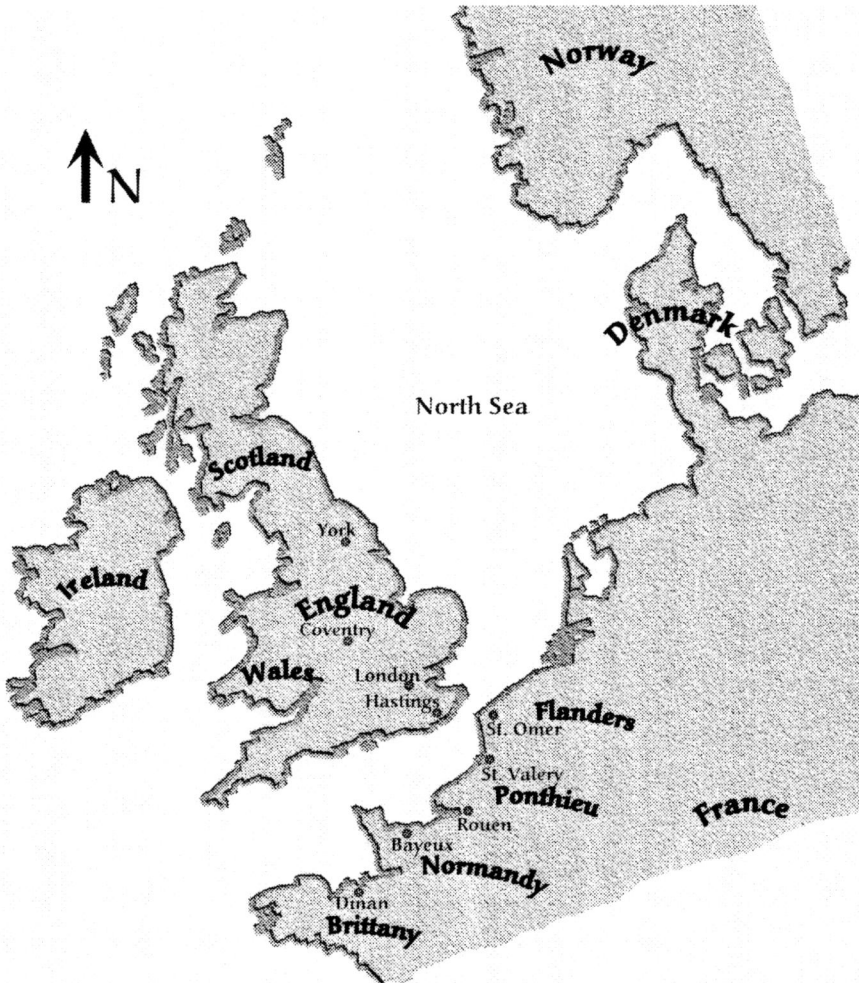

Monarchies around the North Sea in the eleventh century

English Royal Line

Dukes of Normandy

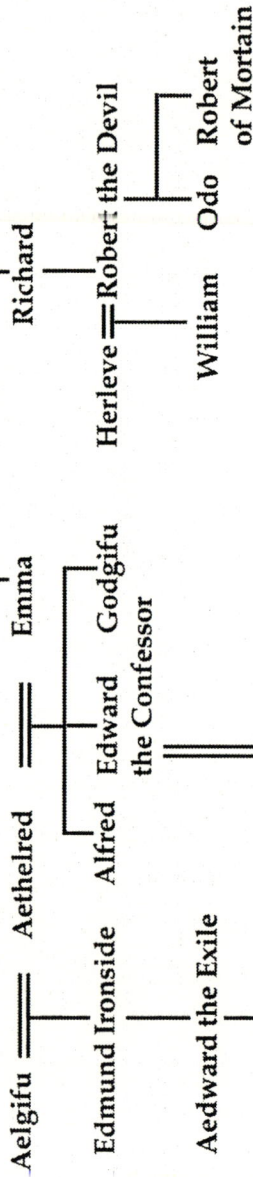

Aelgifu ══ Aethelred ══ Emma ══ Robert the Devil

Richard

Edmund Ironside   Alfred   Edward   Godgifu

Herleve ══ Robert the Devil

the Confessor

Aedward the Exile

William

Odo   Robert
of Mortain

Edgar the Aetheling

House of Wessex

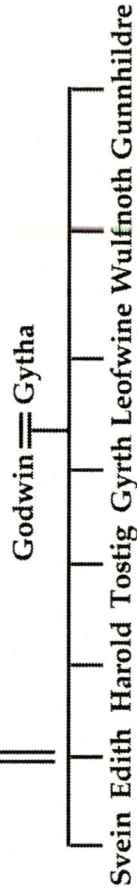

Godwin ══ Gytha

Svein   Edith   Harold   Tostig   Gyrth   Leofwine   Wulfnoth   Gunnhildre

House of Mercia

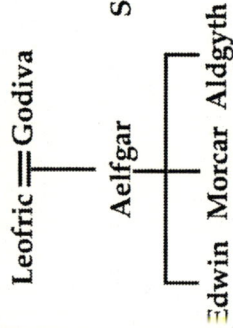

Leofric ══ Godiva

Aelfgar

Edwin   Morcar   Aldgyth

Prologue

▼

The tailor's apprentice opened a shutter and looked out. The familiar street seemed somehow odd. The young man could see the closed windows of the wheelwright's shop across the street, the closed door of the smithy that normally stood open to let the craftsman breath. The quiet inside the tailor's work place was broken only by the giggling of two young girls who ran by outside. Normally bustling with late morning business, the street was strangely soundless with only a few women walking slowly along toward apparently unimportant destinations. There was something peculiar in the air, but the apprentice did not have time to place what gave him that impression before his attention was drawn to some riders coming up the street. A gentle gust of wind brought the dust from the street, kicked up by the approaching ponies, into the young man's face.

The southerly breeze was not itself unusual for that morning; yet, coming from across the Channel it often brought traders and travelers with tales of far away kingdoms of which the young man had only dreamed. The wind this day heralded a new season, and the apprentice guessed that many in Coventry had been out all the previous night celebrating the coming of Springtime. The apprentice glanced over his shoulder, smiling with the thought that the old tailor might have been out all night as well.

Holding the shutter open, the young man peered through the dust to see if the procession in the street might be townsfolk Bringing in the May.

There were only two riders, and it looked to the apprentice to be a pair of women. There were no soldiers or guards. It was a curious thing to see two women traveling without any male escort. Intrigued, the young man stared out the window as the women came into better view.

The woman in front blocked the young man's view of her companion; but by the looks of them, they were not ordinary burghers. The lady he could see must have reached her mid-life. She was dressed in simple attire, but it was clean and ordered as he rarely saw the ladies of the village. The cloth, though cut in an unassuming pattern, looked to be of very rich material and not the simple homespun common for a villager. She rode sidesaddle upon a healthy horse. A strong horse was, again, not a common sight in the Midland town. By the look of it, the woman was probably a servant of a nobleman's household. As the two riders moved by, the woman in back came into view. The apprentice was sure the second woman was younger than the first, although he could see only slim, sleeveless arms stretched out in front of her, one hand on her horse's withers, the other holding the reins of the white palfrey as she guided the beast down the road. The younger woman had an incredible mop of hair that obscured the features of her body. The tailor's apprentice caught sight of her face as she glanced in his direction; olive cheeks and bright blue eyes were framed in the great mane of reddish-brown hair that seemed to be on fire in the sunshine. It all happened so fast; yet time seemed stationary as the man gazed out at the young woman in the street. She was the most beautiful woman he had ever seen, in reality or in his dreams. The scene was strangely ethereal. Had she smiled at him?

The woman looked away. The young man's eyes followed the contours of the long hair that shimmered in the breeze; went wide as the man saw the rider's naked legs across the side of the horse. An uncontrollable feeling of guilt crept over the apprentice. He tried to focus his thoughts, but had no time to determine if he had indeed done something wrong as the guilty feeling rapidly became fear. It suddenly struck the apprentice what it was that had bothered him before.

There were no men in the street.

The young man involuntarily stepped back, letting the shutter he had been holding slam shut just as the older of the two riders motioned toward his open window and cried out. The man did not hear what was said. He backed quickly away into the lightless room, a queasy feeling developing deep within him.

There were no men in the street!

The young man's mind raced. The beautiful woman in the street was surely a spirit, there to take away the men of Coventry! Thom the tailor was gone already. But to heaven or to hell?

Just then, a sound behind him caused him to jump. Something from the Otherworld was in the room and after the young apprentice himself! In a panic, the young man dashed for the back door. The creature shrieked an oath as it grabbed for him, but the apprentice struggled for his life. Kicking and punching, he made his way out the door. The apprentice's hair bristled as he heard the demon cry out his name.

"Lord help me!" the young man screamed as he ran out into the woods.

Book I

▼

AD 1057

Entry I

▼

In which we meet the Earl of Mercia and learn about his young wife

"She did what ? !"

Leofric began to fume, not because he was in a foul mood, but because he had been in such a good mood. The day had begun well as the Earl of Mercia and his party left the two-room hunting lodge outside of Ashby to head for the Nottingham woods. The spring air was fresh on his face, and when the sun actually broke through the overcast earlier than usual, it promised a good day for hunting.

Leofric's bones ached from his hours hunting in the saddle, but the hunting had been good and his pains had been a testament to his physical stamina in having kept up with the younger men of Mercia. Yet, after hearing the latest news from Coventry, he just felt old and sore. He made a deliberate effort to sit up straight in his chair at one end of the main hall in the lodge.

"She did WHAT ? !" Leofric bellowed again louder, standing up to confront the bearer of the bad news. The Earl of Mercia had lost much of his muscle over the years, but Leofric still commanded a presence that many feared.

The man who stood before Leofric was Caedwig, a clergyman of St. Omer in France. His monk's tonsure accentuated the high forehead of his egg-shaped head, and the near-sighted squint did little to soften the somewhat bulging eyes. The eyes and large ears made the cleric look rather like a jester. Still, he was an intelligent man and a messenger of King Edward. This day he had not brought news from Edward, however. Today he came from Coventry with news of Leofric's wife.

"My lord, your wife, the Lady Godiva, did this afternoon ride on horseback through Coventry clothed only in her hair! I swear it is true, for I have only just come from the town, and the whole population is buzzing with the story."

"What in the name of God was she doing?! Naked? In the town? For everyone to see!!" Not waiting for an answer, Leofric bellowed over the monk's head to his servants. "Find my wife, and bring her to me. NOW!"

"Yes my lord, at once my lord!" one of the two servants in the room said as he stumbled into his companion. The two had been collecting the day's kills to be taken out to the separate building that housed the kitchens in preparation for dinner. Aelfgar, Leofric's strapping young son, had stepped into the room, and one of the retreating servants bumped into him, dropping a pheasant at his feet without even realizing he left the room one piece of game short.

Aelfgar bent over and picked up the bird, then swung it up to shake it at his father as if he was holding his mother in front of the man. "Well, Father, what are you going to do with this wife of yours?"

Caedwig stepped back to let the young man address his father. The monk was perhaps a short man, but the son of Leofric at only fourteen years old towered two hands above Caedwig. Aelfgar was much like his father had been as a young man: Of medium build, but already displaying a strength of purpose that commanded respect. Caedwig looked at Aelfgar's face to see if the anger was true, noticing as he suspected that Leofric's son was trying hard not to grin. Seeing his father's stricken look, Aelfgar lost the battle and burst out laughing. The handful of thanes in the room began to laugh as well. The talk at the Earl's court was that Leofric could not control the wife half his age.

"Father, Father, Father! You look as if you just lost your earldom! Perhaps Godwin himself contrived to have you marry the Lady Godiva. There is no time to fuss over his family's scheming when you are too busy trying to control your own wife! Interesting plan. I would not have put it past Godwin's abilities!"

Leofric fell back into his chair with a thud. The Earl's face showed deep lines cut as much by strain's blade as by the scythe of his sixty-one years. His last great coup six years earlier which brought about the exile of his chief rival Godwin and his entire family was a crowning achievement for Leofric. The very next year, however, the Earl of Wessex and his sons were back with their lands and power restored. Leofric's only conciliation was that Godwin himself died the following year.

The Earl's expression showed Aelfgar that he had tread on precarious ground. "Ah, I was only jesting. Everyone knows that you beat Godwin at his own game, and got his entire family exiled from England, even if only for a short time! It is certainly not your fault that King Edward had no spine to stand up to his wife's father Godwin!" Aelfgar glanced toward the monk who was the King's messenger, but Caedwig seemed not to have taken note of his remark against the king. "As for my mother, well, we all know why it is that you go to bed so early after dinner every night when you are so obviously wide awake!" Aelfgar winked at his father. "I think it is clear you are the master of every room in this house!"

"Is it?" Leofric had lost the edge on his anger, but he was still simmering. He grabbed at his son's sleeve and pulled the young man close so he could speak softly. "She tries to influence my decisions as if she would rule alongside, perhaps instead of me. I am Earl here, not her!" Leofric's voice had risen higher than he had wanted, and he looked around the room at his thanes and men-at-arms. The company of men who had been quiet, straining to hear what passed between their Earl and his son, suddenly became wrapped up in a half dozen separate and lively conversations amongst themselves.

"That is right, Father." Aelfgar shook the pheasant he was still holding, threw some of his father's words back at Leofric now. "Wives are like this bird...beautiful in flight but made to be caught and used to sustain us men! Like a stubborn workhorse, you must simply draw the reins a bit tighter when they get a mind of their own, and strike them when they refuse to do your bidding. That is all.

"I must admit, though", Aelfgar chuckled, "this latest stunt is an interesting one!"

Leofric's temper flared again. "What in the name of God was she thinking about today? Aelfgar, she rode through Coventry...naked! Can I let that kind of exhibition go unpunished?!"

"But, my lord, you did suggest she do just that!" Caedwig broke in.

Leofric turned to the monk and stood up again. "What are you talking about? Why would I tell my wife to flaunt her naked body in front of God and everyone? You may be the messenger of the King, but be careful what you say to me in my house!"

Aelfgar stepped between his father and the monk, although he knew his father would never strike a clergyman. "It is true, Father. Last night at dinner, in front of the entire household, you did make such a suggestion."

"Are you telling me I am mad? Why would I have ever uttered such a crazy notion unless I was mad?"

"No, not mad. But you were a bit drunk, Father."

Aelfgar's broad grin took the edge off of his father's fury. Leofric sat down again, and looked from his son to Caedwig, waiting for an explanation. Caedwig had no personal ambitions, and that allowed him to expend his energy fully in the name of King Edward. That strength of purpose supported him in confrontations such as the one he found himself in now.

"My lord," Caedwig said quietly, "you know that I have been at your court for a couple days now urging you to remit the high taxes on the people of Mercia. King Edward desires that the heavy tax burden on his subjects be lifted. All of the earls of England are to comply with his initiative."

"I cannot have a conversation with you that you do not mention the high taxes! My people are not taxed too much! The people of Mercia help to pay for the protection of their own homes and villages from the Welsh, and other foreign raiders. Surely King Edward knows this. I tax them no more than necessary."

"Oh, but you do, my lord." Caedwig was ready to press his point. "I have traveled through your lands over the past week, and it is clear that the people are overburdened. The Welsh have not been so active lately to demand that the protection of the people come at such a high tax rate. If you would just open your eyes, you would see that the people of the Midlands are suffering. Only today it was that I saw in Coventry—"

"In Coventry you saw a Benedictine monastery which I have sponsored!" Leofric snapped. "I didn't hear any of you clergymen complaining when I used tax money to build that!"

Caedwig was nonplused. "It is the people that I saw in Coventry—"

"Damn the people of Coventry! What has this got to do with my wife!" Leofric was standing up again, and again his son stepped between the Earl and the monk.

Putting a hand on his father's shoulder, Aelfgar said, "It was last night, Father, as I said."

"The subject of the high taxes came up, and the Lady Godiva chose to champion my cause," Caedwig said confidently. "She suggested that you go out and see the suffering of the people."

Leofric began to boil again, "I remember that you hounded me about the taxes until I could hardly enjoy my dinner! And I remember that my wife supported you over her lord and husband only because she is pious and you are a representative of the Holy Church. Did I then force her to display her naked body to the world as punishment for not agreeing with me?"

"Almost." Aelfgar was beginning to laugh again, realizing that his father really had no memory of the latter part of the dinner.

Leofric sat down again. His knees really ached. "Explain yourself, son, and be quick about it!"

Aelfgar put a hand up toward Caedwig who was about to speak again, and stepped over next to his father's chair. He respected his father, but he was enjoying this. It was not often that his father drank to excess. "Let us see…it was sometime after your tenth or eleventh cup of ale, Father." Leofric scowled, but Aelfgar continued with a smile. "You beckoned for my mother to accompany you to yonder bedchamber. But she held back, and we all heard her say that she was sure the Earl would not retire before satisfying the entreaty of the King's messenger."

Caedwig cut in. "And that entreaty is that you promise to lower taxes!"

Aelfgar put up one hand to silence the monk, and his other hand on his father's shoulder who was about to stand up to face Caedwig again. "The Lady Godiva did suggest that you travel to Coventry and look over your people and lands to see what taxes may not be necessary. I fear that I may have made things worse by suggesting that perhaps you would take more note of the people of Mercia if they all looked like your wife. When we all laughed at that, you yourself added…let me see…what did you say exactly? Oh yes: 'The day mi'lady Godiva gallops through Coventry as bare as a babe will be the day that I remove the taxes.' It sure sounded funny at the time!"

"As it was meant to!" Leofric was beginning to remember something of the interchange. "It was only said in jest!"

Aelfgar laughed again. "But apparently mother knows not your sense of humor! She did take your meaning literally, it seems."

"As did I," added Caedwig. "Although it should not have required this sort of display by your wife, I do expect you to stand by your word."

"You put her up to this!" Leofric was up once again and stepping toward the monk holding out an accusing finger. Aelfgar was right behind him, putting his hands on his father's shoulders to calm the Earl down.

"Father, relax. I am sure Caedwig did not incite my mother to make her shameless ride. No." Aelfgar smiled his big broad smile again. "You must take this up with our Lady Godiva herself."

"Indeed I will! And, where is she? I sent for her long ago!" Leofric glared around the room, daring anyone to meet his gaze, but at the same time expecting an answer. The room was filled with a large dining table in the center. There were a handful of men in attendance besides Aelfgar, Leofric's thanes from Leicester and Nottingham shires who had gone hunting with their Earl. The men shuffled their feet and looked from one to the other, shrugging and waving their hands. The servant Leofric had sent out of the room earlier to fetch the mistress of the house was hovering at the door. Neither did he want to come in and face the Earl's anger upon receiving the bad news he carried, nor could he leave without delivering that news to someone. He tried in vain to catch the Lord Aelfgar's attention before Earl Leofric noticed him.

"You there!" It was too late for the servant, Leofric had spotted him and was coming toward the door. "Did I not send you to bring the Lady Godiva to me straight away?" Leofric reached the doorway and planted his feet in a wide stance, with his hands on his hips clenched into fists.

"Where is she? Speak up, man!"

"My lord—", the servant's voice cracked and he swallowed through a dry throat. "My lord, the Lady is...not here."

"What?" Leofric exploded. "Where is my wife?!" He grabbed the servant and shook him back and forth.

"Where is the Lady Godiva?"

"Ah, Lord Leofric, she is not in your private chamber, nor is she in the kitchens. The groomsmen at the stables have told me that the stall where her horse should be is indeed empty. Her attendants seem to think she is still in Coventry, probably at the lord Earl's residence."

Leofric released the servant with a strong push out of the way, and the man scurried out the door and out of sight. The Earl of Mercia turned to the men in the room with a grave look as if he were in a war council. "Men, we ride for Coventry at once! Someone bring me fresh riding clothes!"

Entry II

▼

In which we meet the Lady Godiva and the Welshman named Davydd

Lady Godiva was seated on the edge of her bed, trying with difficulty to pull off her left riding boot. Her long hair kept getting in the way as she struggled with the tight boots. As the boot came off with a pop, she wondered why she had bothered to put them on at all after her ride through Coventry when she wore nothing. The maidservant Hildreth reached to help with the right boot. The young woman leaned back with her elbows on the bed and pulled her foot out as Hildreth stumbled back with the empty boot in her hands. The afternoon sun shown through the bedroom window to light up Godiva's thick light brown hair that jostled back out of her face, offering a sharp contrast to her smooth, olive tinted skin. Her hair had a hint of red that gave it an unearthly glow in sunlight. Her features were even, with a strong chin line yielding to soft cheeks that framed her full lips. Her symmetric nose was not large, yet not too small to be lost between her large, blue topaz eyes. Long eyelashes accentuated those glowing orbs that looked up to her maidservant with feigned innocence.

"Well, Hildreth, he told me to do it!"

"You are a grown woman. Do not act like a child! You know his lordship will be angry!" Hildreth had reached her forty-second year only a month ago, but she still felt young and strong. She had filled out in the past few years, but she swore to herself that she would never get as fat and homebound as some of the women she had grown up with in Chester. That is why Hildreth had welcomed the chance to serve the Earl's young wife after her own husband had passed away.

Hildreth had ridden right alongside as Lady Godiva left for the town of Coventry that morning, and she had known what her lady was planning. She also knew better than to think the Earl would take it lightly, and she felt it was her place to admonish her rash mistress.

"Lord Leofric has probably returned from his day of hunting already, and I expect he has heard the story by now. Better if it had come from your mouth and in private, my lady."

"No, it does not matter. As long as I get his attention. Leofric only wants me to warm his loins when he climbs into bed, and warm his backside before he gets out in the morning! There is more to me than that! Yet, the only way I can accomplish anything is by using my body against Leofric. The only reason Leofric had endowed the building of the monastery at Coventry is because, if he did so, I promised to stop praying aloud while he had his way with me. If the only way I can get the taxes of Mercia lowered is by riding through Coventry like a shameless Danish harlot, then so be it." Godiva dropped her head into her hands to hide her tears, and her mass of hair sprawled out about her like a curtain.

"Ah Hildreth! I am worth more than that!"

Hildreth dropped the boot she was holding and stepped back to the bed. A small cat, black save for little white mittens and a white belly, had been asleep on the oak settle next to the door of the room. Awakened by the falling boot, the feline sensed Godiva's distress and jumped onto the bed to curl next to the young woman. The cat began to purr, offering the kind of support only he could. The maidservant brushed Godiva's long hair aside and sat down next to the young woman, reaching her arm over to try and console her mistress.

"There, there, dear. I know how it is."

"Do you? You were married, but to someone you chose. It was my father's wish, as Leofric's thane in Coventry, that I marry Leofric, and who was I to gainsay his authority?" Godiva became aware of the little animal pressing his head against the back of her hand. She brought her hand up to rub the cat's eye ridges, and the animal's purring became a roar.

"I knew my husband was many years my senior, but I had expected he would have an ear for my thoughts. He does not know a thing about me. He takes me almost every night, and I satisfy him as a proper wife should. But he never once tries to please me. I do not think he would be able to if he tried. He would not know how! Mayhap I could have loved Leofric; but, Hildreth, I did not know what love was all about when I married the man fifteen long years ago!"

"And now you do?" Hildreth was thinking about Davydd, and was sure Godiva was too. "You must be careful, young lady. You are the wife of the Earl of Mercia! People are starting to talk about how you spend so much time with that young minstrel from Wales."

"Oh, I know you do not approve of Davydd. But, the time I spend with him is all too short, and he is harmless."

"Not so harmless if the Earl finds out about the attention you give to this foreigner. What do you see in him, anyway? The man has nothing. He can offer you nothing…nothing but heartache."

"No. He offers me the respect I give to him. We talk about things, and he listens to my thoughts. That is something my husband has never done. I have often wondered why I did not grow to love Leofric as my father said I would. I respect Leofric as the Earl of Mercia, but I do not respect him as my husband; and he surely has no respect for me or he would treat me differently. Respect. Maybe that is the root of true

Love." The cat began to press his claws gently into Godiva's hair sprawled out on the bed.

"Listen to yourself talk of pretty words like 'love' and 'respect'. You have to be realistic. If you want to be the mistress in the house of the Earl, then you must act as such. And all that entails is to be humble before your husband and bear his children if the Good Lord wills it."

"But I do not just want to be the mistress in the house of an earl! I want more out of life." Godiva saw the skeptical look that came over her maid-servant's face. "Perhaps when I was twelve years old I dreamed about what it would be like to be the wife of a rich thane, or perhaps even of an earl. But I am grown up now, as you so often feel the need to remind me. I know there is more to life than just the richness of fine sheets and the brightness of gold jewelry. Is it a sin to want to find Love in this world?" Godiva broke down again in sobs. Her hair rippled like Autumn leaves blown in the breeze.

"No young lady." Hildreth took her mistress' head in her lap and stroked her temples. "It is not wrong to want to be loved. But you must realize your position and seek the goodness in what you have. You are not wanting for anything, as many of your ancestors were. You have a husband that does not beat you, and that is a mercy. My own had broken the rule of thumb on occasion to chastise me with a switch as thick as his wrist! You have me and your other servants who do love you. And the people of Mercia adore you! Even if your stunt today does not sway the Earl, you will be remembered for ages by your people as their champion! In the crowded marketplace of Coventry today I heard the people associating you with the legends of Aethelflaed, the daughter of Alfred the Great! You have much more than most young women could ever dream of achiev-ing."

"I know, I know. I have much; but I lack something truly important!"

"And this Davydd can give you this all important thing that would make everything you already have pale in significance?"

Lady Godiva looked at Hildreth, but realized her remark was not meant to mock her, there was too much concern in her maidservant's eyes. The young woman got up and went to her bedroom window to gaze out at the countryside. The cat looked up, meowed in disappointment.

"I do not know, Hildreth. Yes, Davydd offers me respect…respect for my thoughts and an interest in my feelings; but sometimes I wonder if he too is lacking in qualities I find important. He seems to lack a sense of loyalty and purpose. If I could take some aspects of Davydd, and perhaps some aspects of Leofric—" Godiva sighed. "Am I just a silly girl to think I can have everything the way I want?"

"Silly? No, let us say simply a bit unrealistic. Look, child, every woman would like to find the perfect man; but, I am not sure the 'perfect man' exists. Men, on the other hand, have no problem finding women to suit them. The 'perfect woman' would be a young, clean girl with a slim body and a comely face, large firm breasts and a lively disposition in the bedchamber. When it comes down to it, the last of these qualities seems to be the most important. If a man does not find that he is married to this 'perfect woman', then he finds one in a brothel. It is not so easy for us women. We marry with the hope that we will come to love the man we share our bed with. If not, well, we have our home and our children. You must take what you have got, count your blessings and be as happy as possible."

Godiva walked back to the bed where her maidservant and the cat still sat. When the animal stood up and looked at Godiva expectantly, she picked him up and held him over her shoulder. "I do not believe that every man is so shallow! Do you really think that summarizes all men's desires?"

"Yes, I am afraid I do, my dear. Oh, each man, with his distinct character, may appear to have desires that are different from other men; but when it comes down to judgment, he is looking for one thing only in his woman. Your Welsh minstrel, for example. It is his character which allows him to show respect for your thoughts and feelings. But do not get it in your head that he does so purely out of respect for your mind! It is my firm belief that that man wants your body; and, once he gets that, he will be off again to his foreign land!"

"Yours is a cruelly pessimistic view of the world, Hildreth! I am surprised I had never noticed it before. Nevertheless, I—" Lady Godiva stopped as she heard a knock at the door to her bedchamber. The cat turned to look toward the doorway, pupils wide.

Hildreth stood up and started for the door as it began to open. "Lady Godiva? My lady?" A man's rich, bass voice filtered through the crack in the door, the words sounding strange with the thick Celtic accent.

"Ah, speak of the Devil!" Hildreth mumbled as she moved to bar the doorway. "How dare you enter into my mistress' bedchamber unannounced!" The cat scrambled out of Godiva's hands to hide under the bed.

"Peace, Hildreth," Godiva called. "Please let the man in. With you here as a chaperone, there can be nothing unseemly about this meeting. Besides, the room could use a more jovial personality in it to brighten it up right now!"

Hildreth glanced back at Lady Godiva, squinting her eyes in silent defiance. She would not question her mistress in public as she would in private. "As you wish, my lady, only remember my warning."

The man at the door stooped a little to keep from hitting his head to the top of the doorway as he entered the room. He was indeed a handsome man, Hildreth had to admit: Tall and agile, with hair as dark as a raven. He was slightly too thin, the older woman thought, suggesting he only developed enough muscle on his bones to wield a lute. His large brown eyes seemed to look right through her, and it was clear to Hildreth that the foreigner knew she did not approve of the attention he lavished on her mistress. But then, she did not really try hard to hide her disaffection. Davydd entered the room and made a formal, yet ever so slight bow toward the maidservant as he passed her by to approach the Lady Godiva. To the young woman the minstrel dropped to one knee, at the same time reaching out his right hand to catch her left in a gentle caress.

"My lady, it is good to see that you have not come to any harm after such a brash undertaking as you made this day." As the Welshman bowed his head over the Lady Godiva's hand, his eyes were drawn to her bare feet that shown below her riding shift. Seeing a part of this young woman naked that would normally be covered had a direct effect on his loins and caught the man off guard. When he was away from Godiva, he would tend to forget just how strongly the young woman's body could affect him. He lingered for a moment longer than necessary while his lips brushed over the soft skin of her hand. Before raising his eyes to hers, he tried hard to suppress the shudder of desire that threatened to overtake him each time he set his eyes on Godiva.

"Lady Godiva, you are more beautiful each day that I am fortunate to behold you."

"Your foreign manners are far too kind, but I thank you for suggesting that my humble appearance is more than that of a simple farm girl. I am dusty and tired from riding in the country today, and I cannot possibly look that good right now!" Godiva had grown accustomed to hearing compliments from the Welshman, and she found she rather liked them. Her husband had never made any comment that was not purely a lewd or suggestive remark.

"Riding in the country indeed!" When Davydd stood up, he towered over both women. "Is it true, my dear lady? Did you ride through this town today without the encumbrance of your riding attire? It is a small wonder that you did not incite a riot in the street! I am not sure I will ever understand you English women!"

Lady Godiva looked up at the exotic foreigner and met his gaze. "Have you come to berate my choice of action as my maidservant has done already?" Hildreth started at that, since she had not cautioned against making the ride, only against underestimating the Earl Leofric's reactions. But she could see that her lady was only teasing a bit at her expense, and she stayed quiet in the corner of the room to which she had retired a moment earlier.

Davydd swung his arms out in a gesture characteristic of the expressive foreigner. "On the contrary, Great Lady! It is my thought that your actions do speak out as loudly and clearly as a bard calling to the gods. It is also my hope that you will allow me to write a ballad of this day so that the poetry of your youthful endeavor can reside forever in the hearts of your countryfolk! Oh, to have been there in Coventry to see your glorious ride through the market place!" Davydd glanced down the length of Lady Godiva's loose fitting dress, trying in vain to envision just how she looked clothed only in her hair, which is long, but not long enough to have covered her entire body. Another stirring in his loins at just the thought of the girl's bare legs gave him a hint of what the sight in Coventry might have done to him had he been there.

Hildreth could not keep quiet. "It would have made no difference if you had been in Coventry. The lady's escort cleared the streets ahead of her so that my lady's ride this day was completely innocent."

"Cleared the streets, you say?" The Welshman gestured with his right hand toward the center of town, while bringing his left hand to his head to brush back his wavy hair. "Was there no one to see the remarkable spectacle? I was a bit jealous thinking of the others who might have seen my lady; but was there no one to attest to my lady's proud display? More's the pity." Davydd's eyes focused once again on the young woman's bare feet. "The Lady Godiva would have had the whole world at her feet!"

Lady Godiva sat down on her dressing chair and crossed her legs, reaching her arms out to clasp her hands around her upraised knee. Feigning shock, her eyes went wide as she gazed up at Davydd. "You do not think I would taunt the men of Coventry as a woman of pleasure in the market square?!"

Hildreth had followed the foreigner's gaze. "Indeed, it is that which we hoped to avoid. Yet, there is perhaps more wanton abandon right here in this room than there had been in the streets today!" The maidservant reached for the night slippers at the end of the bed and bent in front of

Godiva to put them on, putting herself between the man and the woman on purpose.

"No! Please forgive my thoughtless suggestion!" Davydd had been watching the young woman's feet as she moved to sit down, and he had not realized that Godiva was teasing until he looked up to see the sparkle in those wide eyes. Hildreth, on the other hand, was completely serious. "Ah, my lady," Davydd continued, "I only thought that your actions should have been witnessed by someone so that the ballad I write of this day will be known to be true!"

Lady Godiva smiled, "Not to worry, my dear minstrel. Hildreth did but mean that the men of the town were ushered out of sight. There are plenty of women in Coventry who will attest to my deed this day. Hildreth herself rode right beside me. Perhaps you can get the story first hand from her as material for your ballad!"

"Do not involve me in any work with this…this foreigner! I do beseech you, my lady, ask your guest to leave so that you may freshen up after the long day. You must be ready to greet your husband the Earl when he comes home."

"Leofric is off hunting, I do not expect him to be back soon." Godiva glanced over her shoulder where she could see the afternoon sun just over the window ledge.

"Do not fool yourself, my lady," Davydd said. "I am sure a messenger has already brought the news of your ride to the Earl, and we know he is a jealous man when it comes to his beautiful young wife." He gave her a wink. "Do you know what you will say to him?"

"What she will say is for his ears, not yours!" Hildreth was getting annoyed with the Welshman's casual familiarity with her mistress. "Please, my lady, ask this man to leave. I would like to go draw water for your bath, but I cannot leave the two of you unattended."

"Very well, Hildreth." Lady Godiva stood up and slipped her arm through Davydd's as she ushered the man to the door. "Please go now, my good man, and look for me at the dinner table. We will talk then about more interesting things than my deeds this day."

"I will find it hard to keep my eyes away from you, my lady." As they reached the door, Davydd spoke a little louder, "Your maidservant does not care much for me, I fear. But, I do thank you for this audience. As always, I am your servant." He bowed low over Godiva's hand, pressing once again the smooth skin to his lips. "Until dinner then!"

When the Welshman had gone, Hildreth took hold of the hands of her mistress and paused a moment to look into the young woman's eyes. "The foreigner is right about one thing, my lady. You should be thinking of what you will say to the Earl your husband. Perhaps you could say that monk did pressure you to do this deed."

"Hildreth! For shame! You ask me to put the blame for my own actions on an innocent man? Caedwig did only commend my plan to heed my husband's drunken suggestion. Besides, I do not want my efforts to get Leofric's attention to come to naught. He must know that I am serious."

"Yes, but the Earl is a proud man. You must also be ready to give in somewhere, yield something to him lest he take his frustration out on your attendants, and perhaps even yourself! The Earl will need to feel he is in control of some of this affair, at least."

"You are right, of course. I will think on it."

Hildreth left the young woman alone with her thoughts. Lady Godiva sat down at her dressing table and looked at her reflection in the shiny hammered and polished metal on the wall. She had never had such a mirror as a young girl, nor had her mother. Her fine clothes and jewelry she had only because she had become the wife of the Earl of Mercia. So many other women would be content with that. Why was she not satisfied? Why did she feel the need to assert some kind of control over her husband, when it required her to do such outlandish things as she had done this day? She deplored having to use her sexuality to get through to Leofric, yet that seemed the only way he would take notice of her feelings. The young woman in the reflection stared back at the Earl's wife with the question in her eyes: "What is it exactly that you do want, Godiva?"

Entry III

▼

In which the Earl of Mercia faces his wife

The ride from the hunting lodge outside of Ashby to his residence just north of Coventry would normally have been a pleasant one for the Earl of Mercia. This evening, however, Leofric was already tired from his day of hunting, and he was beginning to regret having not waited until he was more rested before departing for the town where his wife was sure to be. He shifted his weight upon his pony and let out a soft groan.

"What was that, Father?" Aelfgar was riding next to the Earl, the handful of thanes with them a few paces behind. The monk Caedwig brought up the rear of the group along with the Earl's manservants. "Are you sore from the day's riding," Aelfgar chuckled, "or are you apprehensive about meeting Mother?"

"It is the ride, of course," Leofric grunted.

"You have grown soft, Father," the younger man teased. "The land here in the Midlands is not so rugged as near our home in Chester among the foothills of the Cambrian mountains of Wales. Many still think of you as the Earl of Chester, but lucky for you they do not know you have left all the border control in my hands!"

The Earl took the bait. "If you expect to be the next Earl of Mercia, you must learn to deal with our Welsh neighbors. That is the only reason I have left Chester to you of late." That, and the damper climate that wreaks havoc with my joints, Leofric thought.

Aelfgar laughed. "I still think it is my lady Mother you are thinking about!"

"Bah," Leofric exclaimed, kicking his mount a little harder than necessary. "I will take control over Godiva's stunt, turn her actions into deeds done in my name. If any man saw her naked, then some heads will roll!

Leofric continued as his son caught up and matched his pony's now faster pace. "Truly, it was not just of your mother that I was thinking. The news that you brought to me from Sandwich was good to hear. I am glad to know that the Bishop of Worcester will be back in England soon. Bishop Aldred has been gone now over three years! But our efforts have finally born fruit. The extra taxes I have levied over these past years have allowed me to raise the ransom demanded by Hungary for the release of Aedward the Exile."

Though young yet, Aelfgar had already learned to enjoy the taste of the intrigues of English politics. "I daresay your old rival Godwin will turn over in his grave when the grandson of Aethelred comes back from his exile in Hungary!"

Leofric laughed. "Would that I could be at the crypt to feel the stones shake! When the old Earl of Wessex had his daughter Edith married to King Edward, I thought then that all was lost. With a Godwin in almost every earldom in England, and a Godwin as an heir to Edward, I truly did worry about the future of the country itself. But, it is obvious now that Edward will not sire a son, nor apparently any child in this lifetime. Having Aedward back in England will put pressure on the house of Godwin. The King's nephew is the most logical heir to the throne. We must make it clear to Aedward who it was that afforded his release from

Hungary. Before the sons of Godwin can get to him, we must meet Aedward and set him firmly on our side of the fence. The royal Golden Dragon Banner may yet fly next to the Banner of Mercia."

Aelfgar asked the question that he had heard all too often himself. "Father, when the time comes, will not Harold Godwinsson of Wessex back his cousin and friend Svend, the King of Denmark, as the next king of England?"

"Perhaps, my son. Godwin himself always backed the Danish line. But with Edward's reign having restored the English royal line of Aethelred, I do believe the English people will not want to go back to Danish rule. I do not think the Witan would ever back the Earl of Wessex in such an endeavor."

The young man laughed. "Well, perhaps now you should stop thinking about English politics, and look to the concerns of your household." Aelfgar pointed ahead. "We are almost to Coventry. There in the distance is a group of your men now, coming out to greet you. Have you a suitable punishment in mind for my lady mother?"

Leofric scowled, then forced a smile. "Even as I think to chastise my wife, so too do I look forward to bedding her this eve," the Earl of Mercia laughed. "It is a struggle, my son!"

"I too would seek the comfort of my wife this night, if she were here." Aelfgar thought of the young girl who he had gotten pregnant earlier that year. She was not a bad match, and he decided to marry her; especially after her father, an influential merchant in Chester, put some pressure on the Earl of Mercia. Now she was getting heavy with child, and not quite so much fun in bed. "A pity she is in Chester! Perhaps a young wench down at the hothouse in town will be interested in warming me up this eve."

A group of four housecarls rode up to meet the Earl's incoming party. The soldiers were in similar attire, unencumbered with any warrior chainmail and having on only leather jerkins underneath simple riding cloaks. Each had a short sword in a scabbard at their waist, and light leather helmets capping their heads. Leofric chose to be infuriated by the soldiers' particularly slow pace, and he kicked his tired mount on to meet them. As the Earl approached his men, he recognized Gunthnot, the captain in charge of his wife's personal escort. The young man was of mixed Danish and Anglo-Saxon blood, the distinction having lost much of its significance over Leofric's lifetime.

"You, Gunthnot! Have you nothing of importance to say to me that you amble toward your Lord Earl as if he were just a traveling bead trader?! Why did none of my sworn men bring me today's news from Coventry?"

When Gunthnot took command of the Lady Godiva's personal guard, he did swear to the Earl Leofric that he would serve the lady until the day she might have reason to dismiss him. In the young captain's mind, that put the lady's desires above the lord's. Gunthnot had come to admire the Lady Godiva, and he enjoyed commanding her personal guard.

"My lord. I had arranged to send a messenger to you straight away, but the Lady Godiva did ask that I hold off until tomorrow."

"She did, did she? And did you think that a messenger sent to me tomorrow would suffice? I should ring your neck with a tight rope, boy!"

"My lord, I have sworn to follow the Lady Godiva's orders and wishes. You yourself did have me swear such an oath. If I had thought your household or Earldom in danger, you know that I would have notified you at once. As it was only a simple—"

"A simple what?" Leofric bellowed. "Did you not think your lady's actions today would have been of interest to me?!"

Gunthnot was adamant. "My lord, it was nothing. I assure you my men did act in the best interests of the Earl even as we followed our lady's bidding. I do not know what you have heard, but—"

"Damn you, man! I have heard nothing, since you failed to think it was necessary to send a messenger to me at Ashby!" Control yourself, Leofric thought.

"My lord," Gunthnot began again, but was cut off as Leofric urged his horse into a canter.

"I do not want to hear anything more from you now, captain. Bring your men, and escort me to my manor. There the story will be told in full. If you have more to say, you will have your chance before I decide whether or not to remove you from my service!" Leofric kicked the flank of his horse again, and the animal galloped away from the group of men standing their mounts in the field.

Leofric found he was steering his horse on a course to bypass the central part of town. He slowed and stopped, glancing toward the road that went right through town. With only a slight hesitation, he redirected his horse toward the town common. Better that his thanes see he is not so embarrassed that he cannot face the burghers.

Coventry, primarily a farming and pastoral community, was completely different from the Earl's residence in Cheshire. The thriving metropolitan city of Chester was the one thing Leofric did miss after moving to the Midlands. After marrying Godiva, Leofric and his new wife sponsored the building of a Benedictine monastery at Coventry; an establishment which brought prosperity to the area and which ultimately made the town into a regional trading center.

Leofric liked to take credit for his far-sighted plans; yet, the Earl still missed the chance to mingle with the variety of peoples in Chester: Welshmen, Irish, some Scots and other foreigners, as well as those of Anglo-Saxon and Danish blood. At least Davydd the Welshman and a few other courtiers that followed him to the Midlands from Chester offered him a change from the simple folks by whom he found himself surrounded.

Not helping the mood of the Earl of Mercia, the weather had changed from the afternoon sun to an overcast, damp evening. As Leofric started down the main street of Coventry, it began to drizzle, leaving the old man soaked fairly quickly.

Late in the day, and with the wet weather, there were very few of the townspeople in the street or out in the market square. A man herded a pair of droopy oxen that grunted with each step as they pulled a rickety dray full of building stones. A younger man was busily scrambling along the north wall of a small structure that adjoined the shop of the blacksmith. The young man was clearing crumbled parts of a wall at the blacksmith shop, preparing for the new stones the ox-driver was delivering.

Neither the ox-driver nor the younger man seemed to notice Leofric and his small retinue. Leofric scowled. So much for his display of control.

Tallow candles burned in most of the buildings along the route, their meager light diffracting along the edges of small animal skins hung over the cottage windows. Smoke billowed from most every stone chimney as the burghers sat down to their rough hewn log tables for a dinner of fresh bread and mutton. The walls of wattle cemented with clay, and the thick thatched roofs kept most all of the family conversation within each private abode, except at the alehouse. There, sharp bursts of laughter and drunken singing could already be heard for a good distance down the street as some of the men of Coventry chose to begin their evening with wine and ale instead of goat's milk and meat. Leofric thought of what Caedwig the monk said about the people of Coventry. "The people do not seem to be struggling too hard," the Earl mumbled to himself.

Leofric glanced over his shoulder at his son Aelfgar who had slowed down a bit as they passed by the brothel that adjoined the alehouse. The younger man caught his father's look, and he smiled. "You know, Father, it has been a long day, and lousy now with this incessant mizzle. I do feel my bodily humors directing me to the warmth of yonder hothouse! If only I did not so strongly wish to see your meeting with my lady Mother this night!"

"Do not act as if the interactions between your mother and myself are put on for the amusement of the household, my boy!" Leofric reprimanded the younger man with feigned indignation. He was still angry with his wife and exhausted with the days riding; but he could hold nothing against the light of youth in his son's eyes. The Earl sometimes found himself needing to draw strength out of the energy that seemed to exude from Aelfgar. "You are young, Aelfgar, and there is plenty of time to know the delicacies of women. But go now, if you cannot hold out, and warm yourself by the flirting fires of the females in that house. I myself will be wanting a good meal!"

"Oh, I suppose I can come back here later after we have supped and you have spoken to Lady Godiva. Show or not, I truly do not wish to miss the interchange!"

The company had left the main street behind and had come up to the courtyard of the manor house where the Earl had taken up residence since his wife's father passed away. A housecarl at the gate recognized the master of the place, and had swung the gate wide as the riders approached, calling for the young groomsmen to come out and fetch the tired horses. Leofric jumped off his horse and grabbed at the closest stable boy.

"You there! Let the others take care of the horses. I want you to go and tell Lady Godiva I do wish to see her straight away." Even as he spoke, a plan was forming in the Earl's mind. Leofric grabbed the boy's shoulder. "No, have my chamber men draw warm water for my bath. I will change out of these riding clothes and cleanse myself. Then I will be ready for dinner. Have the lady await me in the hall."

Leofric smiled to himself. His own chambers directly adjoined those of Godiva. He could easily have met Godiva in her room after he had freshened up. But then he would be on her terms. This way she would know he was right next door and know that he did not desire to see her until he was ready. In fact, he would take his time changing, he thought. Let Godiva wait a bit alone in the hall with the dinner guests. His thanes will be expecting a display just as was his son Aelfgar. Leofric laughed silently, "let them all wait until the Earl of Mercia chose to join them!"

Leofric let the body servants in his chamber undress him. They moved slowly, playing for time while their companions brought in warmed water from the kitchens on such short notice. For once Leofric did not mind their incompetence. He had all the time in the world. When the bath was half full, Leofric climbed in, motioning to the nervous servants to continue to bring in water. It was good to submerge his joints in warmth after the long day. After soaking for a long moment, Leofric beckoned to a waiting servant to bring soap and scrub brush. As a young man he had disdained to take too many baths; but as he had grown older, the Earl found the warm water very therapeutic.

Leofric climbed out of the bath and dried himself on the towel handed to him. His servants spoke not a word, and he said nothing to them until he saw the clean clothes they had laid out for him to wear. Leofric scowled at the dark brown cloth.

"No! I will wear the purple mantle with red dragon embroidery! The material was a gift from King Edward, and in it I do look splendid."

Not waiting for the servants to fetch the clothes he requested, Leofric stamped across the room to dig through a pile of garments in the corner. Finding the one he sought, the Earl slipped into the loose overshirt. He sat down to let one of the servants lace his sandals. Leofric stood up and stretched. The short bath had relaxed him somewhat, and he was not so sore as when he first arrived. He had waited enough time. He was ready to face his wife.

Leofric pushed his way through his chamber men and out of his room into the adjoining dining hall. The clamor of conversation suddenly stopped as the Earl strode around the room to take his place in the fireside seat. He watched the eyes of his thanes as he moved passed them, eyes that watched him in turn. They were anxious yet also much amused by the whole affair. The Earl of Mercia could see that these men respected him; he was not going to lose their faith through any ridiculous actions by his wife. Leofric held his head high as he stepped around the room and came to stand at the head of his table. Leofric smiled broadly, glancing expectantly to his right where his wife's chair was.

The chair was empty.

All his confidence seemed to drain out of him, sapping his strength as well. The Earl of Mercia fell back into his chair, still looking at the vacant place beside him. He felt his seat sore from riding and his elbows and knees ached. Leofric realized he was tensing up. He took a deep breath and tried to relax. He realized he was still staring at the empty seat, and slouching in his chair. He straightened up and looked around the room. There were a couple murmurs from the other side of the room; but all eyes were on him, waiting.

Perhaps none of the people assembled knew he had expected his wife to be waiting for him, Leofric wondered. He had not made an obvious order out of it except in his own mind. He suddenly felt very hungry, and, clapping his hands together, he yelled, "Where are my lazy servants?! Bring on the food! Now! My guests and I are hungry. And let us have some music!"

There was a bustle at the door that led out to the kitchens in the adjoining building. Three servants scurried out of the room; but one hung back. "My lord, do you wish to await your lady, the Mistress Godiva? I am told she will be here shortly."

Leofric slammed his hand down on the table. "Damn it man! If I wanted to wait for Godiva I would certainly not have just ordered the dinner to be served!" Forcing somewhat of a smile, Leofric continued, "The Lady Godiva will join us when she can. My men and I are hungry, but not so hungry that we will eat everything and leave nothing for your mistress!"

One of the thanes broke out in laughter, and the other men at the table followed. The room was filled with jesting and light conversation as the food started to be brought in. Leofric relaxed a little again.

Davydd, the Welshman began to play a light melody on his lute, humming a tune softly behind the Earl's seat. Leofric was listening intently to the conversation next to him as his son related a hunting story to one of the Midland thanes. He was laughing and chewing at the same time, tearing another large bite of meat off the leg quarter of lamb before he had swallowed the last bite. He reached for his flagon of ale and chanced to see his wife step into the room from the outer doorway. Leofric breathed some half-chewed meat into his windpipe and began to choke. As he coughed at the obstruction, he stood up, eyes watering, bracing himself with two clenched hands on the table in front if him. When the spasm passed, he took a long draught from his flagon and dropped it to the table empty. Leofric wiped the back of his hand to his mouth and tried to focus on his young wife across the room. The minstrel had stopped his music, and all were quiet in the room.

Leofric glared at the Lady Godiva. Damn the woman's timing!

Everyone looked from Leofric to Godiva and back to the Earl. Leofric could not take his eyes off of the Lady Godiva. Leofric felt himself tense up, his knuckles beginning to hurt as they pressed against the hard oak table. Somehow he could not think of something to say. Tension began to mount all around the room as the guests began to wonder if they would get to finish their meal in peace. The Earl's son broke the silence for them all.

"Father! I thought you were going to leave us tonight with a gobbet in your throat just as that Godforsaken Godwin did four years ago!" Young Aelfgar laughed a surprisingly deep, strong laugh, and the others at the table joined in.

Leofric rubbed his eyes and looked at his son, then laughed as well. "I still remember his face turning purple as this robe of mine that evening at the King's table. Of course, he choked because he had tempted fate, calling down the Lord to judge his conscience; whereas, I do not know of any reason why the Lord would chastise me this eve." Leofric sat back down and righted his glass, waving to a servant to come and refill the flagon.

"Unless it be that you failed to await your wife before starting dinner." Aelfgar added, smiling again as his father's scowl bounced off his own light mood.

With her son's last comment, the Lady Godiva glided into the room. Davydd began to play a light marching tune. Leofric followed his wife with his gaze as did all the men of the room. To look at her anytime, one would never guess that she was the granddaughter of a farmer. It did not matter what she wore, she always carried herself in an elegant manner that came naturally. The Earl's wife had on a flowing sky blue gown that made her eyes glow like jewels. Yet the gown was of a very simple design, and she was adorned with only a thin choker of gold. She had on none of the gaudy jewelry that the other women of her station so often wore, and in fact very rarely dressed in anything more elaborate than what she had on now. Even their Queen Edith, a rare young beauty and daughter of the late Godwin himself, paled when in the same room as the Lady Godiva. She did not seem to walk; it was more of a sway, like a gentle breeze blowing into the room from the open doorway.

Taking her seat next to Leofric, the music ceased and Lady Godiva spoke. "My lord the Earl knows he can begin his dinner whenever he likes. Please, everyone continue your repast!" A thane took a tentative bite of meat, then looked back at the Earl without chewing. There was a sound as someone set their mug of ale down a little too hard on the table.

Leofric was taken aback. He had not known what his wife might say; but, calm agreement with him would certainly have been the last thing he expected. He stared at his wife.

Even Godiva became a bit unnerved under her husband's scrutiny. "Good Leofric, how was your day of hunting? I did not expect you back so soon from the woods."

Ha! My hunting was cut short because of YOU, Leofric almost blurted out.

Perhaps that is it, Leofric thought. Play along with Godiva for a while, pretend that nothing is amiss, and show them all who is in control.

"My dear wife, I had such a splendid day of hunting that I chose to come back to Coventry early." Just a little lie.

Leofric reached for his flagon of fresh ale and downed the contents in one long gulp. "Where are the servants? Bring more ale here!" Leofric swung his empty mug over his head and brought it down on the table with a crash.

Aelfgar had been smiling expectantly, but his brow furrowed in frustration. This is not what he had anticipated!

"My lady Mother, how was your day?"

Entry IV

▼

Through which Aldbald of Coventry is introduced

"Please! Someone listen to me. It was all my fault!"

Caedwig pushed through the crowd outside the gate to the Earl of Mercia's Coventry manor. How many times had the monk pleaded for lenience? He felt the weight of the whole affair on his shoulders. If he had not pushed for the remission of the taxes, perhaps the sordid circumstances could have been avoided. But Earl Leofric demanded some sort of retribution in order to save face with the people of Mercia, and Caedwig had not been able to help the poor tailor who was brutally blinded that morning; a man who he had just learned had died of his affliction shortly thereafter.

"It was my fault!"

The cleric wondered if he would ever be able to forget what had happened. Yet, now there was a townsman crying from the crowd, claiming that he himself was to blame! Caedwig could not focus well over the distance, but could easily hear the man's cry.

"It was me. Me!"

It had been many hours after leaving the village limits before Aldbald, the tailor's apprentice, fell into an exhausted sleep amidst a field lying fallow. The next day the young man was able to think more clearly about the incident in Coventry. The being he had encountered had spoken his name, not because it had come to take him out of this world; but simply because the being had been Thom the tailor. The apprentice realized then that the man's oath had had something to do with the shutter. Obviously, the tailor had closed the shutters so that no one would look out into the street.

The streets of Coventry were full of talk after the Earl's housecarls took Thom the tailor away. It had been the Earl's wife, the Lady Godiva, who had ridden through Coventry common. The word in the marketplace was that the Earl had discovered through some women of the town that the tailor may have seen the Lady Godiva's ride through the town. Leofric learned that Thom had apparently not heeded the Lady's housecarls who had ridden through ahead of their mistress ordering shutters to be kept closed until further notice. Even the Lady Godiva's maidservant had noticed an open window at the shop of the tailor. And now the news was out that Thom had been blinded. Aldbald felt sick.

"Please. Please! Listen to me," Aldbald sputtered.

The apprentice could not break through the press of the people. Many were angry at the harsh punishment inflicted on the tailor. Others felt it had been the Earl's right as a husband. Still others focused only on the Lady Godiva, calling for her as the champion of their rights.

"Listen to me." Aldbald fell forward to lean against the man ahead of him who would not make way for the craftsman. The big farmer shrugged off Aldbald's touch, removing the support his large back had offered the distraught man. Aldbald fell to his knees, hands pressed against his face to cover his tears, his anger, his shame.

No one but the cleric in the crowd seemed to take notice of the apprentice. Caedwig could not make headway through the crowd either, but he was able to skirt the edge of the group to make his way to the distressed young man on the fringe of the throng. He took hold of the young man's shoulders from behind, assisted Aldbald as he stood back up and pulled the man away from the townsfolk.

"My son, let me help you."

Caedwig could see the man well up close, could tell he was obviously a cottager in the town. Of medium build, his beard and wavy hair helped to fill out the round shaped head. The man's small eyes that were not quite blue and not quite green stared out on either side of a straight nose that came to a blunt end. He appeared to have reached his mid-twenties without getting a broken nose or losing some teeth as was a common enough occurrence; the monk knew a night did not go by without a brawl at the alehouse. Then, the monk guessed, perhaps this cottar did not carouse and drink to excess as did many of his peers. The monk watched as the stricken look in the man's eyes turned to recognition of Caedwig's ecclesiastical frock.

"Oh, help me father!" Aldbald said. "Help me tell them they have punished the wrong man!"

Caedwig caught his breath. "What do you mean, young man?"

"It was all a mistake. They must let Thom go free." Aldbald could not stop the tears now. He started to put his hands back to his face, but Caedwig grabbed him and held him close.

"Do not fret, my son. All will be well. Let us find a better place to talk." The monk led Aldbald away from the crowd to a stand of trees beside the manor pathway. "Here, sit down with me a moment."

Aldbald fell to his knees, then slumped back into a sitting position. "How could this have happened? How? It was all a mistake! Just a misunderstanding. I did not know...I did not know!"

Caedwig knelt beside the young man, placing one hand gently on Aldbald's shoulder. "Please, my friend, relax a moment. Tell me, what is your name?"

Thom's apprentice was breathing rapidly in between sniffles. He rubbed his sleeve across his dripping nose and watery eyes, then looked up at the cleric next to him. The intensity of Caedwig's genuine interest seemed to calm the craftsman.

"My name is Caedwig," the monk said, patting the other man's back lightly. "What is yours, my son?"

Aldbald took one deep breath, then another. "Aldbald."

Caedwig sighed. He understood guilt all too well, especially in this incident. He just did not understand the cottager's reasons for taking the blame. "Aldbald, my friend, why do you castigate yourself for Thom the tailor's indiscretion?"

Aldbald began with renewed excitement. "Because Thom is not to blame! It was me!"

Caedwig waited a moment while Aldbald relaxed a bit once again. "Tell me your story, young man. What happened?"

"I am Thom's apprentice." When the tailor's old nag had caught a burr in its hoof on an evening delivery to the tinker's work place, Aldbald had stayed up quite late to rub a salve into the sore spot and soothe the beast with a soft voice. Sometime in the night he had fallen asleep beside the animal in Thom's small stable. He had expected the tailor to berate him for coming to work late, instead had found the work shop empty and dark.

"When I came in to work yesterday morning, Thom was not in the front of the shop, and I opened a shutter to lighten up the room." When Caedwig took in his breath, Aldbald continued quickly. "I swear it was a mistake. I mean, I did not know the Lady Godiva would be…I did not know I was not supposed to look…I mean, I had not heard that the shutters were to be kept closed!"

Aldbald watched the horrified look transform the cleric's face. "Please, believe me, I did not know!"

Aldbald's imploring tone brought Caedwig out of his speechless surprise. "I do believe you, my son. It is just that—"

Aldbald's eyes went wide. "Please, tell me the Lord will forgive me! It was not premeditated, was only an accident!"

Caedwig squeezed the young man's shoulder. "I am sure He has already forgiven you, my son."

Aldbald sighed with relief and closed his eyes, then opened them all the wider. "But Thom has not! I wonder if he will be able to. He was blinded, they say! How can he ever forgive me?" When Caedwig made no answer, Aldbald began to feel even worse. "How can I ever forgive myself?"

Aldbald stood up and Caedwig followed, keeping his hand in place on the other man's shoulder. "I must tell Lord Leofric. I must accept any further punishment. Thom must go free. Will you help me set things aright?" Aldbald brought his hands together as if to pray to the cleric. "Will you help me?"

Caedwig raised his chin, bent his head back. His hand extended to Aldbald went limp. Eyes closed, he whispered a silent prayer along with his own question, why?

The hesitation horrified Aldbald. "Please, father. Help me!"

Caedwig brought his attention back to the young man. "I will not, my son, I am sorry. It would be to no avail."

"But I must set the story right. Thom must be set free!"

"My friend," Caedwig spoke slowly, softly. "Thom the tailor is dead."

"No," Aldbald gasped.

"It is true. He expired only a short time ago. The blinding itself was not fatal, but the old man's spirit could not live on."

"Oh, my God! What have I done?" Aldbald fell to the ground sobbing, his breathing becoming uncontrollably shallow.

Caedwig knelt beside him once again. "My friend, do not hurt so. There are many who can share the blame for this day's deeds. For your part, you must put aside the idea of telling Lord Leofric anything of what you have told me. It would do no one any good. The Earl believes he has punished correctly, as do the townsfolk. Telling everyone the truth would only make matters worse at this point."

"But, I must set things aright."

"Nothing you can do can bring the tailor back. Do you have family outside of Coventry? Anywhere you can go to stay for awhile?"

Aldbald shrugged. "My life has been spent here. I have no place—"

Aldbald stopped in mid sentence. He thought of the Earl of Northumbria. Caedwig did not press for more, but calmly waited as the young man's thinking began to clear. After a moment, he said, "There is someone, is there not?"

Aldbald had never believed the life of a cottar was for him. Every year Aldbald thought that the next year would be the right time for him to get away. It was quite recent that Aldbald's dreams of travel were ignited. Shortly after he became apprenticed to Thom the tailor, Aldbald had met Tostig, the younger brother of the Earl of Wessex and son of the famous Godwin of Wessex. Tostig Godwinsson had accompanied the Earl of Wessex on a trip to York in late February, and the Earl had stayed for a couple days in Coventry, making it a point to speak with Thom. Tostig had approached Aldbald with a proposition that promised wealth and adventure for the young burgher.

"I do know the Earl of Northumbria."

Caedwig's surprise was evident as his big eyes went wide. "Tostig Godwinsson?"

"Yes. A few months ago Lord Tostig requested that I send reports to him of the activity in Coventry. He was planning on securing the earldom in the north, and he wanted me to help keep him informed about life in the Midlands. Nothing much has ever happened in Coventry, in my opinion, and I told him so. But he insisted, and I decided it would not be such a hard job. After dinner one evening, I had confided in Thom my relationship with Tostig Godwinsson. I was surprised to find out that Thom himself was in the pay of Lord Harold, the Earl of Wessex."

Caedwig nodded. He was not as surprised as the cottar. The cleric knew that the Earl of Wessex felt it was important to keep a collection of men beholden to him within the lands of his only rival in England, the Earl of Mercia. Harold of Wessex liked to keep tabs on where Leofric was and what he was doing. With the Earl of Mercia now spending much of his time in Coventry, Thom had no doubt become an important link in Harold's chain of spies. It was obvious to Caedwig that Tostig only wanted to have an informant wherever his older brother had one.

"Anyway, I guess I envisioned myself traveling to the northern city once a month or so, astride a strong and healthy pony with gold coins clinking in a purse at my belt." Aldbald looked down, feeling guilty for his immodesty.

"Then you have been to York?"

"Never. I had explicit orders to deliver my verbal messages to the wool merchant who passed through town frequently. The traveling merchant, who knows how to write, would take note of anything of importance and deliver the messages to Lord Tostig at York. Apparently there had been nothing as yet that the new Earl of Northumbria had deemed important enough to pay me for. I am not sure why I let myself stay involved with Lord Tostig."

Caedwig grabbed Aldbald's shoulders. "It is a good thing you have. Go to York. Go to Lord Tostig. I am sure you will find refuge in the house of the Earl of Northumbria."

Aldbald narrowed his eyes. "What would he do if I were to tell him what happened to Thom? What if he finds out what I have done?"

"You need not tell anyone the whole story. Let it be what everyone here in Coventry believes."

"But—"

"I told you, the truth in this instance would only make matters worse." Caedwig smiled broadly to help soothe the other man's aching conscience. "You must make a new life for yourself in Northumberland. Leave for York at once!"

Entry V

▼

In which Aldbald travels north

The darkness moved. During the day the rolling hills were beautiful, with trees and shrubs green with life, contrasting with the brown of the ground below which was covered in a thick layer of dead leaves that graded into the soil. The variety of plants and insects amazed Aldbald who had never really taken note of the land before. The wildlife was a mixture of small rodents and birds, scuffling through the underbrush or ruffling through the branches in the trees. No matter what his apprehension, the young man could not help but enjoy each day's travel.

But at night, the darkness was alive. The hills became wolves, the tall trees spirits, enclosing upon the tanner's son inch by inch. The darkness embodied every story he had been told of the wild country, every fear he had of the unknown. He conjured all too many hideous scenarios in which he was brutally torn to pieces by wild animals or turned into a horrible beast himself through the magic of the sprites he could almost hear whispering overhead as he lay trying to sleep. As the day would break, he would find the forest just as he had left it the night before. Yet, each night he found himself in the grip of uncontrollable reactions that kept his sleep fitful and his dreams rampant. And there had already been far more nights on this long trip than Aldbald would have ever guessed.

Aldbald had never been out of Coventry, much less all the way to York in Northumberland. He was born to a tanner a year shy of a quarter of a century earlier, but much of his young life he spent working in his father's shop. Since Coventry had a fairly large market square, his father rarely left town seeking business, and Aldbald himself then never had occasion to go far from the homes of the local farmers.

Aldbald checked his thoughts as they swung back to the circumstances of his departure. He tried not to think too much about the days past. At least the tailor was able to give Aldbald one final gift: The tanner's son finally had a reason to leave Coventry.

He watched the birds overhead, and tried to envision what it was that they could see. It was a curious and difficult thing to try and see the land from other than his perspective looking through the trees. The young man remembered from his talks with the monk Wulfwin that Coventry had been near the southern most part of the Danelaw, a region set up long ago in a treaty between Alfred the Great and the Danes. York, on the other hand, had been at the heart of the Danish lands. Beyond that little information, Aldbald knew no more.

The young man stopped a moment, struck again with a pain of worry. He did not really know much about Tostig. He only hoped the Earl of Northumbria would take a simple cottar into his service. Aldbald straightened his back and shook himself, remembering again where he was and what he had to do. He would have to tell the Lord Tostig the story. At least most of it. Aldbald urged his horse on again. The old hackney had been Thom's; but the tailor would certainly have no use for it anymore.

Heading north, Aldbald crossed the River Trent that wound to the east, searching in vain for the old Roman roads that would take him to York. Still the early miles seemed to have gone by fairly easily, with villeins offering small foodstuffs along the way. It was north of Nottingham that the

young traveler found himself in the more difficult terrain of the foothills
of the lower Pennines range. The young man turned east, pleased to leave
the bracken and bulrush of the uplands behind for the more familiar
countryside hedges of white hawthorn, honeysuckle and hazel. Meadow
pipit, lark and wren calls kept the air alive with sound. Squirrels darted
from oak tree to chestnut, rustling leaves and chattering at the disturbance
in their domain.

The path he followed was no more than a deer trail; a track that was
merely a high ground that served as the watershed for the surrounding low
lands, winding around the marshes and past overgrown thicket to be lost
among the trees and shrubs. The plants were so thick at times that Aldbald
had been forced more often than not to walk his horse through the
growth. He lost his sense of direction, although he vainly sought out the
sun when he could see it through the trees and the clouds. The traveling
was exhausting. He found himself resting almost more than he walked.
His shoes proved to be far less than adequate, and he developed blisters
and calluses he had never experienced before.

Coming upon what he determined was a river leading north, he followed the river downstream and the going became a little easier. The
seemingly endless traveling gave him all too much time to think about the
circumstances which brought him to make this trip.

For much of Aldbald's life, the young man had heard stories of the
wife of the Earl of Mercia. Since the founding of the Benedictine
monastery and especially since the Lord Leofric had taken up a more
permanent residence in Coventry, tales of the young Lady Godiva had
spread throughout the town. She was seen to champion the cause of
those lower than herself, and many people spoke very highly of the
woman. From the loose tongues of the Earl's house servants came stories
of the Lady Godiva's unhappiness in her marriage. Only a couple years
younger than the lady, Aldbald had felt he could understand the girl's
need for recognition and acceptance. The Lady's deeds and her thoughts

as Aldbald dreamed them had sometimes seemed more real to the young man than many things in his life.

The young man had sometimes felt guilty when he would catch himself daydreaming about the Lady Godiva. He would laugh it off; although on occasion he would think about mentioning his thoughts during confession. Yet, since until recently he had never even seen the Lady, Aldbald had felt sure he could not possibly be desiring her in any immoral way. The lady of his dreams had never looked the same. Sometimes she had looked dark, sometimes fair; often he did not notice. He would envision them sitting alone beside a stream, listening to the sound of the water below, the rustle of leaves in the trees above. Sometimes his imagination had placed them alone in a quiet room, talking about life, nature and things that puzzled them.

Aldbald had always understood that it was the concept of woman that pleased him. Women think differently than he did. Their interests are separate from those of men, and not simply because of their position or out of lack of choice. Women act and react differently than do men. The world itself was different in their eyes than it was to Aldbald, and this intrigued the young man. When he once described his feelings to his friend Athlen, the other boy had laughed as if Aldbald were joking.

Aldbald smiled as he thought of his first sight of Godiva. From now on, he knew his dreams would certainly be more specific.

The smile melted off as the young man thought of Thom the tailor. Remembering the evil he had unexpectedly brought upon his friend wore Aldbald out. He passed into a deep sleep in which he dreamed of the events of the past days. Only this time the lady in the street was an angel, and Aldbald relaxed, ready to let the woman take him to heaven. Then a gruff voice came from behind him, and it was not a heavenly creature, nor was it Thom. A large man grabbed him, and Aldbald realized he was not asleep any longer.

"What have we here?" The gruff voiced man was huge, and he held Aldbald dangling in the air. "Ha! We have a poacher! Let us proceed with the punishment."

Aldbald shook himself completely awake. There were four others with the big man, each astride a horse. "Please, sires, I am no poacher. I was lost in the woods…was only sleeping."

One of the other four smaller soldiers laughed. "Sleeping, you were, on the Earl's land. That makes you a poacher."

"No!" Aldbald tried to talk as one of the men left his horse to join the big brute. They hauled the man of Coventry up, tying a rope around his waist, hands and neck. "Please! I beseech you! I have traveled from Coventry, on a trip to see the Lord Earl Tostig of Northumbria!"

The big man roared in laughter. "Yes indeed! I am sure Lord Tostig would like to see you! He often presides over the punishment of poachers and thieves in his realm!"

The others laughed, but Aldbald cried out all the louder. "Please, take me to him. Take me to Lord Tostig. He will know me. Which one of you is in charge here?"

One of the four smaller soldiers dropped off his horse and stepped over to the tailor's apprentice. The soldier picked up the reins of Aldbald's horse and handed them to one of his men still mounted. "You may address your comments to me, thief. I am the commander of this guard. Although precious little good it will do for you."

The captain of the soldiers was not as big as the brute that held Aldbald; but he looked tough, with ruddy skin and a scar under his right eye that went down to raise his upper lip slightly. All of the soldiers had scruffy hair and dirty skin from hours in the saddle. Aldbald wondered fleetingly if he looked as unpresentable. After so many days lost in the woods, he might well have the appearance of a vagabond.

"Sire," Aldbald choked. As he spoke, he tried to motion with his hands and that only made the rope around his neck draw tighter. "I tell you, I am the servant of Lord Tostig, and I do have important news from Mercia. Please release me and take me to the Earl."

"News? What is this news?" The captain was amused. "Tell me your story, and I will weigh its worth. No need in bothering the Lord of Northumberland unduly."

Aldbald waved his arms again, and the rope constricted a little more. "I tell you it is important! But it is for Lord Tostig's ears." Aldbald was not so naïve as to make the mistake of talking all at once. Obviously, his information was the only thing he had with which to bargain. Unfortunately, the captain did not seem to care.

"I have heard enough then." The captain motioned to his companions. "Take him. We will find an appropriate place for the punishment of this poacher." The captain was back on his horse, turning to lead the others out of the woods.

Aldbald croaked. "No! I tell you, Lord Tostig will want to hear this news. He will need to tell his brother Harold what happened in Coventry!" Aldbald croaked as he said the name of his home. The big brute had thrown him on the back of his horse like a sack of newly milled flour, and the taut rope around his neck caused him to gasp for air.

The soldiers laughed as their quarry tried to speak. Their leader came back to where Aldbald lay flung across the tailor's old horse. The captain grabbed Aldbald's hair and pulled his head up, choking the Mercian all the more.

"Did you say something about Lord Harold?"

Aldbald struggled to nod his head slightly. He could not speak at all with his head at that angle. The captain let go Aldbald's head and jumped back off his horse, gesturing a command to his soldiers that they loosen the bonds on their captive. Aldbald gulped air as the tension was released.

"All right, men. Let us see if this wretch is telling the truth. Perhaps a trial here in the woods would not waste too much time."

As the captain looked about him, the brute began a chant, and the other soldiers followed along. "A trial! A trial!"

The soldiers enjoyed a good trial by ordeal. Trials, although meant to allow the hand of the Almighty to intervene on behalf of the veracious person, rarely had the best interests of the accused in mind.

After a moment, the leader of the soldiers cast a frustrated look at his captive, then snapped his fingers and drew his sword from where it hung alongside his horse. It was a great broadsword, requiring two hands to raise above his head. The man swung it down toward the prisoner, and Aldbald jerked as the singing blade hissed by his left ear. The captain jammed the pommel of the weapon into the earth, so that the blade lay edge-up amongst the clover and vetch.

"You three," the captain excluded the largest of their company, "bring your swords here and place them as I have placed mine, one pace apart from each other." The man in charge slapped the brute on his back. "You, watch this lout, should he try to run. We would not want him getting lost in the woods."

The big man turned to Aldbald, smiled a toothless grin and grunted. "He will not get away from me."

The captain approached Aldbald, produced a dagger from his belt and brought the small blade close to Aldbald's chin. "We shall let the fates determine if you are telling the truth." The soldier sliced through the thick cord that bound the captive, just nicking the young man's neck. Aldbald stood in front of the soldiers with the rope still tangled around his waist and wrists.

A soldier stood on either end of the swords, the weapons aligned like rungs in a ladder lying flat on the ground. One soldier held the reins to their horses while the big man stood next to Aldbald hefting a battle ax. The captain went to stand on the other side of the line of weapons.

"All right." The soldiers watched eagerly as the big man pushed Aldbald toward the line of weapons. The captain tried to look serious. "Walk across the sword blades to my side. If your feet are unharmed by the weapons, then perhaps we should take you to Lord Tostig."

Aldbald could sense a reprieve. He raised his right foot to begin the test, but the captain stopped him. "Hold there! Bare your feet, you imbecile! What kind of test do you think this is to be?"

The soldiers chuckled at the apparent stupidity of the commoner. The brute shoved Aldbald off his feet and tore the captive's boots off when the young man failed to reach them due to his bonds. Aldbald struggled back up and looked down at the weapons in the ground. They were huge blades, used more to crush by their weight than slice with their edge. The edges were not keen, but jagged and nicked from over use and neglect. Still, all his weight would be on his unprotected feet as he tried to walk the test. The young man hesitated just long enough for the big man to give him a shove.

"Get on with it, thief!"

Aldbald stumbled forward, resting his right foot on the first blade. Over his shoulder was the big brute with an ax; the men on either side were eager to see their captive fail the test, their eyes bright with excitement thinking how much more fun is the punishment for lying than for poaching. Poachers were men who might be admired still; liars warranted no consideration. The commander of the men was quiet ahead of Aldbald, waiting on the other side of the four swords lying cross-ways between them. If he lost his balance and fell, Aldbald's whole body would land directly on the blades.

"Now, wretch."

Aldbald took a quick breath and stepped onto the first sword. He let out the air with a gasp as he felt his weight press his foot onto the weapon. The blade may indeed have been dull, but he could feel its cold surface, almost hear it cry out for his blood. He had to move. The young Mercian hopped as lightly as he could from sword to sword. It was only a moment, and he was on the other side.

Aldbald's first thought was that he had succeeded. He made it without stumbling, and had not really felt the blades cut into him. He took a deep breath, then realized he did feel something wet on the soles of both his feet. In a panic, he turned to examine the sword edges. Aldbald was as surprised as the soldiers were disappointed to find no blood on the blades. The brute vaulted over to Aldbald and knocked him off his feet, grabbing one of the flailing appendages as the captive tried to recover.

"Damn! Look at his feet! They are so callused and blistered that I will bet he never even felt the sword edges! I demand another trial. A different trial!"

The captain, a head shorter than the brute, showed no fear of the bigger man. "You demand? Bah! Get yourselves back on your horses. All of you! This was a fair ordeal, and the man has passed the test." The three smaller men retrieved their weapons but the brute stood firm.

"I tell you, look at these blisters! They have been broken! Does that not mean the weapons did harm him?"

The captain picked up Aldbald's boots and tossed them to the captive. To the brute, he said "The blisters he did get from the Lord as he walked. They were there to protect him against just such an ordeal. He has passed." It was final. The brute grumbled, kicking Aldbald in his sore left foot before climbing onto his horse. The captain stepped by Aldbald as he reached for his own mount.

"I thank you, sire." Aldbald said, relieved to have found the man finally on his side.

"You have nothing to thank me for. You are still a prisoner. If the Lord Tostig does not know you, you may suffer far worse than a poacher's punishment. Poachers often survive their penalty. Lying, deceiving cheats are dealt with in a special way. I have not known any to last more than half a day."

The captain rode off, with the others behind. Aldbald was allowed to ride his horse sitting up-right, although his hands were still encumbered. The big soldier rode just behind him, hoping he would try and escape.

Aldbald prayed that Lord Tostig would remember him.

Entry VI

▼

Where Aldbald brings the news of Coventry to Tostig and Harold Godwinsson

"Excuse me, sire. If I may interrupt—" The commander of the housecarls of York was cut off in mid-sentence.

"Damn it, man! Can you not see I am concentrating?!" The man who spoke sat stiffly, hunched over with shoulders tense and arms tight. He was staring at the table in front of him, his straight, shoulder length hair tucked behind his ears to keep it from falling into his face. Aldbald recognized the man he had met a half year ago. A small bit of stubble threatened to break through the sunburned flesh of the long face, growing in patches that made it look like the man's chin needed cleansing; but it was unmistakably Tostig Godwinsson. It was clear to Aldbald why the young Earl preferred a clean shaven face; he obviously had a difficult time growing a full beard. His deep set eyes were squinting as if trying to focus beyond the chessboard in front of him to the motives behind the mechanism of the game.

Aldbald relaxed for the first time in quite awhile. He had finally made it to York! What a long trip it had been. Looking about the room, the cottar from Mercia felt he was to be in good hands. The guards had brought him into the solar. A brightly embroidered wall hanging, brilliant in the substantial light afforded by the large windows, showed what looked like Viking raiders laying waste to a town. The chairs were of plush velvet; the dishware on the table beside the Earl of Northumbria was of silver. Everything looked rich. Yes, Aldbald thought, here I have found a place to stay.

Aldbald could not believe the man sitting across from Tostig was related to the same family; yet he had seen the Golden Dragon banner of Wessex hanging from the pole outside Tostig's manor house. Aldbald recognized it as the symbol carried by the Earl of Wessex, and the captain of the housecarls had told him the man in the room was indeed Harold Godwinsson. Harold was lean and muscular, with broad shoulders and a solid build. Whereas Tostig was a bit awkward looking with his pointed nose and sharp chin, Aldbald could tell that most women would think Harold was very good looking. The older of the two brothers had a prominent nose, straight and strong, a legacy perhaps of the Roman occupation of the island. Harold's left arm was stretched out across the chair back, his wide chin rested on the upraised palm of his left hand, careful not to crumple the neatly trimmed mustaches. The thick, wavy hair was almost the color of his tanned complexion, a slightly darker shade of the same bronze. Here was a man who obviously spent more time out of doors than inside. But the morning had brought quite a storm, and Harold and his favorite hunting companion were forced to spend the day inside subject to the hospitality and company of the Earl of Northumbria. Harold reclined in his chair, sitting back as he reached his right hand down to scratch the young wolfhound behind the ears. The dog was seated beside Harold's chair, tongue spilling out the side of its mouth and eyes watching the newcomers to the room. Both the dog and the master were anxious to be done with the game so they could get outside now that the weather had cleared.

Harold smiled at Aldbald and the pair of housecarls, relishing in the distraction from the boring game. "Perhaps I might attend to this business at hand while you finish your move, brother." He made no move to get up, but his head turned to scrutinize Aldbald and his left hand dropped to grip the arm of the chair.

"No!" Tostig interjected, a bit too forcefully. He continued easier. "No, dear brother. You are my guest and should not be troubled with the affairs of my estate. Please relax and take no notice of these servants of mine. I will address them in a moment." Tostig brought his attention back to the gameboard, irritated at the interruptions. Who had designed such a ridiculous game, he wondered. A game should be a diversion, not a difficulty!

The commander of the guard stood by quietly, awaiting the Earl of Northumbria's pleasure. Tostig seemed at a loss, his eyes roving over the gameboard, forehead furrowed in frustration. After quite a few minutes, Tostig moved his horseman to take a pawn marker and bring his piece within striking distance of Harold's inner line where the king had stood since the beginning of the game.

Tostig sat up straight and smiled at Harold, clenching his fist on the game piece he had just removed from the board. He turned to scowl at his henchmen and the scruffy man they held between them. "Now, what is the meaning of this disturbance?"

Harold kept his attention on Aldbald. "Yes, what is it? Who is this miserable fellow you bring before your Earl my brother?"

Tostig shot a glance back at Harold. "Please, Harold, do not trouble yourself. It is your move, after all."

Harold took a moment to look over the chess board. It was covered with stone-carved pieces representing the powers known in England for the few hundred years past: kings and queens, bishops, housecarls on horses, and soldiers on foot. Harold hesitated only a moment. He brought his queen to capture his brother's last bishop.

"Your King is in check, Tostig," Harold exclaimed.

The Earl of Northumbria had turned back to his captain, but he missed what the housecarl was saying. He could not believe his prize piece was in jeopardy; and with the loss of his only remaining cleric! "Damn!"

Harold continued, "You say you have been working for the Earl of Northumbria? Where do you come from, my boy? What is it that you do?"

Tostig shrugged. The game was stupid. He stood up to face Aldbald. "Who is this man, captain?"

"I do not know, sire. He says he knows you."

Aldbald cleared his throat. "Lord Tostig. I am Aldbald from Coventry—"

"If you know me, then you should know that you should speak when you are spoken to! When I want you to talk, I will ask you a question."

"Yes, sire."

"Well?"

Aldbald was confused. "Well what, sire?"

"You insolent wretch!" Tostig seized the Mercian by the collar and shook him. "Who are you?"

"My Lord Tostig! I am your servant from Coventry. My name is Aldbald."

Harold's eyes widened. "A servant in the midlands, Tostig my boy? What are you up to?" The older brother feigned shock at the news of Tostig's secret.

The Earl of Northumbria smiled as much to himself as to Harold. It was time to impress his older brother. He looked at Aldbald again. "Yes, I know you. Of course. You are my man from Coventry. Why are you not in your home town doing your job?"

The captain of the housecarls looked surprised. "Then you do know this man? He told us you would want to see him, but I truly did not believe it. We caught him poaching game in your preserve beside the Humber."

Tostig sat back into his chair. He was a short man, and hated always looking up to those around him while standing. At least when seated, his stature was not so obvious. "Of course I know him. Whether or not I want to see him is another question! Poaching you say? You know how I deal with poachers. Why bring him to me?"

The captain of the guard bowed slightly. "Yes, sire. I will see to it at once." He turned to go, clutching Aldbald by the arms and shoving him back toward the door.

Aldbald did not know what the Earl did to poachers, although he had almost found out earlier that day. From the trial that he had undergone, he was sure he would not want to find out what a punishment would be. "Lord Tostig! I am no poacher! I bring news from Coventry!"

Tostig had turned his attention back to the game board. "Damn!" he muttered under his breath.

"Wait!" Harold called to the guards. "Bring that man back here." Tostig glared at his brother, and Harold spoke kindly. "Surely you would want to hear the news from Coventry, brother?"

Tostig sat back in his chair. "Of course. Oddwall, is it? Tell me, why do you poach my game in the morning, then waste my time seeking my favor this afternoon?"

Aldbald was hustled back into the room. "Lord, Tostig. I was not poaching. I was merely traveling. Making my way from Mercia to York. I do bring important news from Coventry. It is fortuitous that the great Lord Earl of Wessex is here in York, for I believe this news will be of interest to him as well."

"I shall be the judge of that!" A surprised look from his brother made Tostig more congenial. "I mean, why is it you think that news to me from one of my men would interest my brother?"

Aldbald took a deep breath and swallowed hard through a dry throat. He wanted to tell the story, yet he had feared the Earl of Wessex might take out his reprisal against him. Meeting the man, however, Aldbald felt more comfortable. Harold seemed to be very understanding. "My lords, I have news of Thom, the tailor of Coventry." Harold stood up at that, so Tostig had to stand as well. He was a half-foot shorter than his older brother, and that infuriated him.

Before Tostig could say anything, Harold stepped closer to Aldbald himself. "What do you know of Thom, and why do you think I would care?"

Aldbald involuntarily stepped back a pace, and a guard grabbed each of his arms to hold him. "My lords, it was quite a few days ago now. You see, I have been on the road for some time. And off the road as well! The trails from the midlands to Northumbria are far from ideal. I must have gotten lost two or three times in as many days. And the directions I received along the way from the villeins and cottars of the land left a lot to be desired. It seems like no one has traveled outside their own communities much! I will tell you, I was close to giving up in the Nottingham woods until I stumbled back upon the River Trent and followed it North to the Humber."

His fist still clenched over the last game piece he had captured, Tostig hit his hand on the table, just forcibly enough to shake the chess pieces a bit from their positions. Pretending not to notice the mess of the game-board, Tostig almost screamed, "Did you come all this way to give me a lesson in geography? You are a babbling fool! Captain, give that man a shake to settle the rocks in his head before he utters another word!"

Harold raised his hand to stay the willing guardsman. "Careful Tostig, my dear brother. Your man-at-arms will think you are serious. There is of course no reason to shake the news out of the man. It will come in its own time, like a meandering river does naturally find the sea."

Tostig glared at his brother for over-riding his wishes, then glanced at the table where the chess pieces were askew. He smiled to himself, then relaxed and assumed a contemplative look. "Of course, Harold. The man must have important news to come all that way to see me."

Harold did not seem to notice the emphasis on the last word. "Continue, young man."

"Yes, sire. I am sorry, Lord Tostig, if I do speak off the point. The truth is, my employer Thom the tailor is dead."

Tostig found he was pleased to hear it, and he watched his brother for some sign of anger at the loss of his man in Mercia. Harold showed nothing, merely put his hand on Aldbald's shoulder and waved the housecarls off. "Dead, you say? Please, tell me more. What has happened?"

"Lord Harold, I apologize but I did learn from Thom himself that he did have an association with you. I thought you would want to know of his untimely death."

"Indeed I do. Untimely did you say? How did the man die? You can tell me, my friend."

Tostig interrupted, wanting to regain the position of inquisitor from his brother. "Was it foul play that brought the tailor to his untimely end?"

"Actually, I heard that he was blinded by the Lord Leofric of Mercia. He died later."

Harold stiffened slightly for the first time since Aldbald entered the room. "Leofric? And why would Leofric blind the tailor of a Midland town?"

Tostig had noticed his brother's reaction and smiled. "Surely the Earl of Mercia did not react so, simply out of dislike for the man's craftsmanship? Did he find out that Thom had, perhaps, other interests besides working with clothes?"

"No sir! In fact, it was because of Leofric's wife, the Lady Godiva."

Harold sat down and began to pet the dog again, both looking completely relaxed once more. "And what part did the mistress of Mercia play in this affair?"

Aldbald hesitated to say what exactly had happened. "My lords. It seemed that Lord Leofric had reason to suspect that Thom did catch his wife in a compromising position. The punishment laid upon the tailor was blinding. Unable to recover from the shock of the cruel sentence, Thom did expire."

With sudden insight into the game of chess he had been playing, Tostig pictured the pawn pieces as not just the simple markers that they were, but as real townsfolk, figures of people just as the soldier pieces, the bishops and the king and queen. Small, almost inconsequential people that played a purpose in a larger game. People like the tailor of Coventry. The Earl of Northumbria smiled again, tossing into the air the game piece he held in his hand. He caught it and tossed it up again. "I believe Thom was a…friend of yours, Harold? My, my. The Godwins butt heads with Leofric of Mercia once again. Well, brother, what will be our reprisal?"

Harold looked disinterested and noncommittal. The Earl of Wessex knew well that the pawns in the game were expendable. "The man fulfilled a useful purpose to me; but I have others in similar places." Tostig's smile faded. "Still, it is a shame for an Englishman to die so. Of course, if I find out the death had anything to do with Thom's relationship with me, I will meet Leofric to discuss it."

Tostig smiled again. "Ah, and I will be there beside you! Just like old times when our father kept Mercia under the dominance of Wessex. Now, brother, let us finish this brain-teasing game."

Harold brought both arms down to cup his dog's head between his hands. The dog slobbered all over Harold's forearms as the man shook the floppy ears from side to side. Not looking at his brother, Harold said, "I fear your exuberance has overturned the setup. Perhaps we can start where we left off. I believe my maiden did just allow me to relieve you of your remaining bishop, placing your royalty in an extreme position." Harold let the dog go and reached to right the pieces, feigning concern for their proper relationship. "Shall we see if we can right the pieces and continue? I do not think they are too mixed up."

The smile that had been lighting on and off across Tostig's face left once again. He hated it when Harold tried to show him to be the less perfect brother, especially in front of servants. They were both sons of Godwin! Still, Tostig thought, Harold must be somewhat put out with the news from Coventry, and the younger brother could take pleasure in that. "No, dear brother. We can start a new game tomorrow. I am sorry if I shuffled this one up. Now you will never see how I was going to turn your trap back upon itself! Anyway, you will not be at your best after hearing this disturbing news. I would not want to take advantage."

Happy for the reprieve from playing out the game he knew he had won quite a few moves back, Harold granted his brother the small victory. "You are right. If you do not mind, I would like to talk with this young man here for awhile longer."

Tostig waved his hand toward the cottar. "That is no problem. My servant is your servant. Let us all sit down. I will have ale brought—" Tostig was cut off by a servant at the door to the room.

"Lord Tostig. The Lady Judith requests that you attend her. Now."

Tostig, mouth poised with the words of the unfinished sentence, stared at the man at the door.

"Shall I tell her that you are coming straight away?"

Tostig recovered with that. "I will not have you interrupting me when I am with guests. Do you hear?! Make yourself useful and go and fetch some ale for your Earl…and his brother!" The last added quickly, as Harold met his brother's look with a smile.

"Sire." The servant at the door did not move. "I have many errands to accomplish for the Lady Judith. I request that you have one of your personal servants or one of the housecarls bring Lord Harold his drink. I suggest that you attend your wife."

Tostig was on his feet, waving his pointed finger at the man at the door. "You can tell my wife that I will leave this room when I am finished in this room. And not before then!"

"Very well." The servant frowned. "The mistress will not be happy."

Tostig raged, "Leave me, you fool!" But the servant was already gone. The Earl of Northumbria glowered across the room at the empty doorway, then turned his back on the door and looked toward Harold. "You were saying?" Tostig's glazed eyes stared through the other two.

"I was saying only that I wished to speak with this man from Coventry. Aldbald is it?"

"Yes, my lord."

"Tell me what happened. How did our mutual friend Thom compromise the Lady of Mercia? Was he working on a dress for the woman? As you already have said, you know that Thom had occasion to give me information regarding the Earl of Mercia himself. Are you sure the tailor's death had nothing to do with that?"

Tostig glanced over his shoulder at the door, then back in front of him. He remembered being so proud that his father Godwin had chosen him over Harold to marry into the Flemish house to seal the friendship between Godwin and Count Baldwin of Flanders. He learned years later that it was a truce made under duress by William of Normandy and Godwin only saw it through to secure his position in exile on Flemish soil until he could bring his family back to England. In other words, Tostig had been expedient and expendable.

The Earl of Northumberland's gaze was completely unfocussed, and Aldbald directed his answer just to the Earl of Wessex. "Lord Harold, believe me when I say I do not think that Earl Leofric sought to attack you by killing the good tailor."

"Yet he had to have a strong dislike of the man to blind him to death!" There was one other reason that made sense to Harold. "Tell me, could Thom have been a lover of Leofric's wife?"

Tostig stood up abruptly. "Excuse me, Harold. I just remembered some urgent business I wanted to attend to this afternoon. I will see you at dinner." The Earl of Northumbria made a quick exit, slamming the door behind him.

Aldbald paused, watching his master leave the room. Harold brought him back to the story. "Do not worry about Tostig. His urgent business is to run to his wife. My little brother may be the Earl of Northumbria, but Judith of Flanders is the ruler of him!" Harold switched back to the business at hand. "So, Leofric's wife was seeing the tailor behind closed doors?

I would not have thought it possible. Thom was not in his prime, and I do believe the Lady Godiva is very young."

"Oh, sire! The lady is young indeed!"

"Still, anyone might seem young next to Leofric. Or perhaps she is not so attractive, and the old tailor was all she could find who would have her!"

"Forgive me, sire, but you have it all wrong! The Lady Godiva is the most beautiful woman I have seen in all my life." Aldbald had hardly seen the woman in the streets of Coventry, knew her more from his dreams of her than anything else.

"No," Aldbald said emphatically, "the Lady was never unfaithful to Lord Leofric. Believe me. I do not think she could be. The Lady Godiva is a wonderful woman. A champion of the common folk; a friend to the people of Coventry. The Lady Godiva is a pious woman; a respectable woman. And beautiful, like an angel! You should have seen her riding through Coventry that day—"

Aldbald stopped himself, but it was too late. He had not planned on telling the whole story, or at least had not figured out how to say it. Yet, he could see that Harold sat expectantly now, and he would have to continue.

"Yes? What ride through Coventry? What was the lady up to?" Harold leaned closer to Aldbald, resting his right hand on the younger man's shoulder. "You still have not told me how our friend Thom met his fate."

"I am sorry, Lord. It was a beautiful thing, actually. The Lady Godiva did ride through Coventry on her sleek white mare—" Aldbald paused again.

"And Thom saw her do this? I find it hard to believe the Earl of Mercia would blind every man who casts his eye upon his wife? To be blinded unto death must be a horrible way to die! Leofric must be an incredibly jealous old man!"

"Well, sire, there were some special circumstances regarding this particular ride."

Now even Harold was getting impatient. "Yes?"

Aldbald coughed. "Well, Lord Harold. You see, the Lady Godiva chose on one certain day to ride through Coventry…well, sire, naked she was! Naked as the trees in winter time."

Harold laughed, slapping his knee as he sat back in his chair. The dog next to him clapped its mouth shut in surprise at the quick movement, then let his tongue hang out once again. "Now that is interesting! I was really beginning to wonder what kind of intrigues might have been brewing in Coventry! If the Lady Godiva is so beautiful, how is it that every man in the town did not meet the same fate as did Thom the tailor?"

"Oh! You see, the soldiers of the Earl came by and cleared the streets of all men. Shutters were drawn on every cottage in the town during the ride."

"Interesting!" Harold tried to picture his own Edyth riding a horse naked, but could not envision it. Too bad about Thom, he thought. "All the shutters were closed except those of the tailor?"

Aldbald shifted nervously in his seat, and coughed. "Sire, Lord Leofric had fair reason to believe that Thom did peek at his wife; but I can honestly tell you that he did not. It was just a…just a misunderstanding!" Aldbald fidgeted. How could he tell the great Earl of Wessex that it was he, Aldbald who had looked as the Lady passed through town?

"Pity about Thom. He was a nice man, and a good Englishman." Harold sat back staring at the thatchwork in the ceiling.

"Interesting," the Earl muttered. "You say the Lady Godiva is beautiful? Leofric rarely takes the woman with him anywhere, so I admit I have not seen her since she was a child."

"Oh! Very, my lord!"

"And young? She must be approaching thirty years old by now, I would have thought."

"She looks to be no more than eighteen years of age; yet from what I have been told, I know she must be at least my own twenty and four years. I will tell you, sire, never have the years dealt so kindly to a woman."

Harold shook his head. "But, why would the lady do such a crazy thing as ride naked through town? It does not sound to me to be a normal way of passing the time for an earl's wife! Is this Lady Godiva touched in the head?"

"Oh no! Again, sire, you misunderstand! I learned that Lady Godiva strove to convince Lord Leofric to remit the high taxes on the townsfolk. A very noble and goodhearted thing. I understand Lord Leofric did dare the Lady, and so she rode through Coventry upon her white mare."

"And peeping Thom was punished for spying? Then I must take some of the blame for the poor tailor's demise, perhaps."

Aldbald was quiet, did not know what more he could or should say to the great Earl of Wessex. Harold smiled at him then, thinking of the scene in Coventry. What a woman she must be to ride naked through the streets! Harold could not imagine a pretty young woman in the home, and bed, of his father's old rival Leofric.

"I had never really thought much about why that old man of Mercia never seemed to bring his wife to any public place with him. I think perhaps I might like to visit your town of Coventry one day soon. Perhaps I might meet this Lady Godiva."

*   *   *   *

Tostig stomped down the hallway outside the solar, swearing under his breath with every step. Damn! Why had he neglected to find out where his wife was waiting? She would be angry with him now. Each time his right foot hit the floor, he muttered an oath and punched the wall with his right fist. "Damn!" Where could she be? His eyes were wide, but unfocussed.

"Damn, damn, damn, damn—"

"Oh! My goodness! Lord Tostig, you startled me!"

Tostig was surprised too, as the wall he was hitting suddenly became a woman coming out of an adjoining passageway. The man jumped back, bumping his head on the wall sconce protruding into the corridor.

"Excuse me! I am sorry. I did not notice anyone there...I was...distracted."

"Distracted would be to put it mildly, Tossie!"

Edyth Svanneshals was the only one the Earl of Northumbria would ever allow to be so familiar. Not even his wife would get away with treating him so. But, coming from Edyth, Tostig could not find a reproach. The woman had fair hair and bright, emerald eyes that sparkled in the candle-lit corridor. Her skin was a smooth, milky-white, and her long elegant neck had earned for her the endearing title Svanneshals, Swan-neck, by the time she was twelve. Edyth was a distant relative of his, and still as beautiful as in their youth together when she was his first infatuation. For the man, the infatuation had grown into love. Edyth, Tostig thought, had seemed to prefer his company for many years. The Earl of Northumbria had believed at one time that the two of them might marry.

Somehow things had changed; and the results were clear. Edyth Swan-neck was with Harold. Even now it seemed to Tostig that his brother would lay with whomever he pleases; and Tostig guessed that many do please him. Yet, Edyth had stayed with Harold all these years even though Tostig knew that the woman was aware of Harold's excursions throughout the bedsheets of England. Tostig wondered why. Why would this incredible woman stay with the likes of Harold?

The Earl of Northumbria felt pretty sure that he did know why. It tore him up to envision it. The only thing that made sense was that Harold, then the young Earl of East Anglia, had seduced the fair Svanneshals, taking away the flower of her youth. Edyth could do nothing but commit herself to Harold ever after. Tostig could not blame her for that. He could, and did, blame Harold. Yet, Edyth seemed happy, and Tostig himself was now married to Judith of Flanders.

"Tostig? You are looking at me, yet through me; beyond me! Do you not know your dear cousin?"

"Oh! Again, I am sorry, Edyth! Forgive me for my rudeness. I do indeed recognize you. How could I not? Always the fairest lady to grace these dingy halls of York."

"You flatter me beyond my due, Tossie. The mistress of York always looks stunning, and I see how you do dote upon her!" Edyth pouted. "If I were a different woman, I might be jealous." The woman's chiding was rewarded with a surprised look in Tostig's eyes. Her cousin had always been an easy man to read, and thus easy to tease.

"Edyth!" Tostig stepped closer to his cousin. *So, she does remember their time together,* he thought. Tostig made an effort to reach out his hand towards hers, but she had moved past him and down the hall toward the solar.

"Are you done with that man of mine? Where did you leave Harold? Now that the weather has cleared, I thought he might spend some time with me outside."

Tostig coughed, putting his outstretched hand up to cover his mouth. "Harold is in the solar, Edyth." *Damn the man!*

Edyth turned back to Tostig, her hand to her forehead. "By the way. I passed your wife only a moment ago. Judith seemed upset about something. I think I heard her mention your name. You might want to go and see what she wants." Edyth herself would never be so domineering with Harold. He would never put up with it, for one thing; and, she would not be happy tying him down either. The man had to be free. Then, when Harold came to her bed, she knew it was because it was what he wanted to do.

Tostig remembered why he had been hurrying out of the solar. Judith was waiting. Judith was angry. Angry at him. Again. He needed to catch his cousin before she was gone. "Edyth! Where did you say you saw Judith?"

Edyth was already far down the hall. She called back over her shoulder, "The Lady Judith was headed to her chambers when I did see her last. I am sure you will find her there still."

Edyth Svanneshals entered the solar quietly; but Harold's hound gave her away, pricking his ears and turning his head slightly. His tail began to bounce in recognition, and the clap of the whip on the floor caught Harold's attention. He smiled as he watched the woman approach. The two men stood up to greet the elegant lady. She was dressed in a simple gown of soft dark blue satin that made her pale skin all the more pronounced. Her long neck was adorned as usual with a black choker clasped with a small diamond.

Harold pulled Edyth to him and kissed her on her cheek. "Edyth, my love, meet Aldbald of Mercia."

Aldbald bowed low, taking the woman's outstretched hand and pressing it to his forehead. "My lady. It is a pleasure to meet the wife of the Earl of Wessex. Forgive my appearance. I have just completed a long trip and have yet to refresh myself."

Edyth looked at Harold in surprise at the use of the term wife. Harold seemed not to have noticed. He clapped Aldbald on the back. "This young man has come all the way from the midlands. From Coventry, to be exact. We were enjoying a simple chat. Something I do not seem to find much time for of late."

Edyth sat down next to the toppled chess set. "A simple chat, I am sure. Tell me, Aldbald, were you two talking about women?" The woman was teasing, yet she caught Aldbald's nervous glance at Harold, and Harold spoke a bit too quickly himself.

"My dear Edyth, we were talking about news from this man's home town. It seems my friend Thom the tailor of Coventry has come to an unfortunate end. Aldbald came all this way to tell me."

Aldbald recognized that he should not mention the Lady Godiva. "That is true, my lady; although I was initially seeking out my Lord Tostig of Northumbria. I was glad to find the Earl of Wessex here in York as well."

Harold smacked the other man on the back again. "Aldbald will dine with us tonight."

"My lord! I cannot. I am a simple cottar. I would feel out of place in the company of earls and their fine ladies."

"Oh? Have you found my company so distasteful?" Harold made himself look angry.

"No! Sire, it is just that—"

Harold smiled. "It is just that I would prefer your company to that of my brother. You would be doing the Earl of Wessex a great service! Besides, I feel like we might have more to discuss concerning…Thom of Coventry."

Before Aldbald could protest again, Harold slipped his arm around Edyth and guided her to the door. "So, Edyth. The weather has cleared and I want to get out! What do you say we saddle up a couple horses and go ride about Yorkshire?"

"Harold! You know I do not ride well. I was thinking we might take a small lunch out to the lake and have a picnic."

The disappointment showed only briefly on the face of Earl of Wessex. Edyth may not ever ride naked on a horse; but many a picnic of theirs had certainly ended with her naked on the grass. "Anything, dear. Just let us get out of here." The shaggy hound jumped about the two, barking and salivating in excitement. "It looks to me like we all need to get out." Harold winked across the room at Aldbald as he passed through the door. "Except the young man from Coventry. Get yourself cleaned up, man! You look a mess!" And Harold was gone.

Entry VII

▼

In which Harold and Tostig speak of Hungary

Aldbald had been manservant to Lord Tostig for only a couple months, but he had come to be familiar with the way the Englishmen of Northumberland spoke. The young man was amazed at how different the people of St. Albans sounded from the countrymen north of the Humber. He had no trouble understanding what was said around him in the crowded alehouse; yet to find Englishmen speaking so differently from one end of the kingdom to the next amazed the young man.

Tostig met Harold over a drink, and the two brothers were talking at a corner table within the large room. The Earl of Wessex was spending the night in the back guest room of the place, which appalled his brother Tostig who preferred more private accommodations. Harold enjoyed mingling with the common folk, often finding their company much more pleasing than that of those of his own station.

Tostig was agitated; but to have been any less would have been unnatural for him. Harold, looking for distractions from his conversation with his brother, noticed the young man from Mercia nearby in the room.

"Ah, is that not my friend Aldbald? Come, sit down here with us!"

Tostig was surprised. "Harold! The man is a servant. He will find refreshment at the table with the other servants. We are Godwinssons! Need I remind you that we are above people like him?"

"Not that far, Tostig." Harold said, annoyed with his brother's attitude.

The young man from Coventry glanced from the Godwins to the rest of the room. Smoke from the poorly ventilated brazier pooled in the rafters above, descending to mingle with the raucous banter below. Men from every walk of life found something in common at the alehouse. If not their taste for the strong drink, then their desire to escape from their homes for a short time; be away from wives and families and forget the hardships in their lives. Aldbald himself was drawn to the alehouse as the only place to find dinner so late in the day, however meager it turned out to be. The young man could see the other men from York sitting across the hall, mostly soldiers of Lord Tostig's house. Sitting prominently among them was the big brute who had been so intent upon Aldbald's punishment in Yorkshire, a man he learned was called Bufread Bloodyaxe. Aldbald had no interest in sitting with that man this eve, but the exotic minstrel entertaining the group held his attention. A Welshman proclaiming himself as Davydd the Dreamer was putting the soldiers' exploits to music as they laughed and threw coins at the foreigner.

"Thank you, Lord Harold, but I will sit on the other side of the room with the company from Northumberland."

Tostig glared at Aldbald. "That is exactly where you will go!"

"No matter." Harold waved his hand over his head as Aldbald stepped away. "Perhaps I will join you there, shortly." The Earl of Wessex leaned back and brought his hand up to stroke his mustache, a little impatient to be away from his brother's company.

Tostig grabbed his brother's hand to bring him back to their conversation. "You said that we would meet Aldred together! Could you not have waited until tomorrow as we had planned?" Tostig had not touched his drink, so frustrated and infuriated was he at being left out of his brother's plans.

"Tostig. It was nothing. I spoke with Bishop Aldred of Worcester only briefly. It seems he was surprised to see me. He had expected to find the Earl of Mercia, of course. Bishop Aldred did let on that he was heading to see the King. I believe he is awaiting the Earl of Mercia now, wants to speak with Leofric before he approaches King Edward. In fact, I have learned that Leofric is to arrive tonight."

Tostig smiled, glad to have information that his brother lacked at the moment. "Yes, Harold. That is the truth. I heard the news of Leofric's retinue in the streets as I made my way to this ale-house to meet you. I tell you, Mercia is scheming behind our backs." Tostig's smile vanished. "Did you see the man from Hungary?"

"Aedward? No. Bishop Aldred kept quiet about Aethelred's kin, and I did not press the issue. Tomorrow, as you said, is soon enough. I am not even sure yet if Aedward the Exile is back in this country."

"Oh, I think he is." Again, Tostig's smug look as he revealed something of importance to his brother. "I had one of my men follow the Earl of Mercia to find out where he was heading while I made my way through the damned crowd in the square to get to this ale-house." Tostig paused for effect, but found that his brother looked uninterested. "Harold, my man told me that he heard Leofric speak of heading to Bromely on the morrow. If the Exile is not here in St. Albans with Bishop Aldred, then I will wager he is in Bromely. What better place to hide Aedward than in a small village south of London? Obviously, Leofric thought to protect the Exile, while still having the man be close to the King at Thorney Island. Only, the Earl of Mercia did not count on my finding out about Bromely!"

"If Leofric has a scheme such as that, then he is more a fool than I would have believed. Surely he knows that Edward left last week for Gloucester."

Tostig had not known that King Edward was not in London, he glared at Harold. Damn his brother for making him feel like the fool the Earl of Mercia certainly was! "Are you sure the King is not in London?" Harold did not answer, just looked at his brother.

Tostig rallied. "Okay, Harold. So King Edward is in the west of England. That gives us more time. First impressions are important. Aedward the Exile needs to be shown where lies the strength of England. It is not in Mercia but in the house of Godwin. Bishop Aldred is overstepping his bounds in keeping the Exile from us; and Leofric is behind it, I am sure."

Harold took a long draught, laughing as he wiped foam from his mustaches. "Aedward the Exile may not even speak English, Tostig. The grandson of Aethlered has spent all his life in exile from England, ever since the years of Danish rule. What shall we say to him?" Harold laughed again. "Relax, brother."

Tostig was insistent. "I tell you, Harold, Leofric is cooking up something with that damned Bishop."

Harold set his mug down and stared at his brother. "The Earl of Mercia and Bishop Aldred can make no moves without the support of the Witan."

Tostig scowled. "Remember, it was that damned man from Mercia that swayed the Witan against father only five years ago. We were all exiled!" The younger brother spat into the floor rushes. "That is something which must never happen again!" He was vehement. "I will never again submit to exile from my home!"

Harold tried to soothe the younger man. "You worry too much, Tostig. You always have. Do not be so passionate about things, you will drive yourself into an early grave. Anger will not solve our problems; logic will. Leofric is an old man. His son Aelfgar is striving to be more important;

but neither carry enough sway in the Witan right now to set us to worrying about our future. With our younger brother Gyrth the Earl of Kent,
you in the north and myself in Wessex, three Godwins hold two thirds of
England. As I said, Leofric is an old man. Who knows, he may not last out
the year. You can be assured that when Leofric does leave this world, his
death will be good for the house of Godwin. We might move fast at that
time, keeping Aelfgar in East Anglia while Gyrth takes over Mercia."

Tostig's eyes were alight with the thought of it. "Or myself—"

"Perhaps, if you do wish it; then Gyrth would take Northumberland.
Either way, we might move the next Godwin into his own earldom. With
brother Leofwine then made Earl of Kent, England will be all but unified.
Even with Aelfgar's seed in East Anglia, we will never need to worry about
the house of Leofric again. Nor will we have to worry about any scheming
with Aedward the Exile from Hungary. Aedward would know that he
must reckon with the House of Godwin."

Tostig was excited. "Perhaps we might yet bring our youngest brother
Wulfnoth out of France to take his rightful place among the earldoms of
England. In that case, there might not be any room for Aelfgar. Would not
father be pleased?! What a grand plan. Only Leofric does stand in the
way."

Harold scowled. "I will tell you what would have pleased our father. If
our brother-by-marriage, Edward the King, would sire a son!"

Tostig looked contemplative. "I cannot believe sister Edith is barren.
She will not talk to me about her home life. I fear she cannot conceive."

"No, I do not believe that is the problem. Edward wears his chastity as
prominently as his crown. Edith might have done just as well to stay in the
nunnery she retired to when the rest of us were sent into exile with father."

"Do not remind me of that time, Harold." Tostig took a drink of ale,
his eyes merely slits staring straight across the room at nothing. "You
know, Harold, the young Aedward had been sent to Sweden by Canute. A
pity he was not done away with at that time instead of being shipped off
to Hungary. If not for this Exile that traces his blood back to King

Aethelred, perhaps Edward would be seeking a Godwin as his heir even without a child of our sister Edith, the Queen. King Edward and I have come to be very close." Tostig slammed his fist down on the table.

"I am telling you, Leofric has something in the kettle, stewing as we speak! I fear he has been cooking up his broth for a long time, and he may well be ready to serve it up before we can determine what is on the menu!" The Earl of Northumbria was waving his arms, gesturing wildly. Harold grabbed the other man's hands and held them firm.

"Leave it, Tostig! Don't you ever quit?" Tostig relaxed slightly, and Harold withdrew his hold. The older brother rubbed his stomach. Harold looked past his brother, but he had lost sight of the bar-maid he had been eyeing all evening as she went off with the loud Welshman whose purse was now heavy. "Ah, now you have done it, little brother. You have gone and made me remember my hunger."

"I am serious, Harold." Tostig spat on the floor. "Leofric is consolidating his strength, and I will bet the Exile from Hungary will play a role.

Harold refilled his mug. "Perhaps tomorrow we will meet this Exile. Do not fear, Tostig, I am sure that Godwins will still hold the power in England, whatever kind of man Aethelred's line has produced." Harold laughed and drained his glass.

The younger brother was thoughtful. He drained his own cup and stood up. "I would go to see the Earl of Mercia tonight. It looked like Leofric is treating this trip from the Midlands as a holiday. As I passed the man in the streets, I saw at a distance that his wife and courtiers did accompany him into town. That self-righteous old man acts as if he already has reason to celebrate. Perhaps a little threatening will remind the Earl to stay in his place."

For the first time this evening, Harold thought, Tostig actually offered something of interest to the conversation. "The Lady Godiva is here in St. Albans?"

"Yes. I have heard Leofric can be especially disagreeable when his wife is around. I think the man is in his dotage. It will be my pleasure to see the old man try and face up to Tostig…and Harold, Godwinsson!"

Harold recalled the tale Tostig's man from Coventry had relayed. It was only a short while ago that Aldbald had come from the Midlands with his story of Lady Godiva's curious ride through the marketplace of Coventry. This might be his chance to meet the interesting woman. "You just might have something there, little brother. Let us go and see the Earl of Mercia tonight."

Entry VIII

▼

In which Harold meets the Lady Godiva

"No, the Earl is not here." Gunthnot, the Lady Godiva's guard, stood barring the door to the small cottage used by the Earl of Mercia when he passed through town on his way to London. "He went out to an important meeting, and I know not when he might return."

"Damn!" Tostig punched his fist into the doorjamb. "Harold, he is gone to see Aldred! I am sure of it. Do you still believe they are not scheming between them?"

"I told you not to worry, Tostig." Harold said under his breath. The Earl of Wessex faced the guard. "Perhaps the lady of the house could offer more information?"

Gunthnot was about to decline, ready to slam the door in Harold's face, when a voice came from within the room behind him. "You there, guard. Who is at the door? If it is that Welshman, tell him to go away." A maidservant pushed the soldier aside and yelled out into the darkness. "It is much too late for callers—" The woman's reprimand trailed off as she realized she did not know the men at the door. The one in front had a kind, handsome face and Hildreth's curiosity won out.

"May I help you?"

Harold hesitated. This surely could not be the woman of whom Aldbald had spoken so highly, could it? Tostig asked the question Harold couldn't seem to word. "You are not the wife of Leofric are you?"

"Certainly not," Hildreth scowled. It was the funny looking one of the two men who had spoken. Hildreth found no reason to be pleasant with him at such a late hour. "My lady is relaxing after the day's journey. Who might you be?" She addressed the question to the handsome man.

Harold answered, "I am Harold Godwinsson, and this is my brother Tostig of Northumberland. We were seeking Earl Leofric; but the guard there could not tell us where we might find the man. Who might it be that we have the honor of addressing?"

Hildreth was surprised, and a little flattered. It was Harold of Wessex, appearing so friendly and speaking so formally with the maidservant. "Oh, my! The Earl of Wessex! I am pleased to meet you." The woman bowed low. Tostig glared at her obvious exclusion of him. "I am Hildreth, maidservant to the Lady Godiva."

Harold bowed slightly to the woman, and Hildreth blushed. "And, would you know where your Earl has gone this evening?"

"Well, sire—" Gunthnot still hovered beside the open door, threatening to close it on the callers; but Hildreth shooed him away, then smiled to Harold. "I am pretty sure I heard Lord Leofric tell my lady that he was heading to the chapel, there to meet the Bishop of Worcester."

"Just as I thought!" Tostig slammed his right fist into his left palm. "Harold, did I not tell you that they are up to something? Damn!"

Harold was about to snap at his brother in impatience, when his attention was drawn behind Hildreth and into the small cottage where he could hear a woman's voice softly humming. His brother's oath brought him back outside. "Excuse me a moment, Hildreth." Harold smiled at the maidservant and took his brother aside.

"Tostig. Maybe you are right after all." The younger man's eyes lit up at that recognition from his brother. "Why do you not take a couple of your housecarls and go to the town chapel. See what you can find out."

"At once, Harold! It is what I thought we should do. You will fetch a couple men as well?" The last was more a statement than a question, which is why Tostig was so surprised by his brother's answer.

"Ah, no. You take as many of your soldiers as you feel you will need. I will stay here a moment and talk with...this maidservant. She may know something that would be hard to learn from Leofric himself." Harold could see a worried look transform his brother's face.

"Yours is certainly the more important mission. Tostig, see what you can learn at the chapel, then press on to Bromely. I will leave Leofric to you. Maybe the man is planning something. As I told you before, it will be nothing that we cannot handle. Still, it would be nice to have Leofric out of the way so we would not have to worry about him. In the meantime, I will finish here, then proceed to Gloucester to head off our friend the Bishop. I am sure now that Aldred will be making for the king's court. We can meet again there, you and I. I am counting on you, Tostig. Together, there is nothing we Godwinssons cannot handle."

Tostig stood up straight, the gleam in his eyes tempered by the shadows. "Of course, Harold. I will find out what I can, and do everything I have to do. You can count on me. I will take care of things in Bromely. When next we meet, everything will be under control." With an exaggerated flourish, the Earl of Northumbria turned and disappeared into the darkness.

Harold came back to the woman waiting at the open door. "Your mistress...could I have a word with her? I will only be a moment."

Hildreth smiled. "I am sure my lady will have the time to speak with the Earl of Wessex. Please, come in." The woman held the door ajar, letting Harold step inside. It had been a hot day, but it felt cool inside the mud packed cottage. Harold was disappointed to find the Lady Godiva was not in sight. Had she left by the small back entrance? No, the humming began again, coming from behind a silk curtain on the left side of the room.

"My lady is finishing her bath, sire. I will tell her that you await her convenience." Hildreth smiled again, and walked across the room to step behind the curtain.

Harold, standing in the doorway, could see the entire house-room, lit as it was by an oil lamp on a small table in the center. The room was modestly decorated. It had only a little bit of color to break up the monotony of gray and brown, in the form of a rich curtain with a simple but bright red and gold woven design. A chair near a dressing table to Harold's right, and a bed across the room completed the furnishings. The guard who had barred the door stood casually near the back entrance, and a small black cat lay asleep on top the dressing table.

A faint smell of lilac filtered up from the clean floor rushes as Harold walked into the building. There was not much room for more wood than was already in the small pile of aged pieces next to the brazier. The cottage was used mainly in the warmer months, when the Earl of Mercia would join the king on his mid-summer hunt. There was little cookery; Leofric would undoubtedly attend meals with the king. The main use for the small cottage was to sleep—with the Lady Godiva.

As when Harold had first spoken with Tostig's man Aldbald, the Earl of Wessex found himself intrigued by this woman of Mercia. He could not hear what was being said behind the curtain by the two women, their muffled voices mingled with the splash of bathwater. Harold realized he was mildly excited. What would she be like, this wife of the old goat Leofric? Aldbald had proclaimed her to be of surpassing beauty. Perhaps he should not expect much, Harold thought to himself. What would the simple cottager from Coventry have to compare with the Lady Godiva, anyway? Bent-backed farmer's wives; craftswomen with callused hands and sores on their feet. What would be the fairest maid young Aldbald would have met? No, Harold guessed, Aldbald could not have had many experiences with pretty women to make a reasonable comparison.

Under the watchful eye of Gunthnot, Harold stepped over to the dressing table chair. As the man pulled the chair out to sit, the cat on the table jerked awake. The feline pupils dilated to register any threat, and the little brain was quick to note that Harold was not someone he knew. Harold was startled as the cat dashed off the table in front of him to hide under the bed. Harold shrugged, then sat himself down at the table and began to stroke his mustache.

There was a mirror of polished steel on the counter, and the Earl of Wessex stared back at Harold. The mirror was a luxury not unknown to Harold. He had bought a similar one for Edyth Svanneshals a few years back. The man smoothed his mustaches as he thought of the women he had known. There were many, although not so many as others might guess. Still, he had found his share of pleasure among the other sex. Harold had to admit to himself, there were indeed some attractive villagers. In his travels across England, it had not proved difficult finding pretty young ladies with whom to spend his free time. *Perhaps Aldbald does have a good idea of what makes a woman attractive. After all, did he not meet Harold's own Swan-neck?* Aldbald had been impressed with Edyth's beauty, so he had told Harold; yet he had not seemed over-awed with her as he had with the sight of Godiva.

Harold, fingering the all too normal items on the dressing table, did not realize there stood a woman behind him until something caught his eye in the burnished metal. He stood up quickly, turning to face the young woman. The Lady Godiva smiled and moved back toward the bed on the other side of the room from Harold. Hildreth smiled again at Harold, then stepped behind the curtain to clean up after her mistress. There was a strained silence as the young lady eyed the Earl of Wessex with interest, finding the man's surprised look humorous.

"Has the famous Earl of Wessex come to beg some face powder from my humble possessions?" She was slightly mocking, mostly joking. Harold grinned at his own predicament, caught with his hands in the makeup. His face turned serious.

"You have discovered me, my lady. At night I do dress as a woman, and I found myself in dire need of rouge for my cheeks."

The woman was amused, pleased to find her husband's rival to have a sense of humor. She sat down on the bed and motioned for Harold to seat himself again.

"I have heard the tales of the Earl of Wessex being a great man who does know the English people well. Now I think I know why he is so understanding. Any man who is sensitive to the ways of women is most certainly a step ahead of those who do not recognize their importance." Godiva gestured toward her stock of makeup. "Please, sir, help yourself. Then I will help you with anything else you desire in comprehending the females of the realm."

Harold finally let loose his great smile, teeth shining in the room's night lamp light. "Believe me, my lady, there is not a day goes by that I do not learn something new from the fairer of the two sexes." And yes, perhaps you could teach me something, Harold thought to himself. Here is a woman who rode through a town square, naked, just to prove a point or to get her husband's attention. No woman Harold had ever met would even have thought of such a thing.

The Earl of Wessex scrutinized the young woman with increasing interest. Her features were not exotic, her face not so uncommon; yet, in her simplicity, she did seem especially pleasing to look upon. Her smooth olive skin looked ageless. The man was sure it was soft to the touch. Her body was hidden within a large bath robe; but Harold could tell from the woman's neck and arms that she was lean and healthy. Even so, she was not that different from many other women he had known. At least the younger women. How old had Aldbald said she was? She must be almost thirty. Yes, she did look very good for almost three decades of life.

Her hair, wet from the bath, was still obviously extraordinary. That Harold had to admit to himself. Long and thick; not simply brown, but tinged with red highlights that caught the flicker of the lamp light, sparkled with fire. His Edyth had less hair to work with, and still he would find her fussing with the strands for hours out of each day. Lady Godiva must be forever cleaning and brushing her incredible mane to keep it so shiny.

Yet, again, hair alone does not a beauty make. Perhaps it was the way she carried herself, strong and sure of her position, that intrigued him. Whatever it was, Harold realized he was entranced. Something about the hair, the innocent and intelligent face, the hint of her body beneath the robe…altogether, that truly did seem special. At that moment, Harold envied his father's old rival. Leofric was an old man, but he sure had something here to keep him content during his declining years.

"I am curious, Lord Harold. Truly, what does bring you into my humble company? Hildreth has told me that you know my husband is not here."

"Yes, I do know that Leofric is out, my lady. I confess, I merely had a great interest in meeting the Mistress of Mercia. Your reputation," Harold paused, picturing the woman naked on horseback, "as a champion of the people precedes you."

"Does it?" The lady's face showed true surprise. "I would have guessed my Lord husband's reputation would be known in Wessex, but surely never my own."

Harold smiled. "You might be surprised at how reputations are made and do spread."

"Oh? And what have I been able to accomplish that would draw such attention? My husband Leofric does take care of all the business of Mercia. There is nothing left for me to do. What is there for me to be known for?"

Harold was interested to find the woman was serious. The Lady Godiva, though not angry, was certainly disappointed about something. For some reason, the Earl of Wessex found himself uncomfortable knowing this young woman was not happy.

"My lady, I have a feeling that you are not content in your station as wife to the Earl of Mercia. Does not the second richest earldom of England suit your interests?"

Godiva smirked. "Ah, but I am not the Earl of Mercia!"

Harold laughed at the thought. "Of course not! But you are wife to the earl. You have borne the man a fine son. You have fulfilled your duty to your lord."

"Yes, my duty." Godiva looked amused. "Tell me, Lord of Wessex, do you talk with your wife? Do you listen to her thoughts? Do you know her desires?" The woman noted Harold's confusion and strove to settle his thoughts. "Truly, my lord, I am only curious. I do not mean to pry into your personal life."

Harold sat back, contemplating the woman's questions, and the thoughts behind those big eyes. "I gather you are frustrated. I admit, I know not why. The common folk of the Midlands seem to adore you. You are the Lady of the Mercians to them."

Lady Godiva cocked her head, her brow wrinkled slightly in thought. "Funny, my maidservant Hildreth never ceases to remind me of that. Have you been talking with her behind my curtain?" Harold started to speak, wanting to clarify his question, but Godiva went on. "No matter. You are right, and I do give thanks for the love of the people. My husband has administered the borderlands now for many years. Not always so leniently at times, perhaps; but mostly he has been fair and just. Even so, it would give me much pleasure to discover that my reputation, such as it may be, will outlive Leofric's in the eyes of the people."

Harold broke in. "My lady, I want to assure you that your reputation, at least among the people of Coventry, is of a great woman. Did you not remove the taxes which weighed so heavily on your people?

Godiva's playful smile faded. "Indeed I did, and for a great price."

"I heard a man did die because of it," Harold prodded. "Is that true?"

The lady shuffled her hands in her lap. "That is something I do try to forget. It was such an unfortunate mistake."

Harold remembered then that he had never quite learned from the young man Aldbald why exactly the tailor of Coventry had died. Maybe from Godiva, Harold thought, he could learn more of why Thom was killed. "A mistake? Surely Leofric did have just cause in ordering such a punishment as I heard befell the man. Were you and the dead man…friends?"

"Heavens no!" Godiva looked angry, but not at Harold, at herself. "I had never even met the man. I am still not so sure that he had seen me either. I had no intention of bringing anyone any harm."

"Did your husband have any particular reason for wanting this unfortunate man out of the way?"

"Only to soothe his own ego." The room seemed to become more dark as the lady struggled with her regrets. "No, I am sure the people of Coventry will not remember me for that crazy stunt I pulled in their town."

The Earl of Wessex might never learn the whole story of what happened in Coventry; but he was content to know that the Lady Godiva seemed truly upset about the whole matter. Harold felt the need to brighten things up. "My lady, I think you are wrong. You are an impressive woman."

"Lord Harold, you do flatter me. Can you honestly say that you know the mind of even your own people in Wessex? If so, you are truly a different man than the Earl of Mercia."

Harold smoothed his mustache hair unconsciously. "My Lady Godiva, I am certain that I am a very different man than Leofric. Perhaps when you and I become better acquainted, you will see what manner of man I am."

Lady Godiva stood up, and Harold followed. "I do not see that happening, sire. You may indeed be different from Leofric, and you look to be someone who is not following in the footsteps of his father either. Still, I am the wife of the Earl of Mercia. While Leofric lives, my house will ever be at odds with the house of Godwin." Godiva ushered Harold to the door, speaking on to keep him from uttering the dispute forming on his lips. Godiva put her hand to her mouth. "Shoosh!" The lady strained to hear outside the cottage walls. Harold heard nothing.

"My lady, what is it?"

"Oh, nothing. I did think that I heard my husband return. He may come any time now. I regret to say he would not find the presence of the Earl of Wessex in his bedchambers as amusing as did I. Please, Lord Harold, go now. It was a pleasure to have met you."

Harold again began to protest, but Godiva opened the door. She smiled. "For now, Lord Harold, let us part as we met, with humor." She smiled. "If ever you need to borrow some makeup, do not hesitate to ask it of me."

The two of them laughed at that. "You are too kind, my lady." Harold reached to hold Godiva's hand to his lips. He was right. Her skin was amazingly soft. "I will look forward to meeting you again."

"If the fates do decree it, Lord Harold."

The streets of St. Albans were empty, leaving Harold's mind to wander as he joined his small guard that awaited him, and made his way back to the alehouse where his retinue was staying. Harold had known his father to have loved life as Earl of Wessex. Godwin had found it exciting, invigorating. For Harold, the constant power struggles inherent in his position grew tiresome at times. He was different than his father; more lenient to foreigners in England, and much more friendly with Aethelred's line than had been Godwin who, till the very end, had favored the Danish royal line. Under King Edward, and with Harold's strong rule, England was at peace and prosperous. The situation in England now was different than in the days of Harold's father.

Yet, Harold found he could not freely talk with the wife of another earl, an earl that was not a Godwin. Simply because Harold was a Godwin made the other house hostile. It just did not make a lot of sense to Harold. Leofric, of course, would have too many memories of struggles with Godwin. Perhaps the man would never be able to get over the ingrown feelings of resentment toward Harold's family. On the other hand, Leofric's son Aelfgar was a different matter, the next generation. It is entirely possible, Harold thought, that the House of Godwin and the

House of Leofric could begin to coexist in mutual friendship once Leofric was gone.

Harold realized he would not want to present his brother Gyrth to the Witan as the next Earl of Mercia upon Leofric's death, whenever that might be. Gyrth could take East Anglia, and that would still leave Kent for Leofwine. Aelfgar could make a good Earl of Mercia, and the House of Leofric might easily be reconciled with the Godwins for once. The Lady Godiva, free of her old, stifling husband and with the Godwins as friends, would no longer have any reason to keep from talking with the Earl of Wessex. It could only make England stronger.

The soldiers riding with Harold were quiet; but the Golden Dragon banner above him was loud, snapping erect in the wind as they rode across the town. Harold glanced up at the royal symbol of the English kings and smiled to himself. He would mention his ideas to King Edward when he arrived in Gloucester. Harold would make sure to let the King take the credit for such a reasonable plan.

Entry IX

▼

Where King Edward is introduced, along with his wife Edith

Caedwig resisted the urge to light some candles to illuminate the murky air. He would suggest it; but not just yet. Edward sat with his eyes closed in the dark, on his grand marble throne that was the only piece of furniture in the King's audience hall. Outside, a storm raged, whipping trees with the strength of the wind and tearing at the thatch on the roof. The storm had swept quickly across the Cotswold Hills, keeping the King from his planned day of hunting. The small monk stood quietly by his side, letting the King take his own time to come out of his melancholy mood.

"Caedwig?" Edward's eyes jumped open, his arm reached out into the gloom.

"Yes, my lord. I am here," the monk answered.

The King relaxed. "Good. Of course you are. For a moment I thought you had gone." Edward continued in Norman-French, and Caedwig switched from English to the other language.

"No, my lord. I am here still."

"You are my one true friend, Caedwig." Edward shut his eyes again. "You and the Lord Jesus himself."

"The King has many who are friendly to him. I am only one of those."

"Ah...many who are friendly. You know, they sent me to Normandy and left me there all those years. Even my mother deserted me."

Caedwig was never sure ahead of time in which direction the King's mind was going to wander. The monk struggled now to see where this was leading. It had been fifteen years since Edward was back as King of England; his exile in Normandy was long ago.

"Yes, sire. You were put through many trials and much tribulation; but your strength of will and sound heart brought you through."

"Yes, with the Lord's help." Edward was silent for a time after that.

Caedwig asked slowly, "What is troubling you today, my lord?" The monk placed his right hand lightly on top of Edward's head.

"I am afraid, Caedwig." The King whispered, and the clergyman leaned closer to hear. "Caedwig, will you hear my confession?"

"Certainly, sire." The monk was glad for the cover of darkness in the room which was fitting for the act of contrition.

"Forgive me Lord, for I have sinned. It has been much too long since my last confession." Caedwig suppressed a smile in the dark. The King's last formal confession was only three days ago, and Edward spoke to Caedwig as his confessor at least once a day beyond that.

"What would you like to tell me, my son."

"My brother and sister were with me in exile; yet no one was nearer to me than the Lord. Jesus was my friend when all others were gone."

"I know, my son. That is when we met. What should trouble you now?" Caedwig was truly puzzled.

"It is that old feeling again." The King sighed. "I fear it never goes away. I strive to do better every day, but still I find a stray lustful thought creep into my conscious every once in a while. That is far too much. Many years ago, while alone in Normandy, I pledged myself to the service of our Lord, and gave up my chastity into his keeping."

Caedwig coughed quietly. "My son, you have not the vigor now that you hoped to curb as a young man in Normandy. What is it that worries you of late?"

Edward was silent for a moment. The wind whistled through the branch latticework above them. "Do you remember my coronation?"

"My son, that was many years ago, yet still it is strong in my memory."

Edward swallowed hard. "I thought my young man's urges behind me even then; until I did see the young wife of the Earl of Mercia. Do you remember the Lady Godiva? She was a mere girl, only beginning her second decade of life. I was appalled that Leofric would take this girl to his bed; yet at the same time, I found I did get excited as I watched her at the dinner table."

"Yes, Edward. I remember you spoke to me at that time. The Lord recognized your honest desire for forgiveness for your lustful thoughts, and He did absolve you then. That should not weigh upon your thoughts anymore. Put it behind you."

Edward took a deep breath. "I know. If it had ended there, I would not be worried for my soul."

"Lust is ever present in this world, put here by Satan to tempt men into evil. You, Edward, can be pleased with yourself for being much stronger than most men in fighting off that particular demon."

"Even so, I feel so weak sometimes."

Caedwig cleared his throat, tried to swallow from a dry mouth. "The weakness itself is not a sin. That is our human failing, and why the Devil can win good men over to him."

"Yes." Edward was silent again. "Only a short while after my coronation, I was again tormented by Satan."

"Oh?"

"That Godwin—" Edward began. The monk smiled to himself. He was used to Edward referring to the late Earl of Wessex in that way. "He presented his young daughter to me. The old sinful feelings rushed back, just as I thought I had beaten them. She was so young…is so young! She has become like a daughter to me. And still I am shocked to find I do watch her with lustful intent when I let myself go unguarded."

The cleric was especially glad for the cover of darkness in the room as the conversation moved toward the subject of the Queen. "But Edward, my son, Edith was made your wife! The Lord delights in man and woman joined in bonds of holy matrimony. It is one of the great sacraments. Edith may yet look young, but she is not a child! Even at your wedding, Edith had been somewhat beyond the normal age to be married. You must see that the Lord looks favorably upon you. Marriage is a wonderful thing, and it is important for England as well. And—", the monk paused, "the Queen needs you."

"Ah, but chastity is a virtue, is it not?"

"Yes, and duty to your people is important as well. You have no heir, Edward; but Edith can give you that. Edward, one of the greatest gifts you can give the Lord is to bring a child into this world He has created."

Edward sighed again. "If only I could do that without any personal pleasure."

The monk was feeling a little frustrated. "Jesus will not forsake you should you choose to spend carnal time with your wife. I assure you of that, my son." When Edward did not respond, Caedwig finished, "I only ask that you think upon what I have said."

Edward took a deep breath. "I will pray for strength and guidance, and search my conscience for the truth."

Caedwig took that as a small victory. "That is all the Lord desires of you this night."

"Thank you Caedwig. I am sure the Lord will send me a sign."

The monk made the sign of the cross in the air in front of Edward. "Be at peace now, Edward."

"Yes, for the moment." Edward looked about him as if for the first time noticing the lack of lighting. "It is dark in here Caedwig. Why don't you join me in the solar. I am afraid I have not the concentration today for chess, but we could have a rousing game of drafts."

Caedwig smiled again. He had known Edward for almost twenty years. In all that time, the monk had yet to see Edward finish a game of chess.

"I am sorry, my lord. There is truly nothing that I would like more, but I am afraid that you have business to attend to this morning. Shall I light some of the sconces in the room?"

"Oh, very well."

Caedwig left the hall briefly, returning with a lit taper. As the room brightened, the King appeared out of the shadows. Edward sat in the stone seat, resting his long chin on his left hand as he slouched slightly in the grand chair. His right hand was unconsciously fingering the garment he had on, the gold neck chain he wore. Edward was not comfortable in all the regal finery he wore; but Edith thought it important that he dress the part of king, and he did so for her sake. His graying beard was out of fashion for the English aristocracy. Caedwig thought it particularly interesting that Edward, who had grown up in Normandy, seemed to look a bit out of place amidst a fashion that was influenced, at least in part, by the clean-shaven Normans at court.

The King's eyes drooped, giving him a look of constant sadness and making him seem tired all the time. Edward's mind had wandered off, outside the confines of the room, away from the kingdom. Caedwig cleared his throat to bring Edward's attention back to Gloucester.

"My lord, the Bishop of Worcester wishes to see you at your convenience."

"The Bishop of Worcester?"

"Yes, Bishop Aldred. He is back from Hungary."

Edward sat up. "Oh, yes. Caedwig, see that he gets something to eat. The man from Hungary is probably hungry!" The King smiled at his attempt at wordplay.

Caedwig forced a smile. "Sire. I think he wants to talk with you."

"Ah yes, of course. Bishop Aldred. And what was he doing in Hungary?"

Caedwig cocked his head. "My lord, do you not recall Leofric of Mercia suggested to you that Bishop Aldred be sent to retrieve your kinsmen in exile?"

"Ah yes! Of course. That Bishop Aldred. What has the man to say to me today?"

Caedwig stepped back toward the door. "He is just outside. Let me bring the Bishop in to speak with you, sire."

"Please do." Edward again leaned his chin upon his hand.

The door was open only a moment before Bishop Aldred was through it with a flourish, his traveling cape flowing behind him. The man was of average height, with an overly rotund mid section that made him look shorter than he was. His face was dominated by a huge nose and a big smile. Aldred swooped up to Edward and bowed as low as his middle would allow.

"King Edward! Good it is to see you again after my prolonged absence."

Edward hesitated, his mind searching for his store of English vocabulary. "My good Bishop. What news have you brought to England from the continent?"

Bishop Aldred smiled, and bowed again. "My lord, I bring you great news! I have secured the release of Aedward your nephew, his son Edgar and his two daughters as well. This is a happy day for the descendants of Aethelred!"

Caedwig coughed, stepped away from the doorway, bowed his head. "Excuse me, sire, my lord Bishop, the Queen of England approaches."

"Bishop Aldred, Edward my husband, good morning to you both." Queen Edith entered the room upon Caedwig's announcement, paused only briefly beside the monk. She walked over directly to kiss her husband on the forehead. She took a place beside Edward, resting her hand on the King's shoulder. Edith had on an elegant white wrap that covered her neck and shoulders, her brown hair pinned up and under a delicate wimple. Beneath the wrap, a deep purple gown hung loosely on her sprite figure. A veil partially hid her dark eyes; eyes that were unmistakably the most prominent feature she had inherited from her father. Large and intelligent, wide yet restrained, keeping the thoughts within her head hidden even from those near to her.

Edward patted her right hand with his left. "Ah my child. Please come and stand behind me. The good Bishop has brought news from Hungary. It seems Aethelred's blood has grown strong in more than just your husband. Aldred has retrieved the lost members of my family. Exile is such a horrible thing. I am so glad my nephew and his family could come home to take their rightful place in England. Though, I daresay they will have a difficult time making the adjustment. I lived so long in Normandy; yet it was not my home. When I came home to England, I found I missed Normandy. Strange—" Edward trailed off, his gaze undirected.

Aldred jumped back into the conversation where Edward had left it hanging. "Oh yes, the transition will not be easy, but it will be satisfying, especially if your nephew knows just what his rightful place in England will be."

Edward was lost in thought. Queen Edith spoke for the King. "Well, of course Aedward and his family will be welcomed into the King's own household, given all that descendants of Aethelred deserve."

Aldred smiled. "That is what Aedward would want to hear, I am sure. His six year old son Edgar is a marvel. He will grow to be a fine young Englishman."

"I am sure he will." Edith said.

Aldred continued. "Yes, yes. A fine young boy." The bishop hesitated, then pressed on. "My lord, I have heard some disturbing news since I returned."

Edward shook himself, and shrugged. "Oh, and what has disturbed you?"

"I heard that you have promised the King of Denmark that he might inherit the throne of England when you pass on to your reward." Aldred bowed slightly to Edith. "In lieu of children of your own, of course." The queen turned her head slightly away.

Aldred paused to let his accusation sink in. He had spent three long years negotiating the release of Aethelred's grandson, and it was disheartening to think that his efforts might mean nothing for England. When the King offered no response, Aldred continued.

"Is there any truth to this rumor?"

Edward's gaze focused on the Bishop. "What rumor?"

Bishop Aldred shifted his feet and rubbed his nose across the sleeve of his cloak. "Ah, is it true that Svend of Denmark does expect to follow you as King of England?"

"That is absurd!" Edward waved his right hand in the air as if he was brushing away a fly.

"Besides, our friend Svend is far too busy fighting off marauding Norwegians to worry about England." The Earl of Wessex entered the hall unannounced. He gestured to Caedwig as he passed through the door, nodded curtly to Bishop Aldred, bowed low to the King and leaned over to kiss his sister's cheek. Edward's long face brightened at the sight of his right hand man.

"Harold! Good to see you! But where is your brother Tostig? I plan a hunt as soon as this wretched storm abates, and Tostig would be sorely missed were he not to join us. I thought we would head to Savernake Forest. Oh, Harold! You should have been with me last week up on Cranborne Chase! To hear the sound of the hounds baying as they scrambled after the largest red fox I have ever seen! It was exhilarating. At one point I had my bow trained on the beast, but I could not bring myself to fell such a beautiful creation."

Harold laughed. "The mighty hunter! My God, I fear you are getting soft in your maturity, Edward."

The King seemed to take that to heart, his face clouded over with concern. "I shall pray for guidance." Edward's face lit up again. "But tell me, where is your brother?" In the past few years the King had gotten along well with all of Godwin's children, but Tostig remained his favorite, mostly because he looked and acted least like Godwin himself who had caused so much trouble for the House of Aethelred.

"My lord, Tostig had some business to attend to south of London, but he was to meet us here straight-away afterward."

Bishop Aldred raised an eyebrow. "What business south of London? Your brother would not have been heading to Bromely, now would he?"

Harold merely smiled. "Tostig will be here shortly, and we can all sit down and chat about such things, Bishop Aldred. In the meantime," Harold handed a parchment over to the King, "here is a letter from Normandy. I intercepted a courier on his way up from the coast. I thought I would deliver the note personally."

Edward snatched the letter from Harold's grasp and tore open the seal in excitement. "It is from my friend William."

"Yes, indeed it is." Harold stepped next to the King so that he could read the note over Edward's shoulder.

Edward paraphrased the contents out loud for the benefit of the others. "It seems William has his hands full of fighting the French king." Edward looked up. "You know, life in Normandy is a constant struggle, whether as a ruler or as an exile—" The King's gaze floated into the rafters above, where rain was beginning to soak through the thatch in a couple places and drip onto the floor below.

Harold had continued reading. He grabbed Edward's shoulder. "My lord, the Norman seems to allude to a promise you made him a few years back. A promise of a sort that he seems intent upon your keeping. What might that be?"

Edward shook himself and began reading the letter again. "I do not know. Let me see. We used to hunt together—"

Harold was insistent. "William seems to have written a lot about his desire for more than the Dukedom of Normandy. He seems to be concerned about whether or not you have sired a male child."

"Yes, he does." Edward looked toward Caedwig for strength.

Harold restrained himself, keeping his voice casual. "What do you make of that?"

Aldred spoke up then. "Yes, King Edward! Another rumor I had heard while abroad was that Duke William expects to be King of England one day!"

Harold glanced at the Bishop, then looked back at the King. "Surely that is not what this letter is all about, Edward. We have all known that story to be a court joke!"

"Indeed," Aldred responded, "until this letter here."

Harold grabbed the King's arm, squeezed a little too hard. "Edward," the Earl of Wessex spoke very slowly, "what does this mean?"

Edward's eyes startled wide. "What does what mean?"

The Earl of Wessex swept his right hand through the air. "First Svend in Denmark; now William. Do they both expect to be heirs to the English throne?" Harold leaned close to Edward. "You cannot continue to promise the throne to whoever is at hand. I might next expect to hear the news that King Haraald of Norway does claim the crown as well!"

Edward swatted at the same nonexistent flying insect about his head. "That is absurd!" A great clap of thunder shook the hall as the King spoke. "Why should a king of Scandinavia, or the Duke of the Normans inherit the Kingdom of England? Are there no English men in the kingdom that we need to recruit able bodied leaders from overseas?"

Bishop Aldred was satisfied. "Indeed, there is now, my lord. Aedward is a fine, strong man, as brave and courageous as had been his father, your half-brother Edmund Ironside. You will be pleased when you meet your nephew. I am sure of it."

"And when will I meet this man?" Edward asked enthusiastically.

"Soon, sire. Earl Leofric was to meet him in Bromely, and there they would depart for your court here in the west. They should arrive at Gloucester in a few days."

"Good."

The Bishop waved his cloak about him and bowed to Edward. "Sire, if you will excuse me, I will retire now. I have had a long journey, and I do need to rest."

"Certainly, Aldred. We can talk later of Hungary and things." Edward leaned back in his chair.

"As you wish." Aldred bowed again, nodding then to the others. "My lady, Earl Harold—" and the Bishop was gone from the hall.

Harold turned to face his king. He was not so satisfied. "Edward, what is this all about? In truth I need to know. Svend, and William—"

Edward was confident. "Rumor is the work of the Devil, Harold."

The Earl pointed an accusing finger at the parchment still in the King's hands. "And what does that mean, then?" Harold had for so long not wanted anything to do with Normandy. His father had taken up refuge in Flanders during their family exile, marrying Tostig to a woman related to Duke William's own wife. But, Harold went far away from the French coast, had chosen to travel to Ireland with his other brothers. After all, Harold's youngest brother Wulfnoth, and his only nephew were taken as hostages to Normandy at that time. Many of the Normans at the English court had become his good friends; but there was no love in the Earl of Wessex for Normandy itself or Duke William.

Edward's confidence turned to confusion. "Harold, I will think on this, and pray. I am sure the Lord will clear this all up with a sign for us."

Harold was skeptical. "I tell you, Edward, we ourselves have the reason to confront our all too human problems. The Lord need not be troubled at every turn."

Edward looked hurt. "You have been reading too much of that Roman Boethius. He was not a good Christian, remember that. Look to the Lord, Harold, and you will find your answers."

Harold shrugged. "You seek your answers from the Lord, and I will search my own soul to find mine. Perhaps I will find the Lord there in the end, and we two will yet agree."

Edward scowled. "Do not speak so lightly, my friend. If you truly mean to seek the answers in your soul, a holy pilgrimage would give you that chance. Perhaps that is just what you should do."

"What? Go on a pilgrimage?" Harold laughed.

Edward's scowl deepened. "Harold, I think that perhaps a trip to the Holy Lands in the east, or to Rome would give you the time you need to search that soul of yours. The Lord does help those who help themselves. Your time given to the Lord on pilgrimage would be a sacred thing that God will look on very kindly."

"Is the Lord not right here in England that I need to travel so far to seek him out?" Harold smiled. "When I find need of a vacation, I will consider going on pilgrimage."

"Ah, Harold, I do worry about you sometimes."

"And I you."

Edward looked contemplative for a moment, then decided on a new tactic. "Harold, did you ever notice that the moon does rise an hour later each night than the night before?"

"Well, yes, Edward. I suppose I have noticed that. What of it?"

"Do you not see? Nature is not constant, not controlled. Order and meaning in this world can only come from the intervention of God. We must pray for miracles, Harold, for through miracles our lives will be kept on track."

"My God, Edward! You be careful of what you say. I might believe you do mean it."

"Oh, but I do, Harold. Heaven help England if someone were to rule who did not believe these things."

Edith frowned at her brother. "Harold! Do not pester Edward like this! Please!"

Harold ignored his sister Edith and tried once more to get through to the King. "And what of the sun that rises so faithfully each morning?" Harold wondered how it was that the learned man could seem so blind.

Edward slapped his hand to the arm of the stone seat. "Yes! That is precisely my point. You see, it is a miracle of God that brings the sun up each day to cast the Devil's darkness away."

"Forgive me, Edward. On one hand you speak of the inconstancy of the moon as a failing of the Natural order, yet in the next breath you praise the daily rising of the sun."

"Indeed." It was all so obvious to Edward.

"Yet, they are both of Nature, are they not? It remains simply for us on earth to understand the rhyme."

"There is where you are wrong, son. I know I have studied more than you have. Let me explain—"

Before Edward could restate his thesis, a shuffle outside the hall drew the attention of all of them. Caedwig was at the door, but he failed to bar the way before the muddy young man pushed into the room. The newcomer had obviously been riding hard for an extended period of time. His face was drawn with lack of food and water, his eyes sunken with lack of proper sleep.

"My lord, King Edward!" The man gasped, "I have dire news. Tragic news!" He took a deep breath. "The Lord Leofric of Mercia and your kinsman Aedward, the one who was exiled—they have both been found dead south of London!"

Entry X

▼

Through which Aelfgar expresses his anger at Gloucester

The storm that had blown in two days before seemed at its leisure to move on. The rain came, sometimes hard like the flow at the base of a waterfall, sometimes soft like the dew settling on a rare clear night in Autumn; but continually for days it did come. King Edward sought out his confessor each morning, thinking that God was punishing him, making it so he could not follow through with his hunting plans. This kept Edward testy and disgruntled, whereas it was the news from London that upset the rest of the company at Gloucester.

Tostig Godwinsson had arrived that afternoon bringing with him only a rumor that Leofric had died of natural causes in his bed chamber. The Earl of Northumbria had offered no more reliable information than the courier had brought, but he did leave everyone with the knowledge that what they feared was indeed true: Aedward the Exile and the Earl of Mercia were dead. Harold of Wessex had spent the morning arguing with Bishop Aldred over what was to become of the last of Aethelred's line.

King Edward had already offered to raise the child of Aedward in his house; but the Bishop of Worcester seemed intent upon having more offered than just that. With Leofric gone, Aldred's position was not as strong, nor very certain. Both he and Harold knew this. Even so, it bothered the Earl of Wessex that neither of them could figure out what had happened in Bromely, and that made his arguments distracted and inconclusive. Harold looked expectantly toward his brother as he and the Bishop entered the King's audience hall. Tostig sat next to the King, in the place where his sister the Queen should have been, his squinty eyes sparkling with mischief, his teeth showing through the thin-lipped grin. Queen Edith stood behind and to the left of Edward, her long fingered hand resting lightly on the King's shoulder.

The two newcomers addressed the King and Queen, bowing in unison. Bishop Aldred did not bother to acknowledge Tostig, but Harold quickly turned his inquiring gaze to the man seated next to the King. Before Harold could speak to Tostig, a commotion behind him at the door drew the attention of everyone.

"Damn this weather, I could have traveled all the way to London if not for the washed out roads from Chester!" Aelfgar pushed through the crowd of courtiers, never once noticing Harold, Bishop Aldred, or anyone else, so intent was he upon the response of the King.

"King Edward, is it true? Is my father dead?!"

Edward had never felt close to the house of Leofric, did not know Aelfgar that well; only recognized that he had been the offspring of old Leofric's coupling with the child Godiva of Coventry. Appalling, he thought to himself. Nevertheless, the King could sympathize with the young man's loss. Edward's own life had changed dramatically with the loss of his own father, Aethelred. Young Aelfgar would be worried about his position, just as he, Edward, had been. At least Aelfgar did not have a mother to cause such heartache as Edward himself had experienced through his own mother, Emma of Normandy. Emma had turned around and married the Danish usurper who had helped bring Aethelred down, then backed her children of the Danish line over Edward and his brother.

The people in the hall waited expectantly for Edward's reply, no one envying his position in the least bit.

"Yes, young man. I am sorry to say the word from London is that the good Earl of Mercia, your father, is dead." Edward stared at the boy, could think of nothing more to say. Without any more news from London, it was hard to determine how to respond to the boy.

Aelfgar had not allowed himself to believe it, yet now could not escape seeing the King's sincere expression of sympathy. His shoulders dropped, and for a moment the tall, lean young man looked as childlike and innocent as he truly was. "But how?"

Before Edward could explain and offer a word of condolence, Tostig laughed from next to him. "Perhaps it was the plague."

Harold saw something he did not like in his brother's expression. He knew Tostig too well not to recognize when he was trying to stir up trouble. With Tostig's words, Aelfgar noticed that son of Godwin for the first time, then saw Harold stepping up to stand beside Edward. Behind Edward stood Edith, daughter of Godwin. Harold shot Tostig a look of disapproval, but before he could offer something to smooth out the conversation, the young son of Leofric exclaimed in anger.

"Plague, is it?!" Aelfgar waved his hand at each of the Godwin siblings, then back to King Edward. "There is indeed a plague upon England, and it is known by the name of Godwin! I see it now. I have no doubt that the Godwin plague may have brought death to my father! May you all rot in Hell!"

"Careful, Aelfgar." Harold held up his hand. "That is no way for the new Earl of Mercia to act. Sit down and we will discuss it between us all."

Tostig's eyes bulged with shock upon hearing his brother call Aelfgar the Earl of Mercia. He tried to cry out in his rage, could not form the words. Edward began to speak, and Tostig relaxed, sure the King would set things aright.

"Let us not be hasty about this, Harold. Young Aelfgar needs time to come to terms with his father's death first." Edward paused, there was a rumble of thunder as the rain renewed its intensity. "I need to come to terms with the Lord! Then we can talk about the earldoms of England."

Tostig smiled. Whatever Harold was thinking, Tostig was sure Edward was still looking toward the younger Godwinsson's interests. Aelfgar stepped forward, no less angry.

"No! Damn you all! We will talk about Mercia now! I demand that you, in front of all assembled here, confer upon me my father's lands and titles." Aelfgar caught himself directing his statements toward Harold. The young man stepped back and turned to King Edward. "Tell them all I am Earl of Mercia."

Edward stood up. With his restless mood due to the poor weather, the King was not going to let the young man tell him what he should and should not do. "Aelfgar Leofricsson, I had indeed spoken already about my intention to name you the next Earl of Mercia." Tostig's wide grin sagged as his mouth dropped open. "But I will not declare it for you now, and never under duress. You will not dictate terms to me. I am King! I will have my servants prepare guest chambers for you. I suggest that you retire to them and cool off. We can talk more later, perhaps." Edward sat back down, pleased at how he handled the situation. He looked to see if Harold was impressed, but it was Tostig who was especially pleased, for he could see that Aelfgar would make it difficult for himself, and that would leave the door open for Tostig to come in.

Edward's smile faded slightly, for Harold was not so happy with the situation. Nor was Aelfgar. The Earl of Wessex could see that Aelfgar was at a loss for the moment, he stepped up to the younger man.

"Aelfgar. Do not harbor such resentment towards my family. And do not fear for your place. Edward will confer upon you your rights and privileges. I assure you of that."

Despite the fact that it had been said by a son of Godwin, Aelfgar relaxed with the words that seemed so clearly in his favor in front of everyone assembled in the hall. The King furrowed his brow, wondering if he should be angry with Harold for speaking in his name. Tostig fumed for the same reason, stood up and pointed at Aelfgar.

"Lucky for you that you were not in Bromely with your father. Perhaps the plague would have taken you as well!"

The young man reacted at once to Tostig's goading. "Damn you!" He spat at Harold. "Damn all you Godwinspawn! God damn you all to the furthest reaches of Hell!"

Edward jumped out of his chair, pushed Tostig and Harold aside to stand before Aelfgar. "You will stop saying the Lord's name in vain. Stop these vulgarities in my presence! Do you hear?"

Aelfgar, with the passion of youth, stood his ground. "Yes, I hear you, King Edward. And may God grant to me the knowledge that he may damn you as well!"

Harold came between Aelfgar and the King, lest the young man do something as foolhardy as try and strike Edward. To quench the burning embers, Harold turned to speak to Edward, but the King was clapping his hands.

"Guards! Take this boy from my sight!" The soldiers from the doorway were upon Aelfgar instantly, one holding each arm as they dragged him from the room. Harold reached for Aelfgar, but the housecarls bullied the young man from his grasp.

"You Godwins have not seen the last of me! Do you hear?!"

Harold turned back to Edward, who stood red-faced, watching the guards drag the young man from the room. "Sire. Edward! Do something! Say something to clear this up. Surely you do not mean to have that young man handled as he is. He just lost his father for mercy's sake. We can expect him to be angry and confused."

The guards slowed as they heard the Earl of Wessex entreat the King for clemency. As they paused, Aelfgar cried out again.

"You let them kill my father, Edward! I will not forget that!"

Edward's eyes cleared, looked to Caedwig in the corner, focused on Harold. "You are right." The hall was still except for the scuffling as the boy was dragged from the room. Edward moved toward the door.

"You there, guards. Hold that man at the door a moment." Edward crossed the hall and stepped beside the son of Leofric. Anger had transformed the boy's face making him look like a demon. He spat at the King's feet as Edward approached, with a curse sworn upon the Lord God's own person. The anger swelled in the King again. "Yes, I will give you what you deserve, young man."

The King laid his hand on Aelfgar's forehead. "I, Edward, King of England and overlord of the borderlands, do confer upon you, Aelfgar Leofricson, the title of Earl of Mercia, including all the lands and responsibilities with which that title does correspond."

A murmur of shock shook the others in the hall, but Aelfgar was so stunned he could say nothing, only stared wild-eyed at the King. Harold had not expected such a quick turn around, but was pleased, was already wording in his mind what he would say next to keep the entire assembly under control after the strange interchange. Tostig was more flabbergasted than even Aelfgar. He dashed to Edward with a protest on his lips, just as Harold reached the King's side with the smile of approval Edward had sought before. The brothers were stopped in mid stride as Edward continued.

"Now that you are formally made Earl of Mercia, I do hereby formally send you into exile! You seem obviously to be possessed by some demon. You must be banished ere you bring dire consequences upon my kingdom. Guards, see that this outlaw leaves this house and this country!"

Entry XI

▼

In which Aldbald and Caedwig speak for the second time

The young man had been welcomed into the monk's brightly lit cubicle, and he held his hands together to keep them from shaking as he spoke with Caedwig. Aldbald knew that the monk whom he had befriended was the King's confidante, but he did not care. Nor was the young man of Coventry concerned with the inter and intra family rivalries amidst the houses that held the earldoms of England. This night he had been intent upon having the man of the cloth write for him a letter of love. A note he had to deliver, even though it proclaimed a longing he was sure he could never hope to satisfy.

"I would be happy to write for you a letter, my friend." Caedwig stopped. "Love is a confusing thing, no matter the object of that love." Caedwig paused again, looking beyond Aldbald.

"Perhaps the unattainable love is the best," the monk said.

Caedwig sat at his desk surrounded by candles that lit the room as if it were day so that the cleric would be less hindered by his weakening eyesight. The two were very close in the small room, and Aldbald could see a slight frown come over his friend's face before Caedwig brought his gaze back to the young man and smiled ineffectively. "For in the unattainable we strive for goodness always, just as in our devotion in this life to the Lord."

Aldbald cocked his head. "Did not Bede say something like that in his teachings?"

The question focused Caedwig's full attention on the young visitor to his quarters. "Indeed, he may have. I am not sure." The monk laughed then. "I daresay I thought it might have been my own notion! You surprise me, my friend. You come to me for help in writing, yet you seem to know the writings of Bede. Can you read then?"

Aldbald laughed as well. "I fear I do not. I only know snatches of stories I have heard. When I had free time as a boy, I liked to visit an old monk named Wulfwin, and he would tell stories of ages past and people long dead." Aldbald was sure his own predisposition to talk overly much may have come from his association with the old clergyman. Caedwig's expression reminded Aldbald of how the old cleric had looked when they would talk.

"Yes, Bede was a man who had lived many years earlier when the Kingdom of Northumbria was dominant on the island," Caedwig explained. "Your home, Aldbald, was in the middle of one of the great kingdoms which arose following the great migration of Germanic peoples from the continent. The region south of the Humber became known as Mercia, where the Angles called themselves the border folk, settling in the midlands and bordering on Wales. The West Saxons later supplanted Mercia as the dominant kingdom, and even now Wessex is the richest prized earldom of England."

"But," Aldbald interjected, "Wulfwin told me that Mercia was the second most important earldom in the country. Did you know that if not for the raiding Northmen, Mercia might have retained its position as the strongest region in England?"

Caedwig laughed again. "Indeed I do know."

Aldbald shuffled his feet and looked down. "Of course you know. What am I telling you for?"

The monk smiled and went on. "It was the Danish peoples from the Scandinavian countries who raided churches and monasteries, destroying libraries and weakening the Angle settlers. Alfred the Great of Wessex was the first to hold back the Danes, and the Northmen soon began the conversion to the one true faith as well. So, in the end I believe England became the stronger." Caedwig was pleased to see the intense interest in Aldbald's wide eyes. "What do you think?"

"I think it is all so exciting. I just wish I remembered more of what Wulfwin taught me."

"Perhaps you should learn your letters, my friend. Then all that knowledge would be open to you."

"You are playing with me, Caedwig. Reading and writing are for clerics and nobleman, not for cottars and villeins."

"Oh? Did you not know that Alfred the Great translated many Latin texts into English specifically so that the common folk in the land would have access to the writings?" Aldbald's disbelieving look brought a smile to the monk's face. "It is true, my friend. There is a world of knowledge waiting for anyone who chooses to learn. Come to me whenever you feel the call."

"I am afraid I will not have much time as a servant of Lord Tostig. Even when there is nothing to do, he is not one to let me have much time to myself for studies. But, I thank you for your thoughts." Aldbald turned away, feigning hurt. "Unless you are suggesting that I learn to write because you do not wish to help me this night."

The monk knew he was being teased. "Come here," Caedwig laughed. "I will write your love sonnet. But beware my friend, you just might win the lady to your side! Then you might never find the time to learn to read!"

Entry XII

▼

Where the Godwin brothers speak of the business in Bromely

"Now I have to go out in this accursed weather, just to patch things up with Chester!" Harold was storming down the hallway toward his bed-chamber, with his brother following behind. Tostig struggled to match the other man's long-striding pace.

"Surely you do not mean to continue this favoritism of Aelfgar? What has gotten into you, Harold? Leofric is dead, and his son banished! What a triumph for the house of Godwin!"

Harold turned so abruptly that Tostig fell upon his brother's out-stretched, accusing finger. "What has gotten into you? Damn it, man, I had secured Gyrth in East Anglia and Leofwine in Kent. What matter that young Aelfgar retained Mercia for the house of Leofric? Better that, since it would have kept England united and strong, not broken the kingdom apart as do these petty family rivalries."

"Petty family rivalries? But Harold! With Aelfgar gone, I can take Mercia! It will be just as we spoke in St. Albans. There will be no rivalries, because there will be only one house: That of Godwin!"

"No, Tostig. I secured the Earldom of Northumbria for you, and there you will stay until I choose to find you a different place. When Edward cools down, I will get him to recall Aelfgar to Mercia. Then I will ride for Chester to bring the news personally to the house of Leofric. I will need to know there are no hard feelings. We need the borderlands secure against Welsh raids. And, with the house of Leofric firmly planted in Mercia it will not do to have Chester our enemy as well."

Tostig let his anger flare, his face turning red as he screamed. "All you ever think about is yourself, Harold. Damn you anyway! It was not you that brought the destruction of our father's oldest rival. It was I! And Godwin would be proud of me now, even as you try and sweep me into the floor rushes!"

Tostig's burning complexion became more dull, Harold's gaze draining the color from the other man's face. The Earl of Wessex breathed heavily, swallowed hard as if tasting bitter herbs. He searched the younger man's mad eyes for some remnant of common sense. The silence was so palpable, Tostig forgot to breath for a moment. When he remembered, he still found it difficult as Harold grabbed his jerkin at the throat and pressed it into the younger man's Adam's apple. Harold spoke very slowly.

"What exactly happened in Bromely? What have you done?" Harold raised his brother slightly off the ground. "Tell me you did not kill Leofric!"

The last of the color spilled away from Tostig as he spurted the words, "I never laid a hand on the man!"

Harold did not let go. "Then what did you do?"

"Leofric would not see me. I swear it. I…I only sent him a bottle of my best wine—"

The pupils of Harold's brown eyes dilated. "Tostig! Not poison! My God, what were you thinking?" Harold shook his brother, bouncing him against the stone wall of the hall. "Why, Tostig? Why?!"

"Is the world such a worse place with Leofric gone from it?" Tostig tried to regain some of his former exuberance. "Harold! The man is gone. Forget for the moment how it may have happened. Think what that means for us. You heard King Edward today. If he is willing to sever connections between England and Leofric's blood, we should embrace the opportunity that gives us. With Leofric gone, no one stands in our way! Edward has always looked kindly upon me...us. I tell you Harold, the next king of England could be a Godwin, even without a son borne by our sister!"

Harold shoved his brother away and took a step back. His face showed such dread that Tostig himself was frightened. "What is it, Harold? Why do you look at me so? Is Leofric's death so appalling to you that—"

Harold interrupted the other man, his voice almost inaudible. "My God, Tostig! Did you kill Aedward the Exile as well?" He asked the question, but he already believed it of his brother.

Tostig, too, was shocked then. "No! I tell you truly, brother, I have no idea how or why Aedward died." Harold's horror changed to frustration and anger. He moved back beside his brother, and Tostig pressed himself against the hallway wall trying in vain to keep some distance between the two of them.

Tostig cried, "It is true! I do swear it. I never once even thought to kill the Exile!"

"What is done, is done." Harold leaned close to speak quietly into Tostig's ear. "There is no use mulling old and bitter spices. But, Tostig, if I ever learn otherwise, you will sorely regret having done the deed."

"No, Harold, no! It is the truth." As Harold turned to leave his delinquent brother behind, Tostig followed along bantering to try and gain back some ground lost to Harold. "Still, is not Aedward's death fortuitous? Surely you must see that!"

Harold spun around and grabbed his brother again, shook the younger man. "What I do see, I see for England, not for Wessex alone, nor the house of Godwin, and certainly not simply for you, Tostig! I see a descendent of Aethelred dead, and for no apparent reason. A man who might have worked for our interests; worked in England's favor. Without him, and with no heir of Edward's body, who shall succeed Edward as king?

"I see the Earl of Mercia dead, apparently with no natural cause. Thus, the son of Leofric is angered, justly so it seems, and ever again at odds with Wessex just as in the days of father. I will go to Chester and hope to reconcile affairs with Aelfgar and…Leofric's widow. Perhaps we have not lost their confidence completely as yet. How can England become strong when faced with internal division? Damn it, Tostig. Why can you not see these things?

"I will tell you what else I do see. I see an Earl of Northumbria who is dangerously close to losing all. You, Tostig, had better watch where you do step. You are only an earl through my sufferance! Now begone!"

Harold turned once again, waving his hands toward his brother as if he was trying to get rid of a bad odor. Tostig watched his brother go. When the Earl of Wessex turned the corner at the end of the hallway, Tostig gestured lewdly and spat into the rushes upon the floor.

When Harold arrived at his bedchamber, he found Edyth Svanneshals was not alone. A hooded man stood in the shadows beside the hearth. Edyth met Harold at the door with an embrace, a whisper in his ear.

"Harold, you have a visitor."

The Earl of Wessex had not yet had a chance to extinguish the ire his brother so easily built up within him. He was in no mood to play any games of mystery.

"Do not stand there, lurking amidst the drapes of your concealing clothing. Who are you, and what is it that you want of me? A visitor in my room at this hour must bring more sorry news, the last thing I do need right now! Speak to me, openly and quickly, or leave me be."

Edyth whispered a word of restraint, then let Harold go as he moved to meet the other man stepping into the center of the chamber. A gloved hand pulled back the hood, and two confused eyes peered across the room at the Earl of Wessex.

"My lord—" Aldbald's voice cracked. He swallowed forcibly, began again. "My lord, forgive me for this intrusion upon your private quarters."

The young man looked so distraught, Harold's own foul mood softened in an effort to calm the other man. The Earl reached over and grasped Aldbald's shoulder, squeezed lightly.

"What is it Aldbald, my friend?"

Aldbald looked from Harold to Edyth, then back to the Earl. Normally not at a loss for words, the young man now knew not how to begin. After a moment, Aldbald continued.

"My lord, there are so many stories spreading through the servants of this place. It seems no one is certain what has happened today. I, for one, know only that my lord Tostig has told his servants and retainers to be ready to leave Gloucester within the hour! It is so late, and the weather is terrible. No sane man would choose to leave in this storm."

Harold sighed. "There you have it, then. You have said it perhaps better than I could have explained it all. No sane man would choose to travel in this weather."

Aldbald looked more worried. "Then, the King has sent him away?"

Harold smiled sadly. "No, King Edward did not send him away."

"The Lady Edyth tells me that you and your brother did not see things the same this afternoon with the King. Perhaps you have sent him away?"

Harold shrugged. "Tostig leaves by his own accord. My brother sometimes lets himself become overzealous regarding matters in which he should not be involved in the first place. Edyth is right, and I daresay I kept my temper just long enough to meet him alone in the hallway. I did indeed reprimand the man, but I did not send him from Gloucester. That he has chosen to do himself."

When Harold saw the young man's stricken look, the Earl spoke softly. "Do not worry, Aldbald. Tostig is not out of favor with King Edward. Nor is my wrath over his actions irreparable. Certainly you should not worry that your place in his service will be in question. I only wish that your master was a little more—" and Harold laughed deeply, breaking the tension in the room. "A little more like his older brother!"

Aldbald hesitantly joined in the laughter. "I fear that brothers are rarely alike, my lord. Perhaps that is England's loss! Thank you for your kind words, though. But, in truth, it is not just for my position that I do worry. The news from London is all over the household. I know that the Earl of Mercia is dead. Is it true also that Leofric's son is banished from the kingdom?"

Harold sighed again, sat himself down hard in a chair by the fire. "For the moment. However, you can be sure I will see that Edward does recall young Aelfgar." Harold cast a quizzical look at the other man. "Why do you worry about the son of Leofric? Did you know him in Coventry?"

"In truth, I did not sire. It is more that I was worried about his…the family of Leofric. After I learned of the death of the Earl of Mercia, I had expected to accompany Lord Tostig to join you and the King in Chester to pay our respects at the funeral services for Earl Leofric. Indeed, I had hoped to deliver a letter to…someone of the late Earl's household. When I heard the rumor that Lord Aelfgar was banished, I knew not what to expect. Then, in addition, Lord Tostig's decision to leave at once came to me. I feared I could not deliver my letter."

"Leave your letter with me, and I will deliver it personally to Chester."

"Thank you, my lord. I fear I did not know how to approach the Lady Godiva—" Aldbald looked embarrassed, and Harold was at once more curious.

"Your note is to the Lady Godiva?"

Aldbald's embarrassment changed to worry. The Earl of Wessex may count him a friend, yet he was still only a common man. What would Harold think of his interests in the woman of Mercia?

"My lord," Aldbald was reserved, cautious, "if you could deliver the note to the maidservant of the Lady, that is all I ask. But, do not open the letter, please." Aldbald caught himself as he realized he was instructing the Earl of Wessex in what he could and should not do.

Harold only smiled, this was something he could understand. "Ah ha! So it is a love letter, is it not? And to the maidservant Hildreth? Of course, it must be, by the look of your fiery complexion. She is a…stout woman, a good Englishwoman, though. She does seem much older than you, however." Harold continued when he saw Aldbald blush even more, not willing to answer to clarify the Earl's mistake. "No matter. A good woman, none-the-less."

Harold became serious. "My friend, I fear I do not head to Chester under very good graces with the Lady Godiva. Nor do I expect to see the maidservant Hildreth. But, never fear, Aldbald, I will deliver your love letter, and I am sure the arrow will hit its mark. You do surprise me, young man. I did not know that you knew how to write!"

"My lord, in truth I do not." Aldbald looked down at his feet. "I had a kindly monk, Caedwig is his name, transcribe my thoughts."

Harold looked hurt. "Then you would let a monk in on your thoughts, let him know of your love, but you will not confide in your friends?"

Flustered, Aldbald shot a glance back to Harold. "Oh no. You misunderstand. Yes, Caedwig did help me write my feelings, but he knows not to whom I do send the note." Aldbald quickly changed the subject. "I do wish to learn to read and write, Lord Harold. Perhaps the Lord Tostig might grant me some time alone in which I could study. Do you think that I should ask it of him?"

Harold looked at the man with sympathy. "Aldbald, my friend, you should definitely try. Tostig hated having to study, perhaps it would give him pleasure to see you struggling to learn your grammar as well. And the monk Caedwig is a good man. He would probably be interested in tutoring you if he has the time, or he could send you to someone who would. But, do not let Tostig think that you truly want to learn. Then he might keep you from it, just to show you that he can. For now, rest easy, my friend. Though Tostig retreats to his northern home, I will stay on to smooth things over with King Edward and the house of Leofric."

Harold at once became reserved, his gaze unfocussed. Aldbald shifted his feet. "Well, sire, I thank you for your time and encouragement. Oh," Aldbald reached under his cloak to retrieve a parchment he had folded and stuffed in his jerkin. "Here is my letter."

When Harold made no effort to grab the letter, Aldbald nervously placed it in Edyth Swan-neck's outstretched hand.

"I will see that Harold delivers your letter, Aldbald. Go now, I think the Earl would like to be alone."

"Thank you, my lady. My lord—" With one final glance toward Harold, Aldbald shrugged and left the room.

Edyth closed the door and turned back to her man. "What is it, Harold?" She reached over to gently caress his forehead, the touch of her hand bringing the man out of his distracted gaze.

"Oh, nothing. At least nothing I cannot handle, my dear. I was just thinking about Tostig. He never ceases to vex me of late." Harold laughed sarcastically. "Perhaps I should be glad to have Tostig to bring such excitement to my life; but I fear I am a bore at heart, would sometimes much prefer a more simple existence."

Edyth smiled, hugged the man. "And I, too, my love. Then perhaps I would see more of you. Will you be off so soon for Chester?"

Harold brought Edyth around the chair and sat her on his lap. "I had planned on it. Now, I think I should first travel to London, make sure everything is settled there after the unrest due to the deaths of Leofric and Aedward of Hungary. I have not yet heard from our friend Robert FitzWimark whom I left in St. Albans. I am sure he has heard the news and will be seeking to discover what happened. I must go to London to help him sort things out.

"In the meantime, I will draft a letter to Chester. Let the King's change of heart sink in and tempers cool; then I will travel to see the family of Leofric."

Harold stroked the woman's cheek, cupped her chin in his hand and raised her face to meet his gaze. "I am sorry I must travel so much, Edyth. Right now I would give anything to spend some time with you."

"Well, you are not the insane man your brother is to travel in this weather. At least I know I have you until the storm breaks!"

"That you do!" Harold swept his fingers lightly down along the woman's elegant neck, reached to unlace the woman's shift. He saw the paper in her hands. "And what is this?"

"This is the letter that Aldbald wants you to deliver to the maidservant of the Lady Godiva of Mercia."

Harold stared at the parchment. "Ah, yes…Godiva—"

Edyth gave the man a playful shake. "Godiva's maidservant, Harold. Do not forget. Young Aldbald is counting on you."

Entry XIII

▼

In which Harold travels to Chester to try and console Godiva

Within three days of having spoken so harshly to Aelfgar, King Edward wondered at the circumstances of the young man's absence from his court. As soon as the weather broke, Edward was off hunting. Although the court looked upon Edward's change of heart as true repentance for his rash commandment, Harold knew it was more the man's complete lack of memory of the entire incident. Edward's mood made Harold's job a bit easier, although it was not for a couple weeks that the Earl of Wessex finally made the trek to Chester. His letters, and those he had gotten King Edward to sign, had been received, and all of England knew that Aelfgar was the new Earl of Mercia, declared by King Edward and ratified by the Witan. Chester had not been represented at the meeting of advisors, but the only one who had minded the Earl of Wessex speaking for the son of Leofric was Tostig Godwinsson.

With the coming of the sun and the clearing of the latest clouds, Harold was upon his sturdy pony heading north from Gloucester along the borderlands with Wales; through Hwicce, March and Cheshire. Although Leofric had moved his court to Coventry, his son preferred the family residence on their lands in Cheshire. It was there to which Aelfgar had retreated; there that Leofric's body had been interred; there where Harold hoped to speak to Lady Godiva.

The Earl of Wessex hardly saw the countryside he traversed, so intent was he upon the reason for his trip: to make amends with the house of Leofric. As much as he hated the thought of what his brother had done, Harold did find it mildly pleasing to know that the old Earl of Mercia was indeed dead. Tostig would be surprised to learn, however, that his brother's pleasure came in Harold's belief that the Lady Godiva may herself be happier with the man out of her life.

He had planned to delay his arrival in Chester long enough so that the funeral ceremonies for Leofric were long over. Harold did not think it wise to show up until after the old man was laid to rest and feelings had calmed. Although he learned little more, the Earl of Wessex had made the trip to London which had given him further reason to delay his trip north. Still, when he walked his mount through the outer gates to the Earl of Mercia's manor accompanied by only a small group of his housecarls, it did not upset him in the least to learn that Aelfgar was out hunting.

The guard at the inner gate was worried. Harold realized that Aelfgar had undoubtedly left orders to restrict the Earl of Wessex, not let him enter the house. Yet, the man savored his life and freedom, and knew not how to restrain the most powerful of Englishmen.

"Do not be disturbed." Harold smiled in his disarming way. "Should the young master of the house arrive before I have gone, I shall clear you of any blame."

"But, sire—" The guard was unsure, stepped back only one pace.

Harold laughed. "You can be sure his anger will be directed towards me!" Satisfied at that, the soldier opened the gate to the inner walk.

"Where might I find the Lady of the manor?"

"Lord Aelfgar's wife?"

"No, the Lady Godiva. I would speak with the widow of Leofric."

"At this hour, sire, I would say she should be in her chamber preparing for the evening meal. I shall send for a servant to announce you."

"That will not be necessary. I would arrive before my announcer!" Harold strode across the lawn, turned to call back to the guard. "You can call a servant to attend to my friends there, however." Harold gestured to his soldiers. "They will be needing supper themselves."

Harold thought he recognized an air of gloom hanging over the household. Perhaps the death of Leofric was a more solemn affair than he had guessed it would have been. Either that, or the news that Aelfgar was recalled had not totally sunk in, or been believed. Bad news is always easier to accept. The people of Leofric's household in Chester, as well as on the family's other manors and lands, would be wondering what was in their future. The letters from the King would help, but only time would show that Edward and Harold intended to keep the status quo. But, Harold's presence to reaffirm the King's wishes was important, and the Earl of Wessex made the trip to the borderlands for that reason. That, and to see Godiva.

Harold was surprised to find neither the housecarl Gunthnot nor the maidservant Hildreth in attendance upon their lady. When the Earl of Wessex knocked on the door to Lady Godiva's chambers and announced himself, it was Godiva's own voice he heard.

"I am sorry to bother you, my lady, but I would speak with you now, if I may."

"Please wait. I will open the door in a moment. I am...not dressed."

The added comment distracted Harold. An image came to him of the woman unclothed and riding her horse through the middle of the streets of Coventry. In his distraction, Harold failed to notice the muffled sounds of scuffling behind the door; the hushed whispers. He was surprised when he realized the woman in his vision resembled his Edyth. Then the door opened, and it was Lady Godiva who peered out.

"My lord, you were not expected I am sure. What reason have you for seeking me out? Is Aelfgar not here to address the Earl of Wessex?"

She looked just as he remembered her from that evening in St. Albans, except that her hair was coiled in a huge bun, hastily pinned up under a lace wimple. "It is true, my lady, your son is not at home. Even so, it is you I had hoped to have words with just now. May I come in?"

Godiva had not realized she had been blocking the door in such an overprotective way that Harold's expression showed concern. She wanted to allay his suspicions; and he wanted her to feel more free to converse with him. With that between them, she opened the door, trying hard to act noncommittal, and he entered her chambers with a disarming smile.

"My lady. Again, forgive this intrusion."

"I will, once I know what it is for. Why has the Earl of Wessex come all the way to Chester this day? You missed my husband's funeral. Perhaps you are here to gloat?"

The woman's words cut the Earl as easily as would have a sharp dagger. Harold had not expected that kind of response, was hurt and showed it. Godiva regretted her statement almost immediately.

"My lady, please tell me you do not believe that."

Godiva's stern front broke. "I will tell you, Lord of Wessex, I truly do not know what to believe."

"Unless the courier met some unfortunate circumstance, it is my belief that Chester, and your son, should have received word from King Edward. Aelfgar is restored to the King's favor. You do know all this?"

Godiva turned around to walk away from Harold. The man glanced around the room, and was again surprised to find the woman was alone, without even her pet cat for company. Her mass of hair suddenly fell as the hastily placed pins slipped, the wimple floated to the floor. The hair was still surprisingly controlled, braided in a long rope falling down to her thigh. She wore a simple lavender house dress, with a delicately crocheted neckline to match the wimple now on the floor. A gold chord clung about her small waist, but she wore no jewelry. As she spun around and the hair fell, it flayed behind her like a whip. Godiva was unconcerned, could not help but show her frustration.

"Yes, we received word from Edward. One moment my son is to be made Earl, the next he is exiled. A day later he is recalled. Shall I assume that you are here to cast him into exile again?" Harold's hurt look increased, and Godiva softened again.

"I am here, my lady, to reaffirm the courier's message. Surely you can guess that Edward merely acted out of rashness. Your son, and my brother I fear, did make the matter worse. Still, I recognized that Edward meant not to bring his anger to such a drastic step and I did help him to see the necessity of keeping closer ties with you...and Chester. I swear before God that Aelfgar has received all the lands and duties that are his by right of being Leofric's son and the new Earl of Mercia."

"Those are strong words, and I should thank you for them. Yet, how can I be sure it will be as you say? You swear before God; but does the Earl of Wessex act before God or before Man? My husband, with his many faults, did at least live in fear of the Almighty. But you...I just do not know—" She looked away from him, searched for an answer in the dried floor rushes.

Harold could not argue with the woman's knowledge that he was not as God-fearing as many. He picked up the fallen wimple, brought it over to hand it to Godiva. "Perhaps I am a bit too worldly, my lady, but then know that by worldly standards what I say is true. Your son Aelfgar is and will be the Earl of Mercia. Edward confirmed this, and a meeting of the Witan reaffirmed the same."

She accepted the lace work as if Harold handed her a document from the King. "Yes, I must take heart in that. It is all I have got."

"Count on it, my lady."

The Lady Godiva relaxed, began to finger the end of her long braid. Not looking up, she said, "Still, had Leofric not died my son would have had more time to become ready to be Earl. He is a man, but all too young.

And rash—" This was more to herself than to Harold, but he had to respond.

"Yes, my lady. That touches on another subject I wish to broach with you." Harold hesitated, unsure how to explain that his brother had brought Leofric to his end. The last thing Harold wanted was for the Lady Godiva to think that he himself, the Earl of Wessex, had also had something to do with the business.

With Harold's statement, Godiva became suspicious and defensive again. "You want to talk about my son's age? That is of no consequence. Aelfgar will do fine. He will be a strong Earl. If you Godwins would just give him a chance! Above all, he will not be a puppet to the Earl of Wessex!"

Harold was taken aback by the woman's vehemence. "Please! My lady! Believe that I do back your son. It is the other thing you mentioned, your husband's untimely death, that I would discuss."

Again defensive, but now for herself, Godiva turned away so Harold could not read her face. "And what do you want to know about Leofric's death, that you do not already know?"

Harold mistook her question for one of sarcasm. "What do you mean, that I do not already know? I will tell you honestly, my lady, your lord husband's death came as a complete surprise to me."

Confused, Godiva turned to look back at Harold. "Of course. A surprise it was to us all."

Harold felt horrible simply having the bloodtie to Tostig who had done the deed, was sure his guilt showed in his expression. He held his head low. "Perhaps not a surprise to all." He raised his chin and looked Godiva in her big eyes. "I will tell you, somehow I will make that death aright. When an earl of England dies, with no retribution, there is no safety or law and order in the realm!"

Godiva was guarded again. "What? What do you mean?"

Harold swallowed hard. How could he tell her? "Tell me, my lady, did...a messenger send a bottle of wine to the Earl at Bromely ere he died?"

When the lady's eyes widened, Harold felt sure she had finally made the connection, even had she not until just then. But he had to make sure she did not include him in the dastardly affair.

"Now, remember, my lady, I was in Gloucester by that time—"

Godiva's frightened look turned slightly confused. "How did you know about the wine then?"

Harold could not help but look guilty, he was sure the woman might mistake this for complicity in the deed. "I fear the knowledge came to me too late. But, I will make retribution, I promise you."

The Earl's look was so intense, Godiva shuddered. "What knowledge is it that you have now, my lord?"

"I am sorry my lady." Godiva's scared expression stung the man. "Had I been there in Bromely, your husband would not have tasted his death in that way."

Godiva wondered at the man's conviction, was afraid at where the man was leading the conversation. "You do not believe it was an accident? I have heard no rumors suggesting anything different. Surely the Lord did choose that time to call my husband to His side."

She was playing with him, Harold could tell. She must already know of the poisoned wine, already suspect him. She had every right to make this as difficult on him as possible. He could still hardly believe it himself. Yet, the truth had to be spoken or they would never be able to move beyond the incident.

"No, my lady, I do not think it was your husband's time, even though I do hope he was well received into the Kingdom of Heaven." The unbecoming guarded look came over Godiva's face again, and Harold spoke quickly to get it over with. "I am afraid the wine was from my brother; but I had no knowledge he was up to such a thing. I assure you!"

The tension broke as Godiva sputtered out her held breath.

"What?"

Harold met the woman's gaze directly. "I said, with the deepest regret, that the wine was sent from my brother, Tostig."

Godiva watched the man for some outward sign, wondered at his seeming reluctance to speak. Did he know what happened or not? She was tired of this game of hound and fox. Flustered, she waved her hands at Harold, spoke sarcastically. "What would you have me say? Maybe if my husband had not sent the bottle away unopened, I might have been able to taste the contents and thank your brother whole-heartedly!" Her blue eyes shimmered with held back tears. "What matter where the wine came from?"

Harold dropped to one knee, hung his head before the woman. "Please, my lady! It does matter where it came from! I had nothing to do with—" The Earl's exclamation was cut off as the lady's words soaked in. He raised his head to look at Godiva.

"The bottle was sent away…unopened?"

Now it was Godiva's turn to have the other's words soak in. Why was the man so concerned about the wine bottle? She hesitated. "Yes. Leofric was busy with…well, he had his attention on me. When my maidservant brought the wine, he did not want it. Leofric did not want it to…impair his abilities that evening. So, he sent it away."

Harold was completely confused. "Then, what happened was just as the courtiers have said? It was Leofric's heart? He did expire…naturally, while he was with you?"

Godiva sat down on the edge of her bed, recalling the night in Bromely. "Yes, my husband's heart gave out. It was an accident, really." She was embarrassed and afraid.

Harold could not believe the news. He suddenly felt a whole lot better. "My lady, I see that talking about that night distresses you. We will talk no more of it. I only want you to know that, if any foul play was afoot, I would get to the bottom of it."

Godiva studied Harold's face, looking for some sign to understand just what he was after. It had seemed like he knew what had happened, he had pressed the point about the wine bottle to draw her out, then he retreated before delivering the final blow. Why?

"Lord Harold, what is it that you want?"

Noticing Godiva's embarrassment, Harold could picture the scene in the bedchamber: The old man Leofric trying one last time to couple with his young wife, finally losing all abilities and his life as well. "At our last meeting, you suggested that I might be a stronger man if granted more of the sensitivities of the women in England. Mayhap I am of late trying to see more and more through the eyes of a female." Harold thought it best to leave the specifics out of this conversation. Perhaps one day they would speak of it again. "I want your close friendship, Lady Godiva. That is all. After what we have said here, I do believe I might have it. What say you?"

Godiva smiled cautiously. The man did know what happened, but maybe he would not tell. She was hesitant. "Yes, perhaps we can be friends, Harold of Wessex."

Relieved, Harold turned to go. "Again, and again, my lady, I apologize for this interruption upon your privacy. Let us remember tonight, though, and call it a beginning of a new accord between you and I...that is, between our two houses."

Godiva spoke from her heart. "Lord of Wessex, you are a truly strange man, mayhap exceptional. I look forward to expanding our relationship, to seeing you again. When we met last I could not say that. Somehow now I can."

"Indeed, and it gratifies me to hear it so. Now I will go to confront your son and hope that he too will be as reasonable!" Pausing at the door, Harold turned back to Godiva. "I will count the very hours between now and our next meeting, Lady Godiva."

*   *   *   *

The man behind the curtain cowered against the wall in fear. "I am lost! The Earl knows everything! Did you not hear his questions? How did he find out what happened? Oh, I am lost. He is after me, most assuredly! You heard him say he sought retribution. How can I escape the wrath of Harold of Wessex?"

Godiva held the curtain she had pulled back from the alcove, shook the fabric so that it whipped lightly against the man hiding in the corner. That action was enough to stem the tide of Davydd's excited banter.

"Shoosh! Calm yourself for mercy's sake. Yes, it seems that Harold does know of the whole affair; but, it also appears he would place my good will above his interest in dealing retribution. After all, it is my honor at stake as well as your safety should the story come out."

The Welshman pushed past Godiva into the room. "Damn your cat! If he had not been so jumpy, not awoken at the arrival of your maidservant who brought the bottle of wine, he would not have alerted Leofric to my presence in the room! Damn the skittish animal!"

"If you want to be upset, do not take your frustration out on the cat. You can curse Leofric for coming back earlier than he had intended, leaving you stranded in my chambers. You can curse me for allowing you in my chambers late at night. And while you are at it, do not forget to curse yourself for coming to me in the first place!"

Davydd's eyes dropped, and Godiva stepped away from him. "I am sorry. I did not mean that. But it is true that you and I are to blame. Leofric was not a young man. The sight of you in his wife's bedchamber was too much for his old heart. You and I should have known that might happen. We should have been more careful."

"What shall I do? Harold may not tell, or he may choose to hang me!"

"I think not. But perhaps you should go away for awhile. Go back to your homeland of Wales. I will be near, here in Chester. Let things settle down a little, and let us see what is in Harold's heart and on his mind."

Entry XIV

▼

Where Aelfgar confronts the Earl of Wessex

"Ah ha! So that is it. I had thought my home had the smell of a dead animal; and here it is before me: A Godwin." Aelfgar stood at the doorway, barring Harold's exit from the house. "Tell me, Wessex, how do you sleep at night with such a stench ever present?"

Harold expected the young man to be belligerent, and he had come ready to absorb whatever oaths that Aelfgar would produce. He decided to make light of the slur. "You are right, I fear. It has been a long time since I had a proper bath."

The younger man let loose his anger then. "A proper bath for you would be one in your own blood!" The son of Leofric came into the front room, hand on sword hilt, his eyes daggers already piercing Harold's flesh.

Harold stood fast. "Careful, Aelfgar. My good will extends far, but stops at threats to my person."

"Oh? Your good will? That seems a contradiction in terms to me!" Aelfgar was a pace away from the Earl of Wessex, hand still upon the sword at his side. As he began to raise the weapon, Harold grabbed the young man's wrist, keeping the sword only half drawn.

"Get a hold of yourself. Do not act like a boy. If you want to be treated like a man, then you must act accordingly." Aelfgar was furious at having his wrist held tight, his hand immobile. He felt himself too weak, too young, when facing the son of Godwin. The eyes of Leofric's son did not betray this lack of confidence, only glowed through a haze of hatred.

Harold let go the younger man's hand with a jerk, stepped past Aelfgar spreading his hands wide. "My God! What would you desire of me? To apologize for Edward's actions?" He turned to look Aelfgar in the eyes. "I will not do that. Do you want me to offer you more than Mercia? You will not get it. Aelfgar! You have followed your father as Earl of Mercia. Be content with that, and do not look upon me as your enemy. Times have changed. You and I are not Leofric and Godwin. We are Aelfgar and Harold. A new generation in a new England. A stronger England. Your mother and I have reached an accord. I think you and I might as well."

Aelfgar stepped back to give himself some swinging room. "You say you are not my enemy? Well, you are no friend to me either, I am sure of that. I have to ask myself what you have in mind, that you would speak to King Edward on my behalf. You expect to achieve some personal gain in this, and I have yet to figure out your plan. But I will not sit by and belabor the point. Indeed, Harold, I am not Leofric. I will not stand idly by while the Godwinspawn overrun England as my father had done over these past years."

Harold shrugged. "Aelfgar, listen to me—"

"No, you listen to me! You say that you have reached an accord with my lady mother? Soon you will wish you had! Soon I will have a great ally, and Wessex may have cause to fear the might of Mercia once again. I have just come back from a meeting with a deputation from King Gruffydd of Wales. I have accepted their proposal to wed my mother to Wales. Even now I begin to make the necessary arrangements."

"You have done what?"

Harold had been prepared to argue with Aelfgar, but he was not prepared for that revelation. The younger man mistook the question as fear. "Ha! So the mighty Earl of Wessex trembles already. Good!"

"Aelfgar! I do not care about your petty negotiations with the barbarians to the West. But, damn it, leave your mother out of it. The Lady Godiva and I will be close, no matter what you think or do. I will not have you dictate to your mother what she shall do, and I certainly will not let you arrange to marry her off."

Aelfgar danced lightly about the room, circling the Earl of Wessex. "Oh, this is already working out well. Better than I had hoped, in truth. You really are afraid of this alliance!"

Harold had heard enough. He stepped toward Aelfgar, and the younger man's hand went to the hilt of his weapon again. This time Harold did not stop the other man from drawing the sword. Neither did he stop himself from approaching Aelfgar, even as the younger man raised his weapon above his head to strike. The Earl of Wessex spoke very slowly.

"If you move even a muscle in your sword arm, you will live long enough to sorely regret your actions." Aelfgar's hand froze. "I spoke up for you to King Edward, and you were recalled. I spoke on your behalf before the Witan, and your position was ratified. I hold your future in my hands, Aelfgar. I could easily have the proclamations declaring you Earl of Mercia revoked, even without Edward's consent! You have stepped up from your lordship over East Anglia, Aelfgar, but never forget you are still below Wessex. You hold Mercia at my whim. Play your games with Gruffydd of Wales, but do not expect me to care, and do not involve your lady mother!"

Aelfgar melted under Harold's determined stare. He backed away, let the sword drop, clatter to the ground. When he reached the door and sure escape, he regained some of his anger-fed bravado. "We shall see." The young man smiled. "Have you ever seen the Welsh at war? The quiet of the trees and hills is suddenly disrupted, and out of the darkness comes death flying like a shooting star in the heavens!"

When Harold did not answer, Aelfgar continued, "Ah, but you will find out soon enough. I tell you, Wessex, my lady mother will enjoy her new life in Wales, and I will enjoy the support of the Welsh long bow! I believe there may be a Welsh arrow with your name on it!"

Harold stepped toward the boy; but Aelfgar dashed out the door. "Go then! Go to your friends in Wales. But do not expect to be welcomed back into England, Aelfgar. You will be treated as you have acted, like an outlaw!"

A loud gasp came from the hallway across the front room and behind Harold, where he had first met Aelfgar. The Lady Godiva stood there, shocked at what she had heard.

"Only a few moments ago you did swear to me, and to God! You swore that you were not here in Chester to send my son into exile again!"

Harold jumped at the sound of the lady's voice. He turned to face the woman's anger, embarrassed and at once defensive.

"My lady, that had never been my intention, just as I said. I do swear it." Harold motioned toward the sword on the floor. "Your son has threatened my life."

Godiva never looked at the sword. "Is the Lord of Wessex going to try and tell me that he was at a disadvantage in my boy's presence? I hardly would believe it."

"Your son is being very difficult. Whether or not I was ever truly in danger does not matter, it is the fact that Aelfgar did threaten me that is important. I cannot let him get away with that."

Godiva's olive skin was red with frustration. "And why did you provoke him? Did we not just discuss how young he is; how much he has to learn?"

"Indeed we did, my lady. But he would not listen to me at all. It was not I that provoked him, but quite the reverse. He spoke to me of his plans to send you off to Wales as a bride to Gruffydd, would not listen to me when I declared that you would have none of that. Surely you can see he has been overly unreasonable."

That surprised the lady. "He promised me as a bride to Gruffydd? Absurd. And even if he did, I would never follow through with the marriage. And, even if I did, what is that to you? Do you use that as an excuse to justify expelling young Aelfgar from his home and inheritance?"

"Well...no. As I told you, he did threaten my life."

"Aelfgar has lost his father, for mercy's sake. And he is still convinced that you had something to do with it. Can you not understand the boy's anger, give him some allowance? You come here expecting my son to be cool toward you. You swear to me that despite this knowledge you do support him. Then at the first meeting, you disavow your oath, sworn to God and to me, and banish young Aelfgar to the Welsh wilderness."

"But, my lady, you and Wales—"

"I do not care that for Wales!" Godiva slapped her hands together. "Do you think that just because my son gets an idea in his head that it will come to pass so easily? No, I will not be friends with the Welsh. Nor does it seem I will be able to find friendship with the house of Godwin as I thought I might. Perhaps, Lord Harold, if you were a better Christian, you would find room in your heart for Christian ideals such as honesty, charity, forgiveness and patience. Not until you learn these will we ever speak again."

Godiva spun around and without looking back at the forlorn man, she left him with a parting thought. "I believe you let yourself in to my home with ease. See that you leave just as quickly."

*   *   *   *

Still fuming from her confrontation with Harold of Wessex, Lady Godiva reread the short letter, then looked up to her maidservant. "You found it where?"

"My lady, when I got back from visiting my family this eve, a chamber maid brought the note to my attention. She said it was for me, left by a man. When I opened the letter, I found another sealed letter within, with only a cursory inscription entreating me to deliver the unopened note to my mistress."

"What did the girl say about this man? Who was he?"

"You can question her yourself, my lady, but I am sure she knows nothing more than what I have told you already. Only that it was a note left by a tall, handsome man who spoke about leaving Chester, but looking forward to seeing the mistress of the house again under better circumstances. It is a mystery, my lady."

"Perhaps that does explain it."

"My lady? What does the note say?"

Godiva continued, although not directed in response to Hildreth's confusion, but more to her self. "Still, the note was not written in Davydd's hand. It looks to have the formal strokes of a monk."

"Oh, then you think it is from that Welshman? That is possible. The maid who brought the letter is of your son's household. She would not know that man by sight." Hildreth gave Godiva a disapproving look. "You are extremely lucky, my lady, that nothing bad ever happened due to your relationship with that man while Leofric yet lived." Hildreth continued, failing to notice her lady's sudden reserved look. "I would advise that you keep your association with that foreigner to a minimum, even now that your lord husband is gone. At least until Leofric's bones have cooled in the crypt."

Lady Godiva was thoughtful, reserved. Not her usual manner when it came to defending her feelings for Davydd before the reproachful Hildreth. "Yes, of course. In fact, he must have been thinking as you when he sent this note through you and not to me directly. And then, even more the careful man, he did not even write it in his own hand but had another do the deed."

"So, is what the maid said true? The man is leaving Chester? Are we truly finally rid of him for good?"

"Not for good, mayhap only for a long while. Anyway, you can rest easy knowing that Davydd is far away. He has gone home to Wales for awhile."

"And the note, my lady? What does he say?"

"This note says nothing specific. It only rings poetically about his admiration of me and his longing to see me again under different circumstances."

"I would say, my lady, that you are better off without him."

"Indeed you would say that. Oh Hildreth. You never liked the man. Just read this note and be content. Though perhaps his shortest sonnet, it seems the most heartfelt and lovely poem Davydd has yet written me. Why can you not see the man is genuine? Your constant banter has even had me questioning the man's integrity; but no more. I will hear none of your complaints and disparaging comments. They are not becoming of you."

"Yes, my lady." Hildreth hung her head, backed away and out of the chamber.

Lady Godiva sighed. At least now, with Leofric gone, she could meet Davydd more openly; perhaps one day actually give herself completely to the man who wrote such simple, yet divinely inspired thoughts as she had before her eyes. The woman reread the letter of love.

In the territory of the Trent
In the time of Edward the King
Amidst the many of Mercia
Ancient abode of the angles
An angel.
Far above me, but before me
On the earth, ever present
In the past, in my presence
Perchance to meet under better pretense
God's gift.

Entry XV

▼ ———————————————

Where Harold makes plans of his own

The air was cool and dry for the late September afternoon. The sky was clear, but the sun leaned to the south, lacking much of the warming capacity it had had through the summer. Autumn was all too short, especially the number of days without the cold, bone-chilling rains of October. Englishmen all over the country worked to bring in the last crops of the year, the winter squash, apples and raspberries; stockpiled wood for the upcoming winter and glorified in the brilliant display of changing colors. The first frost had come early. Most of the trees amidst the Marcher lands had changed color, offering a glorious autumn but perhaps boding a hard winter.

Harold of Wessex planned to make the trip from Cheshire back to Gloucester a slow one, but not in order to revel in the beauty of the countryside. He saw even less of the land about him than he had heading north only a few days earlier, so intent was he upon the trouble he felt brewing in Chester. The Earl needed time to think.

"Lord Harold, it is good to see you!"

Harold was met by his clergyman friend in the entryway to the Earl's traveling lodge in Shrewsbury. Wulfstan was a man whose loyalties were with the Church first; but as an old friend to Harold, his interests in the Earl of Wessex's concerns were great. He was a quiet man, speaking only when necessary. But there was a power in his presence, and he was not a man to be overlooked, even when silent.

Harold dropped the pair of boots he was carrying and grabbed the cleric's outstretched hands. "And for me to see you, my friend."

"I had expected to find our friend Robert FitzWimark with you as well, until I received word from London that he would meet you at your home for the feast of Saint Michael."

Harold moved into the house-room and sat down on the sleeping bench. "Michaelmas, good. I look forward to seeing Rob again. I had asked him to stay in London after the deaths last month, but I will require both you and Rob to help me organize my accounts at the end of the month."

"Harold, you will be pleased, I am sure." Wulfstan smiled broadly. "The Wessex harvest was again good. I believe you will find this will be the best year yet! I will bet you thought that last year's crop would be hard to beat, my friend!"

"That is good news; and good news is something I could use right now."

A knock on the door frame interrupted the conversation, and a servant's head popped inside the room. Harold beckoned with his hand. "Come on in, please. I need to get out of these travel-worn clothes."

The servant stepped into the room, bowed slightly to Wulfstan. "Excuse me for barging in, my lords. Here, Lord Harold. I have brought a change of clothes from your bags."

"Thank you my good man. Now get yourself off to the alehouse! That is an order!"

The servant smiled as he left. "Yes, my lord. Whatever you say."

Harold sighed. "That was quite a ride out from Chester. Nothing like a stuck carriage and a muddy road to remind one that his boots have worn through!" Harold motioned to the new footwear on the floor by the door while he tore off his right boot. "Can you hand those to me?"

Wulfstan moved the boots within the reach of the Earl of Wessex. "So, you left Rob in London. Did you expect any more problems?"

"No, not really." Harold pulled off his other worn boot. "The people knew not Aedward of Hungary, and Leofric of Mercia was not a young man. I am sure that most have forgotten the incidents already."

"But you have not." Wulfstan was matter of fact.

Harold put both feet on the floor and rested his elbows on his knees. "Indeed, I have not. Leofric's death seems to have been an accident, just as the rumors would have it. But Aedward was a young man in good health, I was told. There is a mystery that I would understand. And even though Leofric's death seems not to have been related to any underhanded business cooked up by my brother, I believe that Aelfgar Leofricsson has every right to expect the worst of the House of Godwin and the Earl of Wessex."

"You cannot take the blame for anything your brother does, my friend. Besides, you seem convinced he did nothing. What is the problem? What of Chester? Was your visit there unsuccessful?"

"I did not say Tostig did nothing, only that what he did do seemed not to be related to Leofric's death." Harold sat up straight "Nevertheless, I know that Mercia does have a right to be angry with Northumbria, and I must take responsibility for my brother's actions."

The Earl put up his hand to silence his friend's protest. "I am the one who gave Tostig the earldom. I must assume the responsibility for any result of that decision." Harold stood up and removed his riding cloak. "Anyway, before heading home to Bosham I will speak with King Edward. He must make sure that Aelfgar feels secure in his position. I must make sure that Lady Godiva believes Wessex is indeed a friend of Mercia."

"Lady Godiva, my lord?"

"Yes." Harold threw off his mud-caked mantle. "Although I support Leofric's son as the next Earl of Mercia, Aelfgar is young. It is his mother as head of the House of Leofric with whom I want—" Harold paused as he pulled off his leggings, "to settle matters. Nothing is done that cannot be undone. I will have Edward draft another declaration, send one of my own to Chester as well, confirming Aelfgar in the position of Earl of Mercia."

Harold was thoughtful for a moment, standing naked in the middle of the small building. "Our realm is nominally at peace, but I would see a time when England is truly united." The Earl grabbed the clean clothes off the bench and put them on. "At least Tostig is back in his domain for now. Hopefully the upcoming winter will be a harsh one in the north, keeping that brother of mine at home and out of trouble."

"Indeed!" Wulfstan laughed. "That is if Tostig makes it to York. Rob's letter from London mentioned that Tostig had traveled through there to meet with your brother Leofwine and then on to speak with Gyrth in East Anglia. Is he wanting to stir up trouble?"

Harold dropped back to the bench, picking up one of the new boots as he sat down. "Tostig should be in York by now. You do not have to worry about Gyrth and Leofwine, my friend. They have always been closer to me than to Tostig. Whatever Tostig might say, the words will not sway my brothers without their checking with me first, you can count on that." Harold pulled on the remaining boot.

"For now I have promised my traveling companions an extended lay-over in Shrewsbury. I vowed to meet a handful more ale-friends before I leave."

"Or maybe just one ale-wife!" The captain of the housecarls of Wessex stepped through the door with a wide grin. "Perhaps the woman will have a special brew just for you, Lord Harold."

The Earl of Wessex caught a glance from the cleric, then grinned back at the soldier. "I will be honest with you, my friend. I do wish my Edyth were here tonight!"

The captain's guffaw filled the small room. "Yes, just as I wish I had the traveling sickness which would keep me ailing in bed for the duration of our stay in Shrewsbury!" They all laughed. The captain swung his arms. "Come, come, Harold. Let us be off to the ale-house!"

"My lord, there is one other thing—" Wulfstan moved in front of Harold as the Earl stood up.

The captain frowned. Harold sighed, then smiled at his friend. "What is it, Wulfstan?"

The cleric tightened his cincture holding the frock close to his waist. "It is Stigand, my lord."

Harold's smile vanished. When Godwin stood up to the Norman influences in King Edward's court and brought Harold and his family back into favor after their short exile many years ago, the Norman-born Archbishop of Canterbury fled along with others back across the Channel to their home. At that time Stigand had himself appointed to the not-quite-vacated See, retaining his position as Bishop of Winchester as well.

"What is that old man up to now?" Harold asked.

"As you know, he has always hovered around Edward's court. Of late he has spent even more time with the King. I am not sure you know that he did leave Gloucester with your brother Tostig."

Wulfstan crossed the room in front of the captain, his right hand at his chin. "I think Stigand has his eye on the Bishopric at York."

Harold threw his arms in the air, feigning exasperation. "Is the man not content as Archbishop of Canterbury?"

Wulfstan turned around to face the others from the door. "Aldred of Worcester is furious."

The captain spoke then, mentioning what he was sure the others already guessed. "Bishop Aldred would like to increase his own influence I am sure, after all his efforts in bringing Aedward out of Hungary were lost with the young man's untimely death."

"You are right, Captain," Harold nodded to the soldier. "And no doubt King Edward has not helped matters at all. I presume he has been promising bishoprics in his spare time, which he has had too much of due to the bad weather in Gloucester."

Wulfstan spoke slowly. "Should we be concerned about what Stigand and Tostig might do?"

Harold became serious. "I do not think so. The Witan will not convene, much less be swayed by my brother Tostig. And as for Stigand—perhaps the Archbishop believes that as long as he is in disfavor with Rome he might as well push the level of his own power; but that will not go over very well with the noblemen and other bishops of the realm."

The cleric and the captain were quiet as Harold paced from one end of the room to the other. The Earl spoke slowly. "Aldred has long been friendly with the house of Leofric. Perhaps the Bishop of Worcester may be the connection I need to reconcile some of these matters." Harold stepped up to Wulfstan. "I would like you to help me, my friend. Make yourself available to Aldred, be of assistance with whatever the Bishop might need. I will ask Robert FitzWimark to do the same. Let us court the man's favor. He might prove useful."

"I would be happy to, Harold. After my pilgrimage to Rome this year, I feel refreshed and ready for new tasks."

"You sound as if the pilgrimage was a vacation for you!" Harold teased.

"Of a sort—" Wulfstan was taken off guard by the jest. "It is simply that I feel my mind and soul are more at one with the Lord."

Harold became thoughtful at that. "Wulfstan, my friend, would you say that every Christian should feel as you do? Am I too worldly, spending my time thinking only of Wessex and what is right for England?"

"My lord Harold, your attention to the concerns of our kingdom is certainly of utmost importance—to the kingdom." Wulfstan rested his hand on his friend's shoulder. "Only you yourself can determine what it is in your heart that you might need for your personal reconciliation with God. I will say this: the Lord does help he that does help himself, and a pilgrimage is one way that a person can seek that help. Subjecting oneself to the arduous task of making a long journey solely for the Lord shows humility and contrition. It allows the Lord into one's heart."

"King Edward suggested the same thing—"

The soldier was surprised by the turn of the conversation. "Indeed, my Lord Harold," the captain joked, "and a pilgrimage would give you a much needed vacation from the tiresome problems you face here in England!"

A smile flashed across Harold's face as he noted his friend's mood. He smoothed his mustache with the thumb and forefinger of his right hand. "I wonder how men of other lands deal with internal problems such as face me daily."

Wulfstan nodded his head. "There is much one can learn on pilgrimage, my lord."

"You know," Harold said, "with the Earl of Wessex away for a short time, Aelfgar would have the space he needs for his temper to cool, and his mother would find more reason to look favorably on Wessex."

"Certainly," Wulfstan agreed, "it seems to me any act such as that could only bring you closer to the Almighty, and thus closer to all followers of Christ."

Harold's broad grin returned. He clapped Wulfstan on the back. "And I am sure the Lord God would not begrudge me some time away from the trials I must endure as Earl of Wessex!"

Wulfstan laughed. "Indeed not, my lord!"

The captain grabbed Harold's wrist. "Nor will the Lord begrudge you a couple days rest here in Shrewsbury! Harold, the ale-house awaits!"

Book II

▼

AD 1058—AD 1065

Entry I

▼

In which Godiva refuses Gruffydd, questions Davydd and wonders about Harold

"You have made your son angry."

Lady Godiva knelt at the altar inside the small chapel that adjoined the palace of the King of Wales. She looked around as the silence of the room was broken by the voice from behind. Gruffydd filled the small doorway, his eyes flashed with the flickering of the votive candles along the back wall of the room. Godiva made the sign of the cross slowly, stood up and exited the chapel. Gruffydd stepped aside as she passed, but leaned close so that the woman had to turn sideways to get through the doorway. King Gruffydd followed after her. Godiva felt a slight tug as something brushed her hair, and she knew at once that the man had reached out to touch her thick hair. She stepped into the anteroom of the chapel.

"And you, my lord Gruffydd? Are you angry?" Godiva spoke softly.

"More disturbed than angry, my good woman. Was not the gift I delivered to you exemplary? The peregrine was obtained with great effort from the cliffs of southern Wales. Perhaps you did not appreciate its worth."

Godiva stopped walking and turned toward the king, not at first allowing her eyes to meet those of Gruffydd. "Indeed, it was a fine specimen. I have never seen its like."

Gruffydd smiled, interpreting the woman's motions to mean she was uncomfortable in his presence. He liked that. "It is young enough that it should bond well with you, with a little training on its part and practice on your own. There is nothing more splendid than a day of hawking. Such as today. Midsummer offers more day light for a longer hunt. You will accompany me tomorrow."

It was not a question, but not an order either. Merely a statement which the king assumed to be fact. Godiva was indeed uncomfortable, because she felt a little guilty. She tried to meet his eyes, saw instead that King Gruffydd watched in fascination as her hair bounced about her shoulders. "No, thank you, my lord. I...appreciate your generous gift, Gruffydd; but perhaps it would have been better suited for my son. He does love all birds of prey."

The king could not hold his composure. "Aelfgar is just a fledgling!" He flung his arms out, grabbed Godiva by her shoulders. "It is you—" Gruffydd paused. When the lady met his gaze then, he was the first to look away. The man calmed, released Godiva and stepped back. "It is the female of the species that is larger, more aggressive. She is the one to watch. She is the one to have by your side."

"Yes, but are not the male hawks useful as well?"

"The tiercel is inferior! When one controls the falcon...that is when you have proved your worth to the world!"

Lady Godiva was annoyed by that. It seemed to her that all men marveled at the strength of females, yet continued to repress that strength at every turn. No doubt the strength in women makes men feel threatened, she thought. Godiva discovered through her marriage that a man's belief that he controls a woman seems to be one of the most important things in his life.

"Is it control of the falcon then that makes hawking so enjoyable?" Godiva feigned confusion, acted as if she dearly sought the truth. "I had thought that pleasure came from being one with the bird. Each part, man and bird, doing the job that God did intend for them; neither completely whole without the other."

Gruffydd scowled. "The falcon does what it was trained by man to do. And, it is better off for it. The bird could not live without man, whereas man only requires the bird for entertainment."

"Indeed." Godiva shrugged off the man's stare as well as the conversation. "Then there is much I do not know about hawking, my lord."

Gruffydd softened, misreading again the woman's mood. "I can teach you all you need to know." The man displayed one black tooth as he grinned at Godiva. "Your husband was a great man, but he did not know everything."

"And you do?" Godiva snapped.

Caught off guard, Gruffydd raised his hand as if to strike Godiva. A loud gasp from down the hall held his hand. Lady Godiva followed Gruffydd's gaze to see Hildreth approaching, eyes wide and hand held to her mouth.

Godiva made no motion to move. "It seems to me the King of Wales and my late husband Leofric do have much in common."

Without saying a word, Gruffydd pushed between the two women and left them in silence. Godiva stared after the king, but Hildreth turned quickly to her lady. "My lady! Did that Welshman harm you?"

"No, Hildreth. Nor do I think he would have even had you not appeared. Nevertheless, I am grateful for your arrival. The man was irritating me."

As if she did not believe her mistress, Hildreth looked Godiva over for injuries. "What cause did he have for raising his hand toward you, my lady?"

"What cause?" Godiva laughed. "Why, Hildreth, you should know that the King of Wales is not at all happy that I chose not to accept his betrothal offer."

Satisfied that Lady Godiva was not harmed, Hildreth reached for the other woman's wrist, narrowed her eyes to slits. "My lady, your son is not happy about that either."

"So the King has told me." Godiva stared beyond her servant.

"My lady," Hildreth shook Godiva's arm. "Lord Aelfgar has taken a few of his companions, he is heading off this night to seek passage to Ireland."

Godiva gazed softly at the older woman. She nodded her head. "I expected as much."

Hildreth finally recognized her mistress' mood, knew that Lady Godiva had a lot on her mind. "My lady, you are not very talkative. Would you rather I leave you alone?"

"No, Hildreth, that is all right. I was just…thinking." Godiva squeezed her servant's hand, released it from her own wrist. She walked back to the chapel entrance, but made no move to go inside.

Hildreth's brow furrowed. "Were you hoping to seek guidance from the Lord?"

"Perhaps forgiveness," Godiva whispered too softly for her servant to hear. When Hildreth questioned her, Godiva continued. "Only solitude, Hildreth. The chapel was quiet until King Gruffydd showed up." Godiva breathed deeply. "I am content with my choice to not marry Gruffydd."

Hildreth cocked her head. "Completely content, my lady?"

"Well, no. That is not true, I suppose." Godiva spoke slowly. Hildreth wanted to offer something, help the lady in some way.

"You wanted to aid young Aelfgar. As much as I dislike these Welshmen, the betrothal would have been good for your son." When Godiva did not respond, Hildreth continued.

"You might want to think about remarrying, my lady. It has been almost a year since your lord husband left this earth."

Godiva whirled on the other woman. "There must be another way, Hildreth."

Hildreth took one step away from the lady's intensity, then scowled. "You are still thinking of that minstrel," she croaked. "Is that not so?"

Godiva was exasperated. "Stop that Hildreth. Yes, that is why I accompanied my son to this land. Not to accept Gruffydd's betrothal, but to find my friend. Davydd escaped to Wales last August. It is time that he could come back."

Hildreth threw her arms in the air. "My lady! Forget that man! If he was sincere, he would be here by your side now. All of Wales knows you are here in Gwynedd."

Godiva raised her hand, shook her index finger at her servant. "That is not true. I have noted that Wales is not entirely behind Gruffydd as he would lead my son to believe. There are those in southern Wales that do not recognize Gruffydd as their king. It is my belief that Davydd is there where news of my arrival may not have reached."

"But, my lady," Hildreth pleaded, "you received only one letter from the man. Then he vanished. My goodness," Hildreth shrugged, "you have received more letters from Harold of Wessex since the man left on pilgrimage than you have received from that Welshman!"

Godiva was quiet for a time. She dropped her head to stare at the floor rushes. "You are right, of course."

Hildreth moved beside Godiva, patted her hand lightly on her lady's head. "I am glad that the minstrel is gone," she said quietly. "He was no good for you. But, Lord Harold...that is another story entirely. What news does he send, my lady? What does Lord Harold mean to you?" Hildreth winked at Lady Godiva. "Perhaps you are unable to accept Lord Aelfgar's plans for you because you have plans of your own?"

"Hildreth, do not be silly. The Lord of Wessex only lets me know some of what he has done while on holy pilgrimage. I think Harold wants me to believe he is a friend of Mercia."

"He might be, indeed, my lady! I think the man is honorable. He is certainly handsome."

Godiva laughed. "Handsome yes, and honorable—" the lady's laugh stopped. "Oh, I do not know, Hildreth. I thought I might feel better getting involved with the politics of Mercia, but I find myself no happier since Leofric died. I want to help young Aelfgar, but where should I go? The continent? Hopefully my son will find what he needs in Ireland."

"And, if he does not?"

"I do not know. I suppose I will have to think of Mercia first, and myself second." Godiva's shoulders slumped, her head fell backward. "I may still marry Gruffydd for the sake of my son's alliance."

Lady Godiva straightened up quickly. She reached out and grasped her servant's chin in a tender grip. However, it was less the hold on her chin than the passion in Godiva's face that kept Hildreth's attention. "But not before I have sought out all other possible schemes."

Entry II

▼

When Edyth Svanneshals and Aldbald of Coventry each meet the Lady Godiva

Aldred, newly made Archbishop of York, seemed for the moment to have forgotten that pride was not considered a good Christian quality. His demeanor was that of a triumphant general entering the gates to his home town. But this was neither his town of York nor his home, but that of the King, Edward's Easter court at Oxford. For all his pomp, Archbishop Aldred did have a sincere reason for feeling like a conqueror this day, for it was Whitsunday, and he had just led the people of King Edward's household in a mass to commemorate the coming of the Holy Spirit to the Apostles. He chose to wear a white alb in solidarity with the newly baptized, a group of ten neophytes who followed the Archbishop out of the dining hall where the rest of the King's courtiers had assembled for an evening of festival.

The dinner had been served over an hour earlier, and most everyone had finished eating by the time Archbishop Aldred left the hall. Beside the King sat his wife Edith, and beside the Queen her cousin Edyth Svanneshals ate her light meal. Both women were dressed in bright gold gowns, the color accentuating Edyth Swan-neck's fair skin, contrasting with the Queen's dark eyes and hair. The two women were resplendent, and the mood of the day had them laughing and smiling in animated conversation.

The King, too, was in good humor, having had such a successful hunt the day before. Edward was speaking with the man on his right, gesticulating wildly as they recounted the exploits of the previous day. Robert FitzWimark smiled as he found his own memories of the hunt to be in sharp contrast to those of the King. FitzWimark was friend to both Harold of Wessex and the King. By some trick of fate, the man looked more English than some of the Englishman at court, tall and fair, his fine hair cut straight at the shoulder. But Robert FitzWimark was not English. He was half-Norman and half-Breton, having gained the friendship and trust of the King just as so many other men of Normandy had. When the Earl of Wessex suggested to Edward that he keep FitzWimark close and seek his advice while Harold himself was on holy pilgrimage, Edward was quick to agree. Robert FitzWimark was a good man to have next to the King: He loved to hunt almost as much as did Edward himself. Next to Robert FitzWimark sat Wulfstan, who took over as Bishop of Worcester after Aldred moved to take the See at York. The Bishop nodded every now and then, listening intently, and acting interested to hear the King's description of the hunting adventures.

At the far end of the room from King Edward, Aldbald sat with the remnants of his dinner. The young man did not notice the King and Queen, was instead enraptured with the sight of the Lady Godiva. Staring across the room at the woman sitting down from the King, Aldbald was unaware of the revelers next to him. Two men had shoved their dinner-ware aside, were wrestling with their arms at the edge of the table. A group of people had gathered around, all shouting encouragement to one man or the other, and a small boy suddenly had a fist full of coins, in charge of holding the bets of the men.

As Caedwig approached the young man from the Midlands, he smiled wide. Aldbald's informal tutor was pleased with the young man's progress. With his lord and master, Earl Tostig, gone, Aldbald had found much more time to practice writing, filled much of his free time with reading whatever he could get his hands on. The young man's appetite for learning had seemed only slightly greater than his appetite for eating. The monk was surprised to see that the man had hardly finished the food in front of him.

"Aldbald, my friend. Normally you would be on your second or third helping of food by now! Would it not be your normal way to eat enough to hold you through the fasting of Ember Day three days hence?"

Aldbald focused on the approaching monk, glanced at his dinner, then laughed at his own expense. "I am sure you are right, Caedwig."

"Was the food not prepared well this eve?"

Aldbald shook his head. "On the contrary. You know, Caedwig, it never ceases to amaze me how the King's cooks can serve the same food in so many different ways. Eel, in particular, I have always enjoyed no matter how it is served."

Caedwig turned up his nose. Whether the harvests were good or bad; whether or not the gold and silverwork markets were strong; no matter the price of English embroidery in the shops of Europe; one thing the King of England could always rely on was the tax payment of the millers, whose yearly collection of eels from the rivers of England kept a constant supply of food on many a table. This day it allowed the King to easily feed his huge crowd of guests. Stewed eel broth was served, along with eel pasties and meat pies. Edward and his close associates had their fill of roasted game, huge trenchers of venison and rabbit, hunted afresh by the King's party the day before. If the lower class noticed the discrepancy between the King's dinner and their own fare, no one seemed to care. Caedwig himself would prefer the King's fare over the commoners', but chose not to eat much of anything on the holy day.

Aldbald continued, did not notice his friend's displeasure at the thought of eel. "The art of cooking is fascinating."

Caedwig patted the younger man on his back. "Perhaps that is simply because you do like to eat so much."

Aldbald laughed. "Whatever the reason, I vow to learn some of the arcane secrets of food preparation one day."

"Be careful in that, my friend. The use of spices tend to liberate the animal in us all. If the food is not bland, it is the Devil's work."

Aldbald took in his breath, then laughed as he realized the clergyman was jesting.

Caedwig laughed then too. "Seriously," and he glanced at Aldbald's plate, "tonight you cannot stomach the food?"

"I guess I am...distracted this evening." This night it was neither cooking nor studying, but thoughts of love that occupied the man's mind.

"Pondering weighty thoughts, no doubt. My friend, you have a gift for learning." Caedwig handed the scrap of parchment to the young man. "Every time I read something you have written, I have less and less to criticize. We have seen so little of each other, I marvel at your ability to learn on your own. Or, have you found another to help you with your work?"

"Oh no, Caedwig!" Aldbald was proud of his accomplishment, did not want it tarnished in any way. "I assure you it is all my own work."

"And hard work it is. I can tell you have not been idle. If you did not disdain so to learn Latin, I would again beseech you to consider what I believe may be your calling, to follow the Lord."

Aldbald leaned back from the table, almost falling off the bench as he was bumped by the riotous group next to him. The match had just ended with a jerk as the smaller of the two wrestlers raised himself up off his chair to add leverage, bringing the bigger man's arm down to the table with a smash. At once there were cries of 'cheat' and 'rematch'. The loser swept his big arm across the table, clearing off Aldbald's meal, and growled at his contestant.

Aldbald laughed, smiled back at the monk, motioned to the tumult around him. "Join a monastery, and give up all of this?" Aldbald stood up then as two men near him removed the table top from the trestle. Others around the room did the same, clearing most of the hall for the evening's festivities.

"No, Caedwig, truly I do not feel that is my calling. And it is not simply because I do not want to learn Latin. I do not think my fate is to spend my dying days as a monk, no offense intended, of course."

"None taken. I know the Lord does call each of his subjects in his own way."

"As for my interest in English, I do think I can learn much from the example of Alfred the Great. You know how King Alfred had revived learning and writing in England. He translated so many works into English, began to organize the Chronicle, our people's history."

Caedwig found, as when he first met the young man, that he enjoyed discussing such topics with the eager young mind. "Ah yes, Alfred of Wessex. But remember, the man needed to know Latin in order to make the translations from the Latin texts into English, the translations that you have learned to read so readily."

"Exactly so. He translated the works so that the English people need not know Latin. For over one hundred fifty years Alfred's efforts have survived. It seems a waste of my time to go back to the Latin texts when I can begin at the point that King Alfred left off." Aldbald narrowed his eyes. "You yourself spoke of this to me in order to convince me that I should learn to read and write English!"

Caedwig smiled. "The teacher forever tries to push his student to learn more, my friend."

"Then I will take that as a compliment!"

Caedwig became more serious. "And what of the other body of Latin literature that is unopened to you, young man?"

"I have much to read before I do worry about that. And, in the meantime, there are those such as yourself who will continue to write new works and translate old works for me. I do not fear for not having anything to read in the near future."

"As I have told you, Aldbald, no two translations of the same work are exactly alike. Each has its impression made upon it by the translator. It is good to be able to have some knowledge of each language in order to better understand the whole process, is it not?" Caedwig asked the question, knowing he was already planning to give the debate to Aldbald. He was surprised when the other man gave in.

"There you have me, Caedwig. For, if my learning rate and hunger for more knowledge does one day surpass the clergy's abilities to deliver such information, then at that point I will need to learn Latin as well!"

Having been ready to concede defeat, the monk offered a compromise. "My friend, on behalf of my fellow clergymen, I do take up your challenge. I for one will do my best to keep a step ahead of your studies!"

As the two laughed, Aldbald suddenly stopped, struggled to regain his composure as he saw Edyth Svanneshals approaching from behind the monk. He coughed and stood, bowed his head. "My lady. It is good to see you."

Caedwig turned abruptly, bowed slightly himself. "Lady Edyth, you are looking in good health this eve."

Edyth Swan-neck smiled, green-gold eyes catching the flicker of the oil lamp on the nearby wall, picking up the color of her dress. Aldbald thought to himself how she looked more than just in good health, she looked marvelous, her smile transforming her face into an angelic manifestation. The Earl of Wessex must feel lucky, he thought, to have such an attractive woman share his life for so many years. Aldbald chanced a glance toward the Lady Godiva; he could not help but compare every woman he met to the woman of Mercia.

It was true, the Lady Edyth was beautiful. She looked as regal as the Queen herself, dressed in their similar gowns, and each seeming to rival the other in the jewelry they wore. Aldbald knew that Edyth Swan-neck and her cousin the Queen were roughly the same age, whereas the Lady Godiva was perhaps five, and looked at least ten, years their younger. Still, it was not their years that differentiated the women in Aldbald's mind. The Lady Godiva's simple dress; her delicate silver necklace against her olive skin the only piece of jewelry she wore; these were things more appealing to the young man. Aldbald wondered if it was his own thought alone, or if others did see Godiva as he saw the woman. There was something that set the Lady Godiva apart from her peers, made her even more unapproachable by the simple cottar from Coventry. The Lady Edyth's voice brought Aldbald's attention back from across the room to the woman in front of him.

"You are kind, Caedwig. And, Aldbald, is it not?"

"Your humble servant, my lady."

"Good to see you as well. If Harold were here, we could truly celebrate today, think you the same?" The woman's loneliness threatened to show through her outward calm, and Caedwig spoke her thoughts.

"We all do miss the Earl of Wessex, my lady. England does not seem whole without Harold about."

The woman smiled at the monk, looked at the other man. "And you, Aldbald, do you miss your lord Tostig?"

Aldbald was surprised at first, then realized that Edyth was teasing him. He let a smirk show. "In truth, my lady, it has been somewhat relaxing having Lord Tostig out of the country for a time. With the Lady Judith visiting her family in Flanders, it has seemed much like the court at York has gotten a welcome, and long overdue, vacation."

The woman laughed heartily. "Not just a vacation, I would gather all of Northumbria is in festival, from the tales the merchants tell."

"I cannot say that the people of the north are embittered by their Earl's absence."

Edyth became curious. "Although I know you little, Aldbald, I would have guessed you would be anxious to travel with Lord Tostig. Why did you stay behind in England?"

"In truth, my lady, I believe I would have found it interesting to travel to the holy city of the Pope. I fear, when Lord Tostig reckoned that I would enjoy myself, he felt me unworthy to take the trip, said it was to be a journey for the Lord, not one for our pleasure."

Edyth crinkled her nose. "Tostig is right about that, on one level of thinking. What say you, Caedwig?"

"My lady, it is true that a pilgrimage to Rome should not be undertaken with too light a heart. Still, I do not think the Lord God would begrudge a man his enjoyment in traveling through the wondrous lands of the Almighty's creation. I daresay, Lord Tostig simply did not want his servant to have a simple pleasure such as that."

The woman looked contemplative, then sad. "Yes, Tostig can be like that sometimes. Even more so in the past few years. He, more than all his brothers, seems to have felt the presence of their father following him everywhere. I fear he never felt as if he could please the old man when alive, continues to try after the man has been gone for so many years. And since Godwin's death, Tostig has dwelt in the shadow of his older brother, and that does not sit well with him." The woman smiled then. "Of course, many do sit in the shadow of my Harold. I would hazard a guess that the only reason Tostig chose to go on pilgrimage at this time was so that he would not be outdone by his older brother! If I did not think Tostig would mind, I would suggest to you, Aldbald, that you seek service with my Harold. But, such a transfer of allegiance on your part would not be good at this time, would upset my cousin greatly, I fear. Poor Tostig already resents his brother for a number of much smaller things."

Aldbald bowed his head low. "Thank you for your concern, Lady Edyth. Do not worry, I will not disavow my service to Lord Tostig. Insufferable though he might be on occasion, I have much to be thankful to him for. If not for him, I know not where I would be now. Yet, through service to him, I have met people so out of my station I still marvel at it. Look at me now! I find myself speaking to the beautiful Lady Edyth of Wessex as if she were no more than the wife of a miller in the Midlands."

"Indeed, you do seem a bit too casual."

Edyth was slightly sarcastic, mostly joking; but Aldbald chanced a glimpse of the woman's expression, could tell there was a ring of truth there. The cottar blushed and averted his eyes from the woman. He had always recognized that association with the commoners did not come as easy to the Lady Edyth as it did for Lord Harold. She made a sincere effort now, knowing Aldbald to be an acquaintance of Harold's. Had Caedwig, the King's confessor, not been standing there, Aldbald was sure Lady Edyth would have passed him right by. Aldbald's embarrassment turned to shame. After all, why should he expect any different?

"I am sorry, my lady. I will work on it."

Caedwig put his hand on Aldbald's shoulder. "Be careful, my lady, when this man says he will work at it, he does not stop until he has completed the task! Aldbald has been teaching himself to read and to write, under my limited guidance." The monk added the last bit to curb Aldbald's renunciation. "I was just describing the merits of a lifetime devoted to the Church; but, the man does not seem to see himself a clergyman."

Edyth cupped Aldbald's chin between her palms, gazed into the depths of his eyes. "No, I do not see a monk lurking in there. It takes a special kind of person to devote himself so completely to God. Do you not think so, Caedwig?"

Aldbald and Edyth turned as one to the monk who did not answer, followed his gaze to see that the Queen was approaching. Queen Edith stepped up beside her cousin Edyth Svanneshals. Dressed so alike as they were, Aldbald found it interesting to see the dramatic differences. Edyth Swan-neck had such fair skin, such sleek features. The taller woman, her eyes caught the glow of the lamplight. The Queen's much darker hair made her complexion seem all the darker as well, her own eyes deep wells storing her innermost thoughts. As Caedwig averted his eyes and dropped his head to stare at the floor at his feet, Aldbald took the Queen's hand and bent down to one knee, holding the long, fragile fingers to his forehead.

"My lady! I was just saying how honored I have been in my life to actually hold company with such noble gentry. I am overwhelmed at your presence beside me. I am Aldbald of Mercia, servant to the Lord Tostig of Northumbria, and always yours as well."

The Queen smiled, gripped Aldbald's hand. "Arise, my good man. You are not unknown to me. I have seen you about, in my brother's retinue from York." Caedwig felt the weight of the Queen's eyes fall upon him. "And Caedwig, glad I am to see you as well. It seems like a long time since you have joined the King's court of late. Has Edward kept you so preoccupied with errands that you have not time for...your duties in attendance of the King?"

The monk bowed low, his vision still directed toward discerning the various intricacies of the patterns in the floor rushes. "My lady, I have been busy traveling about King Edward's lands. As you know, his steward has taken ill, and I took it upon myself to see to the King's business. I do apologize for not having been in attendance more at court."

Before the Queen could say any more, Caedwig bowed again. "Indeed, I am sure you are right, however. The King will have need of me. If you will excuse me."

*   *   *   *

Across the room and down the table from the King sat the Earl of Mercia, and next to him his mother. Aelfgar had been watching Edward and those reclining about the King, watching Edyth Svanneshals speaking with Caedwig and the servant. The young man smiled in satisfaction.

"I will tell you, mother, it is nice not having those devilspawn sons of Godwin lurking about to muddle up affairs. What things we can accomplish whilst England is free of that brood! I will wager the lords of Wessex and Northumbria will be surprised to find Aldred, a friend of Mercia, as

Archbishop of York. Sometimes I feel it would be nice to be a bird, hovering over them to see their expressions when they do hear the news!"

Aelfgar at once looked contemplative. "I remember the stories father would tell me. You would never guess it had ever been like that in England. How is it that the house of Godwin has gained so much acceptance in King Edward's eyes?"

Lady Godiva leaned close to her son so she would not have to speak loudly. "Aelfgar, Godwin had always the popular support, at least in Wessex and often throughout all of England. His was a shrewd mind, and that kept him on top of the Witan as well. As for King Edward's affections, well our King has always been too easily influenced by those near to him."

The young Earl of Mercia scanned the room. "The King is indeed too easily influenced, and there is a man in need of rebuke for such behavior."

Lady Godiva followed her son's gaze across the room to the long benches where more important servants and lower-born courtiers supped, where a monk was talking with a simple cottar. She knew at once to whom Aelfgar was referring, looked askance at Aelfgar, leaned close to her mischievous son. "Now stop it, Aelfgar, before you go too far. I will not have you start an argument this day." Her words were reproachful, but there was a glint in her eye, no conviction in the threat. It gladdened her heart to see her son in such good favor at court. His lord father Leofric would have been proud.

Aelfgar did not notice his mother's mood, would have continued anyway. "Why, mother, you do not think very much of my prudence, do you? Besides, what could I possibly say that would offend anyone?" The young man laughed loudly. "Without the Godwinbrood about, who would there be to offend?"

As her son's voice increased in volume, Godiva became serious. She whispered in the young man's near ear. "Shoosh, Aelfgar! You forget the Queen is a daughter to Godwin, and her brothers Gyrth and Leofwine sit down the table from us. I truly do not wish you to start anything this day."

Aelfgar grabbed his mother's hand. "You surely do not want me to start anything! Here I am, so newly returned from Ireland where I found no support for my cause, and you continue to fight with me regarding my earlier plan with Wales!"

The lady spoke in a harsh whisper. "Do not start on that again."

"But, if you would just see fit to marry the man! An alliance with Wales would make Mercia strong!"

"Aelfgar!" The young man calmed under his mother's intensity. Godiva spoke more softly then. "Now, let us have no more of politics tonight."

"As you wish, mother." Aelfgar sighed. He gazed back at the trio across the room just as Queen Edith joined them. "As long as I am not provoked."

Lady Godiva again followed her sons stare. "Surely that monk does not provoke you. Why are you so enraged by that man? I have heard you mention him before. He is fairly innocuous, and surely no threat to you."

"No threat to me?" The young man narrowed his eyes at his mother. "Need I remind you how close Caedwig is to the King?"

"That should anger you none. The man is known for his time spent with the King as Edward's confessor. That is his duty, to the King as well as to God. True, Caedwig does promote the King's will throughout the realm; but that too is no failing on his part, nor is it a threat to you."

"Ah, if it were that alone, I would agree with you. The man, however, is very close to the Godwins as well. That is important to me. Caedwig spends far too much time associating with Harold of Wessex for my liking. I will tell you, mother, one cannot help but wonder if the King's proclamations are from Edward himself, or from Harold of Wessex. With Harold's sister the King's wife, and Harold's good friend the King's confessor, how can I guess that any thing Edward does is by his own will and not from that of the house of Godwin. Look, even now Caedwig converses with one of Harold's servants! Even with the Earl gone, that monk keeps a close tie with Harold's household."

"There you are wrong, Aelfgar. That man may be a friend to Harold, but he is the servant of Tostig. I have seen him with the Earl of Northumbria's retinue, and often with the monk Caedwig. I believe they are friends. Do not be so quick to count new enemies for yourself. There will be plenty of them to worry about without your adding more yourself."

"A servant of Harold or a servant of Tostig, it does matter little to me. The man is a servant of the house of Godwin. Even Harold's harlot is with the other two. Do you truly believe that they are not conspiring together? With father gone, we have to be wary of everyone. We are like sheep in a den of wolves, mother."

"Stop it Aelfgar, this instant. I will not have you speak this way. Edyth Svanneshals is no more a harlot than half the women in the kingdom. The Earl of Wessex and Edyth have been together for many years."

"And why does the man not have the Church consecrate their union? I will tell you why! Because Harold wants to be free to sleep with whomsoever he chooses!"

Godiva snapped at her son. "Does your marriage keep you out of the beds of women other than your wife?"

Aelfgar was finally silenced by that. He sat fuming a moment, then whispered to his mother, "Why do I not go ask the Lady Edyth herself."

"Aelfgar, no!" Lady Godiva sighed, waited only a moment, then climbed out of her seat to follow her son across the room.

$$*\qquad *\qquad *\qquad *$$

When Caedwig left to address the King, a strained silence ensued. Aldbald found himself completely at a loss in the presence of the two noble women. The Queen looked in his direction, but her gaze was unfocussed. Edyth Swan-neck too looked distracted, uninterested in carrying on a conversation with only a tanner's son, a tailor's apprentice from Coventry. Feeling like a third wheel on an ox-cart, Aldbald begged his leave of the women, turned to retire from the room. Before he could move two steps, the man became suddenly transfixed. The Earl of Mercia was coming toward them, but Aldbald hardly noticed the young man. It was the woman who followed quickly behind Aelfgar that held Aldbald's attention.

Aldbald had agonized over how he might approach the Lady Godiva, and now she was moving toward him. He knew he had better make a move now, or forever regret his inaction. Still feeling somewhat self-assured having spent the past minutes speaking with the Queen herself, Aldbald stepped past the Earl of Mercia to address Lady Godiva as she approached. Aldbald's ego had been strengthened by his friend Caedwig's appraisal of his penmanship. In one hand he clutched the writing on the parchment Caedwig had corrected, with the other he reached into his tunic to draw out a different note, one the young man had written to give to the Lady of Mercia should he see her this day. Lady Godiva, at first resolute in tracking her son to see that Aelfgar did nothing foolish, became intrigued by the young man who drew near to her. She smiled at Aldbald, and the man's heart leapt for joy.

"My lady. I am Aldbald of Coventry." Aldbald sunk to one knee, bowing even lower than he had for Queen Edith. "Forgive me, but I would give to you a note." Even as he spoke, Aldbald was relieved to see that his resolve had not wavered before he spoke to Godiva. Nor did his voice crack, which he realized after the fact had been a mercy. Aldbald stood, caught the glow of Godiva's sparkling eyes. She did not withdraw her smile, and his own faltered only as he handed the note to the woman. Before she could take it, her son, his earlier mission forgotten, stepped between the two and snatched the note into his own hand.

"And what is this?" Aelfgar's voice was scolding, his disapproval obvious. But, to Aldbald's surprise, the Earl directed his rebuke toward his mother. "Not another letter from Harold of Wessex?"

The interplay drew the attention of the other two women. The Queen looked inquisitive, Edyth Svanneshals disappointed. Queen Edith spoke for the two of them, looking from Aelfgar to Aldbald to the Lady Godiva, unsure at last to whom she should address her question. "Is that a letter from my brother?"

With his attention on the Lady Godiva, Aldbald had all but forgotten the others around him, had not expected everyone to take an interest in his affairs. His face red with embarrassment, Aldbald tried to speak. This time his voice did crack. "No. No, it is not—"

"It is not anything but a ruse by the house of Godwin to get under my guard." Aelfgar cut off the cottar's response, looked at Godiva. "Mother, why do you accept these notes? What is Harold to you?"

"Yes, tell me, Lady Godiva, have you heard from my Harold?" Edyth Svanneshals had only received two letters from Harold since he had gone away the previous year. She was surprised to hear that this woman of Mercia may have received one, or more, herself.

Aldbald's mouth dropped open. Just as Edyth Swan-neck was curious to know more, he too had no idea that Lord Harold may have been in contact with the Lady Godiva. The craftsman from Coventry forgotten for the moment, Godiva ignored her son as well and directed her response to the Queen. "Queen Edith, I know not if that message is one from either of your lord brothers on pilgrimage. I assure you, if it were, that you would be the first to whom I would bring any important news." Godiva nodded to Edyth Swan-neck. "And you, too, Lady Edyth. Do not pay any mind to my son this eve. I fear he may have had too much to drink, and ale-sight is never as clear as men would choose to believe."

"I assure all of you that I do have my full wits about me." Aelfgar was not furious, only forceful. He could afford to be with Harold of Wessex no where in England. He inspected the folded parchment, shrugged. Grabbing Aldbald's shoulder, he waved the note in front of the other man's nose. "In truth, I do not recognize the seal. Who is this note from?"

Aldbald stood speechless. He had been preparing himself to confront the Lady Godiva, not to defend himself before the Earl of Mercia. Aelfgar was younger than Aldbald, but the man from Coventry honored the younger man's blood ties with the noble house of Chester. The Lady Godiva came to his rescue.

"Aelfgar, give the note to me. It is clearly not from Harold Godwinsson, and certainly none of your concern."

The young man smiled at his mother. "I will grant you that it is not from Harold. And a note from this commoner is even less important than that, although not far! Thus, I need not read it." Aelfgar tore the parchment paper into quarters and handed it back to Aldbald. "There, have your note back. What is no concern to me is of no concern to Mercia, nor to my lady mother I am sure."

The Earl of Mercia strode away from them, trying to act more important than he felt. Lady Godiva spoke apologetically to the other two women. "My Queen, Lady Edyth, I apologize for my son's rude behavior. Whether or not he will admit it, he has had too much to drink. He is young still, has not come to know his limits."

The Queen was satisfied, not having felt injured in the least. "Do not worry, Lady Godiva. A man at that age is still testing his limits in all things. We must let them grow. Aelfgar does seem older than his years. Or perhaps I have lost track of the time. How old is your son, Godiva? Does he not already have a second child on the way?"

Lady Godiva sighed. "That is true, Queen Edith. My son, though only in the middle of his second decade of life, does already have one strong boy, and another child due in a few months. You are right as well, that Aelfgar acts older than his years should allow. My son was strongly influenced at a young age by his lord father Leofric, has always tried to emulate my husband. Now he must fill the boots of Leofric, and he is finding it to be no easy task!"

Edyth Svanneshals watched Lady Godiva closely, still wondering why it might be that Harold would have sent her any messages. The Queen misread the confusion on her cousin's face. "Edyth, if I am not offended, I hope that you will not be." She looked from her cousin to Godiva. "Let us put the whole incident behind us as unimportant. I am sure young Aelfgar has no cause for alarm, is only teasing the rest of us with his gratuitous suspicions. Here," and the Queen reached for her cousin's hand, "let us continue what we were about. You were heading out of the hall to get some fresh air, and I daresay I could use some as well."

As the two cousins moved away, Queen Edith spoke to Lady Godiva. "Will you not join us, Lady? Perhaps we can scare up some sweetmeats stored in the kitchen cellar!"

"No, thank you Queen Edith. I am tired, and I do think I will retire early."

"As you wish."

Lady Godiva found that the young servant of Lord Tostig still stood speechless, holding the tattered remnants of his note in the palm of his hand. "Aldbald is it? I am sorry to you for my son's brash actions and accusations." She reached to grab the fragments of the letter. "Who was the note from?"

Aldbald's reflexes brought his hand into a fist, crushing pieces of the already torn note. Godiva smiled softly. "You said you were from Coventry. That is my home, as well. Do you know me from there, perhaps? Was the note from you, Aldbald?"

"No, my lady." Aldbald could not bring himself to look into the lady's eyes. For many sleepless nights in the future, Aldbald would regret his next action. But, at the time, he found he could not do anything else. His will was gone, broken with the fragments of his letter to the lady in his hand, lost through the interchange with the Earl of Mercia, stolen by the thought that the Lord of Wessex had some interest in Lady Godiva.

"The letter is from no one important, it is nothing." Never meeting the woman's eyes, Aldbald kept himself bowed low, backing away until he could flee the room, and the lady's gaze.

Entry III

▼

In which Harold learns of the state of England

"As much as things do change, still everything does seem to stay much the same." Harold spoke not regretfully, but happily, leaning forward to pat his pony's neck. The two men rode a little ahead of the earl's retinue, a small band of his closest housecarls. The Earl of Wessex sat back up straight and breathed deeply of the English air as they made their way to Gloucester where the king and queen were celebrating Lammastide. It was good, Harold thought, to come back to England after over a year and a half to find the kingdom in no sorry state, and in fact much as he had left it. Robert FitzWimark and Wulfstan had done their jobs very well, Harold thought, and his own brothers held together to keep England in one piece. All save Tostig.

"Might I say again, my lord, that if your brother from Northumberland had not chosen to follow you to Rome, my job would have been a lot more difficult, I will wager." Robert FitzWimark laughed.

"Indeed. And lucky I was that Tostig never caught up with me. He would have made my trip much more unpleasant, I am sure." Harold had not stopped at every shrine along the way, nor had he spent all his time thinking about the Lord's work; but instead found his trip useful in studying the style of rule, the way of life, and even some of the women of other lands.

"You know, Robert, there were so many more places I had not the time to visit, but I sorely would have liked to see. My Edyth would have enjoyed the sights and sounds of the world I encountered. If she had been with me, I daresay I might not be back in England yet!"

FitzWimark laughed. "Then I am glad Lady Edyth did not accompany you, my friend. I am glad to have you back, Harold." His smile went away then. "There is the matter of Aldred. I am afraid I may have let him overstep your good will."

Harold shook his head. "Do not trouble yourself over that, Robert. You could not have averted the Witan's decision last year to make Aldred Archbishop of York. He took my gift of a furlong of freedom, did plow, plant and pick the fruits of his labors in the short time I was gone. A resourceful man! One to have as a friend, and no threat to England, I am sure. Besides, you moved quickly to make sure our friend Wulfstan was placed in Aldred's vacated See at Worcester. I am content."

When the other man looked askance at the earl, Harold smiled. "I have returned to England in time for the feast of the first harvest. Let us celebrate the loaf-mass knowing that the fruits of our own labors are abundant, my friend."

"Lord Tostig will perhaps not be so understanding."

"No, you are right about that." Harold laughed. "No doubt he would have expected Archbishop Stigand to hold three bishoprics!" Harold's smile faded slightly. "It seems my brother left on pilgrimage merely to catch up with me. Robert, I do believe my own brother does not trust the Earl of Wessex."

FitzWimark grinned. "Do you know, Harold, that Tostig sent a message to King Edward in which he all but blamed you outright for his trials along the route to Rome."

"Does he think I hired brigands to attack him at every turn?" Harold pursed his lips. "I too was set upon by bandits, but found their ambushes ineptly planned, poorly executed, easily avoided."

"That is where the two sons of Godwin are different!" Robert laughed heartily. "I have no doubt Tostig is cursing you even now, my friend! I am sure he will think it is somehow your fault the winds have been unfavorable for his channel crossing."

Harold shook his shoulders. "As if I have control over the winds in the heavens."

"Your brother may be stranded on the continent until next Spring, now that the sailing season is all but over." FitzWimark laughed all the harder then, and Harold could not help but join him.

"And that will be a mercy!"

"I will tell you," FitzWimark continued after controlling his mirth, "Tostig did leave England in quite a rage. He was pretty mad about your open favoritism of young Aelfgar, thought you were heading to Rome to plot with the Pope to favor the house of Leofric against him, no less."

Harold's smile faded. "Imagine that. Why is it that Aelfgar himself might not believe that. Then perhaps I would not have had the news from you that I did. As I said, things are very much the same as when I left England."

"My lord. I did watch over Mercia, just as you asked. But never did I threaten the young Earl himself. Even so, Aelfgar continued his madcap scheme, strengthened his relationship with Gruffydd of Wales. He has begun to try and use his Welsh support as leverage at King Edward's court."

Harold halted his pony, looked at his friend with a stricken face. "You say he has strengthened his treaty with Gruffydd? Pray, tell me how so?"

"My God, Harold, did I not tell you already? I am sorry. I guess I have been more preoccupied with the results of Aelfgar's pact with Wales than with the specifics of the union. I was speaking of the betrothal, of course."

Harold held his pony in place unconsciously. He was staring at his friend. "Be-troth-al?" he asked slowly.

"Yes. I thought you knew. Aelfgar has promised his daughter Aldgyth to Gruffydd. Even though she is just a babe, it seems the Welshman is content to await her proper bedding time."

Harold sighed with relief, so dramatically that his friend mistook it for despair.

"But, it is not that great an affair, I am sure. It seems that the King of Wales had wanted Leofric's widow, but she declined. With the house of Leofric somewhat split regarding this alliance, and Gruffydd not getting exactly what he had hoped for, this formal agreement between Chester and Wales is certainly not a strong bind. As for Gruffydd's plans, he would probably throw in his lot with Aelfgar no matter what. After all, the Welsh are getting the best end of the deal, while some of Aelfgar's own lands in Mercia have borne the brunt of renewed raiding."

Harold urged his mount to a trot again, and his friend followed to match the pace. "A betrothal between Gruffydd and Aldgyth! You are right, Robert, that is indeed of no concern to me." The Earl of Wessex laughed, then became serious. "But Aelfgar's raiding of English lands, with or without foreign aid, is of enormous concern to me."

Robert FitzWimark shrugged. "Why Aelfgar cannot see what is going on, I do not understand."

"I will tell you this, my friend, the raiding will not continue. I will make it clear to Aelfgar that he does not need an alliance with Wales to keep his hold on Mercia."

"And if he does not listen, Harold? What then?"

Harold caught sight of Lady Edyth, supping on the estate lawn with the queen. "Let us ford that river only if we do find it ahead of us, my friend!" The Earl kicked his pony into a trot.

Entry IV

▼

In which Godiva speaks in confidence to her maidservant

"He is still watching you, my lady!"

Hildreth's whisper from behind brought Godiva's attention back from the letter in her hand to the great hall at Chester where her son was entertaining the Welsh guests. Godiva glanced in the direction her servant was looking, before directing her disapproving look back at Hildreth.

"Now Hildreth! You have spoken unkindly of my Davydd for so long, I do believe you seem to mistrust all Welshmen."

"Well, they are so…foreign, my lady." Hildreth stepped from behind Godiva to stand beside her chair at the dinner table. She leaned down to speak softly. "But it is not just that. It is unseemly that he should look at you so. Perhaps if it was only that Welsh minstrel, I would not mind so much."

"Oh?" Godiva patted her servant's hand. "You would mind. You always did."

Hildreth was relentless. "But, my lady, this is not Davydd—"

"No, it is not." Lady Godiva leaned back in her chair. "Indeed, Davydd is gone, and may the Lord God watch out for him. I am through thinking of him. You were right about him, Hildreth, and do not ever let me forget that. His words, his feelings, they were all as the wind: Strong one day, full of life and lust for living, heavily scented with sweet smells of summer; stale and damp the next, cold and lifeless as a mid-winter breeze. Why I could not see the truth behind the image, I do not understand."

"My dear. Do not chide yourself. True, I was right about that Welshman. His promises were only as constant as his desire to bed the Lady of Mercia. But, he is gone, and better left forgotten. I will not belabor that memory." Hildreth's whisper grew intense once again.

"It is this Gruffydd whom I speak of now. Though he speaks with Lord Aelfgar, his eyes never stray far from watching you. I say again, it is unseemly!"

"Be respectful, Hildreth. He is King Gruffydd, and an important man. We must not upset my son's pact with our Welsh neighbors, simply because you think the way the man looks at me is inappropriate."

"But my lady!" Hildreth's voice rose, was quieted again only by a glare from Godiva. "He watches you as if you were a common serving wench."

"Remember Hildreth, the man had hoped to marry me. I should be flattered that such a great man finds me attractive."

"Do not play with me, my lady. You know that you are quite a comely woman. And I know that you do turn many a man's head. What manner of man would not notice you? But this," Hildreth made a quick, almost lewd gesture, "foreign man pays you not the respect that your station does decree. The man is just this day formally betrothed to the young Aldgyth! His manners are totally inappropriate. His leering across the room at you does you a disservice and shames Lord Aelfgar's daughter." The maidservant hit her fist against her own leg to punctuate the last statement, and the look of satisfaction that flashed briefly across her face made obvious the image in her mind of her having struck the King of Wales himself.

"Nonsense, Hildreth. Now stop it. Yes, King Gruffydd is uncouth, but it is not a trait of Welshmen in general. Only this man himself, which does not make him much worse than many an Englishman here at the dinner table. Especially with this spring betrothal celebration coming so soon after Shrove Tuesday. It has always been hard for men to keep the excessive carousing of that somewhat coarse holiday to merely one day in the week.

"As for shame being brought upon Aldgyth, I am sure that we need not worry about that. After all, what Welshman or Englishman would expect King Gruffydd to show anything but the simplest of attention to his betrothed. She is only a child and it will be quite a few years before she can be properly wed to Wales. If in the meantime I must endure Gruffydd's indiscreet stares, then so be it. I assure you, I can handle that. We must not interfere in my son's alliance with Wales. I am so glad he has made the connection with King Gruffydd even after his original plan was abandoned."

Godiva looked back at the King of Wales who produced a black-toothed smile as he caught her eye. Godiva nodded slightly to him, then turned back to her maid servant, unconsciously turning her chair slightly so that she faced away from Gruffydd.

Hildreth caught the exchange. "See, my lady. It is unseemly. I will talk to Lord Aelfgar about it."

Godiva was insistent. "No. Please, Hildreth, let it go. You know how stifled I had felt under Leofric's household rule. Never did I feel like I could do anything. Aelfgar's desire to wed me to Gruffydd was merely more of the same thing. I could not let the marriage go through. The only thing that counted seemed to be the fact that I am a woman. That is something God did give me, but I cannot be proud of for myself. Still, I found myself less than competent regarding the intrigues of the earldom. Had I not gotten Archbishop Aldred's suggestion to wed Aldgyth to Wales, I fear I would have let Aelfgar down completely. As it is, Aelfgar took the idea and made it happen. I am proud of him, and glad at the way things have worked out. I do not wish to jeopardize this alliance in any way. Aelfgar thinks he needs it, and I want him to feel secure."

Godiva thumbed the folded letter in her hand. "The shadow of Wessex is long and wide. No matter my feelings, Aelfgar may always feel at odds with Earl Harold and the other Godwins. Any success for Aelfgar is a victory for Mercia. We must support my son the Earl."

Moving behind Godiva, Hildreth glanced over the lady's shoulder at the short note in the other woman's hands. "And what are your feelings for the Earl of Wessex, my lady? I expect that is another note from Harold in your hands?"

"Yes, it is. He wishes to meet with me."

Hildreth moved back to where she could see her lady's face. "Will you meet the Earl of Wessex, my lady?"

Godiva was quiet a moment, almost long enough that Hildreth thought to ask her question again. Before she could, however, Lady Godiva spoke.

"I think there is much that Mercia and Wessex might share."

Hildreth sat down on a vacated chair next to Godiva, leaned close as if she were afraid the Earl of Mercia might hear. "When does the Earl of Wessex arrive?"

Godiva did not notice her maidservant's conspiratorial tone. "He was to be here this month," she said simply, "but in this note he apologizes for an extra delay."

"Delay, my lady?"

"Lord Harold has been back in England since summer last, as you know, and he did plan to visit Chester as soon as he could. However, the free time that Harold hoped for has grown more distant. The Earl had barely enough time to get his estates in order after his holy pilgrimage, before his brother returned this Spring. It seems the Earl of Northumbria is blaming his brother Harold for every bad thing that happened to him on his own travels abroad. Interesting how the two brothers seem to be so dissimilar."

"What is there between you and Lord Harold, my lady?" Hildreth winked at the lady. "You have never let me read any of his missives."

"Indeed I have not! They are for my eyes, not those of the world."

Hildreth sat back with a gasp. "My lady. Surely you do not believe I would proclaim your personal business throughout the manor."

"No Hildreth. Forgive me. I did not mean to imply you might be loose of tongue. No, I merely meant that I might do the writer of the notes a disservice by sharing the written feelings with even you."

Hildreth's hurt look brightened. Her eyes sparkled with intense curiosity. "Then the notes are that personal?"

Godiva sighed. "Actually, that is the strange thing, my friend. Even though some are, there are others that are not so."

Hildreth frowned when the younger woman seemed to stop talking, seemed to leave the conversation as if it was done. Seeing her servant's expression, Godiva smiled as she realized she was being so vague. Lady Godiva looked at the folded note in her hand, then held it up and tapped it lightly against her chin. "Hildreth, why do you suppose Harold's notes would be so different. He writes to me of his travels, his desire to see me again; but on one hand some notes are specific yet impersonal, on the other there are those that are more general yet much more personal."

"My lady, are you sure they all come from Lord Harold?"

"Who else?" Godiva acted truly puzzled.

"My lady has many admirers."

Godiva stared at her servant. "It is true that they are often written in different hands. The impersonal, more formal notes like this one are written in a very polished style. Others, though, and the more personal ones, are written in a more informal hand, with much of the feeling expressed simply in the strokes of the lettering. Perhaps Harold does not always have his scribe at hand—"

"And that is probably so, my lady." Hildreth clapped her hands together in excitement. "In fact, that explains everything. The formal letters are more impersonal because Lord Harold does not give all his feelings to his scribe when too busy to write the note himself. When the earl does have the time to write, the notes are more personal as well. It makes sense."

Godiva nodded. "I had thought of that. I have assumed that Lord Harold had his scribe help write some of the letters, although I know that Harold himself is a learned man. Yet I wondered what other explanation there might be." The lady reached over and touched her maidservant's forearm, pulled Hildreth a little closer.

"It is the unsigned letters, the informal ones, which do endear me to the man, Hildreth. They are so…sensitive. I once spoke to Harold about thinking like a woman, and it almost seems as if he does so in those letters."

Hildreth grinned. "Then you will meet Lord Harold, my lady?"

"I have known the Earl of Wessex as a distant figure, a man to contest with for my family's position. I have known the Harold of these formal notes, the first Earl to the King, Edward's right hand man. But I have yet to meet the man who wrote such splendid poetry as in the more personal letters I have received."

Lady Godiva glanced over at her son who was getting louder with every draught of ale. She nodded to Aelfgar as she rose, but the earl was completely oblivious to his mother and most everyone in the room. Instead, Godiva met the eyes of the King of Wales once again. She bowed her head and turned to leave the hall, with Hildreth right behind.

"Yes," Lady Godiva spoke forcefully, "I will meet with Harold of Wessex."

Entry V

▼ ————————————

Where Aldbald travels to meet Godiva, but Harold meets Aelfgar instead

The hall was very different from what he knew in York, Aldbald thought. It was a great hall, portions of the structure dating back to the time when the kings of Wessex ruled southwestern England from within its walls. This was not King Edward's hall, however, but the hall of the queen. Edith spent most of her time by the king's side in London or Gloucester, but she reserved her estates at Winchester as a place to which she could retire when the King was hunting or she desired solitude. The hall was decorated with elaborate embroidery and brightly painted linen sheets. The wall hangings each told a tale from England's past, adding to the aura of age and history that the building itself commanded. Aldbald felt a little strange in the grand room, as if he were intruding upon the queen's personal domain. If it were not for the others there with the queen, he would have left the hall at once.

The great hall at Winchester was filled with courtiers assembled for the Maytime celebrations, but the rains in the northwest had kept the Earl of Mercia from arriving earlier in the week as expected. A rider had come that morning with the news that Lord Aelfgar was only a few hours ride away. Aldbald sat on a bench at one end of the hall and waited, watching the others in the room. King Edward sat at the only table, playing chess with Lord Tostig; but his attention was on Lords Gyrth and Leofwine. The younger sons of Godwin were acting out scenes from their recent hunting excursion. Queen Edith stood behind the king in rapt conversation with Edyth Svanneshals, two maidservants stood close by in the corner shadows. Housecarls of Wessex milled about, but the Earl of Wessex stood apart from them. Aldbald saw that Harold was unusually quiet, and it was the look of contentment on his face that made Aldbald scowl slightly.

The young man caught himself, looked away from the Earl of Wessex. He respected Earl Harold, he had to keep reminding himself, but jealousy was not something he could control. At least in that he found a common ground with the Lord of Northumberland. Sometimes he wondered if perhaps it was simply Lord Tostig's feelings rubbing off. Then Aldbald would remember Harold's interest in the Lady Godiva. Nothing had ever been told to him outright, but he knew. Why of all the people in England, he would ask the wind, did the strongest man in the land desire the woman he loved?

And the wind would answer him. But Aldbald would not let himself listen, did not want to be reminded of his own simple place in the world. At least today he would not listen. Today he would speak with the Lady Godiva. Aldbald swore to himself he would not run from the lady this time as he had at the feast of Whitsuntide three years past. Precious few times had there been for him to try and meet Godiva again since, and then he found he had not the courage. This time, he thought, it will be different.

As the Queen's household celebrated the Rogation Days, Aldbald said his own prayers for his personal harvest. He had accompanied the Earl of Northumbria to the king's springtime court and had met again the Earl of Wessex and others of the English nobility, but it was the Lady Godiva's arrival he awaited so patiently.

Aldbald brought his hands together and stared at them. His prayers were hopes that his labors learning to write were not wasted, that all the notes he sent to the lady had been well received.

"I do believe you have changed into a much more thoughtful man over the past couple years, my friend."

Aldbald was startled, looked up to find Caedwig standing beside him.

The monk leaned close to his friend. "You used to be so talkative, but here you are sitting in quiet contemplation as so often I find you these days."

Aldbald smiled. "You are right, Caedwig. Perhaps I have changed a little. Remember, before a few years ago I was a simple cottar in the Midlands. Now I sit in the same hall as the King and Queen of England. If that is not humbling, I do not know what is."

Caedwig glanced in the direction of King Edward and Queen Edith, then bowed his head slightly. "Humbling, yes.

"Still," the monk's eyes opened wide, "I believe you also have more to think about these days than ever before. Is that not true?"

Aldbald did not answer the monk. A vision of the Lady Godiva standing alone, watching him run from the Whitsunday feast flashed in Aldbald's mind. Caedwig had not expected such a cool response from Aldbald, decided to fill the strained silence himself.

"I was referring, of course, to the latest manuscript I sent. I will tell you, if our friends at Waltham Abbey find I have been lending some of their prized possessions to you, they just might lock me in a cell for the rest of my life!"

Aldbald reached for the monk's hand, gripped it tightly. "Oh, I am sorry, Caedwig. I do thank you for all you have done for me!"

"Ah, then you did receive the manuscript." The monk patted the younger man on the back. "Good. I was afraid for a moment that it did not reach you in York."

Aldbald blinked wide-eyed at the cleric. "You would not truly get in trouble for sharing some written works with me?"

Caedwig smiled, "No, I suppose not. But I have to admit I have not tempted fate," he laughed. "I have not always told my friends what I will do with this manuscript or that one."

Aldbald sighed. "I find the story of King Beowulf most interesting to read, Caedwig. It is hard to imagine that the great man was brought down by events begun with only a simple deed done by another."

The monk sat down on the bench beside Aldbald. "It is often the case, in literature and in life, that seemingly unrelated events connect otherwise unrelated people, bringing about surprising conclusions."

"It is a sad story."

The monk shook his head. "I do not think it is meant to be sad. It is a story of loyalty. One young lad does not leave the King of the Geats, stays to slay the beast. He is the model to which the author of the piece would have us aspire."

"Yes, I see that," Aldbald nodded. "I think every great man should have an equally great chronicler to write his story."

"I am sure that every man would appreciate that," the cleric chuckled.

Caedwig always enjoyed talking with his student, was intrigued today by the younger man's distraction as Aldbald stared at his own hands. Aldbald held his hands up before the monk and turned them over so that the palms were up. "Caedwig," he said, still watching his hands, "what do you make of the art of writing?"

"Art? Yes, there is some art there, but perhaps more craft."

Aldbald turned his hands over again, watched his knuckles as he flexed his fingers. "Art or craft...does that matter?" Caedwig did not respond, knowing that the other man had not finished his train of thought.

"What I am wondering is where the mind comes in to it? I know I need these fingers to maneuver the writing implements, I need these hands to coordinate the required movements. But, without the mind, what is there?"

"Forgive me, my friend, I was thinking about my own writing. What I do is a craft: Translating and copying texts, drafting ledgers and notes from or to the king. Most of this work requires nothing more than the knowledge of letters, the craft to connect otherwise meaningless lines in a way that can impart information. There is some freedom to embellish the pages with designs, and that is where the art comes in to my work, where my mind plays a more important role." Caedwig watched Aldbald who had not taken his eyes off his hands before him. The monk reached over and grasped Aldbald's hands in his own.

"The freedom of expression I have is through that artwork on the margins of the page. But your expression, Aldbald, is truly in the words themselves. Writing poetry is indeed an art form, and I have not the gift for it that you do."

Embarrassed, Aldbald shrugged and pulled his hands away. "I was not fishing for a compliment this night, Caedwig."

"Nor was I only saying something I thought you wanted to hear," the monk answered seriously. "You asked where the mind comes into the writing. I believe it is in the freedom to create that God gave each of us in differing portions. From the little you have shown me of your skills, I believe that you, my friend, have been blessed with a great talent."

Aldbald smiled then, reaching back to join hands with the monk again. "And I thank you for that. But, I only write what I feel. Does not every man have feelings to express?"

"Yes." Caedwig looked away from Aldbald. He glanced at Lord Tostig, but his gaze then came to rest on King Edward across the game table, and the Queen standing nearby. "Not every man is able to express his feelings as well as you might think, my friend." The monk rubbed his hands together and then motioned toward the Earl of Northumbria.

"As a servant of Lord Tostig," he whispered, "you should know that better than most."

There was a glint in the monk's eyes, and Aldbald smiled. "Oh, Lord Tostig is not so bad, once you get to know him."

"And you have a great gift for understatement, my friend!"

They both laughed, but stopped as one with the voice that barked from the entryway to the hall.

"So King Edward, with all these Godwins about, was the Earl of Mercia missed?"

Aldbald stood up as Lady Godiva's son strode into the hall, leaving two companions at the doorway and ignoring all as he passed through the courtiers. Young Aelfgar's attention was on the King and those around Edward.

"Ah. We have the Earl of Wessex hovering, his lapdogs from Kent and East Anglia at his beck and call, and," Aelfgar stopped next to the game table, "the Lord of Northumbria cheating at chess as always."

Earl Tostig jumped up, more angered by Aelfgar's insinuation that his younger brothers followed after Harold and not himself, than he was at being called a cheat.

"You had better watch yourself here, Leofricsson."

King Edward was immobile. Leofwine stepped over and laid a restraining hand on his brother, but kept his eyes on Aelfgar. Gyrth moved to the other side of the newcomer. There was a moment of quiet as everyone in the room watched Aelfgar's eyes follow the movements of the three brothers, then the Earl of Mercia spoke again.

"Three Godwinssons to one son of Leofric. I am not sure I care for the odds." Aelfgar smiled when Tostig grinned at him. He purposefully turned away from the Earl of Northumbria, but not to signal to his housecarls at the door. Instead he met the eyes of Harold who was still leaning against the wall. "Perhaps if the Earl of Wessex joined in I would not feel I was taking unfair advantage."

Harold's laugh captured everyone's attention, even that of Tostig who had almost raised his hand to strike Aelfgar. Then he laughed also.

"Edward, now the festivities can truly begin," Tostig said. "Your court fool has arrived!"

Tostig was rewarded with a glare from Aelfgar, but was disappointed when his older brother moved to take control of the situation. Harold stepped up to Aelfgar, passing his brothers and standing in front of Tostig.

"Indeed, I too am grateful for the mirth brought by the Earl of Mercia. This assembly was becoming a bit too quiet for my tastes." Harold placed his arm lightly around Aelfgar's shoulders to lead him away from his brothers.

Edward began laughing as well then, and the tension in the room broke. "Aelfgar, good to have you finally join us." The King stood up and moved toward the young man. Gyrth and Leofwine stepped aside, but Tostig stayed close, pointing his nose at Aelfgar. The Earl of Mercia shrugged off Harold's touch, turning to face the King as Edward grabbed him and shook his shoulders.

"After all the rain we have heard about in the north, I will bet you are looking forward to a good hunt. The weather here in Gloucester has not been perfect, but it is bearable. We will hunt tomorrow." Edward sat back down in his chair and frowned at the table in front of him.

"I look forward to tomorrow, King Edward," Aelfgar answered, although the King did not hear. Edward's full concentration was directed toward trying to remember what the game pieces before him meant.

Just before the Earl of Mercia arrived, the King's servants had begun to assemble the trestles for the dinner feast. They rejoined their task, collecting the benches scattered around the room and placing them by the tables. Caedwig and Aldbald stepped out of the way as the bench they had been sitting on was moved. The younger man glanced at the door to the hall, but there were only servants coming in.

Aldbald shook Caedwig's hands with a clammy grip. "Excuse me, my friend. I would speak with the Earl of Mercia."

"By all means, Aldbald," the monk responded as Aldbald walked away. "We can talk more later."

As Aldbald approached Aelfgar, Tostig moved close to the Earl of Mercia as well. "Yes," Tostig taunted, winking at his brother Harold, "we have all missed the Earl of Mercia on the hunt. His antics with the Welsh seem to have cooled of late."

Harold turned his attention to Tostig, grabbing his brother's wrist and leaning close so that only the Earl of Northumbria would hear.

"Enough, Tostig!"

Tostig wilted under Harold's scrutiny. "Why must you try the Earl of Mercia's patience?" Harold asked.

"Because it is so easy to anger the boy," Tostig spat. "Leofric's son is not so high and mighty without his precious Welshmen by his side."

"Quiet, Tostig," Harold whispered. "Mercia's connection with Wales may still be something we can use."

"Oh?" Tostig glowered at his brother.

Aldbald drew up next to the Earl of Mercia at that moment. He pulled lightly on Aelfgar's mantle. "My lord? Lord Aelfgar, if I may have a word?"

"Yes?" Aelfgar hardly noticed Aldbald as he grabbed at an ale-skin carried by a servant passing by and strained to hear the interchange between the Godwin brothers. "What is it?"

"Your lady mother," Aldbald spoke slowly as Aelfgar took a long draught, "did she not arrive with you today?"

Aelfgar wiped his mouth with the sleeve of his surcoat. "My lady mother is in Wales watching over her grandchild."

Even as he said that, Aelfgar overheard the Earl of Wessex answer Tostig's questioning look. "I asked the Lady Godiva to go to Wales to keep an eye on Gruffydd."

Aelfgar was shocked, and Aldbald's eyes went wide as well when he heard Godiva's name spoken.

"Bah!" Tostig hissed. "What good is that woman to us, Harold?"

Aelfgar pushed Tostig aside and faced the Earl of Wessex. "Yes, Lord of Wessex, what is my mother to you?" Aldbald stepped beside the Earl of Mercia, intent to hear Harold's response.

Tostig started to say something, but a look from his brother cut him off. Harold met Aelfgar's eyes. "It is nothing, my friend."

"Nothing?" It was Aldbald who asked the question, his unthinking boldness born of jealousy; but no one seemed to notice. All eyes were on Harold.

"Truly," Harold said.

"Nothing?" Aelfgar echoed Aldbald. "I send my mother to Wales to take care of my daughter Aldgyth, and you say you asked her to go!"

"Aelfgar, I asked your lady mother to watch out for England's interests when she traveled to Gruffydd's court."

"England's interests," Aelfgar scoffed, "or your own, great Lord of Wessex?"

"Surely not your interests, Leofricsson," Tostig grinned.

Harold put the back of his arm across his brother's chest, but did not look at Tostig. "I want what is best for England, Aelfgar. It would be to your benefit to remember that."

The Earl of Mercia nodded, walked slowly backward keeping his eyes on the Godwin brothers. Caedwig had moved closer to hear better, had to step aside before the retreating man could bump into him. Gyrth and Leofwine saw the Earl of Mercia back away, came over to flank their brothers while other courtiers went quiet nearby. King Edward was in rapt concentration, but the interchange had caught the attention of the Queen. Edith and her cousin walked over to stand behind Harold and Tostig. Aelfgar's housecarls met him at the doorway to the hall.

"What I remember, Harold, is that we always seem to meet in your lands." Aelfgar raised his arm and pointed at the Earl of Wessex as if with a sword in hand. "You just wait until we meet in the Marches!"

Tostig laughed as the Earl of Mercia left the hall, and Edyth Svanneshals put her hand on Harold's arm. "Can that boy never grow up?"

Queen Edith glared at Tostig. "Young Aelfgar is not the only one that needs to grow up."

Harold turned to Tostig. "I think our brother needs to learn his limits."

Aldbald's gaze had been fixed on the Earl of Wessex as Aelfgar made his exit. Lady Edyth's approach brought his attention to the beautiful woman beside Harold.

"Mayhap we all need to learn of our limitations," Aldbald mumbled as he turned and walked away; but everyone in the group heard him.

Tostig grinned at what was clearly a barb thrown at his older brother by his servant. Harold looked over his shoulder to see Aldbald dodge the out-stretched hand of Caedwig as he left the hall. Harold raised an eyebrow, glanced at the monk; but Caedwig could only shrug.

Entry VI

▼

In which Harold does quarrel with Aelfgar

The two men rode alone along the deserted path. The Earl of Wessex tried to stretch his legs without dismounting. His left knee seemed to be more painful than usual. Harold wondered if it really was somehow worse this day, or was it simply that he was feeling everything a bit more vividly after his long night of drinking with his men. He had had only a little sleep the previous night, but he was anxious to be on his way west.

"Here it is Midsummer's eve, but perhaps not all the sheep shearing is complete in Chester, Rob. It may be that our friend Aelfgar will need some trimming."

Robert FitzWimark grunted in agreement. His own head was clearing fast in the cool morning air. "Aelfgar continues to test your good will, even after all this time. I do believe our young friend should be taught a lesson."

Harold nodded. "I had hoped that my time away on pilgrimage would smooth things over between me and Aelfgar's mother, but I truly thought that the extra time would have helped to cool Aelfgar's anger as well. I have given Aelfgar plenty of time since Leofric's death. Mercia must move on. I believe Lady Godiva is ready to, but Aelfgar seems stubborn."

Harold had not noticed at first that FitzWimark had reigned in his mount. When Harold slowed his pony, glanced back to his friend with an inquisitive raised eyebrow, Robert kicked his beast to catch up once again with the Earl of Wessex.

"So it is true?"

Harold looked at his friend, perplexed. "What is true?"

"That you have kept close contact with Aelfgar's mother?"

"Well, yes," Harold shrugged, "I suppose I have. I asked her to help me watch over Aelfgar's tenuous connection with Wales. I do not trust Gruffydd." Harold frowned. "You knew that, Rob."

"Yes. But is that all there is?"

Harold waved his hand. "Well, I sent a message or two to her while on my travels to Rome, hoping she would be mollified by my pious adventures. I have seen her but once since my return, and that was only long enough to ask her to help us in Wales." Harold paused, seeing his friend's wide-eyed expression. "What of it?"

"My God, Harold!" FitzWimark was incredulous. "Aelfgar has been using that as his excuse for his troublesome expeditions. And it has been getting worse, as you know. Ever since your meeting last year at Winchester he has kept himself isolated in Chester. He seems to think you planned his father's death and are working to get at him through Leofric's widow."

"Tell me something new, my friend."

"Is it all true, then? Wulfstan and I had not given much credence to these claims. I guess I, for one, had thought they were the ramblings of a young man caught in a persecution complex, had guessed they were akin to the tales told by your own brother Tostig. I never guessed they might be true."

"Hold there, friend!" Harold stopped his mount. "You know I had nothing to do with Leofric's death. My God! If I did, you would have been the first to learn of it. I had reason to suspect my brother was involved, but I have learned that Tostig too is innocent. If Aelfgar persists in this belief, it is not because of any shred of truth. And, so be it. There is nothing harder to change than a set mind. Still, I expected more from you, my friend."

"I am sorry, Harold. I did not mean to implicate you. But, what is this connection you have with Leofric's widow?"

Harold looked at his friend, then up to the sky. Without a word, he dismounted and walked his pony off the pathway to a clearing in the trees lining the road. Harold did not need to motion for Robert to follow, the other man had already done so, curious now about his friend's intentions.

"I will tell you, Robert, because for myself I think it may help to speak of it." Robert followed Harold's lead, tied his horse to one of the lower tree branches to allow the animal to graze on the tall grass below.

Harold took a deep breath. "I find I am quite impressed by the woman, Rob. I confess, the woman does enthrall me in some way I do not fully understand. She is very different from other women. Or maybe it is because through her I have seen the strengths in all women that I have too long taken for granted. I only know that I would gain her trust, her friendship. Perhaps there could be more than that between us; but I would have at least that."

When Robert looked at his friend skeptically, the Earl of Wessex became somewhat defensive. "And is that so bad? Too long have Mercia and Wessex been at odds. As you well know, I have brought England a long way beyond where my father did leave the realm. The earldoms are all behind a King that the people adore. The country is at peace. All the earldoms are united, save Mercia. Long have the people of the borderlands backed the house of Leofric. And rightly so. I must strengthen any political tie I can with our Mercian neighbor. Aelfgar is young. It is lady Godiva that heads the house of Leofric at present. By the Lord's dying breath, I had hoped my friendship with Godiva would only have worked to strengthen England. I have no idea why Aelfgar chooses to make me his enemy."

"Because he is young, Harold."

"There must be more to it than that. Young, yes. Brash, yes, and headstrong. But lacking in reason? I do not think so, although sometimes it seems I could say as much and be on the mark when it comes to my brother Tostig. But Aelfgar? No. Aelfgar has his father's wit about him. Did he not inherit Leofric's common sense as well?"

"Harold, it is not that alone, although it may be a part. I think the greater part is merely that the son of Leofric does not know you as do your friends. He cannot trust that which he fears. Yes, Harold, he must fear you. And fear in a young man will most often transform into hatred if left unchecked."

"But I have done nothing to incite him against me. Nothing to make him fear me." Robert raised his left eyebrow, squinting through his right eye. Harold paused, catching the look of disbelief on his friend's face.

"What? What have I done?"

"My friend, you said yourself that you had once thought your brother had been involved in Leofric's death. How much easier for Aelfgar that belief would be. And, why would he expect that Tostig would have acted alone? Surely, where one Godwin goes, the other is sure to be around." Robert held up his hand to stem Harold's disclaimer. "From Aelfgar's point of view!"

Harold was quiet for a moment. "Yes, of course. But, that is one reason why I left on my trip to Rome. I had hoped that the young man's anger and frustration would lessen. Yet, it is obvious that it has not."

"Aelfgar, as I said, suspects you of some conspiracy involving his mother. He can only assume that, whatever you are up to, you have an interest in bringing Mercia completely under control of the house of Godwin, leaving nothing for him and his children."

"And do you deny it, Harold of Wessex?"

Harold and Robert jumped at the sound of another voice. Instinctively, Robert had drawn his sword and stepped behind his pony as he stood, putting the animal between himself and the newcomer. Harold had his hand on his sword, but did not draw it when he saw who it was that addressed them. It was the son of Leofric, although hardly recognizable was he. Aelfgar wore the dress of the woodsmen, the clothes of the Welsh. He must be aged at least eighteen years, Harold thought, and he was growing into a big man. FitzWimark still stood behind his horse, but his hold on his sword wavered as he looked across the glade at the men with Aelfgar. There were only four other men with the Earl of Mercia, Welshmen by their look; but they were well armed and knew well that they had the upper hand should a fight break out. Harold and Robert FitzWimark had been traveling alone, having left orders with Harold's housecarls in Shrewsbury to follow as soon as they were sober.

Even as Harold cursed himself for not giving in when Robert suggested that they wait for an escort, he marveled at the ease with which Aelfgar and his companions had come upon them without either he or his friend, or even the horses, becoming aware of any danger. Harold purposely moved his own hand away from the hilt of his sword, stepped into the open in the middle of the tree-lined clearing. The Earl of Wessex held his arms out away from his body.

"Aelfgar! FitzWimark and I have no quarrel with you today. Put up your weapons and call off your Welsh cousins."

"Ho ho! It will not be that easy for you today, Godwinspawn. These are not the lands of the West Saxons. These are the borderlands, the Marches. This is Mercia. I command here. Interesting that I should come upon the great Harold of Wessex with only one companion! No, it will not be so easy for you to get out of this."

"You are full of courage with your Welsh hounds beside you!" Robert cried. "But they will run when the housecarls of Wessex catch up with us. They can only be but a few moments behind us."

"Ha! Quick thinking, and a good try."

Harold picked up on his friend's ruse, decided to play along in the hopes they could bluff Aelfgar. "Why do you think that we were paused here in this glade? Of course my soldiers are right behind. Do not do anything foolish, Aelfgar."

"Oh, I assure you, Wessex, I do not intend to do anything foolish. It so happens that my companions and I have spent the morning scouting about the area. I do know that you two ride alone." Aelfgar stepped a little closer to the other earl of England, laughed as he saw the look flash across FitzWimark's face.

"Interesting that you do not seem as fearful as your partner, Harold, especially since it is you that have more to be fearful for. But, then, yours was always a cool nature. Nevertheless, I will warrant that you are berating yourself now for making such a fool move as this. Do not be too hard on yourself. Is it not always the case that great men are brought down by simple mistakes?"

Harold had not moved at all, still stood with his hands away from his sides. He brought his arms out even further, in an unguarded gesture of openness. "Aelfgar, I told you that I have no quarrel with you, and I meant it. What is this nonsense?"

"No quarrel? Has FitzWimark not filled you in on the situation in Mercia since your holy escapades commenced? Oh, I think he has. Do not try and proclaim that you have no interest in my alliance with Wales. I will tell you, with Gruffydd on my side, I am stronger than my father ever was! This day we are all witness to the resurgence of Mercian dominance in the governing of England and rule of realm. Oh yes, Harold, I do believe you have a quarrel with me."

"Perhaps there is a quarrel, but not between Harold of Bosham and Aelfgar of Chester. It is a matter between the Earl of Wessex and the Earl of Mercia. A conflict to be dealt with among the men of the Witan, and not to be settled like common vagabonds out here in the forest."

"Call it what you will, Lord of Wessex; but in the end it does come down to a quarrel between you and me. And I, for one, choose to settle it here and now."

"Well, I do not."

"Ah, but as I said, this is not Wessex. This is Mercia. I make the decisions here. My decision is that we fight."

Aelfgar hefted his sword, stepped slowly towards his adversary. Harold then drew his own sword, brought it up to point at Aelfgar's chest as the younger man drew nearer. Aelfgar smiled.

"I have waited a long time for this, Godwinspawn."

"I hate to disappoint you." Harold threw his sword to the ground. "I will not fight you this day."

The Earl of Mercia paused a moment, surprised by the other man's action. Aelfgar then laughed again. "Well, you may not fight today, but you will die just the same."

Robert FitzWimark called to his friend, "Harold, the man has lost his senses. You cannot reason with him."

Aelfgar smiled big. "Your companion is right in part, at least. It is true you cannot reason with me today." With that, and another laugh, the young man swung his sword high.

FitzWimark cried out, throwing his own sword to Harold. "My lord, defend yourself against this mad man!"

With a weapon swinging over his head, Harold's instincts took over. He caught FitzWimark's sword in the air and brought it to parry Aelfgar's attack. Just in time, the younger man's blade came within a hand's breadth of Harold's head. Aelfgar pulled his sword back and paced around his enemy. Given a moment, Harold let the point of his weapon drop down to the ground.

"You can not make me fight you, Aelfgar."

"Oh?" The younger man turned his body in a full circle, using the momentum produced to swing his sword behind him in a slicing motion toward Harold's left side. The Earl of Wessex dropped down and rolled to the side, Aelfgar's sword singing above his head.

Harold came up with his weapon level to the ground, parried a direct thrust as Aelfgar attacked again. The son of Leofric had the benefit of his youth, was at his physical peak and hardened by the past couple years in the woods with the Welsh. Aelfgar pressed this advantage, swinging his sword in a constant barrage; first to the left, then the right, the sword on high, then coming straight in to Harold's chest. The Earl of Wessex found himself being pushed back at every stroke, battling to protect his life as he vainly searched for a way to end the fight.

"Damn it, Aelfgar! Stop this nonsense." Harold's breath was becoming slightly strained, and Aelfgar noticed.

"Indeed, I will. Soon enough. When your blood glistens on my sword." The young man feinted to the left, then swung around in a full circle again, drawing the blade in a wide arc to slice Harold's left arm at the shoulder. A moment of silence filled the glade. Harold's surprised look mirrored FitzWimark's own expression of concern. Aelfgar stared at his quarry.

"Ah! My weapon has tasted Godwin blood. It would be cruel of me were I to not let my sword feast now that it knows what it has been missing."

"Aelfgar, no!" FitzWimark's cry did nothing to halt the young man. Aelfgar's sword was up again and coming down to cleave Harold's head in two. Harold grasped the hilt of his sword with both hands, the pain of his wound forgotten for the moment. He brought the weapon up and over his head to deflect the incoming threat. Knocking Aelfgar's blade to the side, Harold sidestepped to the left, spun around and brought his sword to face his attacker. Aelfgar had put all his strength behind the last blow, lost his balance as his blade was pushed to the side. The young man lost his grip on his sword as he stumbled. Regaining balance, Aelfgar stood looking at his adversary, Harold with his sword raised and pointing at him, while his own weapon lay on the ground between them. Harold let his weapon go slack as he straightened up and caught his breath. But, the blood lust had not yet left the young man's eyes, the smile had not left his transformed face.

"Now, perhaps we can talk some sense." Even as Harold spoke, Aelfgar was jumping forward. The young man dived for his mistakenly dropped sword, rolled on the ground and came up thrusting the weapon toward

Harold's abdomen. The Earl of Wessex brought his own weapon up quickly, meant only to deflect the incoming blade. He was successful in that, but could not pull his weapon back quickly enough before Aelfgar's forward momentum after the roll brought the young man's body directly onto Harold's outstretched sword.

Aelfgar's smile of triumph took a moment to dissolve, then his face registered only surprise. He started to say something, but blood came up and choked the last breath out of Leofric's son.

Lady Godiva's son. "No!" Harold screamed loudly, his voice a shriek, his face looking crazed. The Welshmen who had accompanied Aelfgar murmured among themselves, fearful that the man who just killed their friend might go berserk. Robert FitzWimark dashed to Harold's own discarded weapon, brandished it before the foreigners.

"No!"

When Harold screamed again, the Welshmen dispersed, dissolving into the trees from which they had appeared.

Entry VII

▼

In which we learn that the Lady Godiva has fled

Just as good news might easily move as molasses in January, so too does bad news seem to spread like a brush fire on a dry, windy summer afternoon. Before the Earl of Wessex could arrive at Chester bearing Aelfgar's body, the household of the Earl of Mercia was buzzing with various versions of the story. As with any gossip, the tales were not completely true. A common theme was that the Earl of Wessex was leading an army to Chester; but some had him seeking to punish Mercia while others suggested he was wanting to protect the borderlands. The latter was sometimes accompanied by a vivid description of the Welsh stabbing poor Aelfgar in the back.

When Lord Tostig had learned that the Earl of Wessex was heading to Mercia, he sent word immediately that he would meet Harold. However, troubles in Northumbria delayed his departure, and Aldbald jumped at the chance to act as courier so that he could travel at once to Chester. He had hoped to meet the Lady of Mercia, still desired to make up for his embarrassed departure at Whitsuntide so long ago. Aldbald, bearing Tostig's message to Lord Harold that the Earl of Northumbria would meet him at Shrewsbury a few days hence, had arrived just after word had reached Chester of Aelfgar's death. He knew not what to believe. He only knew that something dreadful had happened to the Earl of Mercia, and that the Lady Godiva was gone.

From information he overheard at Lord Tostig's court, Aldbald knew that there was some kind of tenuous alliance between Mercia and Wales. It was an alliance that, according to the Earl of Northumbria, seemed destined to fail. As Aldbald wandered about the halls of Aelfgar's home, he overheard all the stories passing among the servants. He became certain that the Welsh must have caused the death of the Earl of Mercia and that they may have taken Lady Godiva hostage. Seeking out the rooms of the Lady, he prayed with all his heart that God might keep Godiva free of harm. In a darkened corridor outside the Lady's private chambers, he overheard two of Godiva's maidservants talking about their mistress. In his worry, Aldbald was bold. He knocked on the door.

"Excuse me, my ladies. What is it you were saying about going to join your lady?"

Startled, the young girls exchanged confused looks. They were sisters and the older, more daring of the two spoke cautiously, "Are you a friend to the Lady Godiva?"

"I do count myself friendly to the Lady Godiva." Aldbald sensed the tension in the two young women who were each no more than twelve years of age. The young man saw the wary looks the girls exchanged, and he held up his hands. "I am just a Mercian, overly concerned for your lady's well being."

Content that the man was no threat, the older of the two girls expressed their excitement and fear. "We are leaving on the morrow to catch up with the Lady's party in Wales."

"Ah," Aldbald snapped his fingers, "then it is true! It seems that the foreigners at least have the decency to allow the lady her personal servants. I am gratified to hear that."

The girls were wary again. "Indeed, and why would they not?"

"I admit, I do not know the Welsh ways. I did understand them to be savages."

The young girls shuddered as one. The youngest reached over and squeezed her sibling's hand. "Holy Mary! We have met some Welsh, but only in the bounds of Cheshire. What if they are savages in their own lands?"

The older of the two realized she had to act more secure. "No, I think they have many faults, but I do not want to think the Welsh people are savages."

Aldbald recognized the fear of the unknown on the young girls' faces. "No, of course not. They are just a different people." Not so sure himself, he wanted to try and settle their young minds if he could. "I am sure everything will be all right."

Aldbald suddenly remembered the note he had stuffed into his travel pouch tucked under his belt. Not the message from his lord to the Earl of Wessex, but the one he had hoped to deliver to the Lady Godiva in person. He looked at the girls in earnest. "Please, are there writing materials in your lady's chambers? I would that you could deliver this message to her for me. Let her know that whatever happens, things will be all right." Aldbald glanced around and at once spied the Lady's desk. He dashed to the table and scrawled a note on the outside of the folded piece of parchment, handed the letter to the older of the sisters.

"Please, do not fail me. Take this to your lady, and remember: Things will be all right."

Entrusted with a message to their mistress, the girls felt important, less fearful. "We will deliver your note."

"Thank you." Aldbald turned to go. He knew there was one man who could help him bring the Lady Godiva back from the Welsh wilderness. He had to find Harold.

Hildreth, Lady Godiva's chief maidservant, bumped into the young man in the dark hallway outside the lady's room. Startled by the man, she inquired as to his business, but Aldbald was too intent on his mission, did not hear the woman as he made off down the hallway. Hildreth entered the chamber in a rage.

"Why are you two not packing? The Lady Godiva will need her things. She had not the time to waste collecting her belongings. She is relying on us to help her. We need to be ready to leave Chester early tomorrow. The soldier Gunthnot will be back to escort us to the Lady."

"Yes, Hildreth." The girls spoke in unison. The older fumbled with the parchment in her hand, looking in vain for a safe place to stow the note away.

"What are you clutching at there, girl?" Hildreth reached for the parchment. The girl reluctantly held it back.

"It is an urgent message for our lady. We swore to deliver it to her personally."

"Oh?" Hildreth was not impressed at the girl's protective instinct, not when it related to her lady's concerns. "And who is it from? That cloaked man I passed in the hallway? Who was he? What does the note say?"

The young girl's resolve faltered a bit then. "I do not know, my lady." She glanced at her younger sister, then back at Hildreth. "The man did not say, and we failed to ask." Nor could either of the young girls read, so they had no idea what the man had written on the paper. The older girl stood up straight. "But the man was very concerned about our lady's safety. He bade us tell her not to worry—"

Hildreth snatched the parchment from the girl's hand. "I will take it to her." She read aloud the note scribbled on the outside of the sealed letter. "It says, 'The Lord Harold of Wessex will scour the whole of Wales to retrieve you.' I suppose it does not matter who delivered the note, the warning is real enough. We will not wait until the light of day." The head maidservant reached over to pat the girls on their backs. "Help me pack quickly. We must away at once."

Hildreth let the note fall into the burning embers of the brazier as she hastily ushered the two young women into the adjoining room.

*   *   *   *

When the Earl of Wessex showed up at Chester with Robert FitzWimark and a handful of well armed housecarls, Harold found that the news of Aelfgar's death had preceded him. Harold had hoped to break the news gently to Aelfgar's mother, explain exactly what had happened. Instead, the Earl of Wessex found a hostile household, the servants angry and fearful, and the Lady Godiva gone. Harold sat by himself in the dining hall, sipping ale and thinking. His companions, even FitzWimark, stayed clear for the moment. Aldbald knew no better, approached the Earl of Wessex in earnest. Harold looked up in surprise.

"There is a friendly face in Chester. Aldbald, it is good to see you, even under such circumstances as this. My friend, what brings you to this unhappy place."

"My lord, I was just readying my horse to head out to look for you. I feared something might have happened to you as well." Aldbald cleared his throat.

"My lord, I have heard the servants speak—" Aldbald's question faltered.

"I am sure you have, Aldbald, but I am not so sure I want to discuss the matter right now."

"Lord Harold, you must help the Lady Godiva!" Normally struck by envy, Aldbald this day was glad of his knowledge that Lord Harold was interested in the Lady Godiva. "You can venture into Wales and bring her safely back, can you not?"

Harold stood up so fast, Aldbald backed up a step. "What do you mean?"

Aldbald moved close again. "The Lady Godiva, my lord! Have you not heard the servants in the house speak of it?"

"No. The servants have not spoken to me." Harold bit his lip. "What is this about Wales?"

"It seems she has been taken into Wales, my lord. I spoke with a couple of the Lady's own servants."

Harold slapped his thigh. "Of course! With Aelfgar dead, King Gruffydd would not find his position very strong with only the child Aldgyth under his control. Damn! How could Gruffydd have learned of today's events so quickly?"

Aldbald shook his head and swallowed with difficulty. "Please, sir. You will seek to rescue the Lady? If my lord Tostig were here, I would entreat him to help you. Unfortunately, problems in York delayed his joining you at Shrewsbury as he had hoped."

Harold was not thinking of his brother. He picked up his mug and drained the liquid. "Yes, I will rescue the Lady Godiva." A small piece of the earthenware mug chipped off as Harold brought the empty vessel back to the table a little too forcefully. "I will not let that Welsh King disrupt the peace in my own realm, especially if it means putting the Lady Godiva in jeopardy."

Aldbald suddenly felt like a child. "If I knew anything about fighting, my lord, I would endeavor to accompany you!"

Harold softened at that. "My friend, do not wish it so. You stick to your books. I do not plan for this to be a fight at all."

Robert FitzWimark entered the hall and saw Aldbald speaking to the Earl of Wessex. He approached the two slowly with an inquisitive look. "My lord Harold, the horses are rested and your men are assembled and ready to go. We are awaiting your word."

Harold squeezed Aldbald's shoulder. "Do not worry, my friend. If I can, I will slip in and get out of Wales before Gruffydd has the time to blink!" Harold turned to FitzWimark. "Rob, I have some business to attend to in Wales. Will you accompany me?"

"Wales, my lord?" Aldbald bowed low as Harold led his companion away. When Aldbald looked up again, he saw that the Earl of Wessex was already gone from the hall.

*   *   *   *

The small group huddled in the hollow of the hill against the driving rain. There were sounds of sniffling and murmurs of distaste for the weather. But mostly the people were quiet. A sound came to them over the howl of the wind, and they knew that meant someone was approaching. Lady Godiva reached for a dagger at her belt. It felt uncomfortable in her hand, but she was prepared to use it if necessary.

"It is I, Gunthnot."

There was a collective sigh as the soldier joined them from out of the darkness.

"What is the news?" Hildreth was the first to ask.

Gunthnot directed his response to Godiva. "My lady, with Harold controlling the coast, there is no chance of gaining ship's passage from Gwynedd, even if this storm did abate."

"Then we are lost!" Hildreth exclaimed.

Lady Godiva rested her hand on her maidservants head. "No. There must be alternatives." She reached then for her guard's cold hands. "Gunthnot?"

Gunthnot took a quick breath. "My lady, I have found someone who will guide us into Powys in southern Wales."

"Then we will go there. It is obvious to me that I cannot seek refuge at King Gruffydd's court now. Not with Harold hot on my trail. I might endanger my grandchild Aldgyth. If he captures me in the north, he may easily get her as well. If I can escape to the south, Harold might follow after me and leave Aelfgar's daughter alone."

Hildreth took in her breath sharply. "Would we be safe in the south, my lady?"

Lady Godiva sighed. "At least as safe as we are here—"

"Not necessarily," Gunthnot cut her off. "It appears that all of Wales is not behind King Gruffydd. Those in southern Wales even less so. My lady, this could be a dangerous choice of action."

Godiva managed a slight smile. "Then why do you suggest it?"

"Because, my lady," the soldier grunted, "I have nothing else to offer."

"Then it is settled."

Gunthnot fidgeted. "My lady, I just want to make sure you are aware of what we might get ourselves into down there."

"I do not pretend to know exactly what is in store for us." The Lady Godiva narrowed her eyes. "What I do know is that my son had not found any help in Ireland, so even had we traveled to that kingdom I am not sure what we would have gained. Perhaps on the continent I can find support for Mercia. From southern Wales we might find a channel boat bound for Brittany."

Godiva turned to her retinue pressed close together. "I must go to Powys. I will go to Brittany. But I will not force any of you to join me in this."

There were half-hearted rejoinders mumbled from each of the party. Gunthnot said nothing. Standing close to Godiva, he simply expected her to know that he would stay with her whatever the circumstances. It was Hildreth who then made the most noise.

"My lady! You will not leave me behind in this wretched land. I will go where you go, wherever that might be. I have sworn my service to you. What kind of a servant would I be if I left you when you most needed me? I resent your implication that I—"

"Hush!" Godiva laughed. "Of course I will allow to come along anyone who wants to join me."

There was a short, but strained silence as the others in the group failed to respond the way that Hildreth had. Hildreth noted it at once and turned to chastise the group as a whole, but Godiva stayed her servant's voice with a light hand touched to Hildreth's lips.

"However, I will tell you all," Godiva said, "that I have a great need for most of you to stay behind here in Gwynedd. I would like to know that I leave some of my own servants here to watch over my grandchild at King Gruffydd's court. In fact, I would that a couple fateful servants see to the well-being of Aelfgar's young sons back at Chester as well."

"Are you not taking a risk leaving your young grandchildren in the hands of servants?" Gunthnot whispered to Godiva.

"Yes," Godiva nodded, "but I believe they will be safe enough. Mercia's strength lies in me alone right now. And I am only strong as long as I am free to seek support for my cause."

Hildreth was glowering at the other servants, but in the end most decided to stay back as Godiva requested.

"My lady, I thank you for suggesting the servants stay behind," Gunthnot said as they made ready to leave. "I am not so sure I can protect you, much less the whole band here."

Godiva smiled at her guard, then became quite serious. "We are indeed heading into unknown territory, my friend. With the gold I have brought along, we should find many willing to help us out. I only pray that I will not need your services as a swordsman."

Entry VIII

▼

Through which Wales is subjugated, but the Lady Godiva gets away

Harold of Wessex took a long draught of the strong Welsh mead in a vain attempt to warm the chill in his bones. Wales was an inhospitable country any time, but especially so during the long winter months when the freezing rain was driven by the gusting winds, soaking ones clothing in a second and leaving a man chilled to the bone in a matter of minutes.

The Golden Dragon banner of Wessex hung limp and lifeless above the command tent, its fibers soaked through and frozen, making the weight of the banner more than even the howling wind could move. Huddling near the fire to wait out the worst of the storm, Harold listened to the wind blow through the trees. In each gust the Earl of Wessex could hear the echoes of the Roman legionnaire lamentation: Cambria, their name for the countryside west of the province of Britannia that they garrisoned, but never truly conquered. The might of Rome left most of Wales undisturbed;

yet here in southern Wales Harold of Wessex found himself caught up in a struggle against the Welsh leader Gruffydd.

Harold, in pursuit of Godiva, took his personal guard and Robert FitzWimark into Wales in pursuit. The Earl of Wessex and FitzWimark were now accompanied by Wulfstan and two of Harold's brothers. Gyrth and Leofwine had brought with them more housecarls and had called up the fyrd, made up of the thanes and farmers of Wessex, to swell their numbers for more protection against the Welsh attacks.

"But my lord, the Welsh are on the run!" Wulfstan was shocked to find Harold so unresponsive. "Even now they seek a truce with you. You have won!"

"Yes...I have won." Harold had been staring into the fire, his attention far from his advisors and friends assembled in the tent.

Robert FitzWimark continued, "My lord, the Welsh deputation do wonder what your demands will be, as do your own men, I might add."

Gyrth Godwinsson grabbed his brother's wrist. "The word from the north is that our brother Tostig has found only weather in resistance to his advancement. No Welsh seem to be hampering his march at all, only this damnable weather does slow the Lord of Northumbria down. Your feint into Gwynedd and then our full thrust into southern Wales was a bold move, but one that has paid off. Dare I say it, Harold, but you should offer terms now, and let us all be gone from this wretched land and back home to our own hearthfires."

Harold looked from Gyrth to his other brother Leofwine, to FitzWimark and Wulfstan, at each of the senior thanes present. "You and the Welsh will have my demands by morn. Now, leave me, all of you."

As the frustrated men reluctantly shuffled out into the driving rain, Harold reached for his friend, "Robert, stay a moment."

"Yes, my lord." Robert FitzWimark stood quietly, watching the others exit the tent, waited patiently to let the Earl speak his mind.

"What do you suggest, my friend?"

"Harold, you are in a position to demand obedience from these for-eigners. The Welsh have always been a thorn in England's side, mayhap they always will be. But you have a chance to bring them to their knees before you. That is a great accomplishment, and one not to pass by."

"You know what I did come into this accursed land for. Can I demand that? If not for this weather, I would have been able to catch up with the Lady Godiva, could have outrun Gruffydd's forces, and none of this would have happened."

"Do not complain about the weather, Harold. If not for that, Gruffydd would not have gotten his own forces trapped crossing the mountains to ambush us. With the coming of this storm, the Welsh were faced with death upon the crest of that range or truce with the man who controls the narrow escape valley. The Welsh, who have always been masters of their own lands, now find the elements have worked in favor of the English! An amazing thing, and achieved by an amazing man: You, Harold Godwinsson."

Reading Harold's face, FitzWimark's triumphant expression turned to one of wonder. "Then you would rather Aelfgar's mother than Gruffydd of Wales?"

"Damn it, Rob! You know I did not want a war with Wales. If I had not had good reason to think that Gruffydd had captured the Lady Godiva, I would not have crossed into Wales in the first place. Peace is what I want, not to conquer Wales! Forced to fight the Welsh, I found I could not col-lect the Mercian party before they were lost into hiding in Gwent. My scouts have lost all trace of them, although not before they learned that the Lady and her retinue plan to seek refuge in Brittany."

Harold shook his head. "Refuge! The Lady had not been captured by Gruffydd. She has been running from me all along!"

"Then let the woman go. You and your brothers control England. You have brought the Welsh to their knees before English might. King Edward has bestowed upon you the title of Dux Anglorum, Leader of the English! What matter that Leofric's widow leaves the country?"

"Rob, that is exactly the problem! It must look to Godiva like I arranged to murder her son, planned to subjugate Wales, expected to gain King Edward's favor and set myself up in control of England at her family's expense! It is a matter of honor, my friend."

"You had no part in Leofric's death. As for his son, well, Aelfgar was hunting for trouble and he did find it. Let us call it just that, a hunting accident. I assure you, the histories will not blame the Earl of Wessex for either of those deaths."

"It is not the histories I do care about. The Lady Godiva will blame me."

Robert FitzWimark flung his hands into the air. "What matter what the lady does believe?"

"I do not know, Rob. Truly, I do not know. Except that honor demands that I set things aright. I must explain to Godiva that I did not seek out her son, but that Aelfgar did provoke me and his death was an accident. She must know that I tried to keep from fighting the boy."

"You have made his child son Edwin an earl. Does that not show everyone that you hold no ill will toward the house of Aelfgar and Leofric?"

"The Earldom of Mercia was the least everyone would expect of me as wergild for Aelfgar's death. Even so, the compensation is little enough if the Lady Godiva now believes that I had something to do with her husband's death, as well as believing that Aelfgar's death was a premeditated murder.

"Besides, Edwin Aelfgarsson is just a child. Godiva knows that I will need to retain some control in Mercia until the boy is grown into a man. Yes, I want her to see my good intentions, but she will only see her grandchild as a pawn of the Earl of Wessex, just as it is clear that my paranoid brother Tostig does. Damn it, Rob, you spoke to me yourself not too long ago about just such matters! I have to talk with the woman. If I can just show her my intentions are admirable, that I truly seek to make amends with her family, with her."

"Then, my friend, you must find her. But not now. Have your scouts keep watch for her party. They cannot cross the channel until the coming Spring, and your men cannot last much longer in this country. For now, finish with Gruffydd and be gone from Wales. When Spring comes, it will be time enough to find your Lady Godiva. She cannot stay in hiding forever."

"Yes, you are right. Nor did you have to tell me. In truth, I do know all that you say is true. I do know what I must do now. I must finish with Gruffydd."

"My lord. Harold!" The Earl of East Anglia, stepped back into the tent. "I think that the Welsh are not going to wait for your terms! The sentries have alerted the camp. A great body of men are coming down the valley."

"That would be just like Gruffydd to try and push a hole through our lines in this Godforsaken sleet." Harold stood up and crossed the tent to his brother.

"Gyrth, sound the trumpet. We must ready our men and assemble at the valley's mouth." Harold turned to his friend. "Rob, organize the housecarls. We will position the main body of the fyrd along the canyon walls, with the soldiers across the bottom as a stopper. If the housecarls can hold out, the Welsh army will pile up upon itself, and their movement will be constricted. Then we will loose the fyrd upon their flanks."

Gyrth caught his breath. "It will be a slaughter. Heaven help him, what is Gruffydd thinking?"

Harold looked grave. "He is a desperate man. We have seen evidence of that throughout this campaign. The Welsh people are not as one behind the man, and certainly not here in South Wales where he has no blood tie to the noble lines of the past Princes of Powys. From the Welshmen we have captured, it is clear that they assume if he had not supported Aelfgar in raiding Mercia, England would not now be invading their heartland. Gruffydd knows he must act ere his people revolt!"

Robert FitzWimark spoke low. "Indeed. Well, the Welshmen with our friend Gruffydd will like the cold of English iron no better than the sting of Welsh winds on that mountain top."

Out in the rain, Harold could see nothing beyond one hundred feet from his front row of waiting soldiers. "Gyrth, take charge of the fyrd on the right, Leofwine, take the left wall of the valley. Rob, we will signal the attack through the trumpet sound. Pass the word. The first sound of the trumpet will indicate we have sighted the enemy in the valley. The second sounding will mean the soldiers have engaged the Welsh. With the third trumpet sound, Gyrth, Leofwine, you will have the fyrd attack."

"Yes, Harold!"

"We will be ready."

The waiting was always the hardest part, made no easier by the unrelenting rain. Harold's heart beat faster, he could feel the push of the blood in the arteries of his temples, his neck. He was not afraid of battle, at least no more than any normal man might fear the possibility of his own death, the knowledge that he would soon have to kill or be killed. Harold had never found the battle madness to overtake him, had always his wits about him even amidst the most bloody melee. His lack of blood lust was in part responsible for his regret over the very occurrence of the upcoming battle. Harold realized that he and his English army may win, may defeat Gruffydd of Wales; but many good men, English and Welsh, will fall and for no good reason. Perhaps had his brother Tostig not wanted a piece of the action, not wanted to gain some glory at the expense of Wales, then maybe it would not have looked to the Welsh as if the English were invading. Damn Tostig's timing, Harold cursed under his breath.

No, Harold had to be honest with himself. This time the trouble was not only caused by the Earl of Northumbria. Wessex would never be blameless for this mess. He, Harold, could not help but blame himself for the present circumstances. Harold wiped the droplets of water from his mustache. If he could just have spoken with Godiva.

A captain of the housecarls leaned back to Harold. "My lord, they come."

Harold tapped the shoulder of his trumpeter with his left hand, hefted his sword with his right. The sound of the instrument rang out quieter than the Earl had hoped, its voice carried by the wind and rain to the east.

Robert FitzWimark stood next to Harold. "I hope your brothers Leofwine and Gyrth can hear that."

Harold was calm. "Do not worry, Rob, the word will get passed."

The other man was not completely reassured, still looked somewhat anxious. "Harold, I expected the Welsh to rush us, yet they hang back, are moving so slow."

"Gruffydd is up to something, I will wager. Let us wait a moment and see what manner of garment he does wear. Then we might deduce what the man can hold up his sleeve!"

The English on the hillsides to either side of the valley floor strained to listen for their signal. Only one trumpet sound so far. Gyrth and Leofwine held their positions, each one's thoughts mirroring those of the other. The trumpet sounded so quiet, so distant. What if they could not hear the next signal?

The Welsh heard the faint call of the trumpet as well. They knew there were hostile men on either side as well as facing them down the valley. Time was short. Their progress down the mountain was slow, in part not to provoke attack before they were ready, in part because the icy rain made their footing unsteady. When the enemy trumpet sounded, they knew they had only a short time. Rigging up a device usually used for hurling large stones, the Welshmen launched their message to the waiting English line.

Harold saw it first. "Watch it men, our Welsh adversaries have some kind of battle-device, and they are testing its range. Men, hold your places for a moment. Trumpeter, prepare to signal that we have engaged the enemy."

The Welsh held back as their message dropped within a yard of the line of English soldiers. Robert FitzWimark came up beside the Earl of Wessex. "Harold, what do you make of it? They make no other move."

Without answering, Harold stepped away from the English line and to the fallen projectile. His confusion was genuine, for this was no stone or flaming ball. It looked to be simply a leather sack.

Robert FitzWimark came up behind Harold, and the English line advanced to their leaders' position. The trumpeter awaited his lord's signal. FitzWimark reached down and picked up the sack, while Harold stood over it, watching for the Welsh to make a move. It was weighted down inside by something fairly light. If not for the wind at their backs, the Welsh would not have been able to fling the package so close to the English. FitzWimark's ice-numbed fingers fumbled with the drawstrap. As Robert loosened the sack, its contents fell to the ground at Harold's feet. FitzWimark bent down and grabbed the fallen thing, dropped it almost as quickly as he had picked it up. He stepped back a pace crying "Harold! What does this mean?"

At the sound of fear in his friend's voice, Harold brought his attention away from the waiting Welsh to the object again on the ground at his feet. A shudder went through the English line as the word was spread. Robert FitzWimark was shaken as well.

"Is it a warning, Harold? Are they hoping to scare us? Or is it one of our sentries, the brunt of some ancient druid ritual?"

Harold retrieved the head, grabbing it by the hair and holding it above his own head. "No to all of your questions, Rob. Trumpeter, stand down. Everyone, pass the word to the fyrd, to my brothers on the valley walls, tell them to withdraw. I do believe our Welsh adversaries have chosen their own terms for surrender."

The soldiers near to Harold showed their confusion, and the Earl of Wessex smiled. "This, Rob, my good friends, is the head of Gruffydd!"

Harold's smile turned slightly sardonic. "Is it not strange? While my brother Tostig, who was intent only upon glory, finds himself mired in the mud of northern Wales, it is I who find myself conqueror of the Welsh. Ironic how fate does decree things."

Entry IX

▼

When Tostig learns that his brother does make plans without his input

"My lord, it is well beyond Candlemas and I must begin the plowing of my fields."

The man was speaking, but the Earl of Northumbria was paying little attention. When Tostig did not respond, the villein continued. "My lord, I need a working plow. It is as I told you on Plow Monday following Epiphany. My plow is old, is in need of repair. It was damaged trying to break the frozen earth this Spring."

The earl waved his arm. "And do I look like a carpenter that you would come to me with this problem?"

Tostig sat in the only chair in his audience room, a small area adjoining the great hall. He would normally have liked to make the peasants feel small by holding court in the hall itself. The problem he found with that was that he too, seemed inconsequential.

"No, my lord. It is the blade itself that does need support. I—"

"Oh, then you thought I had the skill of a smith, did you?"

"My lord, it is just that the smithy of York has been ill since Christmas. I do not think the man will recover."

Tostig leaned back. "So I look like a healer, and that is why you burden me with such a long-winded story."

"No, my lord!" The villein coughed. He held his hat in his hand, was crushing it completely out of shape. He started to speak, coughed again, then continued. "My lord Earl, I come to you because I hoped you would help me to purchase a new plow."

Tostig sat up straight at that, feigning interest. "Ah, then it is a money-lender that I appear to be to you! Now I understand completely." The earl glanced at Aldbald standing behind the farmer, winked at the captain of his house-men standing by the doorway.

The villein knew the earl was joking at his expense, felt more nervous seeing the earl signal to the soldier by the door. "I am not expecting a handout, my lord! I will use the plow to till your fields as well as my own when I put in my time for you."

"Indeed you will!" Tostig snapped. An old man in a scarlet satin robe stepped out from the shadows behind the earl to lay a calming hand on Tostig's shoulder. Stigand, the Archbishop of Canterbury had played a more important role in English affairs during Tostig's father's life. While Godwin exerted his control, Stigand enjoyed the authority of the highest See in England while retaining the freedom to hold onto his previous position as Bishop of Winchester. This pluralism had kept the Pope from formally recognizing Stigand in his position in Canterbury, although that did not worry the cleric enough to keep him from accepting the tithes from both Sees.

The villein looked down. "It is just that I understand the King has on many occasions offered help such as this to his sokemen. Even Lord Harold of Wessex—"

Tostig threw off Stigand's hold, jumped out of his seat and was hovering over the farmer in one long stride. The villein saw the earl move toward him, stumbled as he backed into Aldbald, sidestepped then into the hands of the approaching housecarl.

"Captain, remove this man from my court." Tostig waved for them to go. "Give him a shovel from the stables so that he might have something to till my fields."

"Yes, Lord Tostig."

Aldbald moved around the soldier to glare at the earl, had to step out of the way as the captain ushered the poor farmer out of the room. Aldbald saw Bufread Bloodyaxe waiting outside the door with a grin on his face, and he shuddered.

Tostig turned back to his seat, paused before sitting back down. "Oh, and Captain—"

The soldier stopped at the door. "Yes, my lord?"

"Fine the man one piece of livestock. Let it be your choice. I cannot decide if I want roast pig, beef or mutton for dinner this evening. Surprise me!"

"Yes, my lord."

Tostig sighed as he settled back in the chair. When the soldier had gone, Aldbald leaned close to the earl. "My lord, was that necessary?" he whispered.

Tostig slapped his servant across the face. "Do not question my authority."

Archbishop Stigand spoke over the earl's shoulder. "Do not take your frustrations out on your servants, my friend."

Aldbald could not speak, was glad when the cleric chose to reprimand the Earl of Northumbria. But Tostig was not receptive.

"Indeed! Imagine, the man tries to compare my earldom to Wessex! Tries to compare my soke to that of Harold!"

Aldbald could see the earl's face turning red, watched the man fuss with his hair that fell in front of his eyes. The earl's servant understood somewhat

Tostig's feelings for his brother. Aldbald wondered fleetingly if he himself looked as ridiculous when enraged by jealousy.

Stigand patted the earl's shoulder again. "My friend, the peasant meant nothing by it."

"Oh, did he not?" Tostig shrugged at the archbishop's touch. "I tell you, I will not be compared to that…brother of mine in Wessex!"

The archbishop sighed, and Tostig jumped out of his chair and whirled around to face the cleric. "You, Stigand, who have so recently been at the court of Wessex. Do you compare me with my brother as well? Lord Harold, he that Edward has entitled subregulus as in the days before Alfred the Great so long ago!" Tostig menaced Stigand with a fist, then hit himself in the chest. "I could have been underking; I should have been!"

Stigand was calm. "Now, you know that it was the Welsh campaign that strengthened Lord Harold's position in King Edward's eyes."

"It was the Welsh campaign that Harold planned to use to discredit me!" Tostig spat. He began to pace around the small room. "I spent a month clearing out Northern Wales of all hostiles; but does anyone remember that? Oh no, the people only remember my brother bringing the head of the Welsh king home to England on a platter."

Stigand stood motionless. Aldbald turned as the Earl circled around them, and he jumped slightly as Tostig whirled on him.

"Do you know why he had Gruffydd's head?"

Aldbald knew more, he thought, than did his master. The young man knew Harold had thought the Lady Godiva had been captured by the Welsh King. The young man felt very confused to have learned that Godiva had been running from the Earl of Wessex all along. Aldbald knew all this, but had no time to answer even if he wanted to before Tostig continued.

"Because the Welsh gave Gruffydd to him! And do you know why the Welshmen turned on their king?" Again the Earl did not wait for a reply. "Because they had no more will to fight! And do you know why they had no will to fight?"

This time there was a pause long enough to have answered, but Aldbald still stayed quiet. Tostig began pacing around them again. "Because I over-ran their homeland. I hunted their king and chased him into southern Wales. I broke their will to resist." Tostig pointed his nose accusingly at the archbishop as he passed Stigand. "I did it! Not Harold." His accusing nose jutted at Aldbald. "Me!"

Tostig stared at his servant so intensely, Aldbald felt the need to say something. "Yes, my lord."

The Earl grunted and continued his pacing back to the archbishop. "And now you tell me that Harold plans a trip to Brittany this summer!"

"I believe so, my lord," Stigand said. "It is only a guess from what your informants have been able to deduce, but it seems Lord Harold is looking for something."

"Indeed he is! First it was Aelfgar and the house of Leofric, then it was Aldred at York and the Pope! Now no doubt Harold seeks to conspire against me with Count Conan of Brittany."

"Perhaps, my lord," Aldbald interjected, "or something else."

Although Aldbald had held some personal resentment toward the Earl of Wessex, the young man had felt quite ridiculous after the Welsh cam-paign of the Godwinsson brothers. From servants to the Earl of Wessex, Aldbald had learned that the Lady Godiva had not been captured by the Welsh as he had thought. In fact, so he was told, the Lady had actually been trying to elude Harold. Lady Godiva's apparent dislike, or at least disinterest, in Harold mollified the young man even though he knew that it was most likely the Lady that Harold hoped to encounter in Brittany. Aldbald knew also that the Earl of Wessex did not plan his every move to target Tostig. But Aldbald recognized that Tostig could not see that.

"No," Tostig exclaimed, "nothing else! Harold has been plotting against me all my life. Why should now be any different? No doubt he thinks he can sway the Bretons to his side simply by presenting himself as Leader of the English! No doubt he thinks that he can conspire without the Earl of

Northumbria! Well, I will just have to remind him that he cannot rule England without me!"

"My lord, King Edward does rule England!" By the sharp look in Tostig's glare, Aldbald knew he had spoken out of turn, but again the Archbishop of Canterbury backed him up.

"Yes, we must all not forget that Edward is king, not Harold."

Tostig surprised both the other men by calming at that. "Yes, that is true. And, even though Harold has swindled his new titles out of the King, it is still the Earl of Northumbria who is Edward's favorite. Harold will have to face up to that one day!"

Entry X

▼

Where Harold meets the Duke of Normandy

The meeting hall of the Duke's palace at Lillebonne was large; but the presence of the two men filled the room like angry lions in an arena. Harold, the Earl of Wessex, stood at one end of the room with his back to the wall. A sleek, dark greyhound stood watching the Englishman, growling under its breath whenever the man made a move. The candle standing in the sconce behind Harold cast a shadow across his face as he peered up through hooded eyes toward the man who had passed through the doorway on the other end of the hall. William of Normandy paused a moment at the entrance, staring across the expanse at the man of England. The ears on the dog bent back slightly to register the entry of someone new into the room, but the long snout did not stray from Harold's direction. The flickering of the light from the candelabra the Duke held brought a dancing illumination to his features, lighting his eyes with a brilliant fire that Harold was surprised to be able to see across the room. William hesitated only a moment, then began a slow journey around the room along the wall, circling around a large marble table, studying this man whom God had delivered into his control.

Harold watched William with equal interest, yet tinged with uncertainty. His simple trip to Brittany had turned into disaster almost the moment he had left his home in Bosham, cleared free of Chichester harbor and the Isle of Wight. The gentle easterly wind had taken a sudden change of direction, vigorously pushing his small boat southeast. The captain of the boat had tried in vain to scramble back to the English coast, only to find once they sighted land that it was off the starboard instead of the larboard. But the wind was merciless, driving the small craft against jutting rocks and leaving Harold and his few companions stranded on the coast of Ponthieu.

Now the Earl was in the hands of the foreign Duke. With no boat, no men by his side and no money, Harold was completely at the mercy of the Duke of Normandy. Not that he expected William the Bastard to be hostile; but then neither did he have reason to expect the Duke to be friendly. Harold's father, Godwin, had been unsympathetic of the Aethelred line in exile in Normandy, as well as a staunch opponent of the Norman influence at Edward's court. Harold himself, though, had been more tolerant of the foreigners at the English court, and he was sure the Duke would know this.

Although his brother Tostig had met William, Harold had never set eyes on the man until this very night. The Duke of Normandy displayed an impressive figure. He was slightly taller than Harold, and solid, with a strong chest and powerful build. Harold knew William was quite a few years his junior, but the strain of the Norman life in a constant state of war had aged the Duke so that he looked older than Harold's own forty-two years. William's clean-shaven face was not the surprise to the Englishman it would have been only ten years earlier. Many of the younger gentry of King Edward's court in London chose to shave their faces. Harold himself shaved his chin, but kept neatly trimmed mustaches, in the way the women seem to prefer. On William, the lack of a beard left his strong jaw line prominent, with a large chin stuck out in a constant show of defiance. The Duke stopped about five paces in front of Harold, setting the candles down on an end table by the wall. He brought one large hand up to cradle his chin, his left arm horizontal across his chest to support the raised appendage. William began to pace back and forth in front of Harold, never taking his wary eyes off the Englishman.

The silence hung with the darkness of the room, broken by the slight shuffling of the Duke's feet as he paced just as the black of the room was shattered by the meager candle light. Besides the candle on the wall behind Harold and the ones the Duke had brought in, the only other light came from two sconces on either side of the entrance to the hall. William stopped in front of Harold and took another step forward. Although it was only seconds since William entered the hall, the time seemed to stretch between the two men, the hall blurred around them as each focused their complete attention on the other. They studied each other, neither of them willing, nor finding it necessary, to speak first.

There was a shuffle at the hall entrance, both men starting as they snapped out of their fixed trance. "My, my! Why is it that men never think to light up the candles in a room? Perhaps that is why they make tapers so long, because it is known that the women of the court will be the ones to light the wall sconces!" It was Matilda, the daughter of the Count of Flanders and Duke William's wife. She walked around the room lighting candles from her taper as she went, until she reached the other side where the two men were glaring at her. Their silent scrutiny of each other had turned to stunned appraisal of the lady of the house.

Matilda was an attractive woman, Harold thought appreciatively. With her hair pinned up and under a wimple, her long neck and lean features made the Duchess appear tall, reminding Harold of his Edyth; yet, whereas the Englishwoman was indeed tall, Harold was surprised to find the Duchess of Normandy reached only to his chin. Matilda caught the admiring look from Harold and was flattered. "Are we going to leave our guest to stand all night in the dark?" The Duchess of Normandy threw a look of mock reproach at her husband, then turned her head in a sideways glance to wink at the Englishman.

That broke the spell between the two men completely. "Guest? Yes of course! Harold of Wessex! Well met!" The Duke of Normandy patted the head of his greyhound and stepped up to Harold, the dog retreating to sit by the wall. William grabbed the Englishman by the shoulders and squeezed lightly as he shook the man with vigor. The Duke's bass voice was a sharp contrast to his wife's more gentle tone.

Harold brought his arms up to grab the underside of each of the Duke's arms, squeezing just a little harder than he had planned. "Ah, Duke William! It is a pleasure to find myself in your company. I have always looked forward to our first meeting, though I did not expect that the timing would ever be so auspicious for me."

"An auspicious occasion indeed!" The fire in the Duke's eyes as he stepped back from Harold was even more brilliant with the extra light in the room, and Harold wondered again just what he had gotten himself into.

Harold turned to the woman standing next to them. "And this must be the fair Matilda, Duchess of Normandy. May I say, my lady, that I had no idea that such beauty ever came out of Flanders! Your cousin Judith who did marry my brother Tostig is fair; but I am sure she would seem invisible if found in a room with you." Harold reached over to grasp the hand Matilda offered him, resting his lips there only a moment.

"Please, sir, you might find that I believe what you say!" Matilda gazed down, then looked back to Harold through her long eyelashes.

William took control of the conversation. "Harold, Earl of Wessex, Dux Anglorum! What, may I ask, brings the Leader of the English to Norman soil?" The Duke crossed his arms over his chest, fixing Harold with an expression of casual disinterest which was belied by his immobile stance.

They spoke Norman-French. Not because the Duke knew no English. William did know a little, although not enough to hold a long conversation. But, there really was never any question. Duke William of Normandy chose to speak his language, and just assumed that the others would follow along. The Earl of Wessex could speak and understand quite a few languages. London had seen an increase in Flemish, Bretons, Scandinavians and French as well as Normans. Harold had achieved a working knowledge of each of the languages, a necessary condition in order for him to take care of the realm's business for King Edward. He was well traveled and quite used to dealing with men, and women, of different races. The language of the Normans he knew best of all second languages, since for the past twenty years the Normans had been welcomed at the court of King Edward. The king himself spoke less English and more Norman-French than any Englishman Harold knew.

Knowing their language well did not mean that Harold understood the people themselves. The Normans were a strange lot. Of Scandinavian blood just as many an Englishman, yet diametrically opposed in styles of life they chose. The raiding Danes in England had found in Northumbria and Mercia a place to settle and become tillers of the earth. The land was not so inhospitable as in Scandinavia, and England seemed to tame their wild Norse blood. Not so in Normandy. Descendants of Rollo and his band of discontents who fled Norway many years ago to carve out a duchy for themselves in Northern France, the Normans never settled down. Perhaps they had no time to, engaged in the never-ending border disputes and skirmishes with the non-Norman rivals around them. In place of quiet farming in a settled land, the Normans had accepted the chivalric code growing in Northern Europe; a code of horsemanship and war.

The Duke of Normandy was the embodiment of that warrior code. From before William was ten years old, he was fighting for his place in the land; and he had come out on top. What would it mean to the Earl of Wessex now that he found himself subject to this Norman's whim? Harold was not at all sure when he would see England again. William had held Harold's youngest brother Wulfnoth and his nephew Haakon for over a decade already, and they were still guests of the Duke. Why had William kept them so long away from England? What was it the man expected?

Harold had no idea how this interview would turn out. For the first time in his life, the Earl of Wessex felt as if he was in a little over his head. No one in England even knew he had left the country. The people of Bosham would have assumed he was off on an extended hunting trip. What could he say that the Duke of Normandy would believe?

When the Englishman seemed to hesitate, William continued "Perhaps the Subregulus has a message for me from my kinsman Edward in England? I daresay it has been too long since I have heard from him. Yet, having the Under-king deliver a message now could perhaps make amends."

Harold did not like the way the Duke was saying his titles with such exaggerated emphasis, but he had to suppress a chuckle at the last bit. William was only a distant relation to King Edward through his great Aunt Emma who was the mother of the King of England. "Nothing so dramatic. It was merely an unexpected northwesterly gale, I am afraid. I was setting out to hunt in the western woodlands when the wind changed direction; and, between the gale and the captain of my boat, it was the wind that proved to be the better."

"Ah, then you did not have a great retinue with you, I am sure! That is well. Since my good Count Guy of Ponthieu had only a handful of men in his…care, I feared you had lost quite a few courtiers at sea in the wreckage."

"You are right, I lost no one at sea. But I do wonder what is to become of my companions still in the dungeons of Ponthieu."

"Do not fear for their lives, nor their comfort. I am sure that they will be cared for without too much hardship. Guy did claim his right to the spoils of the shipwreck. Apparently, the only thing of value on your ship was you and your men! I was hard pressed to deliver you out of Ponthieu's clutches! But, again, do not fear. Your companions will be ransomed back to you when you return to England."

Harold's eyes widened at that. "And will I be leaving soon?"

William looked surprised. "Ah, but we have only just met!" The Duke's deep voice reverberated throughout the room as he walked over to a large oval table. "Sit down and talk with me! You say the King of England did not send you to me?"

Catching another glance from Matilda, Harold thought to himself that perhaps an extended stay in Normandy might not be all bad. Matilda smiled and motioned toward one of the ornately carved wooden chairs at the table next to William. The Earl crossed the room slowly and sat down in the offered chair, feeling a little uncomfortable now that his back was not to the wall and he did not have a good view of the doorway. "No, gracious Duke, I do not bear any message from King Edward; although I am sure he would send his best wishes for your continued health and good fortune."

"He would, would he?! That is good. Good." The Duke clapped his hands and a servant appeared at the doorway behind Harold. "Bring wine and make it quick!" The Duke rested one elbow on the table, bringing his forefinger up to rest against his lips. "You say you were heading to your western woodlands to do some hunting? I do enjoy a good hunt myself! Yet…How is it that you found yourself out so far from the coast of England that you could not get back? This seems passing strange?"

Surely the Duke did not care how he went about his hunting trips? William was searching for something else. "As a hunter yourself, Duke, you must understand the simple mistake of a man of the land having put himself in the care of a boatsman in the Channel! I do swear I will reserve my travel to horseback from now on!"

The Duke's laughter bellowed from deep within his chest. "Indeed. The Channel weather is as unpredictable as it is inhospitable! Sometimes I think that no one in their right mind would make such a crossing, unless they knew they had divine guidance!"

"Certainly no one would make the trip without a strong cause and a granite will, I agree with you." Harold's laugh joined with the Duke's as William slammed his hand down on the table.

"And here is the wine!" A servant came in, accompanied by another man who stayed in the shadows by the door. The servant set three cups on the table and filled each one with a red wine. Matilda reached for a glass and handed it to Harold, their eyes meeting for a moment before the Duchess turned to offer a glass to her husband. William set the glass in front of him, and spoke in a jovial tone. "So we are in agreement that the crossing is a hazardous affair." Harold took a long draught, and choked a bit as the Duke pressed his point "Yet here you are, on my side of the waters. Passing strange! Perhaps you have come in the hopes of collecting your kinsmen who share my hospitality?"

Matilda picked up the last glass of wine and walked over to stand behind her husband's chair. "Dear husband! If the man says the weather did turn against him, what more is there to say? Surely you do not think that Harold of Wessex can control the elements around him?!"

William laughed again, even louder this time. "Ah yes, the unpredictable weather! Of course." The laughter stopped so suddenly that Harold knew the man was in complete control of himself. "Tell me, Harold of Wessex, do you think it is easier for an Englishman or a Norman to gauge the direction of the wind?"

Harold took another draught of wine, glancing over his shoulder at the man in the shadows. The Duke wanted something from him, and he was all too certain what it might be. For twelve years William had made it common knowledge throughout the continent that he expected to inherit the throne of England from Edward. When Harold and his father Godwin had made their triumphant return from exile in 1052, there was a rumor that Edward had made some promise to the Duke. Since then, it was rumored that Edward had promised something to Svend of Denmark and Aedward the Exile as well. Harold and the other people at the English court knew Edward had a way of dropping casual remarks that he would either tend to forget or that never meant anything to him in the first place. How often had it been that Harold himself had had to ride the length and breadth of England in order to smooth the feathers ruffled by the offhand remarks of the King. Since Edward had not offered any substantiation to the rumors, they were left as just that and all but forgotten. In England, that is. It was clear to Harold now that Duke William had taken his encounter with Edward very seriously. What did William expect from him? To tell the Duke that the English eagerly awaited his foreign rule over their land? That might just be the furthest from the truth. But as for who did have the best chance of being the next king of England, that Harold could not say either.

Harold looked at William and answered sincerely, "Duke, in my judgment that particular science is nowhere near exact enough to guarantee any successful predictions for the people of England. If only we could see the pattern more clearly, perhaps we could plan further ahead than the next harvest," Harold looked over his shoulder again at the man inside the door, "or the next fighting season. I would wager a guess that things are no better for you here in Normandy. One can only step outside each morning to feel from which direction the wind does blow that day."

William smiled. "You may be right at that. At least so far as in trusting one's precious life into the hands of a measly boatswain; and even that does not help when the hand of the Almighty does see fit to shift the direction of the wind on you!"

Matilda could not keep quiet. "My dear husband! What has happened to Norman hospitality?" She got up from her chair, grabbing the wine decanter as she walked over to stand slightly in front of Harold. "Are we to make our guest the subject of an inquisition? Harold has been through a hazardous sea voyage that ended in disaster; been held against his will by your Count of Ponthieu; and now you have him pinned to the chair with your questions before we have even offered him any dinner! Man cannot live on wine alone!" Even so, the Duchess bent to refill Harold's glass. The Englishman caught a glimpse of the woman's ample cleavage through the low neck line of her evening dress. Again, Matilda saw Harold's admiring look, and she lingered a moment longer than necessary. She smiled as he followed her neck line up to look into her eyes. "After all, the man is our kinsman as well!"

Harold became overly sensitive of the man standing behind him in the shadows by the door. As if reading his mind, Matilda continued, "And what of your steward lurking at the door there? Please, William, have him come over and introduce him to our guest before Harold gets the notion that he is not to be trusted in your household."

William stood up, too quickly, his chair tumbling over behind him. "Ah, yes! Come in Osbern and meet our unexpected guest." The man at the door walked over to the table. Harold guessed he was a younger man than the Duke must be, perhaps in his early thirties, with dark features that made him look a bit menacing even out of the shadows. Were all Normans so imposing? Perhaps so, Harold guessed, bred as they were for war. "William FitzOsbern, my seneschal; this is Harold Godwinsson of England." The man bowed slightly, and Harold stood up and offered the same in return. "Osbern, I assume that you have news for me?"

FitzOsbern turned to Matilda. "Lady, please forgive this intrusion. I do regret when the affairs of state do press upon the Duke, taking his attention away from his household even when you have guests."

"There is no need to apologize or explain to the Duchess, Osbern. Matilda does know that rule of this realm comes at a high price paid out of our leisure." The Duchess looked at her husband, then down to her feet. Harold could not help but notice her displeasure, as well as note that the Duke seemed oblivious to his wife's concern.

William took his seneschal aside. "Tell me, what is the news?"

In a conspiratorial tone, FitzOsbern said, "Sir, the Count Conan has raided your western border again. Brittany continues to refuse to acknowledge Norman overlordship."

"No. Count Conan fails to recognize the Duke of Normandy as his superior! Conan of Brittany has been a burr in my hoof for far too long, has he not." It was a statement, not a question. William was looking at the west wall as if he could see the borderlands through the stone of his palace.

FitzOsbern stepped closer to the Duke so that his back was to Harold. "Conan will not recognize your sovereignty over the Breton lands. He makes himself lord of his realm and beholden to no one, when it is due to you he has nothing to fear from Anjou on his southern frontier. The man is an arrogant barbarian."

William stepped back and spoke loudly. "The man is a fool. Ponthieu, Flanders, Maine and Anjou have all submitted to me. Even the King of France dares not question Norman interests now. Perhaps Count Conan needs to be taught a lesson."

"The word from the west is that he has raided Avranches and Dombrent. It seems that Conan does believe Rouen to be far enough from Rennes that his actions will have no repercussion."

"He is wrong." Duke William spoke loud enough for his guest to hear, and Harold was indeed impressed by the strict determination in the man who set himself up as the strongest feudal lord in northern France. "I will send Conan an ultimatum. The man will submit to me, once and for all."

"I will ready a messenger." FitzOsbern stood straight and bowed to his overlord.

William clapped his steward on the back. "Do so, at once!"

As the seneschal turned to go, he nodded lightly to Harold and bowed deeply to Matilda. William walked over to where Harold still stood next to his chair. The Englishman had not moved since greeting FitzOsbern, but William knew Harold had strained to hear everything that had passed between the seneschal and himself. "Harold Godwinsson. What would you do with a troublesome lord of one of your English earldoms?"

The Englishman was not sure who it was that was causing problems, but he thought of his own struggles over the past years with Northumbria, Mercia and the Welsh. Harold was honest with the Duke. "It seems to me that what is needed is not just a threat of force. Do not wait for a response to your ultimatum! Ride right away, and in strength, to make the man come to your terms. Ride fast and be at this man's doorstep as soon as he receives your warning. He will have no recourse but to submit to your might."

"Ha! Good! You know, Harold? I think I am going to like you!" William grabbed the other man's shoulder and gave him another hearty shake. "We must talk more. Forgive me now while I catch up to my seneschal. I have plans to make. Matilda, please see to the comfort of our guest."

The Duchess looked at Harold, then back to her husband. "I will certainly see that Harold is taken care of." She reached over to refill the Englishman's glass one more time. As the Duke left, Harold noticed that William's glass of wine was left untouched.

William caught up with his steward in the room adjoining the great hall. "Osbern, I will have my chaplain William of Poitiers write up a warning to Conan. Get it from him when you have found a suitable messenger. Then, ready my guard, and send word to Beaumont, Gifford and Montgomery. We will forego our planned hunting trip, and will take our sport in Brittany! Let them know we leave within two days with as many men as they can muster."

"If you wish it, my lord, it is already done."

"Good. Who brought the news from Brittany? Do we have anyone who knows exactly where Conan is right now?"

The seneschal looked pleased. "Yes we do. A young lad from Avranches, Hugh, did bring us the news. He left a friend to watch the count's moves so that you would have someone to contact when you headed west."

"This Hugh d'Avranches was so certain I would head out in retaliation?"

"I think all who know you would expect it sooner or later. I must admit, the sooner the better! I am glad you will ride west without delay." FitzOsbern hesitated a moment, then changed the subject. "William, what does the Englishman want? Why was he traveling to Normandy?"

"The man does play word games, Osbern, and I have not ascertained all of his motives. One thing is for certain, he had not planned on winding up in the clutches of Ponthieu!"

"Nor did he expect to be here in front of you with no supporters, I would wager. What will you do with him?"

"I confess, I do like the man upon our first meeting. In these next few days he will see my strength mustering for the Brittany campaign. He will recognize that I mean to have those under me stay under me! Conan will swear his allegiance, and Harold will see what it means to be a vassal of the Duke of Normandy. The Englishman will play a game of not knowing who will be the next king of England. But I know, as he does, that he has held the power even in these years of Edward's reign; and his father Godwin before that. He will have much sway in the English Witan. Now Harold himself is called Dei Gratia Dux! Leader by the Grace of God, ha! Before I let him go home to England, Harold will swear an oath to support me in my claim. Just as Count Conan holds Brittany at my discretion, so too may Harold hold England only under my favor. Then he can call himself the Leader by the Grace of William of Normandy!"

*   *   *   *

Harold sat back down at the table, his eyes taking in the length of the Duchess as she moved to bring her seat closer to that of her guest. "I think there is no need for you to feel like I have not been treated well, my lady. I am sure I have gotten the better portion, with your husband off to attend to troubles of his realm leaving me to share the wonderful company of the Duchess herself!"

"Oh?! And is it my company that you appreciate, or merely that I did speak of getting you some food!"

"Ha! I am indeed quite hungry! But, I do think I could take sustenance from the sweetness of your perfume; be fulfilled at the sight of you."

"I daresay that any woman might offer you those things. Just as Man cannot live on wine alone, he cannot live on women alone either! A good sound meal is certainly a complement to the rest, though. Do you agree?" She winked at him again. Matilda called to the servant who had brought the wine and who was waiting by the door. "See if you can find something in the kitchens left over from our dinner that would be fit to offer our guest. I am sure there was some fried gammon left, and bread; but bring whatever you can find."

"I hope it is not too forward of me to mention that I would never have picked you out of a hall of women as the Duchess of Normandy."

Matilda pouted. "And does my appearance offer nothing to be noticed?"

"On the contrary, my lady. You are surpassing in beauty, and you look so young. I would never have guessed you to be the mother of more than four children! Life in Normandy does treat you well, apparently."

"Well enough, although I fear I have wasted away these past couple years. But I thank you for the compliment."

"Wasted away, my lady?"

"I do not know if William is any more ambitious than the next man; but he has become overly enraptured with his rule. I have felt a little left behind, as if I am not a part of his vision. Perhaps I have not had enough excitement to liven my own life."

"May I say, dear lady, that it looked to me as if you found his lordship the Duke's business distasteful. Ruling a troublesome people is no easy task! You must give the man credit for what he has accomplished."

"I know that William is a busy man, and most everything he does is for Norman, and my own, best interests. I guess I am just a bit jealous. He does seem to have lost interest in me over the past few years as he has become more and more caught up in the power he has over his subjects. He is strong, yet there is always someone ready to oppose his will. It never ends.

"Then, too, William has always felt the stain of scandal, the taint of Robert his father having been sold to the Devil by the man's own mother. The Duke seems ever to look for a sign from God to let him know that his father had truly atoned for his sins, that William himself is not to be damned. I fear sometimes I only add to his worries. The Pope was never happy with our marriage, for we are distantly related, the Duke and I. With William worrying over his own conscience and his taking care of the affairs of state, it seems it has been a long time since the Duke and I have had some serious time alone together."

"Who is this Conan that is causing trouble now?"

"He is the Count of Brittany. Actually, the man has been a bother for many years. I guess I always knew he would come to blows with William. I have not met the man, but he is said to be very obstinate. Somehow I do not think the stubborn bull will stand up to the Leopard, though."

Harold had not heard the latter part of what the Duchess had said. When she mentioned Brittany, his mind wandered. Godiva! Could he find the Lady Godiva after all this time? When he had set out from Chichester harbor near Bosham, he had known where he might look for her, and he had had his half-Breton friend Robert FitzWimark along as a guide. Now, Harold was alone, and he had lost precious time. Would Godiva still be there after so many days?

Harold was surprised to find another person had entered the room. "Agatha, our guest is Harold, the Earl of Wessex in England." Matilda smiled at her daughter, then up to Harold.

The little girl's eyes were enormous in her pleasure at the meeting. "Oh my! I always wanted to meet an Englishman." Agatha curtsied very low, looking well schooled and practiced. "It is a pleasure, your—"

The little girl's nose crinkled a little in thought. "Your Earlship," she giggled. "Oh my! The Earl of Wessex!" Agatha stepped closer to her mother and whispered "What is an earl? Is he important? Like father?"

Harold heard the questions, and could not help but find the little girl adorable. Matilda brought her forefinger to her daughter's mouth. "Shush, my dear! Now, tell me why you are up so late! Where is your room servant?"

"Oh mother! I am a big girl now…I heard there was a guest in the house, and I wanted to come and see."

Matilda looked reproachful, but there was humor in her eyes. "You are lucky your lord father is not here, girl. Still, I too heard we had a guest and wanted to come welcome him to Lillebonne."

Harold laughed, scooting his chair back away from the table. "I am flattered! Matilda, this young woman favors you more than the Duke, and to her benefit!"

Agatha bounced toward the guest at that. He had called her a young woman! "Harold? What is England like? Sometimes I hear my father begin to speak of England, but he always sends me out of the room. Where is Wessex? "

Harold bent down in the chair so that his eyes met those of Agatha directly. They were Matilda's eyes. "Agatha is it? Such a pretty name." The girl looked down at the floor for a moment, blushing ever so slightly. "England is my home, young lady, so anything I would tell you might be a little prejudiced. I come from Wessex, which is in the southern part of the country. It is not, perhaps, so different from your home here in Normandy, except for the great white cliffs overlooking the sea." The little girl was truly awed by the thought of England, which seemed to be so far away from her own home. "As for your other question, an Earl is much like a Duke such as your father."

Agatha stood up straight and proud. " I know a few words in English! My father says it would be good to know some words because he will rule England one day."

The Englishman was taken off guard. Matilda shot off her seat to draw her child next to her. Harold sat, looking at the little girl a moment before he recovered. The man smiled at the girl.

"Well, little Agatha! No matter what we on Earth do believe, time will unfold as it wants, and life will go on as it does."

With an apologetic glance at Harold, Matilda turned her daughter around and changed the subject. "All right, little one. You can talk more with our guest tomorrow. You never told me how it was that your chamber maid let you out so late!"

"Oh mother. I...I snuck away! But only to see the guest. Should I not welcome our distinguished guests just as you do?"

Matilda laughed, and patted her child on the head. "Agatha, it is good that you take an interest in such matters. You will make a wonderful bride one day. As for right now," and the Duchess looked over at the man of England, "I do not think that you should expect to welcome the guest exactly as I will!" Harold cocked his head, wondering if he misunderstood the woman's tone. "It is late, young lady, and you should go to bed."

Entry XI

▼

Where Harold speaks with the Lady Godiva

The thick mist clung about the man, obscuring his movements just as his body was hidden under the cloak of a monk, a large hooded cowl keeping his expression buried within its depths. He paused a moment outside the priory of the abbey, peered into the enveloping dampness in vain, suppressed a shudder. If this were a normal evening it would have been the heavy fog that had chilled the man, sent a shiver down his spine. But this had not been a normal day. Today Harold Godwinsson of England had had his first taste of the chivalric warfare of the continent, and the memory of it stuck with him.

The Duke of Normandy had gathered his forces and made haste to meet the troublesome Count Conan of Brittany. Harold had been a bit surprised when William had agreed without hesitation to let him join the expedition. William supplied Harold with a great war-horse, strong and agile, and nothing like the small ponies the Englishman owned at his home in Wessex. Mounted on the great beast, Harold felt stronger than ever, almost forgetting he was at the mercy of the Duke of Normandy. When the small army had traversed the length of the Duchy and reached their destination, Harold was the first off his steed, grabbing his broadsword in both hands, ready for the fight to come.

Duke William had said something in French that Harold did not quite hear, but when the Normans began to laugh, the Englishman knew he had been the brunt of a joke. The Normans danced their horses around Harold as they laughed, none of them made to dismount. The Duke proclaimed that their English guest was to learn how Normans fought; and that Harold did.

In this society where warfare was part of life, the Church had found the need to impose a Truce of God from Wednesday evening until Sunday each week, allowing the common folk to have some time in which they could plant or harvest their crops, tend to their business without the worry of marauding armies about. William of Normandy planned the expedition to reach Breton lands by Sunday evening. Timed just so, William's forces were refreshed and ready early the next morning, just as scouts arrived back at the Duke's camp with information on the Count's whereabouts, and the Church's Truce expired. They would have through Wednesday to campaign, but it hardly took a fraction of that time for the Norman forces to achieve their goal.

Conan of Brittany did not learn that William was in Breton lands with an army until early Monday morning. The Count had retired to Dinan after a few successful raids into Norman borderlands and had laughed at the letter of warning sent to him by William, which he received only Sunday evening. When the word came to Conan that the Duke was on his way to Dinan with an army, the Count had just enough time to organize his sober men and ride out to meet William. Whether he was actually trying to engage the Duke in battle or merely trying to make an escape from the indefensible town mattered not as the two armies clashed before the gates to Dinan.

For an Englishman, the ensuing battle proved to be quite a learning experience. As the Normans met the Bretons, swords were swung, bows drawn, axes hurled, and men died, all on horseback. Harold was amazed at how well trained was the horse he rode. The animal seemed to understand the complexities of the battle better than Harold did himself, charging with the other Norman cavalry, pausing to regroup, and charging again. Although always in the front of the charge alongside Duke William, Harold proved to be less than useful as he sat clinging to the galloping horse beneath him, finding barely enough time to make a single sweep with his great sword before one charge was over and they were turning for the next. The men of the continent carried much smaller, lighter swords which they could more easily wield while on horseback.

Although the men of Brittany fought bravely, there were far too few assembled to meet the unexpected attack, and Count Conan was forced to surrender his position by mid afternoon. The speed of the attacks, the power of the war-horses, the relentless onslaught of the Normans all did indeed impress Harold as William had expected. Harold found he liked not the vision he had this day of a line of Englishmen, standing to fight as they had done for hundreds of years, facing an army of these mounted men. With the day's campaign fresh on Harold's mind, every swirl of the fog was a horse galloping toward him, a cavalier riding him down.

Here he was, Harold of Wessex, in Brittany, one of the last places of refuge for the British peoples who were pushed out of Britannia by the migration of Harold's own Germanic ancestors over five hundred years earlier. As with all youngsters of his time, Harold had sat in wonderment, hearing about the legends of those that succeeded the Romano-British Emperor Maximus. For a generation, the Britons had held back the influx of Saxons along the southern shores of England. Harold's own lands in Wessex had been the heartland of the last Romano-British stronghold. And why had these men been able to hold the invading Saxons at bay? Because, Harold realized now, the Britons had been mounted on horses!

The cavalry of the Romano-British had rode quickly and fought well, winning many important battles against their Germanic adversaries.

Harold himself made sure that every one of his housecarls had at least one horse, so that he could ride to be wherever he needed to be in England as quickly as possible. But, why did his ancestors not learn from the Briton's example and success? Why did he, the Earl of Wessex, not know how to fight on horseback?

Thinking about it was enough to make Harold shudder. However, just as it was not the weather that pricked the hairs on his arms, neither was it the day's battle that had chilled Harold. He was thinking of the encounter yet to come this evening.

How fortunate he had been, and how surprised, to have found that Lady Godiva was herself in Dinan. Upon Duke William's victory, Harold joined the Normans in their triumphant march through town, with Conan forced to walk behind the Duke's horse, his hands bound to either end of a pole propped between his arms and his back. Count Conan would spend the night in a cellar, pondering his predicament and marveling at his lord the Duke of Normandy's kindly disposition before formally submitting to William the next morning.

Harold had rode beside and behind the Duke, where he could watch Conan of Brittany. The man looked to be older than both William and Harold himself, with an expression on his face of such hatred and resentment that Harold was sure the Duke had not seen the last of Breton campaigning. But for now, and for all his anger, Conan of Brittany was submissive. He was certainly not a fool, and knew well when his cause was lost and he had no chance. The look in his eyes spoke for him: There will be another day William, Bastard of Normandy! Harold wondered how the Duke would handle the man tomorrow if he still had that look of defiance in his eyes after the night.

Recognizing that the battle was over, the people of the town had come out to watch the spectacle. They cheered on William and his entourage, hoping to seem friendly enough that the Duke of Normandy would see himself as a deliverer, not a justiciar there to exact punishment from a town that had gladly harbored the rebellious Count and his men.

Harold scanned the crowd as he rode, shocked to find he recognized a face among the foreigners. It was Hildreth, the lady in waiting upon Godiva. The Englishman was so sure he could not be mistaken that he broke ranks from the procession and pushed his horse through the crowd toward the woman. The lady looked up and, scared, she backed away, dashing through the doors to the chapel adjoining the small abbey in town. It was the three Normans who followed Harold that had frightened her, he later realized. The other men ushered Harold back toward the victory parade with some half-hearted apologies for having to watch him for the Duke.

If not for the strong wine the Normans had found in Dinan, Harold would not have been able to get away from his captors come evening. He knew he could not be gone long before someone would undoubtedly find he was missing. The abbot who kept the night watch was kind, recognizing Harold as other than Norman. From him Harold learned that there was an Englishwoman of some rank taking refuge within the abbey, and that she was often found late in the evening within the chapel praying. It was to there that Harold found himself heading through the dense mist; and, it was the expected meeting with Lady Godiva that had made him shudder.

Harold felt his pulse beating strongly, quickly. Why was he so nervous? He did not understand it. He could see no more than a foot in front of his face, and he kept his right hand on the stone wall as he made his way around to the chapel entrance. Finding the large oaken double doors, he pushed his way inside to find the room illuminated by a great number of votive candles along the walls. The silhouette of a woman met him at once.

"Oh! The Lord has seen my distress, sent me a kindly monk to talk with. Please, sir, I do so need some solace. Will you spend a moment with me?"

In the dark entryway, Harold had been about to remove the hood of his cloak, for it had only been a disguise to help him past the Norman guards. Yet, with the woman's words, Harold was inclined to let his charade fulfill another purpose. Perhaps as a monk he might find out information that Harold Godwinsson could not. Harold was unwilling to admit even to himself that, as the moment of meeting approached, he had become quite apprehensive. With his identity discarded for the time being, maybe both he and the lady would be more free to talk.

"I am yours to command...my daughter. What is it that bothers you this eve?" Harold spoke in Norman-French, hoped that Godiva would not recognize his accent as being not of the continent. He worried needlessly, for Godiva was too intent upon her own problems.

"Good sir, do you speak English? I fear my knowledge of French is only rudimentary, enough to get by in this land. I would have no hope of expressing myself in that language with my mind so preoccupied." Even this much was said haltingly, deliberately, the woman struggling for the vocabulary. The man could not see Godiva's expression in the dimly lit hallway, but her voice sounded so desperate. Harold reached over to grab her hand. Surprised, Godiva sought out the man's face within the cowl. Harold pulled his hand back and turned slightly away.

"Yes, I do speak some English. Please, tell me what it is that is troubling you so."

The lady sighed with relief, sat down in the dark on the bench next to the door. Harold tried to picture her features, paint them in where the darkness left only shadows. On his first meeting with Godiva, she had been kindly and concerned, relaxed yet slightly frustrated. Her charm had been unmistakable and very refreshing to the Earl of Wessex. Still beautiful upon their second meeting, the Lady of Mercia's friendly disposition had been missing. After her husband was found dead, she had been very much upset and distracted. Yet, Harold had to admit she had been all the more intriguing to him at that time, looking so forlorn and confused, worried for herself and her children; yet still strong. If Leofric's death had not been easy for her to deal with, certainly her son's was even less so.

The woman who sat in the darkness beside him was not the same as the woman he had encountered before. Still beautiful, he was sure, but not frustrated or distracted or angry. Now she seemed simply tired.

"What is troubling me? Oh, that is perhaps the worst part of it. Sometimes I feel I do not even know what the trouble is any more."

"Are you running away from something?" Harold tried hard to sound calm and mildly disinterested; but he yearned to know what was in the woman's heart.

Lady Godiva hesitated, thinking in the gloom. "I suppose I was running from someone."

Harold caught his breath. Of course she was running from someone, himself. But what was she feeling now?

When Godiva failed to continue, Harold asked, "Perhaps, my lady, your confusion comes from the fact that your heart has forgiven this person, but your mind has not accepted that as yet."

Godiva sighed. "Yes, perhaps that is part of it. I think it is more than that, though. I have been looking for something as well; unsuccessfully. I have no experience in intrigue."

"Intrigue, my lady?" Harold stood beside the lady. As she turned her head, he could see in the candle light from the wall the sparkle of a tear running down her cheek.

"I am sorry. Here I ask you for your help, and I talk in circles. My mind is not clear, I fear."

Harold took a deep breath. "Perhaps if you told me the person you are running from, my lady. Someone in England, no doubt?"

"Harold of Wessex. I suppose you will have heard of him."

Harold smiled slightly, despite the mood. "Yes, my lady. I do know of the man. He is the son of Godwin and the Earl of Wessex, is that not so? Has the man expelled you from your homeland?"

"No, not exactly."

"What has the man done to you that you would need to run from him?"

"Truly, I do not quite know anymore." Godiva paused a moment, then continued. "He is indeed the Earl of Wessex. Perhaps it is just what he represents that I run from. You see, I was the wife of Leofric of Mercia. Harold and his brothers controlled all of England save Mercia. When my husband died, I fear my family's prospects died as well."

"Forgive me, my lady, but did not Harold champion the son of Leofric when the other earls of England, and even King Edward himself tried to keep young Aelfgar from his inheritance?"

A hint of the old anger colored the lady's response. "Indeed he did, only to take it away again by exiling Aelfgar to Wales. And then my poor Aelfgar was dead."

Harold could not keep from defending himself. "Ah, my lady. Did not your son provoke his peers at every turn?" He had spoken too quickly. Remembering his charade, Harold continued more slowly. "I have heard only good things about the Earl of Wessex, that he is fair and not foolhardy at all. You do not believe Harold acted against your best interests, do you?"

Godiva sighed again. How exhausted seemed to be this woman whom Harold had thought of as being so full of life. "You are right, of course. I have no proof that Harold had anything to do with any of my problems. Still—"

Harold interrupted, "Still you believe it could be true. You believe Harold to be a wicked and merciless madman."

"No, in truth I do not."

The woman spoke so sincerely, Harold breathed deeply for the first time since the conversation began. "No, of course he is not. Harold, I am told, even championed Aelfgar's young son Edwin as the next Earl of the Borderlands. This does not sound to me like a man intent upon the destruction of Leofric's line." When Godiva only sat in silence, Harold continued. "Do you hate the man so much my lady?"

"Hate is a strong word, especially spoken in the house of God." Harold hardly noticed that he held his breath once again. "I believe that I did hate him once; but no more. Yet, I do fear for my son's children. You spoke of Edwin. He is so young, and would easily be made into a Godwin puppet. And what of my other grandson Morcar? Yes, I do fear for Leofric's line. It is my family as well! Aelfgar had found support in Wales, and I had thought to find it there as well. When Harold stormed through Wales with his army, I came to Brittany to seek aid. Count Conan, however, has been a bit preoccupied with his Norman neighbors, as we all saw today. Now I do not know what to do."

Harold cringed as the woman spoke of his having stormed through Wales. It had not been the man's intention to bring Gruffydd down, he meant only to meet up with Lady Godiva herself. It was strange fortune that had brought the Welsh to deliver to him Gruffydd's head, only to keep him from catching up with the Lady Godiva and her retainers.

Whatever anyone else might have thought, Harold himself knew the truth of it all, and he felt the lady needed to be convinced of his good intentions as well. "My lady, perhaps if you were to meet with this Harold of Wessex, talk things over—"

"Oh no! I could not do that. Not while I have nothing to bargain with."

"My lady, perhaps you do the man an injustice. You may not need anything to bargain with. I am a—" the man caught himself. "I am told that Harold is a just and righteous man. Did he not even embark on a great pilgrimage recently? I am sure he is in good favor with our Lord. Can you not grant him what the Lord already has?"

"And what makes you so sure the Lord thinks so highly of Harold?"

Harold coughed. "I only assume, from what I know of the man. Still, he may yet have something in mind to help your grandsons. My lady, if you would just go back to England, talk with Harold, perhaps something satisfactory could be worked out."

"Something satisfactory? With Harold's brothers in control of all the earldoms of England save Mercia, what could Harold possibly offer Morcar? Anything he could offer would be at the expense of one of his siblings, and I do not see that ever happening. Also, if I were to return to England, then Harold Godwinsson could hold me as a captive, use me as a knife at the throat of Edwin in Mercia. No, with me safe on the continent, my grandchildren and their supporters will be more free to deal with the Godwins."

Harold winced. How long would he have to work to break the old family hatreds? The man risked putting his hand on Godiva's shoulder. He suppressed a sudden urge to grab the woman and hold her tight, force her fears for her family from her.

"My lady! You misunderstand. That would never be my intention." Harold swallowed and continued quickly, hoping his slipped words would pass the woman by. "That is not what I would expect at all. I only thought that the lack of communication between yourself and Harold of Wessex might be causing you both undue stress."

The monk was so emphatic that Godiva for the first time began to wonder at the man's allegiances. "Sir, just how is it that a man of our Lord in France has gained so much information about England? I am sure even the Duke of Normandy would not sound as interested in English affairs as do you!"

Harold slipped his hand back from the woman's shoulder to hide it within the wide sleeves of the robe. He stifled a cough as he caught his breath. "You are right, my lady. I am afraid that I do spend too much time following earthly concerns. Sometimes I fear I do not make a good monk."

Mollified by the man's self-accusation, it was Godiva's turn to offer sympathy. "It is true, we all spend too much time worrying about the cares of this world."

"Thank you, my lady, for not thinking too unkindly of me." Harold was glad the woman's suspicions were averted; but he felt the conversation was not yet concluded.

"I cannot say anything for certain, my lady, but will you consider the thoughts I have left with you? Will you consider opening communication? Even as prayer is so important between us and our Lord, so too is communication vital between our earthly peers. My dear…child, I am sure you have nothing to fear from Harold. It is my deepest feeling. Do stay in Brittany for now, if you believe you must, but not too long. Come…go back to England soon!"

Lady Godiva stood up and walked slowly to the doors to the chapel. Harold moved too quickly, reached to open the door for the woman. Godiva smiled, and searched once again among the shadows within the cowl the man wore.

"You are a strange monk."

Harold let go the door and bowed low. "I am sorry, my lady."

"No! I did not mean that as anything but a compliment. You are strange, yet refreshing. I know we solved nothing this evening; but I thank you for talking with me. Perhaps you are right when you speak of communication. I always sought more of that in my marriage. Why do I run from it now? I will watch for word from England. Perhaps one day soon I will do as you say. Thank you again for your time."

"I am yours to command." Harold spoke again the words with which he first addressed the lady that evening, and before he had finished, the Lady Godiva was through the door and gone into the mist.

*   *   *   *

Hugh of Avranches was relishing in the good favor in which he stood with the Duke of Normandy; one day the young son of an unimportant local noble of the town of Avranches, the next he was eating with the great Duke William himself and all the great lords of Normandy called him

friend. It might normally have been a time for a young man to drink to
excess in celebration; but that was not Hugh's way. He had one cup of
mulled wine to wash down his dinner, and that was sufficient. As long as
they were still in Dinan, young Hugh was uncomfortable. Conan of
Brittany was held captive, but there were many who might try and break
the man free. Although Hugh considered the man a barbarian, he knew
Conan had many who supported his anti-Norman philosophy. When the
lad dared express as much to the Duke, he spoke hesitantly and quietly,
lest he find he had overstepped his bounds, made himself look like he
thought he could tell Duke William what to do. Hugh was pleased when
the Duke agreed with his concern, shocked when William chose to send
him to check on the prisoner.

Hugh was still growing, but would never be a tall man. Nor was he
lean; but he found the other lords deferred to him as he walked through
the dining hall. He was in the favor of Duke William, and that made up
for what Nature had failed to give the boy.

As he crossed the bailey to the keep, the swirling fog suddenly became a
hooded man walking across his path. With only a foot of visibility, Hugh
could not help but bump into the lone monk. Strange the man of Christ
was out of the monastery so late, and heading toward the kitchens adjoining the great hall alongside the keep. Hugh started to ask of the man's
intentions, but no sooner had he opened his mouth to speak than the
monk had vanished into the mist. The young man continued on his own
business, and that of the Duke. It was too long since he had heard anything from Conan's guards, and the young man did not want anything to
go amiss for his lord Duke William.

Inside the keep and down underground, Hugh found the Count of
Brittany still secure within a small stone cell. The two guards were alert
and protective outside the door. The young man sighed in relief. Still,
something nagged at him.

Hugh had met the Englishman the day before, and the young man
knew that Harold thrived due to the sufferance of Duke William. Though

not a formal prisoner as was Count Conan, this Harold of England was no more a free man either. Stepping back into the cloud settling within the bailey, Hugh decided to check on his lord's other guest as well. Something seemed wrong someplace. He could feel it in the damp air.

The guards watching the Englishman were not so attentive as were those standing watch over the Count of Brittany. Hugh found the two of them fast asleep, an empty wine bottle at their feet. The young man walked quietly up to the door to the chamber where Harold should have been, was almost surprised to find the door ajar and the Englishman in plain view asleep on the bed beside the wall. Backing away, Hugh stumbled upon a pair of boots wet with mud, hastily discarded beside the door to the bedchamber. He caught himself lest he wake someone, then laughed at his own foolishness. These guards were supposed to be awake! Hugh grabbed a small bucket of water from beside the wash basin and poured it over the nearer of the two soldiers.

"Wake up, you fool!" The young man threw the bucket at the other guard. "Get up, I say. In the name of the Duke, get up. Lucky for you I am not Duke William, for otherwise I would know two heads that might roll tonight!"

The guards grumbled to themselves. They did not recognize Hugh, nor did they know for sure he was in the Duke's service. However, they did know that they should have been more vigilant. Hugh left them to their job and headed to the kitchens. Though the young man was sparing of drink, he did have a weakness for food. Besides, he still had an uncontrollable feeling something was wrong, and the best remedy for that was some food from the building's pantries.

The cooks were working through the night, kneading dough and baking bread for the next day's meals. No one knew how long the Duke would be staying over in Dinan, and the burden of feeding his retinue, his army, was one they found hard to bear. Hugh slipped in the back way and grabbed a loaf fresh from the ovens. The pan was hot, and he bounced it in his hands until he was back outside the door where he let the loaf pan drop into a garbage trough as he slid the warm bread under his mantle. Hugh reached for the pan, cooled now by the damp air. As he pulled the pan out of the garbage heap, the corner caught on a piece of fabric. Hugh pulled out the lot, and wondered at the discarded monk's habit he had found.

Entry XII

▼

In which Duke William becomes suspicious and Harold proclaims an oath at Bayeux

The castle at Bayeux looked in no way like the residence of a Bishop. Duke William's influence had gotten his half-brother named to the bishopric, but Odo was about as worldly and just as warlike as was the Duke of Normandy. Even so, Bishop Odo was a God-fearing Christian, and he endeavored to hold the title at Bayeux in as pious a manner as possible. Where his half-brother William was outspoken and forceful, Odo held himself quiet and reserved. Bishop Odo shared the same coloring as his brother Robert of Mortain and his half-brother William, a color inherited from their common sire. There the resemblance between the siblings ended. Even Robert and Odo had no similar facial features, Robert favoring the brothers' father, Odo favoring their mother. Whereas Duke William had the strong chin and high forehead of his own mother, Herleve, Odo's face was dominated by prominent cheekbones, his almost too-small nose still prominent on his face simply because of his habit of rubbing the orifice between his thumb and forefinger when he was thinking. The Bishop could not hide his thoughts as could his half-brother, the Duke, and the Earl of Wessex soon realized that something was amiss.

Harold had been ushered by Bishop Odo into an audience hall, not unlike Duke William's hall at Lillebonne, and the unrestrained look he caught in the Bishop's brown eyes set him on his guard. It had been just under a month since his disastrous channel crossing that had left him in the hands of the Duke of Normandy. He had been treated well, yet he was not free to go where he pleased. Nor did he know just how his companions left in Ponthieu had fared. Duke William had allowed him to send a message to England, instructing his reeve in Bosham to open up the family coffers and to pay the ransom for his friends. So far, there had been no word from England or out of Ponthieu regarding that deal having been completed. Harold had begun to wonder if the Duke was withholding information. Every evening after the Duke's business was taken care of, he would retire early, leaving Harold to be entertained by the Duchess and the ever-present sprite, Agatha. Harold enjoyed the time he spent with Matilda, even though he learned no useful information from the woman who herself was left out of her husband's affairs.

Harold knew that the Duke's true intentions regarding him would have to come out soon. With the military expedition into Brittany in the past, the friendly afternoon hawking trips could only go on for so long. Somehow, the Earl of Wessex had a suspicion that the pot would boil this very day. The Englishman did not have to wait long before Bishop Odo returned to the room. He was followed by William FitzOsbern, the Duke of Normandy's seneschal, then the Duke himself. Another man followed behind, closing the great wooden door to the hall as he entered. Harold recognized the fourth man as William of Poitiers, the Duke's personal chaplain. Harold and the chaplain had been formally introduced just before the Brittany campaign, although the Englishman had not seen the other man since then.

Harold had not moved since entering the room, still stood in the east entrance to the hall. The four others now in the room faced him from the west entrance, across an oval table in the center. Duke William stepped onto the dais and sat down, motioning for the rest to sit as well. There were three seats just off the dais, one for each of the Normans. Harold sat down on a massive oaken chest on the floor beside the table, relaxing a little as the chaplain pulled his chair closer to the table making a bridge between Harold and Duke William's company. The Englishman waited for the Duke to tell him what the meeting was all about. After a moment, Duke William began the conversation.

"Harold, it seems to me that in the past couple weeks we have come to know each other fairly well, you and I; and yet—" This after another pause, "I still feel we are far from enjoying an understanding between us."

Harold looked from one face to another. Bishop Odo's was the only one he could read, and something in the man's gaze told Harold he had better guard his words even more than normal.

"I would agree. Although, for my part, it seems my interests are quite plain. After all, I am an Englishman. Obviously, what I hope to gain is my freedom to return to England."

Duke William smiled. "And that you shall have, my friend. You have been an honored guest, and will certainly be allowed to leave, when the time comes." Harold frowned at that, but William continued, "Still, I think perhaps that is not all you do seek."

The Earl of Wessex suddenly felt sure he knew what it was that was bothering William. Although the Duke had never seemed to take notice of the time Harold spent with Matilda, the Englishman was certain that many in the Duke's household may have produced some concerns over the Duchess' choice of leisure time activities. Luckily for Harold, the Duke's young daughter had most often been with the Duchess and himself, so he had a ready answer.

"Well yes, William, I admit I have sought out your wife's company quite a bit of late, but the charming young Agatha filled the time more than anything else. I pray you would not take offense at my...interest in your family."

William laughed. "Ah yes! That is something else, too, that you and I need to discuss."

It was painfully obvious to Harold that he had misread the Duke, spoken out about his time with Matilda too quickly, for that was not at all what was on William's mind this day. Something was strangely amiss, but Harold could not quite put his finger on it.

The Duke's laugh was cut off, his stare was indecipherable. "I had wondered exactly what you and Matilda might have been scheming. She tells me that the two of you have discussed the various merits of making my Agatha a bride."

Harold swallowed a little too hard. Although he and Matilda had worked out that story to quench any questions regarding their time together, he had not realized that she had needed to use the lie as yet. "Well, yes, William. Yet, I do know that Agatha, though quite charming, is much too young for us to worry about such things right now."

"Indeed, much too young. But the idea is not out of the question, merits further consideration. A link such as that between Normandy and Wessex could only strengthen my...our friendship, is that not so?"

"That is true, William. But let us not decide the girl's fate tonight. Let her grow up first, enjoy her youth unbridled by responsibilities."

"Too true. Childhood is all too quickly over. Besides, we do have more pressing things to discuss, and I fear we stray from the subject at hand."

Harold scrutinized the Duke's face. What was it William was looking for? The Englishman sighed slightly, stretching his arms out in front of him. They had been over this so many times, why again?

"Good Duke. You know that I do wait for word from my companions left in Ponthieu. If that is what you refer to, you are right. I do seek more than my freedom alone."

Duke William smiled again, clapping his hands and calling to the door behind the dais. "Bring him in now."

Harold held his breath, then jumped up as he saw his friend enter the hall, a young man following behind. "Robert! Have you been in Ponthieu all this time? How are you?" Robert FitzWimark embraced his friend, and Harold could not have hidden his delight if he had tried. "My God, but it is good to see you."

"Harold, I am fine. As are the rest of your company that were held in Ponthieu. Count Guy is a hideous man; but, with your having met his price, he did let us go. The rest of your retainers must already be safely back in England by now."

"And why not you as well?" Harold asked the question, then looked back up to the Duke, redirecting the query to William. The Duke, Bishop Odo, FitzOsbern and the chaplain were all quiet, watching the interchange between the two men of England.

Duke William cast a mischievous look from his companions to the Englishmen. "Not to worry, my friends. Both you, Harold, and you, FitzWimark, will be free to return to England. Just as soon as we clear up a certain matter. Please, Harold, sit down."

Harold met his friend's inquisitive look, shrugged. Harold sat back down, motioning for Robert to sit beside him on the long chest. The Earl of Wessex looked across the room at the young man who had brought Robert into the hall. He recognized Hugh d'Avranches as the young man who had played an important role in the Breton campaign, offering Duke William intelligence reports from the west side of William's domain. Otherwise the young man had not yet even been knighted. What was he doing here? Harold met the Duke's gaze.

"To what matter would the Duke be referring?"

"A simple thing. Probably nothing. Tell me, Harold, besides a handful of retainers, why was it Robert FitzWimark alone who accompanied you on your failed…hunting trip? Of all your closest friends and companions, it seems passing strange that you chose someone who happens to be half-Breton."

Harold sat up straight, checked his motion at the last moment, wondering if the Duke noticed his reaction. How in the world could the Duke have gotten word of his intention to find the Lady Godiva? That, of course, had been the reason he had brought his half-Breton friend along with him on his intended trip to Brittany, the trip he had called a hunting trip to allay any suspicion. How could William know about that, and why would he care, even so?

He would not, Harold thought. The Duke was obviously unsure and merely suspicious. "Duke William, I assure you I am harboring no plots against Normandy. Robert is my good friend. That is all."

The Duke sat forward in his chair. "Ah yes, we are touching on an important subject. I do indeed want your complete assurance that you harbor no ill will toward Normandy."

"You have it."

"Nor any ill will toward Norman influence, in Brittany or elsewhere."

"None do I have."

"And, that you have taken part in no conspiracy that would be contrary to Norman best interests."

"Indeed I have not! What is it that you think I have done?" Harold was so genuinely confused by this line of questioning that Duke William relaxed again, sitting back in his chair. Still, the evidence stood before him and he needed to find out the truth.

"Harold, it has come to my attention that a woman named Aelgifu has taken refuge in Brittany. This, in itself, is unimportant. However, when I find that she was, until just a week ago, in Dinan, I do begin to wonder if perhaps you did not have this information as well."

When Harold only stared in honest confusion, William continued slightly frustrated. "Please, Harold, let us dispense with the game-playing." The Duke winked at young Hugh of Avranches. "I have reason to believe that you may have been sneaking around Dinan, masquerading as a monk. I am sure you can understand my need to clear up this matter. It certainly would not do to have the Earl of Wessex conspiring with one of the last relations to Aethelred's line, perhaps consolidating support for that Hungarian-born Edgar."

Harold laughed as his initial shock at having been somehow discovered in his Brittany charade was supplanted by the realization that his night's deeds were still completely unknown to the Duke. Just as well, Harold thought. It would have been hard to explain what he had been doing that night. Still, somehow the Duke had become suspicious of him. Harold noticed the exultant look in young Hugh's eyes diminish as he laughed. So that was it, he thought. This young man must have been the one he had bumped into in the fog, and who had come and awakened his sleeping guards. Hugh must have put the bits together, but would still have no proof, and no clear idea of what had been the true circumstances. Obviously, since the Duke was connecting Harold with some woman other than the Lady Godiva.

William's face grew irritated at Harold's jocularity. Harold quickly spoke to cover himself and soothe the Duke. "Forgive my laughter, William, but I had thought I might really be in trouble! And, it worried me because I knew not why."

William was not as yet convinced. "Whether or not you are in trouble has yet to be determined."

Harold coughed, forced his smile to subside. "I tell you, William, you have nothing to fear from me. Whether I paraded myself around in a monk's habit or not will be up to our Lord to judge," Harold let a small chuckle slip through to make light of the thought, "but, I can tell you truly that I met no woman named Aelgifu in Brittany, nor anywhere else on the continent. Though perhaps a name for a noblewoman, I daresay it is a common enough name that I am sure I have known one or two women bearing such a title in England!"

The Duke glanced at Hugh who looked down, scuffled his feet at the door. William looked over at his seneschal who merely shrugged, then brought his attention back to Harold.

"No matter. What is done is in the past. However, what is undone is still very important to me. Harold, will you swear to me that you will make no plots against Normandy?"

"I do swear. What would it avail me to do so?"

William went on, ignoring the other man's rhetorical question. "Do you swear to uphold Norman interests, especially as those interests relate to England?"

Now the conversation was getting as sticky and awkward as fingers covered in tree sap. Harold frowned. "William, I have told you that I did not conspire in Brittany against you and in favor of Edgar the Aetheling. However, I cannot give you a guarantee that I must then be firm supporter of your claim to the English throne. We have spoken of this before. The matter is in the hands of the Witan. I have told you this. Do not make me swear something that we both know I cannot mean!"

William saw his chaplain glance over at Bishop Odo, Odo nodded then to his half-brother. William continued, "No, Harold. I will not force you to swear anything you do not mean to heed. Will you swear to me, then, that you will champion my cause at the English court? It is a simple enough request, I think."

It was true, Harold realized. If he did not offer something to William, he could be a prisoner in Normandy for many years to come. Though assured of their well being, Harold had yet to see his own brother Wulfnoth and nephew Haakon, two hostages of William's being held somewhere in Normandy and having been held for over ten years now. Perhaps if he gave in some now, Harold might be able to have them all home in England by the first-harvest festival at Lammastide.

"Duke William of Normandy, knowing that King Edward still lives and may yet beget a son, and knowing too that the great-grandson of Aethelred lives and is getting to be of a proper age; recognizing as well that it is the Witan's choice, not my own or even that of King Edward, that will determine the next King of England; knowing these things and having said them between us, then I do hereby proclaim that I will endeavor to present all your intentions for the English throne before the Witan, and will make sure that your claim does receive full consideration. As far as if there are any other foreign claimants to the throne, I declare that I will champion your cause above the rest. All this, as the Earl of Wessex and a chief advisor to King Edward, I do swear now before you."

"And before God," the chaplain added.

Harold continued, "And before God. May He strike me down in mid stride should I stray from that which I have forswore this day."

Duke William spread his lips in his big, teeth-bearing grin. "Good!" he exploded. The Earl of Wessex thought the man looked like an exultant child having just entrapped a skittish butterfly in a net. "Harold of Wessex, if I had just spoken to you about this three weeks ago, we both could have slept better, I am sure."

"Indeed, mayhap you are right."

William's mischievous look returned. "Now, we both know that an oath to a man may last only as long as this audience will last. However, an oath to God will have consequences through to eternity." The Duke paused, watching the Englishmen glance at each other.

"I ask you, Harold, to stand a moment, and you too, FitzWimark. Now, open up the chest on which you have been reclining."

As Robert lifted the heavy lid to the chest, Harold reached to help him. The Englishmen looked inside, at each other, then up to the Duke in unison, both astonished at what they found stored within the crate. William was delighted with their response.

"Yes, as you can see, that chest happens to be the receptacle of the holiest of relics retained in Normandy. I ask that you remember your oath today, made to me, and made to God upon those sacred bones of our saints!"

* * * *

"May he rot in Hell himself! The deceitful, conniving...I cannot believe what the man has done! Surely, even an oath made upon holy relics is not an oath that need be fulfilled when made under such conditions. The man has cheated you and the Lord—"

Harold held up his hand to halt the stream of complaints bubbling out if his friend. "Peace, Robert. Be at peace."

"But my lord, Harold, do you not see what has happened? Do you not care that Duke William has tricked you?"

The two men had retired to Harold's rooms where there was plenty of space for the both of them. The Earl of Wessex paused by the east window overlooking the keep, where the moon had just risen over the outer wall about the inner bailey. Robert was pacing back and forth in front of his friend, creating a breeze that had already blown out one of the three candles illuminating the room in the dusk of the day. Harold turned around and sat down on the edge of the bed, reached out to grab the other man's wrist.

"Robert! Relax. William may be pleased with himself this evening, believing that he has trapped me with my pledge over the holy relics. Yet, may I remind you that, relics or no, I did make the pledge to God. Even had I not done that, I gave my word to William first, and that must mean something, or I am no man."

That caught Robert's attention and slowed his pace even more than the restraining hand of his friend. His surprise was evident. "Are you saying that you intended to keep your promise Harold? You have no problem with that?"

"That is exactly what I am saying." Harold sighed. "Look, my friend. What did I pledge to do, anyway? I swore to William I would present his claims before the Witan. I have no problem with that, would perhaps have done as much without all the useless theatrics."

"Theatrics? What you say carries great weight in the Witan. My God, Harold, you are the Witan. Yet, if you follow through with your pledge, you will sacrifice your credibility, your control over the rest of the assembly. Do you truly expect the English to accept a foreigner as their king?"

"Of course not!" Harold slammed his fist into his hand. "It is not I who will choose the next king of England, no matter my strength in the Witan. I think I made that clear to William, but I guess I should remind you. If all the Duke wants is a fair chance to let the English people choose him as their king if they wish it, then I will support that completely. After all, William is a friend to King Edward, and perhaps has more of a claim to the throne than does my friend Svend of Denmark."

"But no more than Edgar the Aetheling, or any other Englishman!"

"True. Again, the final decision will be made by the English people. If the Witan sees fit to proclaim William king, however unlikely that might be, remember: A king of England who resides in Normandy would be no king of England! Even should the all but impossible come to pass, that William carry the title of King of England, it will be I, and the other earls and nobles of England who will rule the country in practice. Just as it is now."

"But—"

"But nothing. Do not worry about that now. King Edward is still alive and healthy. I fear he will never beget a child upon my sister the Queen, yet I will endeavor to get from him his desire concerning the succession. The Witan will want to know what is on Edward's mind. He has not been a strong king; but he has been an English king. The common people respect and love the man."

"As they respect and love you, Harold. Edward himself may be weak, but you have made his reign strong."

"With the people's support. Which is why I have no qualms about presenting William's interests before the Witan. The English people will make the right choice for our country. I do admit being surprised that William did not try harder to achieve more. Perhaps, through me, he has finally begun to understand English people and English politics."

*   *   *   *

"I cannot believe you let that Englishman get off with such a useless oath! We had him right where we wanted him. If you had just pressed him a bit more."

Bishop Odo and William of Poitiers had retired from the hall, carrying between them the great chest containing Normandy's holy relics. William FitzOsbern had stayed behind to question his lord, the Duke of Normandy allowing his seneschal more freedom of speech than he would most other men. Even so, William was taken aback by the other man's reprimand.

"Useless? I do not think it was a useless pledge."

"Harold only swore to champion your cause at the English court. That does not sound like an assurance of your obtaining the throne at all. Is that not what you wanted?"

"Oh, but it is exactly what I wanted, Osbern. Remember, Harold is not just the Earl of Wessex, but the most powerful earl in all of England. He is sub-king to Edward. The people have proclaimed him Leader of the English. If Harold champions my cause, then that is the same as having my desires fulfilled."

"I am not so sure. Harold again spoke of their Witan—"

"Harold is earl of the most influential portion of England." The Duke held his fist clenched in front of the other man. "His younger brothers control most of the rest of the country. Do not be fooled by his playacting. Harold controls this Witan of which he spoke. You can count on that." William slammed his hand on the table. "The man merely has to keep up the pretense of this administrative assembly of advisors to the King. After all, he himself is only a commoner. With no royal blood he cannot hope to be king himself. The Witan, an outdated formality, is Harold's instrument for controlling England."

FitzOsbern shrugged, got up to stretch. "I admit, the whole concept of this group of advisors to the king makes little sense to me."

William laughed as he stood up to face his seneschal. "You saw how impressed Harold was with my display of force in Brittany. More than impressed, he was amazed. I think I made it clear to him what an oath to me does mean."

The Duke's seneschal was not completely content. "Yes, but an oath from a count in Brittany is much different than an oath from an earl in England. The distance from Rouen to Chichester in England may be even shorter than from Rouen to Rennes, but do not forget the body of water that separates Normandy from Harold's land. It is not such an easy thing to expect the Englishman to honor his pledge when he knows that he has such natural protection that someone like Count Conan does not enjoy."

"That is why the relics, Osbern. Surely Harold would never conceive of disavowing me and God!"

"But is this Harold a God-fearing man?" The Duke's seneschal pressed.

"He had better be," the Duke said seriously. "What manner of man would he be if he was not afraid of God?"

Duke William took a step away from his seneschal. When he turned back to face the other man, there was such a fire in his eyes that Osbern glanced to see what candle must be causing the reflection.

"Long have I sought a sign from God, that I would know I was in His favor. Becoming the King of England will be the fulfillment of my life's endeavors. To be the anointed representative of God on Earth. It would satisfy an emptiness that lurks in my soul."

Disturbed at not finding the source of the light in the Duke's eyes, FitzOsbern laughed it off with a jest. "It would be far easier to be a man of the cloth like your brother Odo if you want to serve God, William."

"Osbern, my friend," the Duke snickered, "I said I wanted to represent God, not be a servant to him."

Entry XIII

▼

After which Tostig is found to be in Exile

"I am sorry my lady, I had thought the hall was empty." Caedwig bowed his head without meeting the eyes of Queen Edith. "I sought only to await the King, I will retire to my quarters until he does arrive."

As the monk turned to go, the Queen put herself between the man and the door. "My dear Caedwig. Please stay. I, too, await the King."

King Edward was holding his court in the west of England once again, spending most of his time hunting in the forests. Once a week the Queen insisted that Edward sit upon the dais in his conference hall and confer with his earls, his advisors. In this the Queen and Caedwig, Edward's confessor, were in complete agreement. Edith placed her hand lightly on Caedwig's shoulder, his forearms being lost in the folds of his clothing. "Please wait with me."

"As you wish, my lady." Caedwig, head still hanging low, stepped back a pace. Edith sighed, sat down on the window seat. "Please, Caedwig, do come and sit a moment beside me upon the settle. I know that you have many duties, but I would like to engage your services for a very important project."

The monk hesitated a moment, then joined the woman below the window. The room was lit only by the afternoon sun streaming through the aperture, sufficient light on that early Autumn day for the two to see each other quite clearly. Queen Edith wore a rich gown of red and gold, clinging tightly at the bodice, but hanging loose below her hips to just barely brush along the floor when she walked. Caedwig was dressed in his simple brown frock, only today he was without sandals, his feet bare upon the floor.

"Caedwig, why do you keep your eyes averted from me?"

The man cleared his throat, gripped his hands together within the wide sleeves of his garment. "My lady, you wear no veil, no wimple covers your hair. It would be unseemly were I to gaze upon your person in that dress, here with no one else in the room."

Edith smiled sadly. "My dear Caedwig, I find it interesting that you would speak so nobly about the correctness of not looking at me, yet at the same time I know that you have seen me all too well."

"My lady?" Caedwig fidgeted slightly, squinting up at the Queen.

"Ah, and do not feign too much difficulty in seeing. I am confident that, with a glance, you did determine not just that someone else was in this room, but that it was your Queen. Indeed, you also seemed to have recognized I wore no wimple nor veil. Dare I say that I believe you could not only tell me the hue of my dress, but the type of stones in my jeweled necklace as well?"

Caedwig jerked his head, almost looking at the woman. "My lady, you wear no necklace—" The monk's confusion turned to embarrassment.

Edith laughed gently. "I knew you did know."

"You are playing with me, my lady. Did you not have something important to ask of me?" Caedwig stood up, made to go. "If not, I do beseech you to give me your leave to go."

The Queen's smile faded as she watched the young monk before her. "Yes," she said, slapping her hands together and rubbing a sudden nagging itch on her palm. "Down to business. Caedwig—"

"Yes, my lady?"

"Caedwig, I want to commission a work from you."

"Commission, my lady? I am pledged to the Lord, and to the service of our King your husband. I would require no commission for any work I could perform for the Queen. You have but to ask me and if it is within my power to accomplish, consider it done already."

"Yes, we are both pledged to Edward, each in our own way, are we not? Then I think you will have no difficulty performing this service. And, though you are a servant of the Lord as well, you are a man first, and a man has needs. I will pay you for your services since that is all I may do for you in this lifetime."

"My lady, I want nothing—"

"So it appears!" The Queen stood up, her countenance becoming cold. "Give the money to charity and starve, then! I do not care." Edith checked her rage. "I want you to write a biography of my husband the King."

Caedwig was about to protest the idea of payment again, but the Queen's request caught him off guard. "A biography, my lady?"

"Yes, The Life of Edward, King of England. I know not how much time my husband does have left on this earth. I think it would gratify him to see in writing a declaration of all the wonderful things that have been accomplished in his reign as King of England. The country has been at peace under Edward now for almost a quarter of a century. Quite an achievement after the last, disordered years of Danish dominance."

The monk nodded. "It is true, a biography of King Edward would be a testament to English rule in England. But, my lady, much of the praise should go to the house of Godwin as well. Lord Harold is recently back from the continent, and he has even brought your nephew Haakon out of exile in Normandy! Surely you do not intend for me to leave out Lord Harold's accomplishments and great influence in England?"

"Indeed not. Very perceptive of you, Caedwig. Dare I say you have always known what was on my mind...and in my heart." Edith softened even as she said her own words, was happy to see Caedwig's wide eyes finally meeting her own dark pools for a moment.

"Yes, my lady, so I have."

Edith stepped toward the monk, but Caedwig instinctively backed up a step. The Queen rubbed her hands together and looked out the window. The Autumn weather had yet to arrive that year, and the day was surprisingly warm for the late August afternoon. Gazing out the window at the trees still green with life, the Queen said, "Yes, do not overlook the deeds of my good brothers, the great earls of England. I do want the records to show that King Edward was well pleased with, and well served by, the house of Godwin."

"Yes, my lady. I will begin the work at once." Caedwig bowed low, then turned to leave.

"Caedwig?"

The monk stopped without turning around to face Edith. "Yes, my lady? I am sorry, was there something else?"

Before the man realized it, Edith was standing by his side with one hand reached out before him. "Caedwig, take my hand for a moment."

Caedwig sidestepped away from the woman, but Edith followed. "My lady?" The monk was noticeably shaking as he restrained himself from retreating further.

Edith spoke very low. "Have I become so repulsive to you, Caedwig?" Her strength gave way then, a sob broke through her outer shell. Had she known that was all it would take, perhaps she might have shown a tear earlier. Caedwig at once dropped to his knee, snatching the Queen's hand that had gone limp between them, he held it to his abundant forehead.

"Oh, my lady...Edith! Never could you ever be anything but attractive to me."

"You do not show your feelings very well, my friend."

"Edith! You know I hide my feelings to the best of my ability. Nay, not just hide, I do forcibly repress them. Do not forget I am sworn to God, and you are sworn to King Edward. Why do you put me through this…this struggle?"

Edith pulled her hand away. "Why do I put you through this? Oh, Caedwig, you did not always feel like this."

The man was still on his knee, his gaze, now unrestrained, was directed straight into Edith's soul. "No, you are right. I did not always feel this way. There was a time when I could think of nothing but you and your happiness."

Edith's eyes clouded with tears. "And what has happened to change the way you feel?"

Caedwig's big eyes seemed to expand, bulging out from either side of his nose. He stared at the Queen while the silence between them was filled with the chirping of pigeons nesting in the eaves outside the window. The monk stood and gathered the unsuspecting woman into his arms.

"God help me, nothing has changed the way I do feel about you."

Edith let herself cry then, clinging tight to the monk so that Caedwig's embrace might never end. "Then why? Why do you ignore me? Why do you avoid me?"

Caedwig peeled the woman away from him, looked her straight in the eyes, gave Edith a slight shake.

"Because, we have no future together, my lady! Foolish is the man who butts his head against the rock of the mountainside, for it will not yield unto him. But it is even more than that. I pledged myself to God.

"When I left the monastery at St. Omer in Flanders to come to England in Edward's service, I was young, had not seen much of the world outside St. Omer before I saw you in Dover that fateful day. I still remember that day, the sky had not a cloud in it and the crowd in the street was overwhelming; but there you were, standing out like a great marble statue, beautiful and distant. I spent a handful of years admiring you from afar, chastising myself for my thoughts. But, as I grew older, I did move beyond my passion for you. How could I have known that I would later be required to escort the Queen of England to seclusion in a nunnery! You were so stricken with grief, so fearful and alone after your father and brothers were sent into exile. And I, well, I found I was still too young, and my feelings for you had not vanished, had only been buried. Even now I can only hope that the Lord will forgive my young indiscretion. I do go about the world unshod, I wear a hair shirt beneath my frock to chafe my every move. That is my penance. That, and to avoid the cause of my suffering."

Edith's dark eyes developed a look of such pain, the monk hugged her again. "No! I did not mean to blame you, make you out to be the cause of my personal suffering. Nor am I strictly avoiding you, my lady. It is my own weakness for you that I do fight to control; my loss of control in your presence I do seek to avoid."

"Oh Caedwig, it has been so many years since we both lost control that one time. We have hardly been together alone in all this time. I do not demand more of you than I can give myself. We are both pledged to others, as you continue to remind me. Yet, can we not be the friends we once were? Edward ignores me already, I cannot suffer that from you as well. Not anymore. You…you once did profess love for me."

Caedwig released the woman, threw his arms above his head. "Edith! My lady, I do love you still. That is what I have been saying. That is the cross I must bear the rest of my life."

"Then do not leave me with nothing. I need to know that there is someone who cares for me. I am only human, I need companionship, even should it be only the love professed by Plato."

"Alas, my lady, for I am only human as well. That is the great gift our Lord has given us, yet is our one true curse as well."

Caedwig reached out and grabbed Edith once again, held her until her sobs subsided. Voices outside the hall brought the two back to reality. "My lady, the King!" The monk released the Queen, moved away from Edith. She smoothed the wrinkles in her gown. The two had more time to compose themselves than they had feared, for the voices they heard were so loud they had carried clear across from the other end of the palace bailey. It was not long, however, before Archbishop Aldred pushed through the doors from the hallway outside, followed closely by King Edward. Tostig Godwinsson hulked over the King's shoulder, and it was his voice the monk and the Queen had heard ringing out.

"I told you, Edward, do not listen to this...this Archbishop. York is mine! I know its people, I know its needs. The people of Northumberland love me."

"Bah!" Aldred exclaimed, waving his arms in front of Tostig as the three walked across the hall to the dais. "Is that why the people north of the Humber are in revolt against you?" The Archbishop of York turned his back to Tostig. "I tell you, King Edward, a popular uprising such as this has no precedent. Even now the people are marching on Oxford to show their unhappiness with lord Tostig's undirected and totally mismanaged rule of the northern lands. Tostig's misrule has—"

"Misrule? If my people are in rebellion, it is because of men such as you who would incite the innocents against their leader. You draw them out of their byres and hovels, misdirect their simple reasoning against that which is in their favor, and away from the true source of their woes: the Church!"

"You be careful what accusations you make, Tostig Godwinsson." Aldred's face was red. "How can you blame any of this on anything but your misguided idea of justice? You have taxed the people unjustly, twisted the law to your own ends and, worst of all evils, you have even despoiled some of God's holy churches!"

Tostig jutted his nose into the clergyman's face. "Many of my retainers have been killed, my treasury has been plundered, my armory ransacked! Yet you have the gall to declare me outside the law?!"

"It is not I alone, but the people of the north, Tostig."

"The people are simpletons, and I will wager that you, Aldred, are behind this!"

"Enough! Stop this bickering!"

The King had sat down on the stone seat. He looked across the room between the two who were arguing, his face cringing with their raised voices, knuckles white upon the copy of Aelfric's sermons that he had hoped to reread that day. It was the Queen who spoke to quiet the two men as Edith and Caedwig made their presence in the room known.

Tostig and Aldred were surprised by her exclamation, each turned to watch the Queen walk over to stand behind her husband.

"Can you not see you are upsetting the King?"

Archbishop Aldred was the first to recover his wits. "My lady, you are right, of course. Forgive me." He swung his arms wide and bowed his head.

Tostig brushed the archbishop aside. "Yes, sister. Of course Edward is upset. Surely he will not abide the lowly people attempting to take their misguided form of justice into their own hands, against an earl appointed by the King." Tostig sliced through the air before the King. "Edward, you must stand behind your earl. Your friend!"

Edward shook himself. "And who said that I would not?"

"My lord—" Aldred began, but Tostig cut him off.

"No, Aldred. Let the King speak for once!" Tostig was pugnacious. "Edward will not let the people take the law into their own hands! How could he, and still consider himself to be king of this country?"

"Indeed I will not," Edward proclaimed. "If Earl Tostig has been wronged, then the people of Northumbria shall pay the penalty. But I shall be the judge, not them."

Aldred began again, "But my lord, the matter is out of control at the moment. You must find a way to appease the people of the north, then you can render a judgment on this earl of yours."

Tostig pushed the Archbishop out of the way. "No, Edward. You must stop them. You are the King, are you not?"

"Yes! I am King."

"You have control over your subjects, do you not?"

"Yes, I have control!"

"Then call out your housecarls! Have them join my men from York who already are organized here for the march. Send the army to meet this band of outlaws from the north. Crush this rebellion before it spreads. It is the only way to keep your control. Show the peasants force!"

"No! My King, listen—" but the Archbishop's plea was stopped short.

"Yes, yes of course!" Edward stood up, called to his guard at the door. "You there, soldier! Alert the captain of the guard, have him assemble the housecarls and what fyrdmen from the western forests he can muster. Immediately!" King Edward added the last as the young soldier seemed to hesitate.

"Sire, yes, of course! It will be done. But, whom shall I say we do ride against? Surely you will not have us fight other Englishmen."

When Edward did not answer immediately, Tostig sprang forward. "You dare to question the reasoning of your King? Or is it Edward's authority you do disregard?"

"No! No, my lord! I did not mean—"

Tostig snapped at the young man. "Then see that you carry out his wishes at once. You will fight who and when the King does demand of you!" Tostig turned back to face the others, grinned at the Archbishop as the young soldier left the room.

Queen Edith walked over and put her hand on her brother's sleeve. "Tostig, why do you not want to settle this peaceably? Surely there must be a better way than to meet the delegation from York at sword point?"

"Delegation? Why sister, you make it sound like an organized group of burghers bringing a minor grievance to the Shire moot!"

Archbishop Aldred rushed in to make use of the Queen's sympathy, stepped toward Edith, turned back to the King. "Queen Edith, my lord Edward, that is all it is—"

"No." Tostig drew his sword and brandished it far too close to Aldred for the Archbishop to be comfortable. Aldred stretched his arms wide and held his breath, Caedwig was shocked speechless, King Edward seemed to be watching as if the action were a scene in a play, and it was left for Edith to cry out.

"Tostig, do not be a fool!"

The lady's voice brought the monk to life. Without saying a word, Caedwig moved quickly to place himself between the Archbishop and the Earl of Northumbria. Tostig swung his weapon away from the monk, slammed it point first into the floor in front of the King.

"I will tell you again. Edward, sister Edith, this is not a simple delegation to the King's court. This is an angry mob carrying weapons, incited to violence by this man here who stole the bishopric at York." Tostig leaned close to King Edward's ear, but purposely spoke loud enough for all to hear. "I think, Edward, that this man hopes to steal the earldom of Northumbria as well, mayhap place himself up as the next king of England!"

"That is absurd!" Archbishop Aldred pushed Caedwig aside and stomped up to meet Tostig, grabbed the younger man's arm and swung the Earl of Northumbria around to face him. "I told you to beware what accusations you make, Tostig. I enjoy the favor of the Pope, the love of the Almighty above! You, however, may very well be doomed to eternal damnation.

"It is not I, but you, Tostig Godwinsson, who dares desire to wear the crown of England. If I did not know that the last wine young Aedward the Exile had tasted had been sent from Lord Leofric, I would certainly have expected to find it was from you, and poisoned too! Certainly, that would have fit your personality, always taking the coward's way to your evil ends."

All Tostig had heard was the Archbishop calling him a coward. The Earl's eyes burned with hatred. Tostig reached with both hands to grapple the Archbishop, but his assault ended with him merely grabbing Aldred's cloak as he lost his balance on the edge of the dais. Aldred stepped back, and they were all silenced by a resounding bellow from the doorway.

"What?"

The single word echoed throughout the hall, reflecting off the smooth whitewashed walls and reverberating in the air space of the vaulted ceiling. The Earl of Wessex strode across the room to the two struggling men without acknowledging King Edward or his sister the Queen. Reaching the two men, Harold grabbed his brother's clenched hands and tore them from the Archbishop's garment. Holding Tostig fast, Harold looked into the Archbishop's eyes.

"What did you say about the wine Aedward the Exile had drunk that night in Bromely?"

The Archbishop of York was surprised and confused. It had been so long ago, seemed not to matter in the end. "Why, lord Harold, I said simply that if the wine had not come from Leofric himself, I might have guessed there had been foul play afoot, and your brother would have been my prime suspect. As it is, I cannot blame him. The wine was delivered from Leofric by his own wife's maidservant."

Tostig tried to grab for Aldred again. "Then why even bring it up?" His reach fell far too short, as his brother pushed his hands aside, so forcibly, that the Earl of Northumbria lost balance again, fell to one knee. Harold never even looked at his brother. Tostig did not seem to make any connection between his own deed in Bromely and Aedward's untimely death, but Harold did not forget. He stepped over the fallen man and up to the King.

"My lord, King Edward. I have recalled the royal soldiers. It seems the captain of the housecarls had the mistaken idea that you meant to fight your people marching down from the north of England. I explained that the last thing the King did wish for was a civil war."

Tostig chirped a rejoinder, but Edward smiled at Harold. "Good to see you, Harold. We missed you today hunting. What is this about a civil war? Of course I want no civil war. My realm is at peace, will stay that way if I have anything to say about it."

Harold nodded. "As I suspected, and as I did explain to your soldiers and to the Northumbrian people. I have already sent their leaders a message saying that I will mediate between them and Lord Tostig, if they will fall back to Northampton. They have agreed, have sent back a sworn oath that they will respect your final judgment and follow your command, Edward. All they ask is to be heard."

Tostig's face burned bright red, his temples beat with the blood rushing more quickly to his brain. He stood up slowly as his brother spoke to the King, stepped onto the dais to stand beside Harold. Out of the corner of his eye, the Earl of Wessex saw his sister cup her hand to her mouth, heard her draw her breath. The monk Caedwig cried a warning, and Harold, in one quick motion, ducked, turned, and dived into his brother's stomach, knocking the wind out of Tostig as the two tumbled to the floor. The Earl of Northumbria lost his grip on his drawn dagger, just as he lost his breath. Tostig gasped for air and grabbed at the lost weapon. Harold stood up, kicked the blade far out of his brother's reach.

King Edward slowly raised his right hand to point an incriminating finger at Tostig. "Is that a dagger brought into my hall?"

The room became deathly quiet as the two brothers stared at each other and the King's suddenly intense presence hovered over them. The only sound was that of Tostig regaining his breath. Once his breath was back, Tostig's voice returned as well.

"Edward, it is all Harold's fault, can you not see it?" He turned then to his brother.

"Damn you, Harold! You have always hated me! Why?"

After almost being stabbed by his brother, Harold was cold as the dirt floor upon which Tostig still lay. "I have never hated you, Tostig. However, I have come to hate the things that you do, the madness you leave in your wake."

The younger brother stood and pointed his nose accusingly at his brother. "No! You do hate me. When I did gain importance in Northumbria, you felt threatened, even had to back the son of Leofric against my interests in Mercia. Still, I settle into my home in York, but then you contrive to have this walrus," Tostig waved his hand at Aldred, "placed as Archbishop of York to challenge my authority!

"Even our campaign into Wales was tainted by your greedy need for recognition above everyone else, especially me. While I conquered Northern Wales, left no escape for Gruffydd but through your lines where you could then vanquish the man's army, you conspire to gain Edward's approval alone, get him to name you Duke of the English!

"Not stopping there, you back a babe in Mercia upon Aelfgar's death, again against me. Now I see quite clearly that I was wrong in blaming this rebellion in the north on Aldred. It was you, Harold. Yes you! Of course. It was you that instigated this civil unrest, was it not?"

His brother looked so pitiful after the long tirade, Harold's own countenance softened. "No, Tostig, I was not needed to incite your people against you, you did well to achieve that all on your own."

Tostig did not even hear his brother. "Ha! Of course! How could I be so blind? You would take my power in Northumbria, would you not? Well, I will not give in to you, Harold."

The Queen stepped over to try and calm Tostig with a gentle hand on his shoulder, turned to her other brother at once. "Harold, so often it is you who plays the role of peacemaker. Now I would that I had your abilities. Swear to your brother that you had nothing to do with this uprising, and let us be done with it."

"Yes, Harold," Edward said. "I am disturbed by all this yelling in my hall. Please tell me you did not start all this."

Harold glanced back at the King, turned and bowed slightly to him. "I beg your pardon, Edward. For your sake, and my sister's, I do swear to you that I had nothing to do with this revolt."

Tostig cringed at his sister's touch, did not believe what he heard. He shook off his sister's hold and backed away from them all.

The King was not completely content. "Tell me, Harold, that there will be no civil war in my kingdom!"

Harold, watching his brother move away, answered the King but spoke also to Tostig. "I can assure you that my brother will not get the chance to cause another revolt in this realm."

That stopped Tostig. "Damn it, now I understand. You intend to put the other child of Aelfgar in Northumbria in my stead! That is it, is it not? Damn you! Northumbria is mine!"

The words that had begun strong, ended in sputtering, whiney phrases. Harold had no remorse left for his brother.

"Well, my lord King. Your ever-dutiful servant Tostig of the north has detailed a marvelous solution to the present crisis that lays so heavy a shadow upon your kingdom. A solution which I believe would be the exact gesture the northern thanes and villeins would like to see. And indeed, I think Tostig's meddlesome nature would best be quenched in this way."

"I will certainly not allow him to bring a dagger into my audience chamber again!" the King responded.

"No, that we will not allow," Harold said. "Congratulations, my King, on a fine solution to this sticky problem. I assure you the Witan will ratify your proclamation, Edward."

The King smiled at Harold, "Yes, of course. Do I not always know how to handle the problems in my realm?" Edward looked toward his wife, his confessor, seeking more praise; but found only their ashen faces, their eyes agape. Even Archbishop Aldred was staring in disbelief at the Earl of Wessex.

Harold bowed his head to the King. "Indeed you do, my lord."

Caedwig and Aldred were dumbstruck. Queen Edith looked from one brother to the other, knew not what to say. Harold turned around to face his brother again. Tostig looked like a mongrel street-hound, kicked and lying in the mud. The man from Northumbria looked pleadingly from his brother, to the Queen, to King Edward.

"I am your brother-in-law, Edward, your friend!"

Edward began to speak, his thoughts cut off by Tostig's brilliant, blazing anger now directed toward the Earl of Wessex.

"What do you intend for me? Do you expect me to step by and let you place the child of Mercia in my place at York? You know I would never live with that. Would you dare to suggest that I leave England in disgrace?"

Harold dropped a cold stare down the younger man's shirt, sending a shiver up Tostig's spine. "I do not suggest it. I told you once before that what I do, I do for England. If you go, it will be England that demands it of you." Harold leaned toward his brother, speaking softly so that only Tostig could hear. "Although, as Archbishop Aldred has said, it does not appear that you had anything to do with your kinsman Aedward's death, you might find exile preferable to your brother's retribution."

Tostig jumped back. "You would exile me?"

Harold shrugged. "Tostig, you can do what you like, once you leave your palace at York. I will have my personal guard see you to York…safely, as you collect what baggage you will from your former residence."

Tostig marched over to the fallen dagger, picked up the blade and hurled it at Harold. The Earl of Wessex did not move as the dagger flew far off the mark, but reacted at once as he heard his sister scream. The projectile had come dangerously close to the Queen. Harold leaped across the room and backhanded Tostig so hard the younger man fell against the wall.

"Get out of here!"

Tostig recovered, made for the door with his hand rubbing his jaw bone.

"You want me out of the way! You are afraid that Edward might choose me as his successor, and you would never be able to live with that, would you? You do not want me to be King!"

"I said, get out of here, Tostig. I will not say it again."

"Yes, Harold, I will leave." Tostig's grin filled the doorway. "But you will live to regret this day! The Book of Genesis decrees that Man's troubles did begin with a woman. Your troubles, however, have begun this day with the way you have treated me! You have not seen the last of Tostig Godwinsson! None of you!"

Tostig crashed through the doors, stomped down the hallway yelling oaths and crying for revenge all the way. He stormed across the bailey, heading for the stables where his groomsmen watched the horses. Aldbald had organized his master's riding gear for whatever action Lord Tostig and King Edward would take, was walking from the stables to meet his master in the middle of the bailey.

"My Lord Tostig, I passed your brother Lord Harold coming from the stables only a while ago. He moved so in earnest, I could tell he had important business with the King. Otherwise I could not read his face, and he heeded me not as we passed each other. Did the Earl of Wessex bring good news?"

"Good news?" Tostig spat, almost hitting Aldbald. "I will tell you his news. My lord brother has ordered my banishment from the kingdom!"

Aldbald knew that Harold and the King would be none too supportive of the Earl of Northumbria's present predicament, since it was mostly, as far as Aldbald could tell, of Tostig's own doing. Yet, he never would have guessed that Harold would abandon his brother. He said as much to his master.

Tostig spat again, only this time Aldbald made sure he was not in the line of fire. "Abandon me? Harold would abandon his bastard children for his own gain. Of course he ignored you as he passed. You thought him a friend of yours? My brother has no sense of honor, no conception of loyalty, cares nothing for you or me!"

Aldbald shook his head. "I am truly shocked."

"I am not, not in retrospect at least. Perhaps I should have expected it of Harold. I do not believe that either of us truly knows Harold as we had thought. At least I know that you, Aldbald, and my other retainers would never desert me as has my own brother."

When Aldbald did not speak, the Earl of Northumbria turned around and grabbed the other man's shoulder, his eyes burning into Aldbald with a fierce intensity. "You would never desert me, right?"

Aldbald was caught off guard, had still been trying to understand Lord Harold's motives. He coughed, "Of course not, my lord."

"Swear to me, now!"

Aldbald's shoulder was beginning to hurt where the other man squeezed him. "I do swear, Lord Tostig, that I will not desert you, as long as you do have need of me!"

Satisfied, Tostig spun around and stomped away from the other man.

Aldbald did not move at once to follow the man; he watched instead the retreating form of the Earl of Northumbria. He was still in shock regarding the news of Harold's actions. Suddenly a light touch on Aldbald's shoulder where Tostig had gripped him caused the young man to jump. He turned quickly to find the Queen standing beside him.

"My Lady," Aldbald burst out in surprise.

Queen Edith was not looking at Aldbald. She too was watching her brother. "I am worried about my younger brother, Aldbald."

"Is it true, my lady? Did Lord Harold and Lord Tostig have an argument?"

The Queen sighed. "I fear it was more than just an argument this time." Edith looked then at the young man. "Aldbald, I do not know you well, but Caedwig has spoken very highly of you."

Aldbald managed a slight smile. "The monk has been very kind to me, my lady."

Queen Edith squeezed Aldbald's shoulder. "Though I fear for my brother, I feel better knowing you will be beside Tostig wherever he will go. Please, I entreat you, watch over Tostig for me, will you?"

Aldbald was held in place by the Queen's eyes. For a moment he was disturbed seeing his own reflection superimposed with the intense worry within the dark orbs. Still, he felt at once quite important as well.

"My lady, I am your brother's sworn servant, and the Queen's as well." Aldbald bowed his head. "I will do what I can for Lord Tostig."

"Thank you, my friend," the Queen said. She nudged Aldbald slightly. Her vain attempt at a smile was lost in her urgency.

"Go now, and catch up with your lord."

Aldbald caught up with Tostig at the inner gate. The snapping of a banner in the wind caught his attention, and Aldbald followed his master's squinting gaze. Above them growled a Golden Dragon, the royal banner of Wessex, the King's banner.

Tostig hardly noticed that Aldbald stood beside him, so intent was he on the banner above. "For far too long that banner has followed you, brother," Tostig whispered. "One day, Harold, I swear it will follow you to the grave."

Book III

AD 1066

Entry I

▼

In which King Edward the Confessor dies on Thorney Island

King Edward had not been a strong ruler. He had never tried to be anything more than what he was: A pious, God-fearing King who enjoyed the peace in his realm, a peace due mainly to the efforts of the Earl of Wessex. Lacking a statesman's savvy and strength, Edward had often been led astray by self-seeking men around him. Many people would put the Earl of Wessex himself in that category, Harold knew; and he could not in all honesty completely disagree with that assessment. Yet, as Harold gained more power over the past years, rose higher in the King's court and in Edward's confidence, the Earl of Wessex learned to think not just of his and his family's interests, but to envision those of England as a whole. With Harold handling the affairs of state, and Edward as a loved figurehead, cherished by the masses, England had prospered for many years.

The Earl of Wessex entered the King's chambers in the palace on Thorney Island, a structure two miles up the River Thames from London rebuilt by Edward so he could be near to West Minster Abbey, the King's prize creation. Harold was immediately struck by the condition of England's King. Although his brother-in-law was weak-willed, and lacking in strength as a ruler, King Edward had always been physically fit and active, hunting every free chance he had. It was the aura of such pristine health that had been shattered, making them all realize just how fragile is this life to which they all held on.

Harold approached the King's bed slowly, clapping his hand lightly upon the shoulder of his friend Robert FitzWimark standing by the door, and nodding a greeting to the cleric present, Stigand, the Archbishop of Canterbury. Edward was emaciated and Harold felt a pain of pity. The old man was thin, more thin than anyone Harold could remember ever seeing before. The King's cheeks were cleft, his eyes sunken. Surely Edward could not have lost so much weight in this last week of sickness he had just come through, Harold thought. Had it happened more gradually over the past few years, and Harold himself had somehow not taken notice? The Earl of Wessex wondered for a moment, then let it pass. The past did not matter now; it was the present, and the future, that did count.

Edward's first attack came just after the tense situation with Tostig and the northern thanes had come so close to exploding. The King's household and Edward's retainers assumed it had merely been the relief of stress; but then Edward was struck again on the eve of Christmas, fell into a coma only a few days later. The household had been on the edge, waiting for the news the royal doctors had delivered that very day, on the eve of the Epiphany. Edward was at last awake, restless and confused after having shaken free of the oppressive unconsciousness. Before Queen Edith and the King's attendants could arrive, Edward fell into a fitful sleep.

The room was dimly lit so as not to strain Edward's eyes should he again gain the strength to open them. As Harold stepped up next to the sickbed, he smiled softly toward the third person in the room. His sister, Queen Edith sat at the end of the bed, warming Edward's feet in her lap. The King's skin was almost as the white-washed walls of the room, so white that Harold at first could not tell whether Edward was dressed in a short or long sleeved nightshirt, could not tell where the white fabric ended and the King's skin began. Without a word, Harold reached to hold the King's hand. The skin was cold to the touch. It surprised Harold, and he at once leaned close to see if the King was still breathing.

"Yes, Harold, Edward does yet live." Edith spoke quietly from the end of the bed. "The doctors have told me he still retains the cold of the darkness in which he had been immersed over the past few days. I do not know though, his breathing has stayed as faint. I fear for him."

Harold reached an arm over and gave his sister a slight hug, looked back at Edward's drawn features. At least, Harold thought to himself, the man does not look uncomfortable. Not as he had on the Wednesday past, at Childermas on the 28th of December. Edward was overwrought that he could not attend the dedication of his lifetime's ambition, the consecration of West Minster on the feast day of the Holy Innocents. His rage during his weakened condition seemed to have brought on the heavy darkness, and the King fell into a coma before the beginning of the New Year. Now, however, Edward looked almost serene. So much so that Harold felt again the urge to make sure the man had not passed on, freed himself from his earthly pains. The Earl of Wessex leaned close, rested his ear to the ailing man's chest. He could hardly make out the man's breathing, but Harold sighed audibly when he heard the faint beat of Edward's heart. As he lifted his head and moved away, Edward awoke with a jerk, grabbed Harold's closest wrist.

"My lord Edward! You are awake!" It was Queen Edith who exclaimed her excitement, the men in the room were too surprised for words. The King did not respond at first, his eyes were wide, but he stared past Harold to the opposite wall in the room. Archbishop Stigand stepped up next to Harold, placed a crucifix on the King's chest. Stigand whispered his concern for the King to the Earl of Wessex.

"Lord Harold, I should administer the last rites as soon as Edward regains his consciousness. We should delay no more. The royal healers can do no more. Edward is slipping away from us."

The scandal pertaining to Stigand retaining control of the See of Winchester while also claiming the most prestigious title of Archbishop of Canterbury had kept the cleric from being formally recognized by the Pope and was to taint Stigand's career ever after. But even as Aldred, now the Archbishop of York, had gained in power partially at his expense, Stigand remained close to Edward. He was often mediator between the House of Wessex and the King; but always a friend to both.

"No!" Queen Edith overheard the Archbishop's hushed statements, though Stigand had tried to keep his words for only Harold to hear. "No. Can you not see that my lord husband is recuperating, getting better even as we speak? The doctors did say they were not sure he would ever regain his conscious thought again; but look, he is awake now and perhaps hearing everything we are saying." With her own declaration, the woman brought her voice to a whisper. "I will not have you speak about Edward's slipping away."

"My lady, I am sorry. The administering of the last rites is only a precaution, should the unthinkable befall our King."

Harold backed up the cleric's feelings. "Edith, it is true. We do not know the Lord's will. He may choose to take Edward before we have prepared the man for Heaven. You must agree that Edward himself would not want to have missed being shriven."

Edith frowned, looked at her husband. "Look! the King is trying to speak!"

The people in the room crowded around, even Robert FitzWimark moved closer to see, for Edward was trying to sit up. The King was about to speak, looked around the room in confusion. "Where is my confessor? My servants, the members of my household?"

Edward looked so agitated, they all feared the King would bring down upon himself another lapse of unconsciousness. Harold turned quickly to his friend FitzWimark. "Rob, get Caedwig, and have Edward's attendants join us in the King's chambers as well. Hurry."

"They are already assembled outside the room, I will only be a moment."

The King was still gripping Harold's wrist. "Ah, Harold! Is that you, Stigand?"

"My lord, it is I."

"Where is my…Ah, there you are Edith." Seeing his wife at his feet, the King relaxed a little, yet still he tried to sit up higher in the bed. "I knew you would be here."

"My lord husband, of course I am here for you."

Edward smiled at his wife, a look that was not as much pleasant as it was disturbing to look upon within the frail features. With Harold's free hand he pulled up a chair, took the cushion and propped it behind the King along with the other bed pillows. Edward leaned back, but was not at rest, so agitated was he and in need of talking with those around him.

"I have had the most astounding dream. A revelation!"

Harold patted the King's shoulder. "Edward, relax. You will be all right now."

"I fear I have wrought a great evil into the world. God is not pleased with me."

Harold waved his hand at Stigand to keep the man from arguing for Edward to make his last confession. "That is nonsense, Edward. Your realm is at peace, your people content."

Edward did not respond to the Earl, was distracted by those entering the room. "Ah, Caedwig. Come and stand beside me here." The King smiled more strongly as the monk walked across the room, followed by Robert FitzWimark, Archbishop Aldred of York, Bishop Wulfstan of Worcester and a handful of the King's chamber servants. Wulfstan showed no sign of disturbance, but Aldred felt snubbed to see Stigand beside the King, and to have Edward acknowledge the monk and not the Archbishop of York. Though his distaste for the scene showed on his face, no one was watching him, and Aldred said nothing.

The King's voice became strong, astonishing all assembled. "Caedwig, do you remember your companions from Flanders, Rodney and Martin of St.

Omer? The two young monks who accompanied you to Normandy, who befriended me, who died together so horribly in that terrible stable fire?"

"My lord, I do remember. They were friends to both of us."

"They spoke to me in my dream. My monkish friends told me that God has laid a curse upon my kingdom. A year and a day after my death, demons will rage across the land. They will carry bloody swords and bring fire and war and misery to England."

Harold, his wrist still held in a death grip by the King, grabbed Edward's hand with his own free hand. "Edward! You had but a dream, nothing more. You cannot believe that God is so angered with the English people. For what reason? Let us not let your dream become a rumor to spread fear across the countryside."

Edward answered Harold, but directed his words to Caedwig. "I fear it is because of me. I have let the earls and churchmen of my realm become too wicked. Rodney and Martin told me all this." The King turned to look at Harold, sat forward in the bed. "But God will send a sign! He, in His mercy, will not punish England forever."

Edward released his hold on Harold, grabbed the monk's frock with both hands, pulled Caedwig closer to him as if to whisper, but his voice carried strongly throughout the room as it had a moment before. "Rodney and Martin told me what to do, and I will tell you. Go into the woods and find a tall, green tree. Make a cut midway up the length of the tree and carry the top half three furrow lengths away. When the tree becomes whole again, joined by its own efforts, when leaves do sprout and the tree bears fruit again, then you will know that the Lord God would cease to punish England."

Queen Edith gasped, the servants at the door murmured in hushed, anxious voices. Edward let go of the monk's clothes, fell back against the pillows of his bed exhausted. It seemed his energy left his body along with his words, his intensity softened with the information from his dream now in the care of other minds.

Stigand leaned over once again to Harold and whispered, "Do not stake too much on Edward's words. The King is old. He is sick, perhaps raving. I fear he will not have his wits about him for his final confession."

The Archbishop of York came forward then, overheard Stigand's comments. "May I remind the Bishop of Winchester," Aldred purposely using the prelate's older, lower title, "that it is precisely churchmen such as he who have weighed so heavily upon the King's conscience! Perhaps Stigand will remember that before he speaks of Edward as if the King were mad."

Stigand began a sharp, unholy retort, but was silenced by an outburst from Harold. "Enough!" The Earl of Wessex had spoken softly to the side, but with a great force of will directed toward the two clerics. He glanced at Stigand. "I hear what you say, but sometimes I believe there is a fine line between philosophy and delirium." Bringing his attention back to the sickbed, Harold tried to sound sure.

"My lord Edward, do not worry for your realm or your people. Now is no time to think about what will happen after your death, for you have regained your consciousness, your health is much improved. All that remains is for you to regain your strength as well. Before too long you will be out-riding your courtiers on the hunt once again. Edward, you will rule England for many more years to come."

Archbishop Aldred pushed Caedwig and Stigand aside, grasped the King's left hand. "I am sure what the Earl of Wessex has said is true, Edward. And many are the good things that you have accomplished. However, for the records, my lord, you might want to name your successor. I am sure it is something you have thought a lot about, and there is no time like the present for attending to such important matters."

Perhaps Harold and Stigand were surprised at such a change of subject, but the entire group stood silent, each one intent upon the King's answer. Edward looked from one to the other, seemed about to speak when he suddenly snatched his hand from Aldred, scratched in earnest at his side, as a feline would lose all interest in everything else save the relief of an itch. Queen Edith stood up quickly, shot a questioning look toward the King's head chamber maid. The middle aged woman bowed, looked in consternation at the ailing man's bed.

"I am sorry, my lady. With the King requiring his bed twenty-four hours in each day of late, we have found it difficult just keeping the sheets refreshed. There has been no time to lay out the fabric with which to catch the lice."

"We should do something—" Edith began, was stopped with a gesture from her brother. Harold was looking back at Edward who was beginning to speak again.

"Caedwig, my friend. Is it beautiful?"

The monk knew at once what the King was thinking about. "Yes, my lord. It is remarkable." Edward's eyes sparkled. "It is a sight to make the angels sing. Surely the Lord will reward such devotion as that which was the inspiration behind the construction of the Abbey at West Minster."

The King's countenance at once changed. From the glowing eyes of a child who had just trained his favorite hunting dog to do a new trick, Edward suddenly looked like a tired, penitent urchin in the streets begging for mercy.

"No, you are wrong." Edward looked at none of them in the room, through them all, reliving his dream. "Rodney and Martin told me much, but I have seen the Lord's face, and I know it all to be true. The Lord did frown upon me."

"Surely that is not so!" It was Caedwig who continued to speak with the King, but he spoke for the Queen and most of the others present.

"It is true! I have shown too much pride. The Almighty did not allow me to attend the consecration of the Abbey. That was God's rebuke for my sins."

"But, my lord—"

With the realization spoken, the last energy drained from the King's voice, his breathing became quick and shallow again. Edward noticed the crucifix Stigand had laid upon him, grasped it, held it up. Though he still had the strength for so simple a task, his fingers lacked the agility necessary, would not respond to his brain's direction. The crucifix fell from

Edward's hands, bouncing off his stomach to tumble to the floor. Harold moved away from the others, picked up the silverwork cross to lay it back on the King's chest. Edward just stared at the talisman.

"Harold, did you ever wonder why things move downward when they fall?"

"My lord, how else would they go?"

"Why do things not fall upward?"

"Edward, I know not the science to explain it. It is simply the natural thing to do. Falling up would be unnatural. There are forces beyond our control at work."

"Indeed." Edward brushed his hand across the image of Christ on his chest, did not try again to pick it up.

"Do you think it is more natural for men to go down when they fall as well? Why should I expect my soul to rise when my body, everything I see and know, does go down? Are we on the earth never to achieve grace? Are we too closely associated with the underworld, drawn by a force beyond our control, just as the crucifix falls to the dirty floor instead of ascending to the ceiling?"

Harold was not used to arguing with Edward in favor of the mysteries of the Almighty. He most often took the position as Devil's advocate, drawing the King out to see that there are indeed two sides to every coin. It was not out of lack of belief in God, but more because he felt there were many things that Man himself could, and should, decipher for himself, without interweaving everything with pious circumlocution. Even so, the Earl of Wessex did believe that there were some things that Man must take on faith alone.

"Edward, perhaps we on earth are chained by our secular concerns, held down even as we seek only that which is good, that which is right. Yet, when our earthly time is up, when our body does expire, that is when our spirit, our soul, is freed to soar. I need not tell you this. It is our faith, and we must hang onto it until the end."

Stigand came close to Harold, leaned across the sick man. "That is why you must be shriven, Edward. Harold, have everyone leave the room so that Edward may be alone with his conscience, come to be at peace with our Lord."

Harold stood up straight. "Yes. Please, let us all leave the King for a while."

Archbishop Aldred protested, "But, Lord Harold, we have not yet heard everything we need to hear from Edward."

Stigand glared at the other prelate. "After he has been shriven, Aldred."

"Yes, I must make my final confession." Edward's voice was faint, like the wind whispering through the shutters of the room's only window.

The Queen reached for her husband's hand, and the three clerics moved back to let Edith stand close to the King. "Edward, do not leave us today! Promise me you will fight to gain your strength."

The King's voice was almost imperceptible. Those in the room stood closer, straining to hear everything their King needed to say. "My dear Edith, I worried so over not being at the consecration of my...of the abbey. Yet, where I hope to go, the splendor of the Kingdom of Heaven will far outshine any worthless structure I may have built on this earth. You heard your brother, the Lord will not let my spirit stay caught in this old receptacle; but perhaps He will not mind if you lay my body to rest within West Minster. Will you do that for me, Edith?"

"Oh, Edward—"

"No, my dear one. Do not cry. I will make my peace with the Lord, I only hope that the Almighty may forgive England at the same time."

Edward grabbed at Harold's sleeve, pulled the man closer to him. The room was deathly quiet as each person held their breath, struggled to hear what might very well be their King's last words. "Harold. Your sister, Edith...she has been like a daughter to me. An adopted daughter, like this land of England I came to embrace after my young life on the continent. Rich, young, vibrant and alive! Untamed and unspoiled...cherish her and keep her well. She is in your care now. She is England!"

Entry II

▼

Through which a witena gemot does reach a decision

The thanes were the landholders of England, those men that held the land through the beneficence of an earl or the king himself. The thanes were also the ones to be called upon in time of battle to make up the fyrd, an army for the earl or the king.

However, the true backbone of England were the cottars and the villeins, those of the cottages and in the villages who worked in the fields of the thane's hide of land and dealt with the industries that kept the rural English economy thriving. On a day-to-day basis, the common country-man cared little for the dealings at the hundreds court, knew even less of the happenings at the shire court, heard virtually nothing about what went on in the witena gemot, the meeting of the wise men, the advisors and councilors to the King.

Without the external influences as in the old days of the Norse raids, the people of England were content with the system, happy to leave, at each level, the pondering and deciding of weighty matters to those above them. However, with the meeting of the Witan on the fifth day of January in the year after Christ one thousand sixty-six, the English people would perhaps have been a little more concerned over the decision to be made had they known that Edward, their king for almost a quarter of a century, had died the day before.

Assembled on Thorney Island for the King's Christmas court, there were the archbishops and most of the bishops of England, as many abbots, and a large number of the King's own thanes. Although the problem was long in coming, for they all knew that no man is immortal, the King's death seemed to have caught them off guard. The group was in an uproar. Harold, his brothers and the senior prelates of England stood by silently as the men began to congregate in the meeting hall of Edward's palace.

One thane who had just arrived at the meeting was looking around him for someone to fill him in, and the conversation he joined was similar to half a dozen others that filled the room with the chatter of voices. "Is it true? Did Edward have a dream that was a bad omen for England?"

"That is what I heard." Another thane answered the first.

"Yes, because of the corruption of the English Church, God will punish England now that his favorite, Edward the Confessor, is gone." A third thane spat out the words toward the Bishop of Lincoln.

"Do not be so quick to condemn the Church," the Bishop responded, "I heard that Edward's ominous dream put the blame upon all of England for wickedness and lack of Christian ideals."

"I do not believe all of England is so wicked. I am not! Surely the Lord will not punish us all for the mistakes of a few—" The first thane spoke fearfully.

The second thane slapped the first on the back. "Well, I for one will not take much stock in the revelations in dreams. I understand King Edward may not have had his wits about him. He seemed to prattle on about many nonsensical things, so I heard."

"True, true." It was the Bishop again. "Let us dwell on the things we can see, not on the fear of the unknown."

"A funny thing to hear coming from a cleric!" The third thane poked fun at the Bishop, but the man of the Church did not take the bait for a fight.

The second exclaimed. "Ah, but that is what brings us together today! The unknown. Who will follow Edward? He left no heir of his body, but there are others who—"

"Do not go on to say that we should then offer the crown of England to Svend of Denmark. I have seen enough of Danish rule." An older thane interrupted the conversation with a loud sniffle as he rubbed his wrist across his dripping nose.

"Of course we do not want a Dane. But, who?"

The Archbishop of York, striding through the assembly, had heard enough. "My lords, fellow clergymen, noted thanes of England, we are confronted with a matter not unknown to England. Simply one that we have had no need to address for many years now. The matter of losing the king of our land is an incredibly important one, and I am sure we have much to discuss. However, the matter of choosing the next king will not be too difficult for us." Aldred waved his arms around the circle of people in the room. "I am sure I need not remind any of you that there does live a descendant of Aethelred. Edgar, son of Aedward, is the Aetheling, the heir apparent, is he not? I am sure we will all be in agreement, but as a formality I do nominate Edgar as the heir to Edward's throne, and will be the first to accept that nomination in the name of the Aetheling." Aldred swooped his arms around and clasped his hands together before his chest as he bowed his head slightly, smiling from ear to ear. He did not expect the response his statement would elicit.

A murmur swept across the room, and it was Gyrth Godwinsson of East Anglia who spoke the thoughts that were almost palatable in the air. "Aldred of York, we thank you for your nomination. Let me be the first to mention, again, that we all know of, and appreciate, your efforts in bringing back Aedward and his family from their exile eight years ago. However, let us not be too hasty in assuming the succession is decided."

Aldred raised his head and looked about the room at the men who's faces showed no sign of solidarity with his own cause. "I do not nominate the man simply because I rescued him, along with his father, from exile in Hungary. Edgar is a relative of our late King and a man brought up these past years on the royal estates as Edward's own son. Without a natural son of Edward himself, young Edgar is the obvious choice."

Leofwine, Earl of Kent, stood beside his brother. "Yes, I think you have touched on the operative word. Edgar is young."

That brought a murmur again to the crowd. One thane blurted out, "We need a man to rule England!" Others clapped their hands in agreement.

Aldred was flabbergasted. "Speaking to some of you who ratified the proclamations that made the young children of Mercia, Edwin and Morcar, to be earls in the realm, I find it strange that you would be claiming that Edgar is too young."

One of the bishops, feeling uncomfortable speaking out against the Archbishop of York, took strength from the knowledge that those about him felt as he did. "We are talking about the kingship of the realm, not the running of an earldom!"

Aldred glared at the bishop who had spoken, glanced back around the room. "Do not ever think that I consider the deciding of the next king to be a simple affair. I only want to remind you all that Edgar is truly our only candidate."

"Our only candidate? That weak boy who spends most of his time dreaming of Hungary where he was born and raised? Then England is in a sorry state indeed!" Gyrth stepped over to face the Archbishop. "We may never know what manner of man Aedward the Exile was, although I daresay he would have been more Hungarian than English. Still, he is not here and all you can offer is his son. But, my lord Archbishop, Edgar is not a man I would want ruling this country." Again the murmur of consent from the lords and thanes in the room.

Leofwine stepped next to his brother Gyrth. "Sure, Edward brought Edgar up in his house. But, he kept him a recluse, did teach him more of what it takes to be a monk than a king!"

"We need a strong king!" This from a thane of the Sussex forests.

Aldred stroked his chin, pretended to be contemplative, but his next comment was only sarcastic. "Ah yes, strong. As strong as King Edward had been, at least!" The Archbishop floated around the ring of men facing him. "Surely none of you will try to claim that King Edward was strong!"

As the Archbishop made his rounds, his statement ended in front of Robert FitzWimark. "No, Aldred, Edward was not strong. But, then, he had Harold of Wessex. England had Harold! And a good thing too." The thanes and lords stomped their feet, clapped their hands together at that. Many looked to the Earl of Wessex; but Harold, stroking his mustaches, said nothing before Archbishop Aldred pushed on.

"At least the man we elect should have a strength of character and desire for justice. Certainly we can all agree Edward did give us that." The Archbishop finally got a grudging agreement from the group. He pressed his point. "And so could Edgar! He is Edward's kin, a descendant of Aethelred—"

Gyrth walked over to the Archbishop. "No one does deny the boy his blood, Aldred, we merely question his abilities."

"And who would you suggest in his place? Svend of Denmark?" That brought Aldred the response he expected from the nobles in the room. No one wanted to return to Danish overlordship, and the thought of it brought feelings closer to accepting the young descendent of the English royal line, as Aldred had hoped. Even so, there were too many opposed to making Edgar king.

Stigand, the Archbishop of Canterbury, knew that his words might not sway the group, but he offered a compromise settlement that he had discussed with a few of those assembled. He was sure that some would find his answer to be the only reasonable solution. "If I may, my lords, it seems to me that perhaps Edgar could continue as the Aetheling, the heir apparent, with a man of strength named as regent until the boy does grow and could assume full responsibilities should he prove able."

The Archbishop's suggestion brought a loud stammer of confused retorts, questions and comments from each side of him. Robert FitzWimark brought the congregation back to order, turned to Stigand. "I think your suggestion is interesting, Stigand, as do many of us here. Who would you recommend as regent?"

Stigand waved his hand as if it were obvious. "The Underking, of course. Harold of Wessex."

Archbishop Aldred pushed into the center of the room again to gain back the attention of the group. "Please, my lords and favored men of England. Let us be reasonable! Edgar is sixteen years old! How much less a man than any of you at that age? He is a good young man, pious, and Edward did favor him."

The Earl of Kent stepped in front of the Archbishop to confront the men in the room. "Then why did our late King not name Edgar as his successor?" Leofwine threw the question into the assembly, then turned to Aldred to wait for an answer.

Aldred waved his hands. "Who can know the mind of Edward? But, we waste our time. What is there for us to consider, anyway?" Aldred spoke flatly, the discussion pointless. He flared his nostrils, challenging the assembly one final time. "I tell you, the Aetheling is our only choice!"

Again, many of the group looked to the Earl of Wessex, expecting him to at least accept the idea of his being regent. As Archbishop Stigand expected, that would be something the thanes and lords could perhaps accept. Harold had listened intently to the arguments, finally offered something to the debate.

"There is another."

The men who stood with hushed voices reacted at once. The King's thanes all started talking, bishops looked at each other in confusion. Only Gyrth and Leofwine seemed to know what their brother was about to say. They smiled at each other, expectantly, waiting to add their consent to the nomination of Harold as the next King. And why not? The two earls had often joked about it to their big brother. After all, in their eyes Harold had been king in all but name for many years already. The Archbishop of York saw the look pass from one son of Godwin to the other, looked over at Harold and scowled.

"And what man of noble birth would it be to whom you are referring, Harold?" Aldred was not going to let the Witan fall under Harold's charms as do the women of Wessex. But, the Archbishop was as surprised as Gyrth and Leofwine, as the rest of the company, to hear Harold's answer.

"Duke William of Normandy."

There was a shocked silence that lasted only a second before the assembly erupted in wild pandemonium. Harold held up his hand to quiet them all.

"You must be jesting with us, Lord Harold!" Aldred spoke above the now softer murmuring.

"Do you truly think I would joke about so important a matter? No, my good Archbishop, I offer up Duke William's name as a matter to consider seriously."

"But Harold—" Leofwine had taken a step toward his older brother; however, Gyrth spoke first, his words failing him even as he began.

The Earl of Wessex looked from one brother's face to the other, scanned the whole assembly, his gaze finally coming to rest on the Archbishop of York. "What were those criteria for a king of which you did speak? If we think only a moment, we might see that William does perhaps fit the mold. I have met the man myself, and I will tell you of what I know."

Harold had the complete attention of the entire group. "You want someone strong. Duke William has carved out a place for himself in Northern France, and held it secure for many years. His influence even now extends well beyond Normandy's borders. He has a strong will and demands justice.

"William is of noble blood, related to our late King Edward who did love his kinsmen in Normandy well. And, although Edward lacked the strength in his final hours to confirm his choice for his successor, it is true that he may very well have thought highly of William as a potential candidate for the kingship of England."

Harold stopped to let his words sink in. As he expected, no one hurried to second his suggestion. Still, the earl gave them all a moment to mull over his comments. The Archbishop of York, however, did not want anyone thinking about something as ludicrous as what Harold suggested.

"Your sincerity does surprise me, Harold of Wessex, and the Witan does acknowledge the case you make for William of Normandy. Certainly we want a strong man as king. And yes, he should be of noble blood. It is also true that we would like to honor the choice of the late king. All these things are true. However, putting by the fact that Edward did not actually proclaim his interest in William as his heir, you seem to have neglected the most important criterion: The next king of England should be English!"

The Archbishop had walked toward Harold and his brothers, turned then to face the others in the room with the last statement, his big nose flaring, nostrils held high, arms swinging out as if to embrace the entire assembly. A few of the abbots and bishops clapped their hands, many of the thanes began to cheer this. Harold's own thanes present were caught between honoring their Earl's thoughts and agreeing with Archbishop Aldred's suddenly popular appeal.

Harold said nothing, but the Bishop of Worcester stood out of the assembly and faced the Archbishop of York. Wulfstan smiled at Archbishop Aldred. "You do not have to remind anyone here, and certainly not Harold of Wessex, that England should stay under English rule."

Harold spoke then. "The Bishop of Worcester is right, as are you Aldred. England would certainly prefer to have an Englishman as king."

Aldred swung his arms around in front of the men, his triumphant smile filling his face. "Indeed it would, and thus, it is settled." The

Archbishop looked around the room for support, but was disappointed to find many of the faces before him had turned back to see what the Earl of Wessex would say. It was not Harold who spoke next, though, it was Wulfstan. The Bishop of Worcester had come up behind Aldred, and even though the Archbishop gave him a warning look, Wulfstan addressed the assembly.

"Indeed, I believe we have almost settled this matter. Just as the Archbishop of York has outlined, there is a man who fits the criteria for our king better than William of Normandy. An Englishman. One who is strong of will. A man who has shown his leadership abilities, bringing the English to many victories over its enemies."

Gyrth and Leofwine smiled once again to each other. They knew their friend Wulfstan well enough to understand where the cleric was going with these statements. The older of the two brothers began to whisper a chant, and Leofwine chimed in.

"Harold, Harold."

Wulfstan continued, despite Archbishop Aldred's growing unease. "A man who stands before us today, already bearing the title of Leader of the English."

Harold's thanes picked up on the Godwin brothers' chant, clapping their legs in rhythm. "Harold, Harold."

Harold himself looked surprised, stood up to dispute his nomination, but Robert FitzWimark moved forward and finished the Bishop of Worcester's declaration. "A man who, with Edward's dying breath, the King did charge to take care of England!"

Archbishop Aldred reacted to that. "No, Edward was talking about his wife the Queen—" The last of the thanes, the abbots and bishops joined in the chant, drowning out Aldred's rebuttal.

"Harold, Harold!"

The Archbishop of York tried one final time to sway the assembly. "Harold Godwinsson is not of royal blood!"

Wulfstan leaned close to Aldred. "You forget that Harold is related to Canute through his father's marriage into the family of the Danish royal line."

"But—" Aldred began, then stopped himself. From the mood of the group, it was quite clear to the Arichbishop of York that the particularities of the noble-blood criterion had become the least important to the men around him. The hall reverberated with the chanting.

"Harold, Harold!"

Seeing his cause lost, Aldred quickly switched to the winning side. He would go along with the decision, but many things might change between now and the time of coronation, Aldred thought to himself. Pushing Wulfstan and FitzWimark out of the way, he walked over to the Earl of Wessex, swung his arms wide and called over the rising tumult.

"I do hereby nominate Harold of Wessex as our next King of England!" Aldred grabbed Harold's shoulders, looking into the Earl's eyes, then turned to the assembly. "All those in favor, show your agreement."

Robert FitzWimark and Wulfstan joined in the chant, and all the men crowded around Harold. Bishops and thanes congratulated the man, and each other for making such a fine, and quick decision. FitzWimark pushed through the crowd to stand beside his friend.

"My lord, I think the decision is unanimous!"

Harold only then found his voice. "But Rob, I did not attend this moot with the intention of leaving with the title of king."

"No, but you will leave it with the crown securely in your grasp."

"But, Rob—"

Robert FitzWimark laughed. "Harold, you never said so, but you knew you were the one man for the job. Do not argue. Take the crown! You can bring England together, united under one strong leader. This is a great day for the country as well as for you, Harold!"

Harold started to protest again, but those words caught him. He thought, as king, perhaps he could do what the Earl of Wessex could not.

Perhaps he could make amends with Mercia and unite England just as his friend had said. Wulfstan gained the floor once again.

"The coronation should be held on a feast day of the Church." The quieted crew mumbled their agreement with that.

"That is the custom," Archbishop Aldred nodded. "Easter is just three months away—"

"I do not think that anyone in this assembly wants to wait three long months!" Wulfstan smiled at the frustrated look his comment elicited from Archbishop Aldred. The Bishop of Worcester continued, "Let us plan a ceremony today. It is the Epiphany, what better time for the coronation of our new king. The day to commemorate the manifestation of our Lord Jesus to the Magi will be the day we declare England's new king before the world!"

The Archbishop of York's pleas for time dissolved amidst the uproar in the hall. Harold found himself being led away as the wise men of England went to prepare a coronation.

Only a handful of hours later, Wulfstan, assisting Archbishop Aldred of York in the service, asked the huge crowd of people from the London area if they accepted the new king, and they responded with an exuberant cry. Harold swore a triple oath to protect the peace, uphold justice and offer mercy in the kingdom. Aldred, flowing with the tide about him, anointed Harold's head shoulders and hands, praying that the King would defend the Church and the people of England. Invested with the symbols of secular power, Harold found he wore the ring of unity, held the sword of protection, had the crown of glory and justice upon his head, the scepter of virtue at his side, the rod of equity in his lap. Before the people outside London even knew that King Edward had died, England had a new king.

*   *   *   *

The elegant Edyth Svanneshals sat to the right of the new King of England at the evening banquet table. On Harold's left sat Robert FitzWimark. Edyth gazed around the room, sat up straight and smiled in satisfaction. She leaned over to speak into Harold's ear.

"My lord, my King! So many years you have acted the part of king. Now you wear the crown yourself. I am so proud to be sitting beside you this day! The people of England chose you. They do love you well, as do I!"

Robert FitzWimark watched the young sons of Aelfgar as he listened to Edyth whisper to Harold. Edwin of Mercia and Morcar of Northumbria were causing a commotion as they chased Harold's hunting dogs around the room. FitzWimark laughed at their antics, then became more serious.

"Not all of England chose Harold today, my lady. Although the Earls of the northern lands are here on Thorney Island, they were too young to participate in the meeting of the Witan." Then directly to Harold, FitzWimark continued, "My lord, I fear the thanes in the north will feel underrepresented at this most important of moots."

Harold laughed in spite of his friend's honest apprehension. "A fine time to worry, Rob, after you and Wulfstan all but pushed me into this crown."

Edyth looked past Harold to the other man. "But the Archbishop of York himself crowned Harold today!"

Robert looked grave. "That may not be enough to appease the northern lords. They already fear Harold of Wessex might use the young children of Aelfgar as pawns for his own ends. They will need to have their minds set to rest over this kingship affair."

"And you are right, Rob," Harold answered the man's unasked question, "I might not have been their first choice."

Edyth reached for Harold's hand. "Is that why you thought to suggest your sister Edith as the next ruler of England, because she would have the popular support throughout the realm?"

Harold was surprised that she knew of this, but not surprised at the shock he read in the look on Robert FitzWimark's face.

"What?" FitzWimark asked in such a tone that Edyth quickly put her hand to her own mouth.

"I am sorry, Harold," she mumbled. "Queen Edith spoke to me afterward; but perhaps I was not meant to say anything—"

"That is quite all right," Harold smiled at Edyth, then turned to confront his friend's inquisitive look. "Rob, I spoke with my sister after Edward died about what he might have meant in those last moments."

FitzWimark shrugged, "The King was talking about England, was giving the kingdom into your hands, my friend!"

Harold nodded. "That is one interpretation. However, I knew too that Queen Edith did indeed have the love of the entire country, just as King Edward himself had. Could I just leave her out of the whole discussion regarding the succession? After all, it was not her fault entirely that there was no heir of Edward's body. As brother to sister I did plan to heed Edward's final plea to watch over his wife."

"Yes, but—"

"As Earl of Wessex," Harold went on, "I also wanted to offer what support I could to the Queen."

Robert FitzWimark was shifting in his seat. "But Harold! With all due respect, your sister is not like Edward's mother Emma who seemed born to be a queen. Edith is not like Alfred the Great's daughter who was a leader in Mercia and fought the Danes."

"Quite so," Harold said, "as Edith herself did remind me. Which is why I did not bring up the suggestion to the Witan." Edyth nodded, but FitzWimark was shaking his head.

Harold finished the wine in his cup. "The northern thanes shall be given the chance to ratify my election. Now that you have gotten me into this, Rob," Harold laughed, "I daresay I will not let you down. As soon as the winter weather does clear for travel, I will ride to York and call together a witena gemot in the north. Young Edwin and Morcar will ride with me, and I will confirm my interest in protecting their rights in the northern earldoms."

"And if the northern thanes do not ratify your coronation?" FitzWimark spoke too forcefully. He had been caught off guard by the previous discussion regarding Edward's wife.

"They will, Robert! I will bring you and Wulfstan along to speak with them and see that they do!"

Robert relaxed then. "I am sorry, Harold. I did not mean to dampen your victory today. You are right, of course. I daresay Wulfstan would be able to talk a fox out of the bulrushes."

Then it was Harold's turn to become serious as he thought of the Lady Godiva, a woman who was perhaps much like Emma of Normandy or Aethelflaed of Mercia. "Of one thing I am certain, I intend to use my position as King to allow me to overcome past rivalries that have torn England apart."

Edyth grasped Harold's hand again and squeezed. "You mean you will recall your brother Tostig and make amends with him?"

Harold laughed quickly. "In truth, I was not thinking of my brother! I do not know right now what I will do with Tostig. Even though I sent the man away, I would not have been surprised if he had been the first foot in my door this new year, boding ill for me!"

Edyth found it difficult to hide her apprehension. The King of England searched the woman's caring face and he smiled sincerely. Edyth Swanneck was still as beautiful as the day they had first lay together. She was still devoted to him, and Harold found that to give him a very warm feeling.

"My love, Edyth, do not worry so. Tostig will cool, the northern thanes will not find it too difficult to rally around me, and England will be whole and strong. I had never thought to be King, but if I am King, by God I want to rule over a united kingdom."

This answer seemed to relieve the woman's fears and she smiled broadly. Harold was almost convinced himself. Was that not all he wanted? Harold remembered his last meeting with Godiva. She had been hurt and tired, needed some sign that she could bestow her friendship upon the house of Wessex. Never had the two of them gotten the chance to really know each other.

Edyth Swan-neck's happiness cooled again as she saw Harold's distant look, a momentary gaze broken quickly by Robert FitzWimark's call for more wine.

Entry III

▼

When Tostig confronts Duke William of Normandy

The silk bed covers chafed his flesh, the velvet cushions were like weathered boulders. Tostig reached to a porcelain basin to refresh his face and neck, almost wretched at the smell of the rose-scented water. He toppled the brass washstand to the floor in disdain.

"How could I have ever thought to seek aid from these weak and womanly Normans? My God, they disgust me!"

Aldbald was not so repulsed, sitting back in one of the two soft chairs in Tostig's chambers after having stacked some wood by the fire place. The cottar from Coventry was the only servant of Tostig's left. The Lady Judith had stayed with her family in Flanders and there she retained all the house servants that had left England with their party. If not for a small group of young soldiers of fortune who joined them from Flanders, enticed by Tostig's claims of material wealth in England, Aldbald and Bufread Bloodyaxe would be the only men at Tostig's side. Bufread, the man that years ago had wanted so much for Aldbald to lose the trial by ordeal, had never grown to like the cottar, and Aldbald took great pains to keep clear of the berserker.

"My lord," Aldbald began, "fussing and fretting will do your health no good. Give the Duke some time, then present your requests again. I am sure the Duke of Normandy is a busy man with many important situations to which he must attend. I am sure he will see that your cause is just. Indeed, time it is that will also bring your brother Lord Harold around to your side again."

Tostig had relaxed a bit with his servant's words, until his brother's name was mentioned. "The Devil take Harold! And the Devil take back William of Normandy as well! Better had his father stayed in Hell than come back to sire that Bastard."

Aldbald had heard the stories of how Robert of Normandy had been sold to the Devil by his own mother. The servants seemed to think that Duke William found the story upsetting, but Aldbald found the tale a little hard to believe. He became more insistent.

"Please, Lord Tostig! Do not say anything so rash. Lord Harold will recall us from exile, I am sure of it. I do believe he must have been pressured into arguing with you. He will find mercy soon enough, and we will all go home. As long as you do not provoke him."

Tostig spat. "Bah! No one pressured my brother. Edward himself was on my side! Oh no, Harold chose, all on his own, to see that I was sent from the English court. He knew all too well that Edward did favor me over him, and that has rankled in him for many years. I will wager everything I own that Harold himself incited my people against me! With me out of the way, and the young whelps of that damned son of Leofric under his wing in Mercia and Northumbria, there was nothing to stop Harold from claiming the throne of England in my stead!"

"My lord, your younger brothers—"

"Gyrth and Leofwine have always idolized Harold, God knows why! Ever since our older brother Svein died, and then father, those two have been misled by Harold's false pretenses."

"Mayhap you have not agreed with everything your brother has done," Aldbald's brow furrowed as he thought of some of his own feelings over the years, "but Lord Harold has always seemed to be genuine to me."

"You too have fallen easy prey to his wiles. Just as cousin Svend of Denmark thinks he has a friend in Harold. Imagine that Danish upstart sending a messenger to me with an offer of an earldom in Denmark. The man could not even face me himself! I tell you, he knows that he has been played the fool by Harold; and he knows that I know. How could I live in Denmark knowing I ran away from Harold to hide under a weakling like Svend?"

Aldbald knew that this was the root of Tostig's current tirade. Tostig had felt ignored at the English court, would not endure that treatment from anyone else. In Flanders Tostig was treated well and offered land and honor as a kinsman by marriage to the Count of Flanders. Tostig refused Flanders' hospitality, and then went on to decline an offer of a Danish earldom as well when they had visited Svend, the King of Denmark. Either of those posts would have given wealth and honor enough to settle most men. But not Tostig Godwinsson. In Denmark, as in Flanders, Tostig was offered honor, but not support for an expedition against Harold of England. Tostig had grown more bitter during their stay at his kinsman's court in Normandy. Here in Rouen, Duke William, although friendly enough, seemed more distracted by his own business than responsive to Tostig's interests.

"No," Tostig continued, "I will tell you, as one who knows Harold well, the man is not to be trusted. He would not even recall me now that he has taken the crown for himself! I will have to fight for my rights! And that I will do, with or without Duke William's aid."

Aldbald knew this was coming, but still it shocked him. That Tostig would think first of fighting instead of working more diplomatically with his brother Harold was a shame. Still, he knew that Harold was level-headed, and so reconciliation was possible. Aldbald recalled his own promise to the Queen. Edith might be the much needed buffer between the two brothers.

Tostig caught Aldbald's look of fear and mistook it for fear for his master. "Do not fear for me, young Aldbald. The people of England do love me still, and I will return triumphantly as the day I and my father returned only a few short years ago! Then let Harold beware! I told him once that I would never put up with exile again. He thinks he is laughing in my face now; but I will laugh last. You can count on that!"

Tostig suddenly became thoughtful, his anger draining away for the moment. He walked over to the window overlooking the castle's north wall. The sun was low in the west, and Tostig thought of his home in Northumberland. He began to speak, but this time it was not really to Aldbald, but more to himself, and the breeze blowing from England.

"All I had wanted was to be in control north of the Thames. With Mercia in my hands, I could have been Lord of the Danelaw." Again Tostig's anger flared up, as with a campfire stoked by a gentle breeze. He whirled around to face his servant.

"Damn it! Harold and I could have ruled England together! But no! He had to have it all for himself. Just like it has always been, even as children. For too many years I have stood by as Harold carried the Dragon Banner of Wessex for Edward, when it should have been me. Not content with that, Harold foments rebellion within the ranks of my own Northumbrian thanes, and backs the House of Leofric over his own blood ties. And, somehow he even got Edward to side against me! Well, I will not be Harold's alderman!"

Tostig stepped close and hovered over Aldbald. "Sure, the Witan chose Harold; but I will guarantee there were only Harold's supporters present! He made sure of that by packing me off to Flanders! Damn Harold, anyway! He is no better than the thanes that deserted the great Bryhtnoth at the Battle of Maldon, leaving their war leader to fend for himself before his enemies. Harold knows nothing of courage, honor and loyalty." Tostig suddenly became contemplative, then more angry than ever.

"My God, he may be worse than I have suspected. He may have killed Edward himself in order to take the throne before I could return!"

Tostig chose that moment to produce a sinister laugh, so out of place with the mood of the conversation that Aldbald was even more frightened. "Ah, but even as the unlucky Bryhtnoth then died for lack of supporters, I will be triumphant!"

Aldbald was still in shocked silence when Tostig kicked his servant in the shin. "Did you not have anything to do? Damn it, lad, get on with your duties. I cannot attend to my future and take care of mundane matters like the laying out of my dinner clothing as well. I must go and talk with Duke William one last time. Before this week is out, with William or not, I sail for England!"

*   *   *   *

The dinner table of the Duke of Normandy was set as usual, with all manner of fish and game set among fine linens and silver servingware. There were honeyed apples for dessert and mulled wine to wash it all down. The prize pheasant served to the Duke himself lay almost untouched on William's plate. The Duke sat surrounded by some of his closest companions, the others in quiet, yet animated conversation since the dinner began. William himself was quiet as he watched his companions. His chin jutted out in front of him as he sat with arms crossed over his chest and eyes mere slits.

Roger of Beaumont picked up the courier's letter, glanced at it again, then threw it back down with a shrug. "William, what does it matter?"

Walter Gifford finished the thought. "Yes, I understand that Harold may have spoken with you about the possibility of marriage with your daughter; but what matter that Harold will not now accept a betrothal with young Agatha? Is that not a minor grievance? The man swore upon the bones of our holiest Norman saint that he would back your claims to the English throne. Then just as easily he takes the crown himself! Surely you do not worry simply about your daughter's plans for marriage!"

The Duke's steward answered for William. "Roger, Walter, all of you, listen," William FitzOsbern began. "Of course Harold has perjured himself, and upon the holy relics of Normandy. Yes, of course he should have honored his oath to William. But think on it: Without William there to uphold his claims, how could any of us expect Harold of Wessex to do anything but what he has done. Perhaps if Edward had died in a more congenial time of year, Duke William might have been able to make the journey to London and events would have been different. Alas, the Lord God would not have it that way. The main problem now is for William to save face. Agatha's marriage to England would have offered a tie that William could use."

The Duke looked across from one familiar face to another. "FitzOsbern is correct. My daughter's marriage to Harold would have bought us some time; given me a chance to consolidate my strength in England. As it is, I have no such strength, and Harold does know this. The man is a worthy adversary. Unfortunately for me, I have a channel of water to cross to challenge him. Harold does know that, too. Nevertheless, no body of water will keep me from my rightful place in England! If it comes to that, who of you will stand with me?"

William did not look at his seneschal; he had already discussed the matters with FitzOsbern, knew the man was with him no matter what. The Duke's brother Odo, Bishop of Bayeux, was the first to affirm his support.

"You know that I stand beside you, and I will speak for your other half-brother who is not with us now. Robert of Mortain will support whatever you choose to do."

William quirked his lip at his brother, turned to Beaumont. "Roger?"

"I am with you, my lord."

"Good. And what of Montfort?"

Hugh of Montfort simply nodded.

"Montgomery?"

"Whatever you feel is necessary is what I believe needs to be done, my lord."

"I am with you as well." Walter Gifford punctuated his affirmation with a fist on the table.

Duke William hunched his shoulders and sat back, pushing his chin out once again in what on a child would have looked like a pout. "Now that I have your unconditional pledges of support, I will tell you honestly that I do not know exactly what will be my next course of action."

The Duke shrugged as Gifford, Beaumont and Montgomery exchanged surprised looks. "Do not be alarmed. I assure you I will do something! There are other pawns that can be played in this game of chess with Harold of England."

"Godgifu, the wife of Eustace of Boulogne, and the sister to King Edward of England." Hugh of Montfort stated the obvious.

"Exactly." William nodded. "I do not need to remind you that less than two years ago Harold of England was our guest in Brittany. When I had my hands on Harold, I endeavored to impress upon him the strength of Normandy. I believe I succeeded in that. I thought that the threat of war with me would keep him to his oath. Barring that, the relics were meant to clinch the pledge, making Harold realize that a break of the oath would not just be a lie to me, but one to God as well."

"However," William went on, "at that time, our young friend Hugh of Avranches did have reason to suspect that Harold was up to some late night charade as a monk. It is most probable that he was even then working for a closer tie with our Count of Boulogne. That might explain Harold's reluctance to support my claim."

Gifford shook his head in confusion. "Yes, of course. We do know that. But what of Boulogne?"

"It seems very possible that Eustace of Boulogne may have offered Harold more than just threats and concealed holy relics." Montfort spoke in answer to Gifford, but he was looking at Duke William. FitzOsbern nodded.

William continued. "Yes. Eustace has a tie to England through his marriage to the sister of Edward. Harold has no direct connection to the crown except perhaps his popular support. It may very well be that Harold and Eustace worked out some plan to share the crown. I had thought that Harold might support Aethelred's line in Edgar, but obviously he chose to take control himself. I fear I may have underestimated this Englishman. I do regret, now, that young Edgar's father Aedward died so suddenly upon his return from exile in Hungary. I do believe that our friend Harold would not then have been in as strong a position. Nevertheless, I must take a bit of time to decide just how and when I shall push Eustace, and what my next letter to Harold will contain. I will not roll my dice until I know the odds of my winning the throw."

"You can bet we will put some pressure on Boulogne!" Gifford hit his fist to the table again.

William FitzOsbern reached over and grabbed Gifford's fist. "We will bind Eustace to our cause in some way, or he will be…taken care of. For, as with everyone, Boulogne is either with the Duke or against him. There is no middle ground. The same goes for Harold of Wessex. If the next step is to attack England, Duke William will expect you all to be beside him."

In all the discussion, the exact logistics of bringing the Norman army into a position to threaten Harold had slipped by them all. Montgomery looked from FitzOsbern to Bishop Odo, and back to William. "You do not mean—"

"Impossible!" Beaumont grabbed William's hand still holding Gifford's wrist.

Hugh of Montfort was the calmest. "I guess it is the only way."

William started to speak, but then let FitzOsbern clarify his intent. "Duke William has already begun to assemble the boats necessary, take stock of what we will need for the voyage. The lords of our neighboring realms will be convinced of his ability to see this adventure through. We will get them all to offer men and have them send money and supplies to build boats for the expedition."

"But what about men like Conan in Brittany?" Hugh of Montfort spoke, the others were still dumb-struck. "He would never sit idly by with the Duke of Normandy gone from the continent."

Duke William smiled then. "If any of our neighbors are disgruntled, I will see that they are—how did Osbern put it?—taken care of. What I foresee will be a great undertaking, but I assure you—"

Before the Duke could continue, the conversation was interrupted. Tostig of England had come from across the room, one hand carrying a goblet, to suddenly stand before them. The Englishman took a sip of the strongly spiced beverage, but could not stomach any more of it. He had already drunk to excess, chose now to be offended by the wine. He threw the goblet to the floor. This night the son of Godwin was not going to be ignored.

"Duke William! I want an answer tonight!" Tostig screamed in English. "Will you join me against England. I would take back what is rightfully mine."

The Duke's face was indecipherable, even had Tostig tried to read it. But he did not, nor did he attempt to read the mood of the group or he might have stayed away for the time being. But that was not Tostig's way. FitzOsbern and the others said nothing, merely gaped at the rude interruption to their important conversation.

After a moment, William sighed. "And what," the Duke said in Norman-French, "is rightfully yours, Tostig Godwinsson?"

Tostig hesitated a moment with the sound of the foreign tongue, and it looked to those around him as if he had forgotten what it was that was rightfully his. Regaining his composure, Tostig blurted out, "England!"

Tostig pointed his nose at the north wall of the hall. "Harold has taken England from me, and I will not let him have his way." Although learning languages did not come easily to the man, Tostig spoke the Duke's language well enough. As with the other lords in the English court, Tostig had learned to converse in the languages of most of the peoples around the North Sea.

"Oh? And what will you do?" William was amused, winked at his seneschal as if the Englishman would have some better plan than they would come up with for the Duke himself. There was a light in the Duke's eyes. He could see their guest had had too much to drink, was playing with the man.

"I will tell you what I will do! I will return to England. With or without the help of anyone. Damn it, I will go back, even if it be with only my servant who smells of the tannery!"

William stood up so quickly, neither Tostig nor the Normans expected it. The Duke met the Englishman with a cold stare, all mirth gone from his face.

"Do you have a problem with tanners?"

"Well, no—" Even through the mulled wine, Tostig knew enough to back up a step; but William followed, keeping their faces only a foot's length apart.

"Do you find people of the tannery to be offensive?"

"Well, I only meant—"

William grabbed the shirt near Tostig's throat. "What did you mean?"

When Tostig only swallowed hard, William continued. "I think I do know what you meant. Where is your servant from the tannery?"

Tostig was confused, knew not what it was that put the Duke on edge. "He…he sits over there, on the other side of the room."

William let go of Tostig with a shove. "Take me to him, I will see that you apologize."

"I will most definitely not!" Without the Duke looming over him, some of Tostig's bravado returned. "What is this all about, William? Damn it! If you will not help me, I will be damned if I will let you humiliate me!" Tostig turned to go. Odo of Bayeux was up at once and holding the Englishman. Tostig shot the Bishop a look of pure hatred.

William waved his brother off. "Let the man go." Then, to the Englishman, "Go, Tostig, and be gone from my court as well, if the smell of the tannery so displeases you!"

As Tostig stormed out of the room, William whispered to his brother. "Odo, go ask that man there to join us over here." When FitzOsbern started to protest, William cut him off. "Do not let me think that you too have a problem with sons of the tannery!"

FitzOsbern was impatient. "Do not be simple, William. You know that is not it. I would that we continue our discussion!"

The Duke smiled at his steward, then looked at each one of his friends in turn. "We will talk and plan more later. Let us finish our dinner in peace now."

Aldbald moved stiffly, in fear and trepidation. The man he recognized as the Duke's own brother ushered him over to stand beside Duke William himself. The Duke stood up, his mere presence making Aldbald feel only two feet tall. William gestured to the doorway where Aldbald had seen his lord Tostig exit the room, then pointed at the young Englishman himself. The Duke spoke in his quick, incomprehensible Norman-French tongue, his voice beating the air before Aldbald. Obviously Tostig had in the end offended the Duke of Normandy in some way, and this caused trouble for the other Englishmen associated with the man. Aldbald shrunk before the foreign being, gesticulated an apology, his body immobile but his eyes darting about him as a cornered rabbit seeking an escape. The brother of the Duke coughed to get William's attention, spoke a short comment, and Aldbald was shocked to see the Duke smile.

"Ah, my good brother reminds me that you do not speak the language of Normandy, young man. I will continue in your English." Duke William spoke in a broken English, in simple terms and somewhat haltingly, but Aldbald found he could understand the man well enough. "Please, sit next to me for a moment, and we will talk."

The Duke motioned for Aldbald to fill a vacant chair, and sat back down himself. Aldbald was relieved, yet still quite anxious. What could the Duke possibly want to talk about with him?

"Bring wine!" The Duke called to a servant, reached himself to pour the beverage for Aldbald. "Here my friend, drink."

Aldbald was so taken aback by the Duke's use of the word friend, that it was only after the glass was filled with the mulled wine that Aldbald responded.

"My lord Duke, I fear I do not have a history of drinking to allow myself to hold my own under the influence of the wine. I do thank you for your hospitality, but truly, the one glass of wine I have had already is more than sufficient for me this eve." Aldbald was looking at the glass before him, regretted his words almost as fast as he had spoken them. Which was worse, he thought, to lose one's control due to intoxication, or to lose the favor of the Duke by refusing to drink with the Norman? Again, however, Aldbald was shocked to see the Duke smile at him.

"Good! I like men who desire to keep their wits about themselves at all times." William pushed his own untouched wine glass away. "How about some more to eat?" The Duke slid his practically untouched manchet of food in front of Aldbald.

The Englishman's eyes went wide. "That I will take, and gladly!" Although he had already eaten his fill, the chance to have a taste of the Duke's pheasant was something Aldbald could not let pass by. The food in Normandy was spicy and flavorful, filled with the exotic tastes that his friend Caedwig had warned against. Aldbald was conscious of the others near him at the table, yet the Duke's closest associates seemed to ignore the Englishman as they did the empty bowls on the table. Aldbald relaxed a little more, began to break apart the bird before him. If this were to be his last meal, he thought to himself, at least he would try and enjoy it.

"Thank you, my lord Duke. You are very kind."

"Ah, it is nothing. Just a bird. Little enough to offer a kindred spirit."

Aldbald stopped chewing, tried to speak with the gob still in his mouth. "Kindred, my lord?"

"Indeed! I am given to understand that you hail from the house of a tanner."

Aldbald swallowed his half-chewed mouthful. "Well, yes. My father was a tanner; but I am a tailor by trade, until I did enter the Lord Tostig's service."

"I do not give that for a tailor," the Duke snapped his fingers, "but tanner's blood is nothing to be ashamed of."

"Oh, no sir, I agree. But, why is it that you care for the tanning trade, my lord?"

"Of course, you would not know, now would you. I myself am the son of a tanner's daughter." The Duke sat up straight and stuck out his chin. "My enemies like to play on the story, but it really matters not to me."

Aldbald stopped eating. "My lord, if I may say, I find it very hard to believe that you were once the simple son of a tanner's daughter! You…you are the Duke of Normandy!"

William smiled at the Englishman. "And more than that! Ponthieu, Boulogne, Brittany, Maine, Flanders, Anjou and even France itself are all ruled by lesser men, men who acknowledge me as their superior. It took many years, make no mistake about that. A rough road; but I, a modest son of the tannery, have persevered!"

As William answered the younger man, Aldbald at once remembered just how great was the man to whom he was speaking so casually. The Englishman's mouth dropped open, his stare fixed on the Duke of Normandy. William could not mistake the awe displayed in the other man's expression. The Duke reached over and squeezed Aldbald's shoulder.

"I had a dream, a destiny, if you will. Do you not have any dreams, my English friend?"

The hand on his shoulder loosened Aldbald's tongue. "Dreams, my lord Duke?"

"Yes, dreams! Goals which you feel destined to achieve. Things for which you would give your very life!" William squeezed harder upon Aldbald's shoulder, his words so intense that the Englishman was moved to speak what was in his heart.

"Yes, my lord, I do have dreams. What kind of a man would I be without them? They may seem far simpler to you than any of your own; still I may never achieve them even as you achieve yours. So, to me they are grand enough."

"I am sure." William smiled down upon the lowborn Englishman. "Tell me your desires."

"My lord, I do wish to return to England. It is my home. I do not want to live anywhere else. But, I am the sworn man of Tostig Godwinsson, and while he is in disfavor, I am also kept from my home."

The Duke laughed heartily. "I will tell you something, my friend. If you survive the next year while following that man, yours will be the greater achievement between us!"

"My lord?"

"Your master is looking for trouble, and I would guess he is the type to find it. If I were to give you advice, my friend, I would suggest that you leave Tostig Godwinsson to his own fate, and you take your chances on your own."

"Ah, that is easy to say, my lord. But I have no money, no land, no home. Without the favor of Tostig, I am less than nothing."

"I am not so sure you are much better with Tostig."

"That may be, I do not know. But for now, service to him is the only way I see for myself to get back to England. Besides, I have sworn the man an oath to stay by his side. I cannot believe Lord Tostig will stay out of favor long. Once back in England, perhaps then I will leave his service. I would dearly love to begin a new life in a small village; mayhap take a wife. If only the Lady Godiva was not so far above me." Aldbald was looking down at his plate, did not notice the guarded look wash over William.

"Who was that you mentioned?" the Duke commanded.

Aldbald became fearful, having heard of the Duke of Normandy's anger. "My lord, I did just mention the Lady Godiva of—"

"Godgifu?" Duke William translated the name slowly, watching the foreigner with increasing interest.

"Well, yes, my lord. It means God's gift, and a more appropriate name there could not be for the great Lady of Mercia."

William had stood up as Aldbald answered, towering over the now quite nervous Englishman. The others at the table were at once on their guard. With the last, though, William asked, "Lady of Mercia? Then you do not speak of Edward's sister Godgifu, she who is married to Eustace of Boulogne?"

"Oh, no, sire! I was speaking of the Lady Godiva of Coventry in Mercia…in England."

William relaxed, sat back down in his chair. "Who is this Godiva of Mercia?"

"My lord, you asked me to tell you my dreams…well, they are filled with visions of Lady Godiva. She was the wife of the Earl Leofric of Mercia in England, he who passed into God's lands nigh on eight years ago."

"Oh, you do dream high after all! The wife of an earl for the son of a tanner! No doubt, you hoped then to take the earldom as well. Perhaps it is possible—"

"Now you mock me, my lord. It is true, I do dream. Again I say, would I be a man if I did not? But I have no interest in being an earl, would never even think of it. Anyway, I know that Lord Harold does also have some interest in her. I daresay he would have a better chance of finding her favor than I."

William stood up again. "Harold of Wessex?"

"Oh, I guess I should say King Harold." Aldbald spoke too quickly, forgot about the rumors he had heard passed by the servants in the Duke's house to Tostig, forgot that Duke William was not at all happy with Lord Harold being made King of England. William's face clouded over, and Aldbald feared again the storm that might break. But, Duke William turned away, the young Englishman, whose name the Duke had never bothered to find out, all but forgotten. Aldbald took that moment to escape, leaving the room as quietly as he could.

The Duke's seneschal was up in a moment and standing close to William.

"My lord, what is it?"

William's eyes were glazed over. "God's gift—"

"My lord? What did the Englishman say to you, William?"

William focused then on his friend, grabbed FitzOsbern's shoulder. "It is nothing, Osbern. I have just learned of another pawn in the game, perhaps."

Duke William turned to his brother Odo and his chaplain, William of Poitiers . "Odo, William, we must talk. We must gain the consent of the Church for this campaign against Harold."

The chaplain spoke softly so the others nearby would not hear. "Duke William, his holiness the Pope will need to have reasons that he can defend easily if he is to back you in your claims for England. It may not be so easy—"

The Duke was insistent. "Then think of something! In England my destiny awaits! I know it, and I will not back away from it!"

Odo's brow furrowed. "I will discuss it with our friend Lanfranc, newly made Abbot of Caen. Perhaps if we can act quickly, without any representatives from Harold's court in Rome—"

"Do whatever it takes." William leaned close to his brother. "Use the portents in the stars if you need to."

Odo cocked his head. "What do you mean, William?"

The Duke smiled. "That fiery beacon that appeared in our skies this week! Did it not appear just as we received Harold's refusal of betrothal to my Agatha? First Harold refuses to back my claim to the English throne as he pledged he would. Then he refuses Agatha. It adds insult to injury. What better interpretation than that the Lord above is ashamed of this usurper in England!

"And the beacon still lingers in the skies." William looked around him at his friends, holding each man's gaze for a moment. "It signals my destiny, my friends. Is it not just like a flaming sword? A sword being handed to me from the Lord God above. I will be God's anointed King of England. I will finally be in the Lord's favor forever."

William took a deep breath. "My people already see this as a sign, let us guide them in their interpretation. It is God demanding that I take up the sword against Harold of England!" The Duke turned to his chaplain. "Let the Pope know that!"

William of Poitiers smiled as he bowed his head. "Yes, my lord Duke."

"My lord Duke—" A shout from the doorway to the hall cut off further discussion.

"What is the meaning of all that racket?" The Duke, followed by his seneschal, strode over to the door where a young soldier had just arrived.

The soldier was obviously exhausted from his travels, and the Duke gave him a chance to catch his breath. William FitzOsbern recognized the soldier as one of the Duke's coast watcher messengers.

"You had orders to only come to the Duke should you have news of England," FitzOsbern began.

The Duke laid a hand on his steward's shoulder and looked into the soldier's eyes. "Tell, me, what news from the coast?"

The messenger grinned. "Duke William. I bring you an Englishman. It must be another spy from Harold of Wessex."

The Duke jumped back with a laugh. "Good! This one we will not lock away in our dungeons! Hold the Englishman without, I will address him in a moment."

William turned to his steward. "Osbern, we will send this man back to Harold with my next message. Harold need not send any more spies to Normandy, I will show him my full strength in person soon!"

*   *   *   *

After exiting the Duke's hall, Aldbald sat on the ground and gazed at the strange star in the sky. It was clear to him from the actions of the Normans who saw it that it was not a normal sight in the night skies over

Rouen. The stars were not much different here than those he knew in England, so he guessed that his people across the Channel could see the inexplicable sight as well. He wondered if they had any better idea what it might mean than did he himself. As Aldbald sat, his attention was drawn to a small group of soldiers who arrived on horseback, with a man on foot led by a rope behind them. Almost more surprising to him than his first sight of the peculiar star was his sudden realization that he actually knew the man standing by the Normans.

One of the soldiers dismounted and tied the captive's rope to a pole before entering the Duke's hall. The other soldiers walked their mounts over to a nearby water trough where they dismounted as well. The guards were in rapt conversation, their attention on the star in the sky; but the captive could not break away, his hands were bound tightly behind his back. Aldbald stepped up to his countryman and spoke in a hushed whisper. He was not afraid to speak in his own language since most Normans understood him less than he did them, but he wanted to talk as long as possible before the guards might usher him away.

"Are you not in the service of Chester? I have seen you in the Lady Godiva's retinue, have I not?"

Startled to hear his native tongue, Gunthnot looked up at Aldbald. "I am Gunthnot of Mercia. And who are you? As soon as these men recognized I was English, they accosted me and arrested me! How is it that you are not manhandled as I have been?"

"I am in the party with Lord Tostig. Have you come here in King Harold's name to recall the King's brother? I told my Lord Tostig that Lord Harold would send someone soon enough!"

"Indeed I am not; but I am interested in the news! I came to Duke William's lands seeking passage back to England for my mistress." Despite the situation, Gunthnot was intrigued. "It seems as if the rumors we have heard in Brittany are true, then. Harold is King in England, and his brother Tostig banished from the realm?"

"Yes, I am pleased to say the first is true; and the second is true as well, although that is less pleasing for me to acknowledge. If I was not in the service of Lord Tostig, I would not now be in exile as well. It is difficult, but I cannot believe it will be for much longer."

"And who is Earl of Northumbria?"

"Young Morcar, I am told, brother to Earl Edwin in Mercia."

"Ha! Then all the rumors are substantiated! My lady will be so happy to hear the news!" The soldier suddenly remembered his predicament as his hands pulled at the bonds behind his back. He glowered at the Norman soldiers.

Aldbald caught his breath. "Your lady is here in Normandy as well?"

"No. She is in Brittany. Tell me, my man, will you take the information to my lady at Dinan in Brittany if I am imprisoned or put to death?"

"I would like nothing more than to do that," Aldbald sighed, "but my Lord Tostig might not let me make the trip."

"Then my mission is lost."

"No, my friend. Perhaps not. I have only been in Normandy a short while, but long enough to know that the Duke does not waste his time in anything that he does. If you were to be imprisoned or, heaven forbid, put to death, I truly think you would not be standing here talking with me."

Gunthnot shrugged. "You are an optimist, my friend?"

Aldbald looked down. "I used to be." He brought his eyes back to meet the prisoner's. "Now I just speak the truth. I do not think the Duke is one to waste his time."

Gunthnot tried to smile. "Then, I will hope for the best."

Aldbald looked down again and shuffled his feet. "Would that I could go to your lady." Aldbald glanced back up and fixed the other man with his gaze. "Perhaps I could write another letter for her, have you deliver it for me should you be set free to return to Lady Godiva." Aldbald reached to grasp Gunthnot's shoulder. "Would you do that for me?"

"Another letter? Have you written others to her? Who are you anyway?"

"I am Aldbald of Coventry. The Lady Godiva may not remember me at all," Aldbald shrugged. "Nevertheless, if I am fated to follow Lord Tostig to his ruin, as the Duke of Normandy has declared, then I would want one last time to write of my love for the Lady."

"Your love? For the Lady Godiva?"

"Please," Aldbald blushed, "I do know it sounds strange, coming from one such as me. Even so, it is true. I have sent her letters of love for quite some time now—"

"Those letters she reads over and over have been from you?"

"For quite some time I have written, but I have been unable to talk with Lady Godiva in person. I tried, once. Perhaps I may never have another chance—" What the other man had said finally struck Aldbald. "Did you say the lady reads my notes over and over?"

Gunthnot saw Duke William come out of the hall and approach the two Englishmen. He pulled at his restraints one more time to no avail. "Your chance to write a note for me to deliver is passed, my friend. Aldbald of England, it looks like you were right about one thing at least. The Duke does appear to have something in mind for me or he would not be on his way over here."

Aldbald glanced over his shoulder and sighed. "Good luck, Gunthnot."

"I am not sure luck has much to do with it."

"Perhaps not." Aldbald leaned close to the other man. "But know this: I have spoken with Duke William myself, and he seems not such a bad fellow. Perhaps it is not luck that has put you in the Duke's hands and me in the hands of Lord Tostig; however, I do believe I might change places with you if given the chance!"

Entry IV

▼

Through which we learn that the English countryfolk are afraid

Harold of Wessex was not used to having a king's retinue follow him everywhere. As Under-king to Edward, he had traveled a lot, and often with many beside him, but always because he had need of every man with him. He was not used to, perhaps could never get used to, the clergy and the gentry following him about simply because he was the King. Harold's own tension slipped through to those of his retinue, a tension heightened by what had become an all too common sight along the old Roman road between London and Gloucester. Here, just outside of Oxford, an old man was taking some time away from preparing his land for the first planting to herd his team of two oxen as the tired beasts labored to haul a huge tree trunk through the open field. The wood was not to be used for building, nor for fencing. It was not to be cut up and used to feed a fire nor to build a boat. The scene might have been slightly different in each case along the Icknield Way, but the result was the same: An inordinate number of half-trees each lying three furlongs from their respective places of origin. Harold knew that was one more reason why the people tried to stay close to him. Perhaps the Lord God would protect those near to the anointed King of England.

Harold, the King of England and still Earl of Wessex, thought it all absurd. He kicked his mount into a trot, leaving all but his closest companions in the distance behind. When he was a good distance from the rest, Harold slowed his pony. Robert FitzWimark and Wulfstan, the Bishop of Worcester, cantered their ponies alongside Harold's to match the King's pace.

"Rob, they follow me like blind puppies seeking the security of their bitch. And the people of the countryside…if they are going to take Edward's vision literally, why have they forgotten that he did say it would be a year after his death and a day before England would need to fear God's wrath!"

Robert FitzWimark chuckled. "Harold, you know that people do hear what they want to hear. They see what they want to see. And, they believe what they want to believe! No matter how well off the people are, they will always seek a reason for what woes they have, something outside of their own abilities to avoid. It offers them security. Still, you cannot expect them to act any different, not after the Easter reveling was dampened by the appearance of that fiery flare in the night sky."

Harold sighed. "If the weather had just been cloudy all week, then no one would be worrying right now! And better for England had it been that way."

FitzWimark's laughter became forced, broke off as Wulfstan spoke. "My lord, surely it must be that God was sending us a sign. You cannot ignore that, can you?"

"I have told you, my friend, this hairy star is not unknown to learned men. I have spoken with many of my friends at Waltham Abbey. Even you should know this, Wulfstan. They cited numerous examples of recorded sightings of a similar celestial display in the past. There was no evidence that any of the previous records related the appearance with the Wrath of

God. In fact, just the opposite seems to be the case in the histories. Why should I believe this was any different?"

The Bishop of Worcester entreated his friend the King. "Harold, that is indeed true, but then it may also be the Almighty's way of sending a sign. It may not bode ill for England, but it certainly might mean more than you make it out to."

"Now you are sounding like Edward, my friend."

"I speak not just for the simple people, I do confess. It seems to me the miraculous message may need heeding." Wulfstan was loath to broach the subject, but it needed to be addressed. "Harold, what of the warnings from the Duke of Normandy?"

"What of them?"

Wulfstan was taken aback by the King's argumentative tone. This was not like Harold, he thought. Robert FitzWimark agreed with the Bishop, was thinking the same thoughts. "I believe Wulfstan is referring to the timing of the light in the sky. Did not the beacon appear just after you sent Duke William your rebuttal? It does seem like quite a coincidence."

FitzWimark waved his hand. "The Witan chose you for England's king, Harold, and the Duke of Normandy be damned. But, upon receiving William's message regarding a plight troth with his daughter…well, if William would have settled for that, would not such a betrothal have given us an alliance with Normandy that you could have used to your advantage?"

Harold acted tired. "And what would you have had me do different? Should I have offered William an apology? I say no. I never promised to marry Agatha of Normandy.

"Yes, an alliance with Normandy might have been important on one hand. On the other, it would be an alliance that would jeopardize the peace in my own realm." Harold motioned to the Bishop. "After Wulfstan worked so quickly to secure the support I needed in the north through the betrothal to Aldgyth of Mercia, I cannot entertain even the slightest interest in Agatha as a possible wife when she is older than Aldgyth. The supporters of the sons of Aelfgar would know the Duke's daughter would be the first to be of marrying age. It would strain the unity within my own kingdom."

The Bishop was at once defensive. "My lord, I know a merger with the House of Leofric was what you wanted. After the Welsh campaign, young Aldgyth was left without a betrothed. Edwin and Morcar were delighted to offer their younger sister to the King of England. It seemed like the perfect plan. If I had known about the expectations of the Duke of Normandy—"

Harold shrugged. "Indeed. And perhaps if I could have waited to marry the Lady Godiva everyone might well have been satisfied. Duke William would have recognized my need to marry to unite the earldoms of England; and, with little Agatha much too young, he would have had to agree there was no other choice."

Harold sighed. "But, that is no matter now. Once the plight troth with Aldgyth was made, I could not then turn and abandon the new agreement with the House of Leofric's son before even the parchment was dry. Not when the connection with the northern thanes is still so tenuous."

Robert FitzWimark followed the King's thoughts, became very serious. "No, indeed not. But, surely you could have stalled William, feigned interest in his daughter for awhile. After all, Aldgyth of Mercia and Agatha of Normandy are neither ready to be bedded. Time, perhaps could have healed many a wound. Instead you chose to pour salt into the Duke's gaping flesh by outright refusing to consider any betrothal with his daughter."

Harold rode on in silence for a time, then turned to look at each of his friends. "Though I cared not for the idea of beginning my reign with an apology to Duke William, neither did I want to begin with a mistake.

"As you both well know, I have had the coast watched for signs of ships out of Normandy. Our spies at the Duke's court say the man is slow to assemble the necessary ships and men. I do think that the letters from William were just a bluff."

Robert FitzWimark grinned. "Your assessment of Duke William's organization does appear to be true. Whether or not that was an omen in the Easter sky, it certainly does not seem to be a warning about any threat by Duke William of Normandy."

Wulfstan, not quite so confident as the other two, simply shrugged. "If I can help make amends, please do not hesitate to call upon me. I know you will prevail. No other's hands are more capable than yours, Harold."

The King found that to be extremely funny. "If only the rest of England were as easy to convince!"

"Oh, I think they will all forget their worries after a month or so at the most." FitzWimark proclaimed.

Harold laughed. "I only hope it is before every tree in England is cut down!"

As the leading edge of the King's retinue caught up to the three men, Wulfstan asked, "What of William, Harold? I know you have said your spies have reported that his progress is slow. But, it is progress. He does not seem to have given up. Do you think the Normans will invade England and try and set William up as king?"

Robert FitzWimark answered before the King could respond. "Even putting the informants' reports aside, how could the Duke of Normandy expect to bring his mounted warriors across the channel to fight in England? Nor can I see Duke William leaving his precious horses behind to sail to England with an army of foot soldiers. I do not believe he will ever gain enough support in Normandy for such a foolhardy expedition!"

Harold became deathly serious. "In truth, Wulfstan, my friend, I do not know. It would be a drastic measure, as our friend Robert says, but one I would not put beyond William's desires. If I learned nothing else from my time in Normandy two years ago, I did learn that the Duke is ambitious and greatly interested in increasing his status. In Normandy he can never hope to be anything more than what he has already attained. He is not just interested in increasing his power and wealth, but it is almost as if he hoped to be accepted by God himself. Being the anointed King of England would perhaps fulfill all his ambitions."

Wulfstan nodded, but FitzWimark shook his head. "I still say it sounds to me like a foolhardy venture, especially trying to gain God's grace through a crown bought with blood."

"The other thing I did take out of Normandy was the impression that Duke William is no fool. He will not try anything he does not believe he can win. That, my friends, is our greatest weapon against him. No, it does not appear that William will be able to muster enough forces, or build enough boats to launch an attack on England. Even so, I have the ships of the Cinque Ports assembling at the Isle of Wight. I have selected some men of the fyrd to take turns watching the southern coast. Should William be sighted, our coast watchers will relay the news to me at Bosham and we will board the boats and travel swiftly along the coast to meet the invasion force wherever it may have landed, from the Isle of Wight to Dover. The Duke's invading army will need time to coordinate their supply lines and organize their defenses. That will give us plenty of time to rally the fyrd."

"Of course, Harold, and a good plan it is." Wulfstan was always playing devil's advocate, but today he truly was concerned for the worst. "Yet, what if William sails before you have assembled your housecarls?"

"If William makes a move soon, he cannot possibly have too great an army, unless he is adept at magic! My spies have been quite clear in letting me know the man's current strength. If the Duke makes an attack soon, the housecarls of Wessex and Kent—"

"And those of the King as well!" FitzWimark chimed in with a smile.

"Yes, and also those I have as the King…those trained soldiers will be more than enough to meet the Duke should he act out of character and attack before he is prepared. Let me say again, however, that I believe William will attempt nothing that he does not believe he can surely win."

Robert FitzWimark was about to add his agreement, was silenced by a commotion in the crowd behind them. The soldiers and courtiers in Harold's retinue parted, grudgingly making way for a courier to the King. The man was dirt-smeared, his horse well lathered after a long, fast ride.

"My lord King Harold! I bring news from the coast!"

Harold, FitzWimark and Bishop Wulfstan reigned in their ponies. The three men looked from one to the other, could hardly believe that their conversation had been so on the mark with the events about to unfold. Wulfstan shot a look of warning to FitzWimark. The cleric had felt there was something poised and ready to break. FitzWimark looked incredulous, could say nothing. Harold jumped off his horse and grabbed the bridle of the courier's mount, held the tired animal steady as the man himself caught his breath.

"Tell me, man, where did they land?" Harold's eyes unwavering, his question the obvious one as he looked at the soldier. Even so, the courier hesitated.

"Then you already know of the raid, King Harold? I did not realize you had received the word. I will tell you, I had wanted to ride much earlier to warn you myself, but we decided to wait and give them a chance to go away."

Harold released the pony and pulled the man off the beast. "I did not need to hear the news to know that my southern coast has been on guard. We all have been expecting an attack! Go away? My God, why did you think that the Duke of Normandy would go away after crossing the channel to attack England? That is why you are part of the chain of messengers, lad. All I need is to know where the Normans have landed, and we will then make our move."

The young soldier was shaken, more by his King's words than the hard ride he just completed. "My lord, forgive me; but it is not the Normans. It is your brother Tostig!"

"Tostig?!"

"Yes, my lord! He landed with a small force of men-at-arms at the Isle of Wight only four days ago."

"Tell me, what happened? Four days ago! Why did I not hear of this sooner? Where is Tostig now? Was there bloodshed?"

"My lord, Tostig had with him some foreigners, men of Flanders it seems. They expected us all to open up our homes to him in welcome. Some of your household in Bosham thought you had called your lord brother back to England. Others felt he had come back uninvited. Yet none wanted to deal with him, so rude he was to them all. The people of Chichester paid him off with fresh food stuffs and some gold trinkets, hoping he would go away."

"Like yielding the Danegeld to raiding Norsemen of old," the bishop whispered as he and FitzWimark dismounted.

Harold ignored the others beginning to crowd around him. He was a controlled volcano. "And did he go away?" The King of England asked the question, but knew well the flavor of the answer he would get. If Tostig had left for good, they would not now be having this conversation.

"Yes, King Harold. But then he called in at Pevensey, then too at Bulverhythe harbor near Hastings. Each time met the same response from your people. My lord, we knew not what to do, how to handle your brother. You left orders to watch for an attack by Duke William of Normandy, not the arrival of Tostig Godwinsson! When it became obvious to me that Tostig was not going back to Flanders, I rode straight to tell you."

Robert FitzWimark licked his forefinger, put his hand out into the air. "Harold, the wind is southerly. Your brother may not be able to get away from the coast. Perhaps he is trying to get back to Flanders."

Harold directed his gaze to the south, felt the breeze on his face. "Perhaps. He seems to be crawling along the coast, heading east. Perhaps he will take the first favorable wind and sail back to Flemish soil. But I will not stand idly by knowing he is raiding Sussex and Kent. Lucky it is there has been no bloodshed yet, but I will not abide my people of the English countryside having to pay him off. Tostig deserves nothing from England! We will ride east at once to head him off at Sandwich. If he rounds the Straights of Dover, contrary winds or no, he will have to face the wrath of his brother the King of England!"

Entry V

▼

In which Tostig burns his boats

A sharp blow to his thigh jarred Aldbald out of his sleep. Tostig stood over him. "Get up, you fool. Assist me."

Aldbald could hear the drunken singing of the Flemish men in the camp on the hill overlooking the River Humber in northern England. The foreigners were reveling in the food and ale they had stolen, and it was clear that the lord Tostig was inebriated as well. Although it was just another expedition to forage for food, Aldbald had not wanted to take part in the latest raid, this time on the homes of the outlying villeins of Kingston, and he had opted to stay with the boats. Curled in a blanket in the bottom of one of the vessels, he had been dreaming of his father's tannery in Coventry. But now, Aldbald awoke to the realization he was still a fugitive, with no land and no where to go. If Tostig could win back some place for himself in England, then Aldbald would be free to move on as well without the taint of being associated with an exile. Right now, he would just appreciate it if Tostig would let him get one night's uninterrupted sleep.

"I said get up!" Tostig kicked his servant again. "Help me move these boats closer together." Tostig's face had a reddish glow from the firebrand he held, his pointed nose casting a sharp shadow across his face.

Aldbald squinted into the torchlight. "But my lord, are they not fine where they are?"

"Damn you! I said help me, and I do not expect you to question anything. If I want the boats dragged by hand to London, you will do it!" Tostig glared at his servant, and Aldbald stood up.

"Very well, sire," the cottar said, then hesitated. Aldbald had long ago stopped trying to understand his master; but tonight he had been dreaming of Mercia. "Perhaps, sir, it could wait until the light of day?"

"No, damn you! Move the boats together. I want it done now!"

Aldbald paused, looking at the bulk of the ship in which he had been sleeping. "Perhaps some of your companions could help, sir. More hands would make the job easier."

"Damn your lazy hide! I will hold the torch, and you will move these boats. Now!"

Aldbald knew Tostig was especially irritable when drunk. At least once the boats were moved, Aldbald thought, his master would find something else to do and Aldbald could go back to a peaceful sleep.

After leaving Duke William's court, Tostig brought his small band of followers to land on the southern coast of England. Aldbald had overheard Tostig tell his followers that he would be welcomed by the people of England, as the man told a glorious tale of his father's triumphant return from exile many years ago. Even if he had expected some support in his own earldom, the Wessex Coast was his brother Harold's domain. Of course, the men of Flanders were not familiar with English geography nor English politics. On their first landing, the Flemish freebooters went ashore with Tostig to find the English people uninterested, their reception of the Englishman and his band of pirates cold. Tostig took that as quite an insult, and more proof that his brother, Harold, had set the people of

England against him. The landing party returned to their boats, with most of the men wanting to head back to Flanders.

It had not been Tostig's will, but the wind that had prevailed, holding in a steady breeze from the south that kept their small band of ships pinned against the English coast. Tostig met more resistance to his pleas for support from the English, and finally gave in to let his men of Flanders plunder the towns they visited. They merely foraged for food, primarily, but it gave Tostig some pleasure to know he was striking a blow against his brother. As they rounded the strait at Dover, Tostig tried to convince his followers that he would find much greater support in his own earldom in Northumberland. The man could talk all he wanted about the plots of his brother Harold, but Aldbald knew too well the sentiment of the people north of the Humber. They had revolted against Tostig, and they would be in no position to welcome him back. Again, however, it was more the wind direction than Tostig's arguments which set the Flemish on their path

Now the boats were beached on the shore of the great River Humber, and Tostig wanted Aldbald to move them. The boats were not real large, but they were still heavy, made of rough-hewn logs strong enough to carry heavy cargo. He grumbled under his breath with each step, but the job was completed in short order. There were only six vessels, and three of the ships had already been close together. In the torchlight, Aldbald dragged the remaining three nearby to form a close group.

"Good. Now, take yourself over to camp and get yourself something to drink."

Aldbald leaned against the last boat in the line. "Thank you, I am not thirsty, my lord."

"Then find something to eat."

"I would rather not. I am not hungry either."

"Then do not eat or drink; but get yourself away from me!" Tostig grabbed Aldbald by his shoulder and shoved him into the darkness. "I want to be alone."

Aldbald stepped back into the torchlight. "I was watching the boats, my lord."

"I will watch them now! Get away from me you insolent wretch!"

"Yes my lord." Aldbald turned his back on Tostig, purposely failing to bow to the man. He had been sleeping soundly, wrapped in a blanket and down in the ship out of the chill night breeze. Now he had no blanket, and nothing to block the wind. There was no way he could sleep by the camp fire where the others were still carrying on in their loud, rowdy manner.

Aldbald skirted the camp, walking on the fringe of the firelight. The men of Flanders were not bad men over all; but the Mercian had little more in common with them than he did with the Englishman Bufread Bloodyaxe who was among them. Yet, he never did have much in common with most of the men around him, Englishmen or not.

One day, he thought to himself, he would find the right woman, and they would go off and live in peace deep in the woods alone; free of all the cares of the world. A strong woman he would find, yet a gentle woman. A woman who believed as he did, who had his sense of morality. Aldbald thought fleetingly of the Lady Godiva. He paused, scuffed his boot in the sand as he thought of the notes he had written to the woman. If he could find a woman like that.

It was a nice dream, however unrealistic. Aldbald had no material goods to offer a woman, and not even the prospect of gaining anything of worth in the near future. They were all fugitives from King Harold and, while the foreigners had a home back in Flanders, Aldbald himself had nothing. For so long he had wanted to get away from the simple life of a cottar. Seeing many different lands could have been interesting. Instead, Aldbald decided he could understand a little Tostig's refusal of the lands and titles he was offered in Flanders and Denmark. Aldbald missed England, and never more so than when he was an exile, knowing he was not welcome back home.

The cottar rubbed his eyes, lubricated by slight tears. Aldbald circled the camp twice, then looked back to where the boats were beached, now in a tight group after his labors. He could still see the point of light that was Tostig's torch by the river bank to the southeast. Aldbald headed toward the river himself, but at a good distance further inland from where his master sat with the boats.

The brightness of his master's torchlight downstream surprised Aldbald, and the cottar realized he must have wandered a bit closer to Tostig than he had planned. A vision of the Queen's worried look for her brother came to the man, and Aldbald decided to sneak a look at what Tostig was up to so late at night without his companions about him. Walking along the bank of the river, the firelight ahead grew stronger; but Aldbald realized he had not been that close at all. It was the fire that was a lot greater than it should have been for a mere torch. Stepping up his pace into a jog, Aldbald crested a small hill to find a bonfire on the bank of the river.

The boats were on fire. Tostig, in his intoxication, must have dropped his torch into one of the boats. The man might be in danger himself. Aldbald let out an uncontrollable yell, and began to run. If he could get there in time, he could perhaps save the rest of the boats by moving them away from the burning vessel.

The running man stopped short of the scene. Every boat was on fire, and Tostig was standing off to the side, his form cast in a bright glow from the conflagration. From his position, Aldbald could not see the wide grin on his master's face; however, he could tell the man must have deliberately set the boats ablaze. They were too far gone for Aldbald to do anything to save any one of them, even if he could have gotten his immobile feet to work.

A shout from the Flemish camp let Aldbald know that the bonfire had been sighted by someone else. Two men stumbled along the foot path to the river bank, leaning on each other for support. He recognized Ranulf and Jurgane. Aldbald, finally finding his feet, began to walk toward Tostig as well.

"Tostig, my friend!" Ranulf stammered in English. Although he spoke the language well enough, tonight his speach was slurred by ale. "Why are you being so unsociable? You left our campfire to come and build your own! Is Flemish company so repelling to you this night?" The two men from camp stopped a few feet from Tostig. Jurgane leaned upon Ranulf who had his legs in a wide stance for stability. Jurgane pointed to the blaze by the river, and tried to speak. Only a mumble came out.

Ranulf continued, "I must admit, your fire is better than ours! Where did you find the wood? We were having a devil of a time finding pieces large enough to keep the fire strong. Of course, my sight has been a bit blurry this evening. I hope you do not mind if we share yours now that we have found you. There is quite a chill in the air, and your fire down here seems so much warmer than up on that windy hillside." Ranulf moved toward Tostig, and Jurgane fell over. Tostig seemed not to have noticed he was no longer alone until Ranulf clapped him on the back.

"Tostig, my friend, do you also have some ale here you did not wish to share? You would not be holding out on your friends, now would you?"

Jurgane crawled over to Ranulf, pulling himself up by holding onto the other man's leg. He pointed at the fire again, trying desperately to speak something intelligible. The words were slurred beyond recognition, but the man's tone was more insistent and the level of his voice was almost a scream.

Ranulf grabbed his friend's ale-stained tunic and pulled as the man stood up. "What is it, Jurgane? Do you see a demon in the fire?"

Aldbald saw the mad smile on Tostig's face as the man watched the blaze. He could not stay quiet. "I think, Sir Ranulf, that the good Jurgane does realize the glorious blaze there is at the expense of our sea vessels!" Ranulf's eyes widened, and he peered through the flames to find their source.

"I think the Lord Tostig could tell us what this means," Aldbald finished.

Ranulf tore his gaze away from the fire, tried to focus on Aldbald, then turned his questioning look to Tostig. "The ale has fogged my vision, friend. Does this man in the shadows speak the truth? Surely our boats are not ablaze?!"

When Tostig did not answer, Ranulf stepped toward the fire, and Jurgane fell over again. Ranulf stumbled back to grab a hold of Tostig. "What is the meaning of this? How did this happen? Every boat on fire? How could every boat have caught fire?"

Finally Tostig moved. He grabbed Ranulf's hands to release the other man's grip, then stepped a bit closer to the fire, setting his gaze amidst the burning embers again. "Yes, our boats are on fire."

Ranulf was sobering a little. "But how?!" He grabbed at Tostig again, but the other man stepped clear.

"I have burned them."

Ranulf's mouth dropped open. Jurgane uttered a gurgle and fell unconscious.

Tostig moved his gaze from the fire to his friend. "Over fifty years ago the great Sweyn Forkbeard landed on the English coast. He burned the boats of his great invasion fleet, leaving the Danes with nothing to do but conquer the island. Which they did! Sweyn's son Canute went on to rule England for a quarter of a century!"

Ranulf's surprise turned to shock. After a moment, he found his voice. "I have heard the story. Forkbeard had an army with him! We are but a small band, and we should be back in Flanders where we belong. We cannot challenge the people of England!"

Tostig was looking across the flames and into the night; he spared only a glance for his friend. "I do not want England. I merely want what was unjustly taken from me. The land north of the Humber is mine. It's people are mine. Harold will see by this gesture that I am serious and a man to be reckoned with!"

Ranulf was unmoved. "But Tostig—"

"Trust me, my friend. Harold will see that I have come to stay. My people will welcome me. Within a fortnight we will be feasting in my hall at York!"

Ranulf looked at Tostig; at the ruined boats; over his shoulder at Jurgane unconscious on the ground; past the lying man to his countrymen still singing boisterously by their own little fire; then back at Tostig. "But Tostig—"

"Trust me."

Ranulf found his words. "But, even if this will be so, would it not be good to have our ships in case of emergency? What will you tell our companions? When the light of day cuts through the drunken stupor of this night, they will look for their boats, their one link with their home, and they will demand to know why!"

Tostig finally turned his attention completely from the burning wreckage. He grasped his friend's shoulders and squeezed. "Trust me, Ranulf. Tomorrow we will go north and west to York. Our friends from Flanders will not miss Flemish soil so when they have gotten more of a taste for what England does offer! Trust me!" Tostig slapped Ranulf across the back as he headed past him up the hill to the others at the camp. Ranulf laughed, but stopped as he turned toward the fire again. He forced another laugh, but it came out as a croak.

Aldbald watched as Ranulf followed Tostig away from the river bank, leaving their companion face down in the gravel. He was confidant that the other Flemish men would not find it too easy to laugh this night off.

Entry VI

▼

Where we find Godiva is unable to return to England

"Mayhap you hit upon the truth during your musings the other day, my good Hildreth. The quiet wife of an Englishman, with a comfortable cottage…a calm life might suit me just fine."

"Yes, my lady." Hildreth stood behind her mistress fumbling with their riding bags.

The Lady Godiva did not look at her servant, was looking north over the rough Channel waters. She patted her pony's neck. "If we could just ride home to England!"

Hildreth scowled. No matter how much she wanted to return to her home, riding long distances on the back of a pony was never something Hildreth chose if she could travel any other way. The beasts they had obtained in Dinan were so jumpy with just the sound of the surf, Hildreth shuddered to think what it would be like to ride to England.

"Yes, my lady," she said dutifully.

When Lady Godiva seemed to hesitate, Hildreth spoke. "My lady. Are you sure you want to leave now? Perhaps we should go back to the inn where we have been staying."

"We must leave. If we do not go soon, we will not find passage across the Channel before the winter storms roll in."

"But, my lady, Gunthnot will be back any day now. He will have secured passage for us. If we leave now, we will miss him."

Godiva threw up her arms, whirling around to face her maidservant. "Hildreth! We have gone through this every day for the past three days! I wanted to leave before now, but you convinced me I should await Gunthnot. However, last week I swore that if our friend did not arrive before Sunday, we would leave without him. Today is Monday. We should go."

Hildreth had dropped her eyes, raised them again imploringly. "But, my lady," she began again.

"No, Hildreth." Godiva turned to face the sea again. "We have been safe enough here, but we are doing nothing. I had hoped to find someone to aid my cause. An alliance outside of England might have given me the strength to keep control of Mercia and retain some semblance of family dignity for my grandchildren. I have accomplished nothing; gained nothing but the knowledge that I am not cut out for this kind of life."

Hildreth softened. "Do not be so harsh on yourself, my lady. Men of power seem to be filled only with self-interest. It is why your son Aelfgar never found support in Ireland, and why he got little in the end from Wales. Why should it be any different across the Channel?"

"You are right, Hildreth," Godiva sighed. "In the end, all this running about these past couple years has simply worn me out. I must return to England. It is there that I belong, whatever the circumstances."

"But, my lady, we should wait for Gunthnot, our protector."

Lady Godiva glanced east. "Something must have happened to the man or he would have been back by now." The lady reached to grasp her maidservant's hands. Hildreth looked down again, but Godiva raised her chin with her palm. "Hildreth, my friend." Lady Godiva paused to wipe a tear away from the older woman's cheek. "I must try and travel without escort. I will not force you to accompany me." Lady Godiva reached into one of the bags Hildreth carried. She pulled out a coin purse, looked in to see several gold coins. "Please, stay behind. I will send for you when I can. This money should be enough to keep the innkeeper of Dinan happy until I can get word to you."

Hildreth sniffled and stepped back, her eyes wide with shock. "My lady, I cannot stay with that money."

Lady Godiva sighed. "You know I have more in the other bag."

Godiva was surprised to see the servant's look change from shock to horror. "It is not the money, my lady. I must stay by your side. I must go where you go."

"I will be fine, and you will be safer and happier here until I can send for you."

The maidservant shook her head. "No, my lady."

"Hildreth, please. Let us not argue."

"No!" Hildreth's eyes closed as she continued to shake her head.

Lady Godiva's hand dropped, the coin purse loose in her palm. "Hildreth, do not act like such a child!" When a tear came again to the older woman's cheek, Godiva sighed. She reached over and gave her maidservant a big hug. "Oh, what am I going to do with you, Hildreth?"

Hildreth returned the hug. "Do not ever leave me behind, my lady. Promise me."

Lady Godiva laughed.

Hildreth opened her eyes. Through her watery eyelashes she saw a man riding toward them from the east. She pushed away from Godiva. "My lady!"

Lady Godiva laughed again. "I am sorry, Hildreth. Of course I will promise!"

"No, my lady. Look!" She pointed over Godiva's shoulder to the east road. "It is Gunthnot returned!"

The man rode fast upon a well bred charger. Before the horse was completely stopped, Gunthnot had jumped off, was kneeling at Lady Godiva's feet.

"My lady! I am here finally!"

Godiva smiled. "Indeed I can see you are here. What happened that delayed you my good man?"

Gunthnot stood, glared over his shoulder in the direction he had come. "Duke William captured me."

The women gasped in unison, Hildreth with her hand to her mouth, Lady Godiva reaching toward the soldier. "But why? Did you break some law of Normandy?"

Gunthnot spat. "Because I was English, my lady."

Hildreth breathed sharply again, but Lady Godiva became matter-of-fact. "Then the tales in Brittany are true."

"Yes, Duke William does plan to take a force to England to fight King Harold."

"Harold Godwinsson is king?" Hildreth asked.

"Yes," Gunthnot beamed. "And that is not all." Godiva was looking past the man. Gunthnot waited a moment so that he would have the lady's full attention. "Young Edwin is truly Earl of Mercia, and his brother Morcar Earl of Northumbria! It turns out there is much substance to the stories we have heard, my lady."

Lady Godiva's mouth dropped open, but she could not speak. Hildreth filled the void with a shriek. "Aiya! I knew that everything would work out for your family, my lady."

"Yes," Gunthnot began, " and the man that told me all of this—"

"Almost everything has worked out," Godiva said quickly. "We are still on the continent." The woman reached for Gunthnot's elbow. "Tell me, when can we leave for England? We must help Harold Godwinsson in any way we can."

"I am sorry, my lady." Gunthnot spoke slowly, not wanting to change the jubilant atmosphere after his preceding pronouncements. "There are no ships."

Godiva squeezed the man's arm. "How can there be no ships on the entire coast?"

"Of course, my lady, there are ships." Gunthnot coughed. "What I meant was there are no ships available. The Duke has confiscated all sailing vessels in all the lands that are subject to Normandy; even any materials with which to make a boat! We would have to go far south and east in search of passage. Then, too, it would be a long trip, and not one to be ventured at this time of year."

Lady Godiva released her hold, stepped away from the other two. "Then we are truly stuck here on the continent?"

"I am afraid that is so, my lady. The man in Normandy has a mad plan. He is building a great fleet with which to attack our homeland."

The hurt in Godiva's eyes was so intense, Hildreth stepped close and hugged her shoulders. Gunthnot spoke softly. "I am sorry, my lady."

"The madder the Duke's plan," Godiva's eyes became slits, "the more intense my need to get home...the more impossible you tell me that will be."

Gunthnot bowed his head. "Again, my lady, I am sorry. There are just no ships here in Brittany for us to take to sea. Even the fishermen and ship captains have all been pressed into the service of the Duke!"

Lady Godiva turned to hug Hildreth with one arm, reached to grip Gunthnot with her free hand. "If the ships are in Normandy, then we must go to Normandy. We have money enough to set a high fee for our passage, a fee that even the staunchest supporter of the Duke would find hard to resist. We leave at once."

Hildreth gasped. Gunthnot coughed. Only a moment later each was speaking, but the Lady Godiva had already turned away from her friends.

Entry VII

▼

In which Tostig decides to leave England

Tostig crashed in the door to the small cottage, a chair that had been hastily jammed to hold the door crumpled under his effort. His shoulder took quite a jarring, and Tostig screamed, more in pain than in barbaric zeal; but the effect on those inside the building was the same. A little boy, cowering under the curled arms of a young woman, cried out as he tried in vain to hide himself completely from the man at the door. The woman clutched her child tightly. Her eyes were wide with fear as she watched the intruder, her lip trembled as she tried to speak through restrained tears.

"Please, take what you will; but do not hurt my child! I beg of you!" The boy began to sob, and the woman pressed his head to her bosom.

"I will not hurt your son," Tostig laughed as he went right to the bread on the table, "and I will indeed take what I want!" He tore a large mouthful of the bread loaf with his teeth.

"Have you no meat, woman?" Tostig looked around for the ale-skin he knew would be in the house-room somewhere. Spotting it hanging beside the hearth, he shoved the woman and her child aside as he reached for the brew. The child screamed again, and that made Tostig laugh the stronger, bread crumbs spilling from his mouth.

"No, do not fear me." He took a long draught of the ale. "I am Tostig Godwinsson, the Earl of Northumbria, and I demand the tribute from my subjects that has been kept from me for too many months!"

The young child began to whine. The woman tried to silence her son, but could not. Tostig walked slowly around the one room dwelling, beginning to relish the sound of fear in the air.

"You are afraid of me, are you not?"

The woman spat on the floor. "Gone are the days my family had to worry about Danish raiders. Now it seems it is our own countrymen we must fear!"

A twisted expression of mirth crossed Tostig's face. The man suddenly felt in complete control of the situation.

"I am your Lord Earl. You will pay homage to me as is your place, woman."

With one hand still holding the ale, Tostig drew his sword with his other and raised the weapon to point at the child's head. Tostig motioned toward the other side of the room with the ale-skin. "Let your son stand aside, and I will not harm him."

With trembling hands the woman pushed her child into the corner and turned back to face her tormentor once again. The expression of dread evident in the woman's features caused Tostig's loins to stir. The man dropped the ale-skin and reached for the woman's old cloth that served as her housecoat. She stepped back and Tostig stumbled.

"Damn you," the man swore as he slapped the woman across her face. "I will take the tribute I deserve!" He grasped again for the cloth and tore at the garment. The woman shuddered as the worn clothing shredded, leaving her naked body exposed to the stranger.

Tostig threw his sword down into the floor rushes and himself onto the woman. The woman struggled with more strength than Tostig would have guessed she had; but that only heightened his excitement. He grabbed at her wrists and pinned her arms, spreading her thighs with his knees. The young woman screamed and the child in the corner wailed. Tostig, raising his mantle, laughed a great hearty laugh.

The cottar woman suddenly became quiet, going limp under the pressure of the assault. Tostig hovered over the woman, savoring the moment before he penetrated her. The man glanced around the cottage. Smoke from burning thatch above began to filter down into the room, giving the scene an unearthly appearance. He could barely see the whimpering child through the billowing gray smoke. The boy sat with head between his knees, beginning to cough more than cry. Tostig looked back at the woman that he dominated.

"That is right. Let your Earl take what he does desire. Everything in this land is mine! It is wrong for any Englishman, or woman, to withhold anything from their lord and master!"

"And what have we here?" An accusing voice from the doorway stopped Tostig as he targeted the woman's loins with his own. The man looked over his shoulder to see the figure in the smoke-filled doorway.

Judith? How could his wife be here? And she had caught him in this act! How will he ever explain?! Tostig's mind raced, all his muscles went limp, and the woman beneath him took the opportunity to struggle free, crawling to join her child in the corner. Tostig kept himself from falling over as the woman left his grasp. On hands and knees, he blinked his eyes over and over, trying to focus on the figure in the doorway.

"Judith?"

A gruff voice barked "What is this Judith?" The apparition dissolved, leaving Ranulf of Flanders standing amidst the smoke in the doorframe looking incredulous. "My God, man! Do you not realize this hovel is burning down about you?! Let us get out of here at once!"

Tostig squeezed his eyes shut, and shook his head. Looking about him again, his wife Judith was no where to be seen, only his companion Ranulf was at the door. Tostig did not need to look to know he had lost his erection.

"Damn it!" he cursed under his breath.

The former Earl of Northumbria snatched his sword out of the dirty floor rushes, and stood up to face his friend. "Yes, I am done here." The two men left the burning building without a glance at the young woman who shook with relief.

The village of Beverley was in a shambles. Many house tops smoldered, fences were torn down and livestock ran amuck. A couple of the men of the village who had come out of the nearby fields to try and protect their homes lay wounded in the streets, their blood mingling with the puddles from the rain which had just begun.

Aldbald, not trying to conceal his distaste for the bloody business, met his master in the street with a scowl. He had been atop a hill to the west of the village. Before the rain came and the fog rolled in, Aldbald had found it to be quite clear, and he could see a great distance inland. He spotted a group of men heading toward the east. It could only mean one thing.

"My lord, I have urgent news."

Tostig was irritated. "What is it you fool? Can you not see I am busy here?!"

"There is a great body of men on the move to the west of us," Aldbald pressed. "They look as if they will intercept us here if we do not flee!"

Tostig straightened up. "Ah, my people! They are coming to welcome me home!"

Ranulf looked around at the carnage that was once the sleepy village of Beverley. He was not so hung over from the previous night's revelry, nor so heady now with the smell of blood and smoke to fail to recognize the warning signs. He shook his companion roughly.

"Tostig! Snap out of it, man! If you will just look about you, you will see that things have gotten a little out of hand. Do not delude yourself into thinking that the English will find what we have wrought here to their liking! This force approaching will undoubtedly be set upon vengeance. My Flemish friends and I will not stay around here and offer our heads to their axmen! That will be the only welcome you receive as well, I am sure." Without waiting for the other man, Ranulf went off to collect his companions.

Tostig seemed to see the wreckage of the village for the first time from an Englishman's perspective. "What have I done?" He was speaking to himself, but Aldbald had to answer.

"You have ruined our chances of being accepted as fellow Englishmen and friends of the country."

"How dare you speak to me like that! Damn you anyway!" He struck Aldbald across the face. "I should leave you to the wolves one day!"

Aldbald stood his ground.

"My lord, we will all be sheep at the mercy of the English wolves who will want retribution for this wanton raiding of yours. With no boats, we have no escape."

Tostig was about to hit Aldbald again when those words sunk in. "No escape—" Tostig was like a statue, hand still poised to strike. He completed the blow after a moment. "Damn you. Why did you not save at least one of the boats for your master?!"

Aldbald glowered all the more at that, but his master did not notice. Tostig turned at once, hurrying to catch up with the fleeing Flemish.

"Ranulf!" Tostig caught up with the others. "Ranulf, we must make it to the coast and steal some boats. There must be plenty of ships for us to choose from. We can get away. Do not worry!"

"Yes, of course," Ranulf answered sarcastically. "I trust you. Let us get out of here!"

Aldbald watched them go. It took a great effort of will to not turn to leave the town in the opposite direction. The young man from the Midlands was beginning to think there must be a line drawn between keeping loyal to a man while retaining honor in oneself. He had sworn to stay with Tostig, but how far should an oath like that take him? Must he forget all his principles because he swore allegiance to an unstable man?

But Aldbald also promised the Queen.

He would need to see Tostig find safety somewhere. Then Aldbald would be free to leave him.

Entry VIII

▼

In which Edith and Caedwig discuss the future

Caedwig frowned when he saw the tension in the Queen's features. Walking the length of her gardens, something that usually relaxed her, today only seemed to exacerbate the tightness of her shoulders, the stiffness of her gait.

"One brother is king and the other is outlaw!" Queen Edith paced back and forth, hands cupped in front of her, unconsciously rubbing her left palm with her right thumb.

"Should I be happy, angry, frightened or sad?" The woman's voice had raised in frustration, her question undirected. Caedwig reached for her as she walked in front of him again. The monk gripped her shoulder in one hand, held her hands in his other.

"My lady…Edith, do not torment yourself. What your brother Tostig has done…well, he has brought the consequences upon himself."

"Yes, and I should have recognized that he needed help." The woman shrugged off Caedwig's hold and stepped away from the monk. "I should have been there for him over the past year. Perhaps none of this would have happened."

"My lady, please do not fret so. You had a duty to your husband, not to your brother."

Edith slumped onto a bench by a fountain, leaned her head forward so that Caedwig feared she had fainted. When he dropped to his knee and raised her chin, he saw the deep pools that were her eyes, a tear running down her cheek.

"You are right. I had a duty to Edward. And in his death I have come to realize what during his life I had taken for granted. He was like a father to me, especially after my own father died. Although there were times he resented my family's influence, he always had respect for us."

Caedwig's hand had moved from the woman's upraised chin to her limp hand. "Godwin was a great man. So too are his sons great," he squeezed her hand, "and his daughter the queen."

"Yes. His sons are great," she repeated. "For my part, I did respect Edward too."

Caedwig squeezed the woman's hand again. "Of course you did. As did I."

"Yes," Edith nodded her head. "Edward was pious, and every one of his actions were a reflection of his belief in the Lord."

"He always meant well."

"Indeed he did. And I know my respect did grow into a love for the man. At least I know that now."

"I know." Caedwig released the woman's hand and stood up, wanting to change the subject. "And you love your brothers as well. That is commendable. To answer your question, I think you should be happy. Harold is king, and he the most level-headed man in England!"

"But what of Tostig?"

"Harold made haste to meet your brother at Sandwich, as you know. The southerly wind from God carried Tostig further north and out of harm's way. Tostig is far from where he might force a confrontation with the king."

"But Harold is no fool, as you know. He will not let Tostig undermine his authority as anointed King of England. My brothers will yet meet in Northumberland. I know it!"

Caedwig was serious. "Ah, my lady, but that is what I have come to tell you."

The woman misread the monk's intensity. "Then they have already met?" Edith caught her breath. "Was there blood shed?"

"No, my lady. Edith, the news from the north is that Tostig is gone to Scotland to take refuge. The northern thanes rallied against him without Harold's presence required. They merely displayed a show of force and Tostig's small band fled."

Edith had not taken a breath yet. "Then Tostig is all right?"

"That is the latest word, my lady."

The woman let out her breath then and breathed deeply. "Thank God."

Caedwig continued. "And the news is reliable. It appears Tostig and all his band are physically well." Caedwig coughed. "Your brother may be hurt in pride, however, as I understand the story."

"Oh?"

Caedwig held back his laughter. "Apparently your brother burned his companions' boats upon landing outside of York. In order to escape the alliance of northern thanes, the outlaws…that is, Lord Tostig and his men, had to steal a small fleet of fishing smacks!" Caedwig smiled then at the picture he conjured of Tostig in command of a fishing boat. "If I know your brother, that will be something he will never forget."

"You are right," Edith replied, deathly serious, "and he will blame Harold."

"But why? Tostig burned his own boats, not Harold!"

"That is not how Tostig will remember it." Edith began rubbing her hands together again. "Tostig has blamed Harold for everything that has happened to him. Ever since father died, Tostig and Harold have grown further and further apart. Tostig resents everything Harold has accomplished, blames Harold for everything he himself has been unable to accomplish." The woman stopped rubbing her palm, brought her hands to her cheeks. "Tostig will never forgive Harold for becoming King of England."

"And you my lady?" Caedwig asked quietly. "How do you feel about Harold as your king? You did seem to wonder if you should be happy."

"Caedwig, you know I am pleased for Harold. And happy for England. In Harold our people have found a man truly worthy of their trust. Not just the fine warleader he was as underking to Edward, but their true and capable king. Yes, my friend, I am happy for Harold." Edith stood up, shook her shoulders.

"And I am content for myself as well," she said, more to convince herself than the monk. "As long as I have Harold and Gyrth and Leofwine, I can live with the knowledge that Tostig is gone. Harold will be able to pardon Tostig sooner than my younger brother will forgive Harold. Nevertheless, when Tostig does come around, my door will be open; and so will Harold's I am sure." The woman moved her hands down along her hips, wiped her sweaty palms on her robe. "As long as Tostig has a chance to cool down."

"Do not fret Edith, I am sure a stay in the highlands of Scotland will cool him off."

Entry IX

▼

Where Tostig meets the King of Norway and all partake of a great feast

The stay in Scotland was a very short one for Tostig and his band of followers. The outlaws from England were made quite unwelcome, and had to travel further north to find more safe harbor for their motley collection of stolen fishing boats. Still with the southern wind at their backs they made it easily to the Norwegian held Orkney Islands. There Aldbald had met his first true Vikings.

The men of Orkney were overall friendly to Tostig, loaning him a better boat and a navigator named Uthgar to get him and his men across the North Sea to Norway; but they were at the same time menacing. Rough and barbaric, Aldbald found himself very uncomfortable in their company. The Englishman was hard pressed to understand anything the Northmen would say, but he could tell by their gestures and tone that they were brazen and uncouth. These foreigners were unclean and completely lacking in any simple social graces, except their offered camaraderie. They seemed more amused than disdainful at Tostig's pitiful sea vessels; almost admiring the man's courage in trusting his life to the small boats.

Uthgar had taken an instant liking to Aldbald, befriending the Englishman and acting as interpreter. By the end of their short stay in the Orkneys, Aldbald found he was more used to the ribald joking manner of the Northmen. He was even getting used to being punched in the shoulder to get his attention, and slapped vigorously across the back with every exclamation. He felt that here was a place he might leave Tostig, if he only had somewhere to go himself. The Orkney Islands were much too remote and alien for him to survive the upcoming winter months on his own. Aldbald somewhat reluctantly found himself traveling to Norway with the others.

Nothing he had seen and no one he had met in the Orkneys had prepared the Englishman for his first sight of the King of Norway. "There is the King!" Uthgar, speaking in English, pointed at the brute standing in water up to his waist.

Haraald Hardrada was big. Everything about him was big. He was bigger than any man Aldbald had ever seen. Standing off the shore in the fjord at Oslo, Haraald looked to be completely naked. The King's mouth was masked by wild and overgrown mustaches, his beard plaited in twin forks grown down to his belly. One thick eyebrow, permanently raised on one side due to a battle scar received many years earlier, extended across his forehead above big and wild eyes. The nose was huge, and deviated at the center to jar toward the left cheek. Haraald's chest, arms, shoulders and back were covered in thick, reddish-brown hair. In fact, it looked to Aldbald like the only part of the man's body not covered in the fur was the palms of the gargantuan hands. The King of Norway stood with arms spread wide as he waded into the ice cold water.

"We have arrived at just the right time to join in Norway's annual celebration." Uthgar bellowed his laughter. "Haraald Hardrada is taking his bath!"

Tostig slapped the prow of the ship. "Steer us over to the man, I wish to talk with him right away."

"Oh no," Uthgar yelled, his speech slipping back into his native Norwegian. "The threat of a thousand wild boars could not get me to interrupt this ritual!"

Aldbald did not know what Uthgar said, but he knew from the way Uthgar spoke what the response meant.

Uthgar leaned over to Aldbald to speak in English again. "Haraald will not go any further into the water, nor will he stay long. However, the cool water will invigorate the man such that he will spend the entire afternoon with his wives."

The Northman waved his hand and continued before Tostig could utter the protest on his lips. "This evening there will be a great feast. You can talk all you want then. A word of warning, however; do not stand too close to Haraald when you speak to him."

Tostig was angry that he would have to wait upon the King's pleasure, and he was particularly unimpressed with the man's awesome appearance. "Surely he is not that dangerous a fellow? Is his wrath to be feared so?"

"Not his anger, but his ardor! His zealous and enthusiastic manner will have him breathing into your face in no time. That is what I do warn you to avoid at all costs!"

Tostig was not listening to the man anymore, but Aldbald stepped closer to Uthgar. "I do not understand."

"Hardrada has picked up quite a taste for exotic spices he collected while fighting many years in the Mediterranean. Whether he truly likes his food as strong as it is, or his mouth is deadened with age so that he cannot taste anything more mild, I know not. Either way, his garlic-laden breath is something to avoid. Believe me!"

Tostig pushed Aldbald out of the way, and the younger man retreated to watch as the boat neared the Norwegian coast. Softly, just to Uthgar, Tostig spoke. "Tell me, my good friend. What does the King of Norway know of England?"

Uthgar was not so quiet. "What do you mean? The King of Norway knows of England what he must know of England. I would wager he cares even less than he knows."

Tostig looked about him to see that no one was within hearing distance. "I mean, what does Haraald know of the English people? Of the English king?"

Uthgar brushed off the question as inconsequential. "King Edward, the saint? I do not think Haraald finds much time to think about the man. He is fairly isolated from the dealings in the rest of Europe. Again, I would wager he is happy that way."

Tostig's eyes lit up. "King Edward, you say? Perhaps I might have some news that would interest the mighty King of Norway."

Uthgar noticed the slight patronizing tone. "Oh really? We shall see, we shall see. I warned you to watch the man's breath. Now I would warn you to watch your own tongue as well. Haraald might enjoy your company at dinner, or he might just choose to rip out your lungs for his own repast!" Uthgar stepped away from the prow to yell instructions to his crew, not letting Tostig make an answer.

The Englishman fumed, turning back to scrutinize the man in the water. This was his last chance. There was no where else to go. Tostig knew he had to convince Haraald to help him win back his rightful place in England. Could the man be that hard to talk to? He must not be that dangerous. After all, the King of Norway had spent the better part of fifteen years fighting Svend of Denmark without being able to conquer the Danes. How tough could a man like that be?

Aldbald kept his eyes on the King of the Norwegians as well. As the boat from the Orkneys got closer, Aldbald found that Haraald was even bigger than he had appeared at a distance. After about five minutes, Haraald turned to walk out of the water amidst the cheers of the crowd assembled on the shore. Aldbald stared at the hairy legs and buttocks. The man looked like a great bear. The King brought himself completely out of the water, then turned to face the inlet to the sea. He swung his arms wide, hands clenched as two massive rocks. He crouched, tensing all his muscles and letting out a ravenous bellow. Aldbald gaped at the tremendous, stiff appendage protruding from the mound of hair between the brute's legs. Everything about the man was indeed immense. Two women broke away from the riotous mob at the shore. They grabbed the massive outstretched limbs, each one raising herself up to hang free in the air. They kicked at each other, swinging and bouncing on either side of the man.

Uthgar saw Aldbald's expression. "Those are the King's two wives. Whichever one can first encircle Haraald with her legs without falling to the ground will be the first he will bed this afternoon. Not that it will matter much. King Haraald will lay with them both two or three times before he is done this day!"

*   *   *   *

Inside the fence of sharpened stakes jutting up waist-high, the hall of the Norwegian king mirrored the man himself. Large, dark and wild; it was ancient and barbaric. The longhouse may never have been considered attractive, but the old building certainly would not be called that now. The fir-studded walls were packed with weather-beaten clay in a vain attempt to keep out the cold north wind. Old thatch covered the steep log roof up to the eaves where carvings of hideous dragons and misshapen creatures hung as the only adornment on the outside of the building.

Within the great hall it looked like an armory, with the walls covered in stained swords, notched axes and battered shields. Aldbald was surprised at how warm it was inside, but it was due mainly to the press of so many sweaty, unwashed bodies. Unwashed save for the King. Haraald arrived at the dinner table refreshed and astonishingly energetic for having spent the better part of the day wrestling in his bedchamber with his wives. The two women looked especially bright and cheerful as they bounced into the room behind their man. Both had obviously been satisfied with their husband's afternoon performance, and gone was the female rivalry Aldbald had witnessed earlier in the day.

With Uthgar of Orkney nowhere nearby, the young Englishman felt uncomfortable surrounded by the gruff Northmen. He was hungry, though, and had had no intention of approaching the King's cooks with a special request for food outside of the dinner hour. Aldbald moved slowly about the room to settle in a chair near the far end of the long table from the King of Norway. Everyone in the hall seemed in good spirits. The hall boomed with talk and laughter. The Norwegians took little notice of Aldbald as he slipped into a spot amongst them.

Aldbald could not tell at first what was being served for dinner. The first two plates of food brought into the dining hall did not even make it to the table. A hush had filled the room as the servants began to enter with the dinner. Then, the bearers were inundated with hungry men, kicking and screaming at their neighbors to get a piece of meat. Five mangy dogs barked and snapped at fallen morsels as well as at the men's legs and hands. A third servant hurled the contents of his platter from the doorway into the room, then ran out of the hall as fast as he could. In the commotion caused by this, a fourth plate of food made it to Aldbald's end of the table before the bearer of the food was trampled. A fifth servant dodged the men crushing his companion and put his tray down on the table, grabbing a chunk of meat as he did so. He backed quickly away, dropping the meat to where the dogs could reach it. The animals fought over the piece, and men tripped over the dogs as the servant made his escape from the hall. Aldbald watched the men near him tear bites of meat. It looked to Aldbald like roast mutton or lamb, charred on the outside and all but raw on the inside.

A great sound came from the opposite side of the hall where the King roared in laughter. Tostig sat to the King's right, and Haraald leaned over and slapped the Englishman on the back.

"Ah ha! I think we have a winner!"

The women next to Haraald laughed, and Tostig smiled broadly. He recognized that he had no where else to turn; but watching the King of Norway, Tostig felt he had found the right place at last. Here was a man who did not know or care much about England itself; but the Northman would love to fight for the sake of fighting, to kill for the sake of killing. Yes, Tostig thought, here in Norway he was confident he had found what he was looking for.

After the first course was brought in, the pandemonium died down. More food continued to be brought in, and everyone had plenty to eat. Even after their bellies were full of meat and bread, the Northmen continued to down huge quantities of beer. The sound in the room became deafening, with men shouting to be heard by the people right next to them. Tostig waited until after the drink drained the energy around the table. Every third man had passed out, and the remaining conversations were subdued. Tostig watched the King, noticing the man was eyeing his wives lasciviously, reaching from one to the other to fondle various parts of their anatomies. If he did not speak soon, Tostig feared he would lose Haraald into the king's bedchamber once again.

On the king's left sat Rodgain the Relentless, a chieftain from a northern tribe of Norway, visiting the king's summer camp. Haraald's two sons sat next to Rodgain. Before Tostig could speak, Haraald was challenged by the man on his left. At this point it was the beer talking, but Rodgain's accusations did represent those of the other Norwegian warlords who were tired of the long break in their traditional way of life.

Rodgain was purposefully hostile. "So, does the King of Norway recognize that there are men outside of Norway that are perhaps greater than himself?"

Magnus, the outspoken of the two sons of the King, stood up with a growl, his hand reaching to grip his battle-ax next to the bench. The other son looked angry, but Olav stayed where he was seated, watching for word from his father. Haraald chose not to be insulted. He leaned close to Rodgain and slapped the man on the back. His loud voice filled the room.

The King of Norway could not whisper if he tried. "No, Rodgain my friend. No Dane; no Swede; no Russian wields as big a sword as does Haraald Hardrada!"

Uthgar of Orkney standing nearby interjected, "Your wives can certainly attest to that, great King!" This brought laughter all about the room. Haraald found it especially amusing, his laughter filling the air around Rodgain.

Even through the fog of the beer, Rodgain recoiled from the king's breath. "Yes, you are Haraald Hardrada, the Ruthless. And never more without compassion for the misery of others than after a hearty dinner when your breath is at its strongest!"

Haraald laughed all the more at that. He was always in such a good mood on his bath day, many wondered why he did not bathe more often. Rodgain was not satisfied, however. He looked across the table in front of the King toward Tostig. "The English have quite a reputation as being fearsome warriors, oh Great Haraald. I have heard stories—"

Haraald's fist came down with a crash all too near the other man's resting hand. "Enough about stories!" The King jumped up and grabbed a great broadsword from off the wall behind him. "This is reality!" Swinging the weapon with both hands over his head, Haraald cut the rope to a hanging candle holder. The candelabra dropped with a smash to the table to punctuate the king's words, plunging the end of the table into shadow.

Haraald brought the sword dangerously close to Rodgain's face. "Reality, Rodgain! All people live in a dream until I bring to them this reality." The King stood poised to strike as a hush fell over the room. In the shadow he thought he could just make out a bead of sweat on Rodgain's upper lip. He relaxed, jamming the sword into the floorboards beside him and resting his hand on the hilt. He looked from Rodgain to Tostig, smiled.

"Here beside me is an Englishman. He does not look that imposing a creature to me! Does he scare you, Rodgain?" Haraald leaned toward the

Englishman. "Tell me, Englishman, are there any of your countrymen that could stand up to me? Would you like to stand up to me in combat?"

Tostig hestitated, wanting to choose words from his Norwegian vocabulary carefully. This was his chance to make an appeal.

"My friend Haraald! I would never hope to stand against you!" Haraald grinned at that and sat back down into his chair, reaching for his glass of beer. "But," Tostig went on, "I would relish the chance to stand with you against a common enemy."

Haraald took no notice of the foreigner's additional comment as he drained the flagon. Tostig pressed his point. "Indeed, I would be honored to have the mighty Haraald the Ruthless fighting beside me against a common foe. Perhaps the infamous King of Norway would enjoy the chance to prove that no Englishman is his match?"

"I need prove nothing," Haraald grunted. "I know. Everyone in this room knows. All who meet me know. I am Hardrada!"

"Is that sufficient, Haraald?" Tostig leaned closer to the King, his sharp features slicing through the shadow between the two. "The King of England does make himself out to be the greatest man alive. He takes what he wants and leaves nothing for anyone else, even his own kin. He has no heart and no soul. Only a great dream with himself ruling the world!"

"Bah!" Tostig pulled back as the other man spoke into his face. "The King of England is an old man, senile, I am told; with no wits and certainly no guts either. I even understand he has no loins! What has it been? Twenty years and he has sired no children?!"

"I believe you would be referring to King Edward?"

"Humph! Who else would I be referring to?"

Tostig smiled his hawk-like smile. "My good friend. Edward is dead. And, though he favored me for his succession, an usurper has made himself King of England in my stead. He places himself above everything and everyone. Even above the King of Norway!"

"Bah! The man is a joke, I am sure."

"He may be a joke, but he is laughing at you and me! Svend of Denmark is afraid of him. Baldwin of Flanders, my own kinsman, will not dare to oppose him. Malcolm of Scotland hides in fear of him. Even William of Normandy does not seem to want to help me against the man! He is a common enemy of yours and mine, and with your help I can defeat this hound from hell. You can help me get my realm! I, and England, will be a friend to Norway for evermore!"

"By Odin! The day I need the friendship of England is the day that frost settles in the fires of the netherworld!" Haraald had refilled his glass, and he drained it once again. Beer ran down the corners of his mouth, soaking the long forked beard and forming two puddles on the table in front of him. "Besides, I do not think any Norseman would want to jour-ney to England to make war. Englishmen, it is said, cannot be trusted; but you can count on them to be weaklings! Where is the sport?" Haraald grabbed Elizabeth of Novogrod, the older of his two wives, and pulled her onto his lap. He pressed his head into her neck, making an oddly pig-like snorting sound while his hands crawled up her thighs. The King kept up his attentions until the kicking and squirming woman screamed in delight. Thora, the younger wife scowled at this display. She pushed Elizabeth off Haraald, bared her chest to the man. Grabbing the hair on Haraald's head, she pulled the King's head toward her and buried his face between her breasts. When the King came up for air, all three laughed and Haraald yelled for more beer.

Tostig had to think fast. If he did not get the king's attention back soon, it would be over before he had begun. The desperate Englishman got up to fetch a boar-bladder decanter that was not quite empty. He filled the king's glass himself. "You know, the mighty Haraald of Norway could be King of England himself!"

Haraald threw his wife off his lap and drained his glass in one gulp. "And of what use would that title be to me?"

Tostig refilled the king's flagon. "Did not your nephew Magnus, with whom you did share the crown of Norway, have a pact with Hardecanute of England? As successor to Magnus, you have inherited that agreement as well, which gives you the right to the crown of England!"

"If Magnus had the right to the crown of England, why did he not rule there? And what does it matter, anyway? If I wanted England, I would take England!" Haraald's fist slammed down on the table again, rattling the empty stoneware strewn about.

Rodgain finally recovered his former arrogance. "Just like he would take Denmark," he said, mustering as much sarcasm as he could through the fog in his head left by the beer. Rodgain directed his comment to Uthgar, but purposefully spoke loud enough for Haraald to hear.

Haraald was up with his sword in hand quicker than anyone nearby could react except Uthgar, who backed off quickly to the other side of the room. Haraald kicked the legs of Rodgain's chair, spilling the man backwards across the floor. The broadsword was high over head, ready to deal the death blow; but Haraald stayed his hand.

"We got what we wanted in Denmark, Rodgain. Booty, women, and plenty of sport. Do not talk of the Danes at my table. They have nothing to boast about to us Norsemen!"

Tostig stood with another flagon-full of beer held out to Haraald. Obviously, the Danish war had left a sore spot on the King. Perhaps he could use that. "Here, now. Have another drink my lord. It is obvious that you did teach the Danes to fear the name of Haraald of Norway."

The King glanced at the Englishman. He swung the sword around to dash the flagon from Tostig's hand, then stabbed the weapon into the floor between Rodgain's legs. "Many a hole we burned there among the kinsman of this Englishman. I left Denmark to Svend because after so many years of plunder by my Norsemen, there was nothing left to take! Remember that, Rodgain!" Haraald glowered around the room, then left the sword where it was and sat back into his chair.

Tostig broke the strained silence. "Indeed. It was the Danish scoundrel Sweyn Forkbeard who killed your own ancestor Olav and split Norway into little pieces. Your half-brother, Olav the Saint had supported

Aethelred of England against Sweyn and his arrogant son Canute, who forced you to flee to Russia, Haraald! The Danes have always needed to be put in their place, and you did just that! But—" Tostig was groping for words. He had not thought this far ahead, did not know what to say to sway Haraald. Rodgain finished his sentence.

"But after two fighting seasons have passed with no campaigns, the men of the North are beginning to wonder about their King."

Haraald glared at Rodgain, still laying on the floor with a sword between his legs all too near his genitals. Uthgar, watching now from the other side of the room, marveled at the man's courage, or insanity.

Tostig continued, "After Svend and his lot have been subdued as you said, you might wonder what the English do think of the King of Norway. If they could see what I see, they would tremble!

"Haraald, the Danelaw can be yours, I tell you. All of England can be yours! Svend is not strong enough to control England, but you could show him. I lack nothing in England save the title of king. I can guarantee you the support of the nobles in England, something you never had during your campaigns in Denmark. The Danes will quiver when they see the might of Norway in control of their kinsmen in England! And I will be caretaker for you from my capital in Northumbria! I offer you success! You could show them all!"

There was a long silence as Haraald seemed to be weighing his guest's words. Tostig stood up straight and smiled. He knew he could win this man to his cause. With the Norwegians, Tostig could finally reclaim his place in England! Haraald's forehead furrowed in concentration, his eyes squinting out over the people sitting quiet in the room. The King stood up as if to make an announcement, then paused again, bent over slightly. Finally, he belched a great belch, farting loudly at the same time. "Ah, that is what I needed! Now I am hungry again!" The King clapped his great hands together. "Bring me more meat!"

Tostig stood immobile, squinty eyes gone wide as he gaped at the King of Norway. *Had the man not heard anything he said? He could not believe* he was losing this last chance for his own glory. "Please, Haraald! Think on it. You spent fifteen years trying to get Denmark, but England lies waiting for you, like a third wife in your bedchamber!" The two wives looked at each other, then scowled at the Englishman's absurd suggestion. Tostig lost all sense of judgment. He reached over and grabbed Haraald, his hand barely able to grip the massive shoulder. "Svend, William, Baldwin, Malcolm, and Harold of England...you can prove to them all that you are their superior!"

"You will never grab at me again, Englishman!" Haraald did not move, except to form the words. "I need prove nothing to anyone. I am not an eyas, but a gyrfalcon waiting to eat out your eyes!"

Tostig released his grip and stepped back a pace, for the first time actually frightened by the great Northman. Haraald glared at Tostig, and the men at the table went quiet, watching. Again, Haraald's good mood won over. The man sat back in his chair again.

"Ha! You did not know that poetry is among my many accomplishments! The great Haraald Hardrada is above all men in everything! Now, Englishman, make yourself useful and fetch me some more meat! If there is none left I will have the cook roast you!"'

*   *   *   *

Rodgain stumbled to the far end of the room, following his friend Uthgar of Orkney. Both Northmen found some room at the table next to Aldbald. Though they both had drunk their share of beer already, Uthgar reached for a half-empty decanter next to Aldbald and began to pour some beer into his glass. Before any had gotten out, Rodgain grabbed it from Uthgar for himself. Uthgar punched Aldbald in the shoulder as he practically fell down next to the Englishman.

"Your companion there takes his life into his hands addressing Haraald in that manner!"

Aldbald was startled and he jumped in his seat. The rowdy Northmen around him had gotten him to drink some beer, even though he tried to make them understand he was not interested. He realized quickly that he did not want to insult any of these barbaric men. Although he had drunk very little, the strong beer was taking its toll on the man's concentration. He had been gazing across the room at nothing, totally oblivious to those around him until the man from the Orkneys brought him out of it.

"I am sorry, Uthgar. What did you say?"

"I said, that your companion there is risking his life. He had better be more careful."

"There have been times when I have thought he would get us all killed."

"The man seems quite strange. I am actually shocked that he is not already roasting over the fire pit! I guess the King is in an exceptionally good mood today!"

"Indeed, the Lord Tostig is more than a bit strange. I fear I have lost everything I ever loved in following that man." Aldbald drooped his head, wishing that the heavy feeling from the beer could crush his memories. Why did so many men like to drink? It seemed to accentuate his depression instead of remove the feelings.

Uthgar laughed, failing to recognize the other man's mood. "Oh? And what is it that you have lost, my friend?"

Aldbald turned to look the man in the eyes. "England. I am afraid I will never go back to my home."

"Is life in England so perfect? Surely you could find someplace else to settle. There are willing women all over, and land and seas to travel! What does England have to offer? You have told me that you come from a simple life. What could you desire of that life now? Living as a wretched craftsman, giving all of your hard-worked profits in taxes to the king."

Aldbald shook his head. "Uthgar, you do not understand. England is my home. It is where my heart yearns to be. I have nothing, save what Tostig chooses to give me. And right now he has nothing. In England I may still have family and friends. King Edward had seen fit to remit many of his taxes, and the people of England have been prosperous for many years. No, Uthgar, England is truly the only place for me. But, I cannot go back. I am in exile with Lord Tostig. Until he makes it back to England, I will not make it back."

Rodgain had been uninterested in the foreigner until he heard something about English prosperity. He came out of his brooding, put his glass of beer down and leaned closer to Uthgar and the Englishman. "Uthgar, I am afraid my English is not so good. What was that about the king and the taxes?"

Uthgar had heard it too. He was amazed, and he punched Aldbald to show his interest. "The king actually reduced the taxes? I had heard a rumor that Edward of England was crazy. Now I know it to be true! No wonder that Tostig fellow is so angry! I guess he lost a lot of revenue."

Aldbald scowled. "Oh, not Lord Tostig. He continued to levy heavy taxes on the people of Northumbria."

Uthgar smiled in understanding. "Then the Earls of England do have control over their own domains—"

"I suppose so. In my time at Tostig's court at York, the King of England never once traveled to Northumbria. Tostig had complete control in Northumbria, until the people themselves revolted and threw him out!"

"Ah! So that is why he is so angry."

Aldbald nodded. "Yes. It was all his fault, but he does blame all his problems on his brother Harold of Wessex."

"Harold Godwinsson?"

Aldbald nodded again. "Right. He is a great man, and a nice person if I have ever met one. Yet, I am sure he will be a strong ruler. He should make a great king for England. But, Tostig claims Harold incited the people of Northumbria against him."

Rodgain wanted to get back to the interesting part of the story. "And what were you saying about the people of England being prosperous? If the earls did not heed the king, then the earls still reaped their own revenues, leaving the common people of England with nothing as always. Right?"

Aldbald shook his head. He found he was getting a bit dizzy with all the shaking and nodding. He had to pause a moment to recover. "No. Tostig was the exception. All the other Earls followed King Edward's lead. All except—" Aldbald paused, gazing across the room, over the North sea waters and through time to that day when he first saw the Lady Godiva.

Rodgain pressed the Englishman. "Except?"

Uthgar too was intrigued. He punched Aldbald's shoulder again. "Except whom?"

Aldbald started to take a sip of beer, but put the glass down before it wet his lips. What he really needed was water, but these Northmen did not seem to ever drink that. The Englishman brought his eyes into focus upon the man from Orkney. "Well, except for Leofric, the Earl of Mercia." Aldbald smiled. "Lord Leofric did not follow his king; but he did heed his wife the Lady Godiva." Aldbald's eyes glazed over as his mind reached out beyond the Norwegian shores again.

Uthgar hit Aldbald across the arm to bring him out of his trance. "Aldbald! There is more to this story than you have told us! Do tell us the rest, before I pass out. Tomorrow we will all have forgotten this night, and I will not know to ask you then for the tale."

"Yet, if I tell you, tomorrow you will have forgotten the story anyway!" Aldbald laughed, seeing his friend's puzzled expression as the man tried to see a flaw in that reasoning.

Rodgain reached past the man from Orkney to poke his finger into Aldbald's chest. "Continue your story, Englishman. I will remind you both tomorrow what we said this evening."

Uthgar laughed, giving up on his train of thought. "Yes, my friend, who is this Leofric character?"

Aldbald raised himself up as straight as he could in his chair. "Let me tell you of Coventry, Uthgar. For my own story does begin there as well."

"Who is Coventry?" Uthgar bubbled the question through a mouthful of beer.

"Not who, but where you might ask. Coventry is my home town in the heart of England. Lord Leofric did pass his last years outside of Coventry on the manor of his wife, the Lady Godiva. When Lord Leofric refused to lower the taxes as ordered by King Edward, the Lady Godiva rode naked through the town to reduce the taxes. She chose to champion the cause of the lowly in Coventry just as Aethelflaed, the Lady of the Mercians, had fought for the people of the Midlands so many years ago."

Uthgar was puzzled. "England is a strange place. I am afraid I do not understand. These women of England must be incredible!"

"Oh yes! Lady Godiva is wonderful. Very pious, strong-willed, and beautiful."

"But, how is it that naked women riding through a town serves to lower taxes?"

Aldbald stared at the man for a long time, wrestling with words that would explain. He could not tell if it was the beer clouding his thinking, or if he did not know the answer. He shrugged. "Anyway…Leofric of Mercia took notice of his wife, and chose to remit many taxes." Aldbald waved his hands before him. "That is what happened. Then the Earl Leofric died that same year. In his bedchamber, they say. No one knew exactly why. It seems to me there might have been some foul play, but the man was old—" Aldbald burped. "I do think I have had enough for tonight. I will hope to see you in the morning, friend."

Uthgar cringed. "I will not want to see anyone in the morning! I will be feeling the effects of this night's imbibing well into the day tomorrow. But, goodnight. I think I will have one more drink with my friend Rodgain here. As long as the damage is already done," Uthgar laughed, "I might as well enjoy it before tomorrow comes!"

Aldbald joined in the other's laughter and began to hic-cup. Still fighting the spasms, he stumbled out of the hall and into the fresh air. Uthgar tried to fill his glass, pouring beer on the table. When he raised the vessel to his mouth, he realized it was empty and tossed it into the wall behind him, just missing the head of a sleeping ruffian. Uthgar took a long draught straight from the decanter.

"Yah ha! To battles, breasts and beer! The three things that make life livable!" Uthgar took another swallow and passed the drink to Rodgain who was no longer sitting beside him.

*   *   *   *

As Aldbald the Englishman left the room, Rodgain brought his attention back to King Haraald. Rodgain had come all the way from his northern tribe to talk with Haraald, and he did not feel satisfied yet. Most all of the veterans of the Danish campaigns, including Rodgain himself, were in desperate need of adventure. None of them had thought much about England, but perhaps that island might serve a Norse purpose.

Haraald had finished his latest course of food, and was leaning back in his chair resting his head back. Thora had fallen asleep holding one of his hands, and his other hand idled among his wife Elizabeth's various bodily features. Tostig had retreated from the room, and the King's sons were asleep underneath the table where they had eaten. Even through Rodgain's beer-fogged vision, he could see that the King was getting lazy. The Norsemen were all getting lazy! A Viking trip to England. That would revitalize them all, he thought. Like the king's annual bath worked wonders on the man's prowess.

Rodgain walked slowly over to where Haraald sat. Candles were relit on the fallen candelabra, still in place where it lay on the table. Haraald took no notice of the man who had aggravated him earlier. His head was resting on the back of the chair, his eyes slightly closed.

"Haraald." Rodgain could have waited until the next day; but the drink in him was still guiding his actions. He found the need to speak now to be pressing him on. "Haraald!" He spoke more loudly. Haraald's eye under the ever-raised brow opened, the other eye the King kept closed.

"Ah, Rodgain. You are truly a menace. Have I ever told you that?"

"Yes, Haraald, I am! As are many of your closest supporters, I am sure. And why? Because we need a diversion! I tell you, King Haraald, the men around you have beached their ships, and that is wearing on the people of Norway!"

The King smiled, looking past Rodgain to a distant scene. "Rodgain, do you remember the diversion I ordered when we attacked the port of...what was the name of that place? Ha, some unpronounceable thing! We stole the fishing boats in the night, and sent them back into the small harbor the next morning aflame! With the wind off the sea, the fire easily spread to the docks and then to the town houses on the coast. Oh, that was a sight to see! It was almost as much fun as when we tied fire to the backs of those birds that were nesting in the thatched rooftops of—

"Damn, I can never remember all the places I have sacked! But the sight when the town went ablaze is etched upon my memory! Do you remember Rodgain?"

Haraald closed his eye again, smiling as he hefted Elizabeth's ample breast in his extended hand. The woman purred. Rodgain moved closer. "Haraald! Listen to me! I say we take on a trip to England. I think the chieftains of Norway would welcome the chance to go a viking again. I have learned that England may turn out to be a wealthy prize to plunder! The people of England are prosperous, and apparently have been so for many years."

Eyes closed, Haraald did not move at all. "Oh? And how do you guess that? England seems to me to be a poor country. Did you hear the tale of the boats which brought our friend Earl Tostig to the Orkneys?" With that, Haraald opened both eyes to gaze about the room looking for the Englishman. "That certainly does not sound to me like a rich country." He laughed. "Where is the Englishman? Go ahead, talk to him about it! I will say this about the man, he does not seem to have a fear of the sea. That is a good trait, at least!"

Rodgain was insistent. "Tostig has nothing because the people of England have thrown him out. I heard a story of a woman in England who rode through her village naked and all the taxes were then reduced—"

Haraald pulled both his arms in to the armrests of his chair. His younger wife shuffled, but fell back asleep across the back of her own chair. Elizabeth appeared vaguely put out by Rodgain's incessant talk. The King brought his full attention to Rodgain. "A woman rode naked through a town? And this reduced the taxes?"

"Haraald. I admit it sounds absurd, but it is true. The people of England have been duty-free for many years now. I tell you England is prosperous!"

Haraald leaned forward. "Hm…naked, you say?"

"Yes. This happened a few years back, and the people of England have since not had any taxes levied upon them! Do you realize what that means? Can you envision the plunder we could take?!"

"Plunder, yes—" Haraald sat back, then leaned forward again. "Who was this woman of England?"

"The wife of the Earl of Mercia. Some Lady Godiva, I believe. I gathered it all happened some time ago. The people of England must be rich by now. Ripe for us to plunder, I tell you!"

"Ripe, yes…I will bet she is ripe!" Elizabeth scowled at her husband's remark, then turned her sour face toward Rodgain, annoyed that the northern chieftain continued to take her husband's attention away from her.

Haraald had indeed forgotten about Elizabeth for the moment. "This woman of Mercia. She was riding a stallion?"

Rodgain was pleased the conversation was going somewhere. He had finally gotten Haraald's attention. "I do not know. Perhaps it was a stallion…but think of it, Haraald! The riches, lying there for the taking in England. I think it is exactly what our people need."

Haraald bellowed in laughter. "What I need indeed! I can see the woman now, a wild bay stallion between her thighs! Rodgain, who is this lady? Where is Mercia?"

"Haraald, I admit I am not sure. The Englishman said something about Aethelflaed of Mercia. Was that not Alfred's daughter?"

Haraald was on his feet. "Of course!" Haraald laughed. "Aethelflaed, daughter of Alfred the Great! I know the legends of her. She was a great Dane fighter, like me!"

"Perhaps this lady Godiva is related to that line; and a relative of Aethelflaed," Rodgain pushed the jest as far as he could, "would trace her line through Alfred to Cerdic the Saxon and all the way back to Odin himself!"

"Ah yes!" Haraald clapped his great hands together, and his wife Thora woke up with a grunt. "The Lady Godiva of Mercia. What a woman! I will bet her husband is a great man. I should meet this Earl of Mercia in single combat—"

Rodgain interrupted, "Well, Leofric of Mercia is dead now, I do believe. Something about having been found dead in the woman's bed-chamber—"

"Of course! The man was slain through the woman's passion! This mad Lady of Mercia," Haraald laughed. "The man could not keep up with her, I am sure. Not like I could."

Elizabeth spoke out then, glancing at Haraald's other wife nearby. "Haraald, you do not need another wife!" Elizabeth had only given Haraald daughters, and she already resented Thora who had born the King his two sons.

Haraald had walked away from the table, and he looked back at his first wife. "You are right, woman!" He smashed his hand down on the table to add emphasis, then looked at Rodgain. "But I am in need of some sport!"

Rodgain smiled. Haraald clapped him on the back. "Too bad about this Leofric of England. I would have loved to have killed him and taken his wife." The King's smile changed to one of excited anticipation as he looked to Rodgain.

"Rodgain, my friend! I think there may be work for us across the seas!"

Entry X

▼

Where the King of England is found to be wondering about William

Harold's subconscious became aware of the water lapping at his feet. How long had he been standing there? He had lost track of the time completely. Coming out of his reverie, Harold looked down at his worn boots, a half inch under water. The tide was coming in, and there was nothing he could do to stop it. Canute the Great had shown his followers that he was not the master of the sea. Why is it that he, Harold Godwinsson, thought he could prevail against what Nature did intend? Given that he might hold back the tide from southern England; what then would be the fate of the west? Would the eastern shores also be affected? Standing on the shore of Chichester harbor near his home at Bosham, the young King gazed south across the all too narrow channel of water. He could almost see his adversary staring back at him, surrounded by knights mounted on impatient steeds that stamped and swayed with frustration in their inaction. Men from all over northern France prepared to help William the Bastard make his unwarranted claims upon the English throne.

The wind blew chill at Harold's back, pricking the hair at the nape of his neck. He shivered slightly, looked up into the sky above where coastal plovers circled overhead. Although he had tried to make light of it, the fiery omen that had appeared at Easter had left him disheartened. He did fear what many said was true, that the sign boded ill for England. If he could have told the Duke of Normandy that he would marry his daughter Agatha, then perhaps all would be well now. Instead, he plight his troth with Aldgyth of Mercia, and he could not back down from that betrothal now. Not if he wanted to avert rebellion in the north. Could he have handled the situation in any other way? Harold thought of the Lady Godiva. Where was she now?

Yet, Harold thought, what of that heavenly display? Was it not seen across the waters in Normandy as well? Could not the omen be in his favor, a warning to would-be invaders to stay away? He had made sure to present that idea as his interpretation of the sign, and the weather had certainly been in England's favor. For two months during the height of the campaigning season, the weather had held for England. The north wind was like a breath from God, a whisper of warning to William: Stay back in your domain. Leave England to Harold and the English. The season to fight was all but over now. Harold had sent the fyrd back to their homes until next spring, safe in the knowledge that the winter weather would make the channel impassable. William would have to recognize the same thing.

A noise behind Harold brought his thoughts back to England. "My God, Harold! I have been looking all over for you!" Robert FitzWimark came down the path out of the mist holding a goblet in each hand.

"The sentries told me that you had gone down to the beach, but I had just about decided they had been mistaken since I could find no trace of your being out here. The rising waters seem to have washed your footprints away, my friend!"

Harold looked down at his feet again; but when he did not speak, FitzWimark continued. "I thought I had better bring something to help warm you should I be able to find you." Robert pushed one of the goblets of ale into Harold's hands. "What in God's name are you doing out here? How long have you been standing there?"

Harold reluctantly took the cup that was thrust into his hands, but failed to hear FitzWimark's questions. It was a moment before Harold seemed to recognize his friend. Grasping the goblet in his left hand, Harold threw his right arm around the other man who was half-Breton and half-Norman, a distant relation to William of Normandy. "Tell me, Robert, what is happening over there in your home?" Harold looked back south across the waters.

"My lord, England is my home!" FitzWimark glowered at his king.

"Of course. Forgive me, my friend. In Normandy, then. What do you suppose is going on at the Duke's court? In the Duke's mind?"

"Harold, just as you know he has built a fleet and is bringing together his forces over there, so too does he know that you have had the coast watched and an army of your own gathered to repel invaders. What can the man do? To attempt a landing upon the English coast would be folly for William. He would find it very difficult to land in one concise strike force; instead would be scattered across the coast needing time to regroup. One of your coast watchers would notify you, and almost immediately your fleet would assemble our army in a position to mop up the Normans bit by bit. Your defense has been more than adequate. William must know this to be true. You have won this round, my lord."

"No, Robert. I fear it was not my calling an army together to watch the coast that held the Duke's ambition." Harold released his grip on the other man and turned to look north, breathing deeply the fresh air. "The wind has been seemingly overkind to England."

Robert shrugged. "Let it be the wind then. The breeze has been against the Duke, and now we enter a season when only the foolhardy traverse the channel seas. I am sure that William has realized his plans have come to naught. Again, what can he do?"

Harold looked out over the water. "And what if the wind does change to southerly? Now that I have let the fyrd return to get their households in order for the upcoming winter, and the fleet of the Cinque Ports has left, my strike force is gone. If William landed tomorrow, I would have nothing with which to meet his army."

"Do not worry so." Robert placed his free hand on his friend's shoulder. "It is a wonder the fyrd stayed assembled for you till the eve of the Nativity of Saint Mary, fully a month beyond their duty. The farmers have been anxious ever since Lammastide! The fact is that the wind does still blow from the north, and the season for launching an invasion of England is over. It is mid-September. Our country is secure until spring."

Robert saw the look come over Harold's face, the slight frown made more obvious by the long mustaches. "And even were it not so," Robert's arms swung wide to either side, spilling a bit of ale as he gestured, "the fyrd can be called up at once to join your housecarls, and within only a couple of days you would have your army again. You can be certain that you will have more relations with Normandy in the future, and who can tell what will be? But for now, savor what you have."

"You are right of course. Should the wind change now, it would be a southern gale to strike havoc upon the Duke's fleet. He cannot attack until Spring." Harold's smile was short-lived, as he turned his attention once more to the south. "I can say the words, but I still feel uncomfortable. Why is that, Robert? Why do I have a feeling that England is not secure?"

"Because you are King. The people have entrusted you with their lands and their lives. That is a great responsibility! Harold, a man like you takes gestures such as that to heart."

"Yes, you are right again. I do. Perhaps that is the root of my problem. Sometimes I do feel like I have brought woe to England through my own actions. If that were true, I could not live with that, Robert."

"Nonsense, my lord! You have controlled England for many years as Underking to Edward, and now as King in your own right. You have brought peace and prosperity to your land and your people. What William of Normandy thinks now he has thought for over ten years. Perhaps he has been a bit misled; but you? Never!"

"Then why do I feel forces brewing beyond my control which do threaten England, even as we speak?"

"I know not, my lord. But, even as you say, these things beyond your control," Robert said the three words slowly, "will stay that way. What Nature intends is perhaps different than what we would have in mind; but we must keep moving forward. It is all we can do. For now, take heart in the fact that Nature has been on your side, blowing a steady breeze in Duke William's face! You must stop your brooding and let us retire now. It is cold and damp out here!"

Harold laughed, only then realizing what he had been holding in his hand. "Again and again, you are right my friend." The King took a long draught from the goblet, draining the ale before gasping for air. "You know, only to you and my Edyth can I speak in this way. Do not fear for your King! At least not as long as the Lord above does keep me in his good graces. My worries are my own, not truly those of the country. Only sometimes do I find that sharing them does ease the burden slightly." Bright teeth suddenly showed through a big grin as Harold hurled his empty goblet into the sea. "That is for you, William of Normandy!"

"I will drink to that, my lord!"

Robert FitzWimark emptied his drinking vessel as Harold grasped his friend and started walking back up the track toward the warmth of the hearthfire.

"Tomorrow we ride for London."

Entry XI

▼

Where Godiva embarks on a plan to leave the continent

The young squire lifted a shaky hand to light the lantern at the masthead. The strong south wind threatened to extinguish the burning brand, succeeded only after the oil lamp blazed alight. Above the lantern was a cross, a blessing from Pope Alexander for the conjured crusade against an errant English. Almost out of reach of the lantern's dim light could be seen the figure of a leopard on a banner at the prow of the ship.

Since mid-August, William of Normandy's fleet had been completely assembled, the men to follow the Duke anxious, but ready. For that time of year, the lack of a south wind came as a surprise to the channel pilots. Even the best of the Fleming helmsmen decreed the north wind could not last forever. For a month, however, the Duke's splendid invasion force sat stranded on the banks of the River Dives outside Caen.

There had not been many ships in Normandy only a half a year ago. Duke William had had to build the bulk of his fleet over the summer months, which was no simple feat even if there had been more ship builders available. The amount of timber required was incredible. The ships in William's fleet were all of the same design, not much different from the Norse vessels that first brought Rollo to the shores of Normandy one hundred and fifty years before. They were double ended, although most lacked the elaborate carvings of dragon heads on the stems and monster tails on the sternposts due to the urgency of the construction. The ships were of many sizes, the larger ones used for carrying more of the most important cargo, the horses. Duke William's ship, the Mora, was one of the few that could be rowed if necessary, having enough men on board to work the oars, and not having the encumbrance of any horses or supplies on the open deck. Most all of the rest of the fleet needed a favorable wind.

That morning in mid-September, the wind shifted, and along with it Duke William's luck. Knowing it would be no good to approach the English coast in the dark, the Duke directed his fleet to sail on the night tide to arrive by morning. Duke William stood below the Leopard Banner on the prow, flanked by his brothers Robert and Odo, his seneschal William FitzOsbern, and the young Hugh of Avranches, who had gained quite a reputation for gluttony and was commonly referred to by his peers as Hugh the Fat. The lit lamp at the masthead of the Mora was a signal to the entire fleet: The Leopard of Normandy was ready to sail for England. The lantern was easily seen by the men waiting along the banks of the river; it was their signal to hoist their sails.

The darkness obscured the variety of bright banners, muted the colorfully painted devices on the shields of the men embarking on the expedition. Equalized by the shades of gray, the men sought each other out for security, commiserating with each other in their common concern over entrusting their lives to the will of the sea and the skill of the helmsmen, about whose art or science the chevaliers knew nothing.

The Lady Godiva was counting on the insecurity of the men in the army. The more they were afraid for their own lives, the less apt they would be to discover her and her companions amongst their numbers.

"My lady, this is madness! We will be found out for sure!"

"Now, Hildreth," Godiva spoke softly. "I told you that you need not go through with this. I did not bring us from Brittany to Normandy simply to watch helplessly as the Duke's fleet leaves for England."

"Yes, but we had hoped to buy our passage to England, not try to stow away like criminals."

"That was before I knew we would arrive just as the fleet is ready to sail. I will give Gunthnot the same choice I give you now, Hildreth. Go with me, or stay in Normandy."

"Yes, but when you proceed with this madness yourself, how can we not follow, my lady? Would that I could change your mind, though."

The two women stood in the dark behind a small fisherman's shelter near the waterside. The small three-sided structure was used by the locals to house their draft animals while they were out to sea. Now it was deserted. It had been quite some time since there were boats available for fishing in Normandy. Godiva and her servant watched as the first boats left the shore and the second group were launched. Men shoved boats of all sizes into the River Dives, hoisting sails and catching the south wind and the ebb tide to follow the Mora out to sea.

"Well you cannot change my mind. For months now I have wanted to gain passage to England, but the Duke of Normandy had confiscated all the boats on the coast! If I had but tried to leave a little earlier, I am sure I could have gained passage out of Brittany."

"The Count Conan of Brittany's death was untimely, my lady. They say he was poisoned by minions of Duke William's for not backing Normandy's exploits. Dare I say it, if that is true, how much easier for the Duke to have us killed should we be found out?"

"That is a chance I must take. I will cross the sea to England with Duke William and his army."

"But, my lady, there will be plenty of ships, and more opportunities, after this day!"

"Not until next spring. I have heard the men muttering in many languages; but a common thread is their fear that even this crossing will meet disaster. The winter winds will soon sweep across the Channel, Hildreth, and I have no desire to pass yet another Christmastide on the continent. With the news that Gunthnot learned of the state of affairs in England, we have every reason to go home. I need to settle things with Harold of Wessex, need to see that my grandchildren are alright." The Lady Godiva narrowed her eyes as she looked out to sea.

"Besides, I cannot stay away from my homeland when I know an enemy of England has amassed an army and is launching an attack on our people! I may have proved to be less than adequate in making alliances that could help my own family; but I cannot stand idle while our country is threatened.

"No, Hildreth, it is now that we will leave. Tonight, on one of those ships." Lady Godiva pointed to the banks of the river.

Hildreth hung her head. "Very well."

Godiva sighed. "Do not worry. I do not think it will be that difficult."

The Lady Godiva studied the ships leaving the security of the land. The first ships out after Duke William were those carrying cargo, mainly barrels of wine, and timber to build defensive barricades. These had been loaded and anchored and were the easiest to get ready to sail. What followed were ships carrying the men and horses that made up the bulk of the invading army.

"You see the boats being loaded with horses, Hildreth? The soldiers are leaving most of the tending to the animals up to peasants. If Gunthnot comes back with similar insight after his scouting about, we should not have a problem. We will simply blend in with the horse servants. Many of the soldiers are speaking foreign languages, so as long as we talk as little as possible, our accents should not cause too much alarm."

"Of course, my lady," Hildreth answered, not entirely convinced.

"Now help me." Godiva became suddenly urgent. She unsheathed her dagger, handed the blade to her servant.

"My lady! You do not expect me to be able to fight, do you?"

Godiva's mood was so fervent she failed to find the humor in her maid-servant's shocked expression. "Indeed not! I want you to cut my hair short."

"My lady?"

"Do it, Hildreth, and do not dawdle. We have not much time. We must disguise ourselves as best we can before we join in the launching of one of the next vessels to carry horses. We will choose one of the larger ships with at least twelve horses to be cared for."

"My lady, perhaps you can cut your hair and dress as a man, mayhap even fool these foreigners; but I do not believe I will be able to carry off such a charade!"

This time Hildreth's look did bring a smile to Lady Godiva. "Hildreth, let us be serious. I do not know what either of us will look like if we try and disguise ourselves. But, we must try, and then simply do the best we can to keep away from the others. If we choose a boat with many horses, I am confident that the foreign soldiers will not question having three extra groomsmen for their beasts. It is a ploy that I believe will work."

"Perhaps, here in the darkness. But what about at first light? How long do you think we can keep up the farce?"

"As long as we must!" Lady Godiva softened at the look of frustration and fear in her servant's eyes. "I do not know, Hildreth. How long is it to cross the Channel waters to England? Just a few hours, and most of it in the dark. We will just have to do our best and face the ramifications of discovery if and when the time comes. Remember, Gunthnot will be beside us."

Godiva fingered her hair in the back near the base of her skull. "Now, cut my hair to here, and be quick about it. It need not be a perfect cut."

"That is good," Hildreth forced a laugh, "because I daresay I will not be able to cut perfectly in this light, even if my life depended upon it."

"Yes, speaking of that, here is something on which your life might depend." Lady Godiva handed the other woman a piece of leather from inside her cloak. Wrapped within, Hildreth found another, smaller knife. She looked at her mistress in surprise, started to hand the package back.

"No, Hildreth. Keep the blade tucked away in your mantle. If you never have a need for it, all the better. But, keep it just in case. It is a good size for you to control should you find you require something with which to defend yourself."

Wordlessly, Hildreth searched the folds of her clothes for an appropriate place to hide the weapon. Godiva turned her head so that her servant could work on her hair. In the dark back corner of the shack, Godiva spotted something that would make their disguise the most genuine. Reaching down to the earth, she winced slightly as she picked up a handful of horse dung. She quickly smeared some on her boots and clothing. When Hildreth reached for Godiva's hair, the older woman gasped for air.

"My lady! What in Heaven's name are you doing?"

"Why, Hildreth, if you do find me repulsive this way, how much more then will the haughty chevaliers! I think we can be assured that this will make our disguise credible."

"Credible, I do not know." Hildreth sniffed. "But it will make us unapproachable, definitely."

"Then we will be safe. Now, cut my hair! As soon as Gunthnot gets back, we will board one of those boats and be gone."

Entry XII

▼

In which Harold of England has a dream

The King of England had kept an easy pace on the trip from Bosham and the southern coast of England, through the forests of Sussex, to London. So many hours, days and years in the saddle took its toll on his limbs, and his left knee hurt more often than not lately. Pressed so by the need to move fast and ride far, it was precious few occasions throughout Harold's life that he had the time to actually enjoy the simple pleasure of travel. Sometimes he realized he would take the countryside for granted; but, having seen many different lands from France to Italy, it was almost painfully clear to Harold that England held his heart. At the same time, Harold realized how much he anticipated his homecoming welcome from Lady Edyth, and he wondered fleetingly if it were not perhaps her company that made life in England so desirable.

Harold and his companions crossed the north downlands and reached London late in the evening. The King went right to his bedchamber to meet the woman who awaited him. Edyth met him with open arms and wild kisses. She did everything within her power to help the man she loved to relax. Harold smiled. The woman had always brought her whole body and soul into their relationship. Edyth was very real in his arms, and he did love her. They had been together for so long, he found it hard to see life without her.

Edyth's touch seemed to melt the man's cares. She had unclothed him, and laid him back among the smooth sheets. There was a wash basin beside the bed. Edyth wetted a small cloth with the warm water.

"I was waiting for you, my lord." She smiled at him across his strong chest as she wiped his feet with the damp cloth. Edyth rewetted the cloth with the warmed water, and ran it along his legs, pausing as she reached up the inside of his thigh. She rested her hand on the man, and he came to life just as she expected.

"Oh, my love," she feigned surprise. "Are you not tired from your journey?" She asked this as she bent over to kiss his lower stomach, his pelvis. "Here is my own private housecarl, standing straight at attention in honor to me! Did my little soldier miss me?" Edyth's smile faded for an instant as she saw the uncomfortable look come across Harold's face. She stroked the man gently. "Oh, I am sure this little guy did not want for companions out in the field." She laid a gentle kiss. "But, did he miss me? Just a little, perhaps?" Edyth kept up her ministrations until Harold could take it no more.

"Enough! Come here." Harold pulled the woman up to meet her lips with is own. "You know that I do miss you. You have put a spell on me, Edyth." He slipped off her light night dress. "Do you know, sometimes I find I cannot even enjoy myself as I used to. Your face comes to my mind, and if you are not there I find I am somewhat disappointed."

"Somewhat?" Edyth leaned away playfully, then became more serious as she looked into Harold's eyes.

"Harold…sometimes I feel like something, or someone, has indeed ensorcelled you. I fear I am not the only one who has some control over the King of England."

Harold leaned over and bit the woman's ear. "You are the only one who has spun a web of wizardry around me!"

"Oh?" Edyth pushed Harold gently back again. "You know I have never put restraints on you; never asked you for any commitment."

"No commitment? Then what am I doing here?" Harold made to get out of bed, and Edyth grabbed him by the waist to hold him back. The man began to laugh.

"My God, Edyth! You are the mother of my children. You are a part of my life. What is this talk of no commitment?"

"I only meant to say that I know our bond has never been blessed, that we are not truly married in the eyes of the Holy Church. As the Earl of Wessex, that never mattered. As King of England, perhaps it does. I know that you have planned for some kind of alliance with the northern earls. I know that you might marry for political reasons. For so long I have enjoyed the pleasures of being consort to the greatest man in England; but more and more I find it is simply you that I do want. I just wonder where I will fit into your future plans. Sometimes lately you have seemed so distant. Sometimes I cannot determine what it is you are thinking; why you are doing the things you do."

"Is that what you are worried about?" Harold laughed deeply, and pulled Edyth to him. "By the Lord's dying breath, Edyth! Even I do not always know what I am thinking or what I am doing!"

"I am serious, Harold."

Harold stopped laughing, and released the woman from his embrace. "Dear, so am I. Truly, forgive me if I have seemed distracted of late. You know, I had never thought to be king. It is such a great responsibility. One I am not sure I do like." Harold leaned back on the pillow. "Until Christmas last, I was content in my position as Under-king. Now, I am not always sure where and how I should stand."

Edyth looked confused. "But Harold, my love, it was you who did handle most of the country's affairs even while Edward was king. Why should it be so different to actually wear the crown?"

"I do not know, Edyth. I do not know. The coins I have had minted with PAX written on them were meant to soothe the people and make them believe in peace. Why do I feel that the Peace of Harold is not something that will be remembered?"

Edyth lay close to Harold, pressing her body against his side. "I am sorry, dear. I began this fishing for something from you to give me more confidence. I surely did not mean to have it turn around so that you would be questioning your own status as king!" She passed her hand lightly over Harold's chest. "You are a good man, and you are a great king for England. The people have put their trust in you because you will not let them down. Already you have shown them your capacity for organizing their protection by keeping Norman invaders from our shores."

Harold kissed Edyth on the forehead. "Perhaps we both worry too much." He kissed her cheeks; her lips. Edyth responded with vigor. When they had both spent their energy, the woman slept. Harold lay back for some time before exhaustion overtook his wandering thoughts to allow him some sleep as well. It was a fitful sleep for the King, however.

*   *   *   *

After many hours, although it seemed only a moment to Harold, Edyth shook his arm to wake him. "Harold? Were you dreaming? It seemed as though you were struggling to breathe! I had to awaken you!"

"Yes, Edyth, I was dreaming." Harold sat up in the bed, breathing deep. "A disturbing dream. A confusing dream." Harold shook his shoulders to loosen up, rubbed his hands together as if to warm the cold feeling left by the dream.

The concerned woman gently massaged his shoulders. "Perhaps you should talk about it, let the demons free from your head—"

"It was strange, disorganized. In my dream I was sleeping as well. Something woke me and I sat up in bed, but could not see the room around me. Someone was blocking my eyes. The person spoke, and it was a woman's voice.

Edyth sat closer, continuing to rub Harold's back. "Mine?"

Harold brushed his hand across her cheek. "No, my dear, I do not think so. But I know not who it was."

"What did she say, this lady in your dreams?" Edyth found herself to be a little jealous, however unreasonable that was.

"I do not remember," Harold paused. "She was singing some song. Softly, like a siren in the rocks. It seemed her hands covered my eyes, but I was unable to move my own arms to remove hers from about my head. I spoke, asking, Who are you? That stopped the singing and at the same time I could see."

Harold laid back down, staring up at the ceiling. Edyth filled a glass of water from the night table and held it out to Harold, but he merely shook his head.

"What did you see, Harold?"

"It was not my own room, but a beach. I was alone; the woman had gone. Waves rushed in around me, tugging at me as they went back out to sea. Each wave was a little bigger, until their strength threatened to pull me out into the water. I could not move; could not back out of the water. I crouched low as the wave hit me. When I looked up, I was in a field, kneeling before a great stone cross."

Edyth gasped. "The Rood!"

"No, Edyth, not the holy crucifix at Waltham, but simply a cross. The monolith towered above me, and it began to speak to me, in a language I could not understand; yet a voice I understood. It was warning me of something. I wanted to ask of it to explain the meaning of the warning; but just then a huge bird, black as the night came out of the north and dived for my head. I ducked, and it was gone.

"At that point, I realized there were many men around me, a hunting party. In front of me was a great, wild, spotted cat. The cat came bounding toward me, and again I could not move. The men around me yelled and threw things at the beast, but it did not stop. As the animal struck me, I went down to the ground, tucking my head in and rolling like a ball. I wanted to come up ready for another attack; however, it was not a cat then, but a huge wave, taller than this house which struck me. I was immersed in water as the wave dragged me out into the murky depths. I found I could not struggle to stay afloat. All my energy was gone."

Harold stopped telling his story. Edyth grew afraid. "Oh Harold! Were…you…dead?"

A knock at the door startled them both. Wulfstan peered in. "My lord? I fear I must disturb you! I have pressing news." The Bishop of Worcester stepped into the room. The candle he held was the only light, and the two figures in the bed were completely in shadow. Harold jumped out of bed, catching himself at the bedpost as his stiff knee buckled under his weight. He did not notice the pain.

"William has landed." Harold spoke it before his friend could say anything else. They all had known it was going to happen.

"No, my lord. It is not the Normans. I bear news from the north. Haraald of Norway has burned to the ground the village of Scarborough in Northumberland!"

The King of England was stunned. His sore leg gave out completely and he dropped back to sit on the edge of the bed. His mind was reeling. What on Earth had brought that berserker out of his frozen fjords?

"Tostig!" Harold's voice was just a whisper in the darkness, but Edyth had heard him. She drew in her breath sharply. Wulfstan heard as well.

"Yes, Harold. The messenger from Northumbria has said that your brother Tostig is indeed with the Norwegian horde."

Harold rallied quickly. "Wulfstan is it?"

"It is I, my lord."

"Of course it is. Call Robert FitzWimark! Tell him to ready the house-carls. We will muster the fyrd as we ride north!"

"Yes, my lord!"

"Wulfstan?"

"Yes, my lord?" The man's head slipped back into the room.

Harold struggled to find some saliva to wet his tongue and throat. "What of young Morcar?"

"Sire, there was no news of the Earl of Northumbria, except that his brother Edwin of Mercia was in Yorkshire with him. I expect the people will rally around their young Earls and make a valiant defense in the north."

"Yes, of course. And I will ride out with support from the south of England as well! Go now, my friend. We will leave at dawn!"

"Yes, Harold!"

The man at the door was gone, and with him the light. Edyth slid down to the foot of the bed and squeezed Harold's shoulders. "What do you make of it, Harold? Tostig, and the Norwegians?"

The darkness hid Harold's expression. If Edyth could have seen it, she would have been surprised to see it looking much less careworn than it had for many months. "What I make it to be is the answer to my questions. That fiery beacon at Easter did proclaim the first arrival of my brother at Southampton. I have been worried about William when the omens have been warning me to watch for Tostig! I am afraid I did not take the man seriously enough. But now I must meet him on the battle field."

"Then you will fight your own brother?"

Harold turned to give the woman a great hug before standing up. "He may be my brother, but he is dangerous for England. I will meet him with an army of English at my back. There is no room for the Northmen on English soil! Tostig should have known that before he ever thought to bring those foreigners here."

Entry XIII

▼

In which the Duke's plans appear to be dashed

"My lady!" Hildreth screamed!

However strong she appeared to her servant, Godiva had been deathly afraid of being caught in her deception before even getting on a boat. Then, she became painfully aware of what it would mean to be discovered after the boat had left the coast of Normandy. Their one protector, Gunthnot, would not be a match for all the soldiers on board, surely. The two women could be manhandled by the men and easily thrown overboard to become food for the creatures of the sea. But Lady Godiva and her companions were pleased to find that the plan worked. The soldiers left them to their side of the boat, keeping the relatively clean horses between them and the filthy peasants. When the last of the Duke's fleet left on the ebb tide of the River Dives, Godiva thought they were safe. The overcast sky kept the night dark, and by the same time tomorrow the three stowaways would be back in England and could easily slip away from the invading army.

As the light of day filtered through the overcast sky over the fleet in the Channel, the last of the ships had already cleared the Bay of the Seine hours earlier, and all were in open water, out of sight of land on any side. That was not what was surprising to the helmsman. What set the men on the ship on edge was that the fleet had broken up in the darkness, and they could only see a handful of other ships near them.

"My lady!" Hildreth bellowed again, as the boat lurched upon the great waves borne of the Channel tides.

"I cannot watch the horses and you, Hildreth," Godiva answered into the wind. "And stop saying 'my lady' !" Hildreth seemed to have forgotten to act out their parts as extra groomsmen for the cavalry's horses. At that moment, though, it did not matter. The soldiers on board were far too concerned for their own safety to worry over the cries of the peasants on the ship with them.

It had not been long before the helmsman of the boat recognized what had happened. The strong wind that billowed their sails had, gently through the night, changed direction, building in strength as it did so. When land was sighted, it was the coast of Normandy to which they were being driven by the now increasingly strong westerly wind.

Even the larger sized boat that Godiva and her companions had boarded was rocking uncontrollably. Horses, sensing the growing fear in the men, began themselves to panic. The beasts began struggling vigorously to free themselves from their bonds, and their agitation added to the overall confusion on deck. Lady Godiva and Gunthnot strained to calm the beasts within their reach, but Hildreth was of no help at all. As the boat rocked to the other side, Hildreth cried out again before tumbling into a thole on the side of the vessel. The oar hole stuck out just enough to catch the maidservant and keep her from falling overboard, but she struck it with her head, fell unconscious to the deck.

"Gunthnot! I will be back in a moment." Lady Godiva scrambled to her maid's side, dragging a piece of rope meant for the horses. She lashed the unconscious woman to the side of the ship, tying the rope securely to the very thole that had saved Hildreth's life, but had left her senseless. The boat pitched as Godiva stood, sending her reeling across the deck to the other side. She crawled back to where Gunthnot still stood holding the reins of four of the horses.

"We cannot take much more of this, my lady!"

"I do know it. I am sure the helmsman will take us in to shore as soon as he can find safe harbor."

"Then let it be soon, my lady! The wind may drive us ashore, harbor or no, and we will be dashed upon the rocks. Even if we survive on this swaying vessel without being trampled by these beasts, we surely will not come through a shipwreck unscathed."

"Yes. We have our hands full keeping the animals as steady as we might, so let us pray that God has directed us to a boat with a pilot worth his weight in gold! In this northwesterly gale, all the helmsman can do is keep the sail at an angle to the wind and follow the shore until we can reach safety."

As fate would have it, on that September morning, the ship of the Lady Godiva followed just the path that Harold of Wessex had traveled two years earlier. There were no safe harbors along the coast before Saint Valery on the Somme, and it was to there that the helmsman steered the vessel. As the ship made its way into the safety of the harbor, they passed close to the shore and could see numerous vessels whose pilots were not so adept, or ships that were just not so lucky, leaving the boats to be crushed upon the rocky shoreline of Ponthieu.

The horses settled down somewhat as the boat entered the more calm waters. The wind that had been so unkind came now from the north to push them into the harbor and into safety. Lady Godiva looked around to the many other ships that had made it to Saint Valery before them. She saw at last the Mora, William's flag ship, and she knew then that the Duke's entire fleet had been pushed away from England by the contrary winds. It would be some time before the Duke of Normandy could assess just how much of his force he had lost this day. No doubt there would be some boats that were lost at sea, and then there were the unlucky ones she had seen along the shore; but it looked to Godiva as if much of the Duke's strike force was yet intact in the harbor.

Gunthnot stepped beside Godiva. "My lady, are you all right?"

"Yes." Godiva answered, speaking very softly.

Gunthnot was winded, but smiling. "We are alive, and the ship is safe. A victory for us as well as the helmsman!"

Godiva turned to look at Hildreth, and over her maidservant to the open sea to the north. The wind blew strongly in her face, and she knew this was no victory for the Duke of Normandy. They would be stuck on the coast once again, waiting for a favorable wind that would probably not come again until Spring. Duke William's grand invasion was dashed by the fickle wind, and Lady Godiva would spend another winter in foreign lands. Hildreth began to stir, just as a cold rain began to fall on them all.

Entry XIV

▼

After Harold met Haraald at the village of Stamford Bridge

The soldier threw the fabric at the King of England's feet. "My Lord Harold, here is the battle standard of the King of Norway, and the man who was unconscious beside it. He does carry your brother's cloak and signet, but the man is not Tostig. I am sorry, my lord. There are so many bodies, I do not—"

"Yes, I know." The King of England stood outside the gates of York on the surprisingly warm and sunny day, the twenty-sixth of September. He was flanked by his friends, Robert FitzWimark and Bishop Wulfstan, and a score of housecarls. The fighting had gone on the entire previous day, ending after dusk as the few remaining Norwegians fled to their ships docked at Riccall. Harold looked down at the Land-ravager banner of Haraald Hardrada, the black raven on the now quite dirty, white background. He recalled the sight he was met with that very morning, the open country about the River Derwent littered with the bloating bodies of the dead. Thousands of good men merely raven's bait now, and the Raven of Norway had landed to feast for the last time. The night before, after the battle was won, Harold remembered joking with his soldiers about the waste of good English countryside if they were to bury the Norwegian dead. Viewing the debacle in the light of day, the King made no more jests. The English had definitely won a great battle, but the land was indeed laid waste.

"So many dead," Harold spoke softly, and his friends followed his gaze down to the Raven Banner. Robert FitzWimark stepped onto the standard on the ground.

"A great victory, Harold!"

"A great victory, but one that was almost in the hands of the Norwegian King." Harold did not look up, almost as if he spoke to the raven on the standard at his feet.   .

"I do not know about Haraald achieving a victory, but I daresay there was a point I thought we would have a stalemate across the Derwent! I was not so sure that one Norse berserker on the bridge would ever be brought down!"

Wulfstan spoke then. "Perhaps King Harold is thinking about what we would have been faced with had the King of Norway gained the captives before we made it to York on Sunday last."

Robert FitzWimark laughed. "It seems that Haraald had thought the fighting over, the kingdom of England won after his short battle with the men of York at Fulford! The people of York say that the Norwegians were festive and relaxed. Haraald found himself an Englishwoman, and that seemed to be all the man did want!"

After winning the skirmish at Fulford, the King of Norway had wanted to be assured there would be no more hard fought battles. He wanted more plunder for his army without the worry of losing too many more of his men. Haraald had settled down to await the delivery to him of some English hostages to assure him the English had capitulated.

"But we cannot look upon the timing of the hostage exchange as merely good luck," FitzWimark continued, stepping closer to the Bishop.

"If Harold had not sent a messenger on ahead of our army requesting the people of York stall any negotiations, perhaps things would have been different. Nevertheless, it makes Harold's victory all the more complete! When the invaders, basking in the sun with no chain mail as if they were on holiday, saw not a few hundred hostages coming toward them from York but an English host thick with shields and spears…well, I will wager the chroniclers will write songs of yesterday to rival the story of the Battle of Brunanburh and Athelstan's defeat of a different alliance of northern enemies so long ago!"

Harold brought his attention to the soldier before him. "I do want Haraald's body found! I promised the man six feet of English earth, and I will fulfill my pledge to him." The King saw the look on the soldier's face. "And, as for my brother Tostig, continue to look for his body as well."

"Yes, King Harold."

"I have had word from Riccall that he is definitely not among the survivors stuck there. I do believe my brother is dead."

"I will continue the search, my lord."

As the soldier gratefully left the King's sight, Harold looked at last to the man that had been brought before him. His skin and clothes were begrimed, his head wounded, a trickle of blood ran down the left side of his head. The man's eyes were swollen, but there was no defiance in them, only extreme exhaustion. Harold stepped over to the captive, quite surprised when he realized that he knew the man. Despite his own mood, the King smiled. He spoke softly, but strongly, so that the other man would know his feelings to be true.

"Aldbald, my friend. Never would I have dreamed that we would meet again under such conditions as these today."

"Nor I, my Lord Harold, and I am ashamed for it myself." Aldbald cringed, his head reeling as he spoke.

Harold frowned. "Do not talk, if it hurts your head to do so, my friend. And do not be ashamed, Aldbald. I knew you were a sworn servant to my brother, and I commend your loyalty. Would that I could have offered him as much as you have. But I could not think of his interests, had to think instead for England."

"That is precisely what I do feel ashamed about. Surely I did not want to abandon my master, yet even so I never wanted to fight my own people. When Lord Tostig—" Aldbald caught himself, looked questioningly to Harold.

"It is quite all right to refer to my brother as Lord Tostig. The man is dead, I am sure. We can give him at least that now."

Aldbald continued. "When Lord Tostig and the King of Norway set out to attack England, I only thought to join the expedition so that I could return to England myself. I swore an oath to your brother, yet how could I attack my own people? But your brother did not let me out of his service." When Tostig realized that Aldbald was going to flee at the first chance, he set a soldier to guard the cottar. Aldbald thought of the berserker Bufread Bloodyaxe who had welcomed the job.

"My lord, Tostig learned that I planned to leave, and he kept me by his side the whole time, right until the end."

Harold nodded. "And how did you come to wear the clothes of my brother?"

"When King Haraald fell and your brother picked up the King of Norway's banner, Lord Tostig bade me hold the Norse standard aloft as he screamed his refusal to your offer of a truce."

"Yes. Had the Norse reinforcements from the boats at Riccall not come just at that time, I am sure Tostig would have seen his cause was lost then."

"Even so, my lord, it was not long before it became apparent that the battle was lost anyway. Lord Tostig switched cloaks with me and made off, hoping to make his escape. Your soldiers were upon our position before I could get away myself."

"And did you see if my brother did get safely away?"

Aldbald hung his head. He remembered seeing Uthgar of Orkney die fairly early. The Norseman called Rodgain the Relentless outlived the King of Norway, but not by very long. Even Bufread Bloodyaxe of

Northumbria died during the most violent fighting toward the end of the day before. No one Aldbald knew had made it alive.

"My lord, I did not see your brother's fate. But I do not think he survived. Your soldiers overran our position too quickly."

Harold nodded. "Yes, my friend, and I am sure that you survived with only the blow of a blunt instrument because my men thought you were my brother. Funny, Tostig had thought to lose his identity and escape, but it was probably his identity that saved your life."

Aldbald hung his head. "Yes, Lord Harold, I suppose so."

Harold smiled for the second time that morning. "Aldbald, my friend! Do not look so glum. I mean it, I am proud of your loyalty to my brother. I would have you come into my service, if it be your wish."

"My lord?"

"I know you have always wanted to learn, and perhaps have not done as much as you could as servant to my brother. In my service, I will send you as soon as I can to learn from the monks at Waltham Abbey. They are my friends, and all are good men, and bright. That will be the first task for you to complete in my service: Learn as much as you can from them!"

Aldbald's eyes lit up. "My lord, thank you!"

Harold reached to examine the man's wound. "You have received quite a blow to the head, my friend. I will have my healers take care of you straight away." Harold motioned quietly to one of the guards, pointing back into York where Harold's house-servants had gotten together with the people of York to organize a place to care for the wounded.

"Treat this man as the wounded Englishman that he is, not as an enemy."

"Yes, King Harold." The soldier stepped toward the gates of York, but Aldbald hung back.

The Englishmen saw the group coming up the road toward the gates of York. Aldbald recognized the three men in front of the small party as the King of Norway's son Olaf the Quiet, and Paul and Erlend, the two young sons of the Norwegian Earl of Orkney who had accompanied Haraald in order that he look favorably upon them as possible matches for the King's own daughters. None of the three young men showed any of the cockiness with which they had begun their latest adventure with the King of Norway. They had spent the night camped by their boats, knowing that they not only lost the battle at Stamford Bridge, but that there would be no more battles. A ring of English housecarls formed around the advancing party of Norwegians, and the King of England walked down the road to meet the procession.

"I have been awaiting the arrival of a delegation from Riccall!" Harold spoke to the men in their own tongue. "What have you to say to the King of England?"

Olaf the Quiet stepped away from the rest to stand before Harold. "What would you have us say? We have lost, and you have won the field. We have come here today to hear what you have to say, Harold of England. Make what demands you will. We must accept." The Norseman glanced up at the gatehouse to York, was quite surprised to not find the head of his father on a pike at the entryway to the city.

Harold followed the foreign man's gaze, saw above them the Golden Dragon Banner standing proud in the strong south wind over York. What more could he want? The invaders were vanquished, and the young northern earls, the grandchildren of Lady Godiva, were alive and secure in their positions. Harold laughed. What better sign could he send to England? Harold motioned to a soldier behind him to fetch the raven banner on the ground.

"Olaf Haraaldsson! Swear to me that you, and all your associates, will never come to England again! Swear this upon your father's standard, and I will let you all go."

The son of Haraald the Ruthless cocked his eye at the King of England. This man who had just won such an amazing victory would not let them all go home, Olaf thought to himself. Harold will keep some hostages, surely. He himself would probably spend the rest of his life as a hostage in England.

"Swear this to me, Olaf!" Harold said again.

Olaf the Quiet dropped down to one knee before Harold, grabbed the cloth held out to him by the King of England. "By the great Haraald

Hardrada, I swear that I have had enough of fighting Englishmen. I swear that I and my countrymen will leave your realm in peace, if you will let us go."

"Then be gone! You will be allowed to go back to Riccall and take what ships you need to carry your surviving companions home and away from England. The wind is favorable for your northerly trip, and I do expect you to make sail before the wind does change. But, be prepared to row against the wind should it change, for I will not have any of you stuck on English soil!"

As the Norwegians backed away, Harold turned to see Robert FitzWimark's look of surprise. "Do not look so, my friend! As you have said, we did win a great battle yesterday, and no one will sing the praises of the mighty English housecarls as will the defeated Norsemen themselves! You can bet they will not again try and attack England."

"But, Harold, without taking captives and collecting ransoms for the survivors, the invaders' ships would be the only spoils of this war we could take. Yet you give them their ships back as well?"

Harold watched the retreating Norwegians heading back to the banks of the River Ouse and the town of Riccall. "How else can we be rid of them? Besides, Rob, you saw how many men they have left. They will only have the men to pilot perhaps one eighth of their navy. Better to let them go with what they can take and be done with them. We will still collect many more than one hundred of their abandoned ships."

Harold's gaze followed after the Norwegians, his cheeks felt the gentle southerly breeze. "Funny, is it not, Rob? All summer we have been glad for the north wind that kept William from attacking our southern coast, only to have the same wind bring Haraald and Tostig to Northumberland. And now I do welcome the southerly wind that will take these God-accursed Norsemen back to their home and away from England for good. I have often wondered at the ability to control the tides upon our shores; but now I do see how much more important is the control of the winds in the heavens!"

Entry XV

Where the Lady Godiva summons the fyrd

The night fog was thick. Each sound brought the Lady Godiva's head around, expecting to see Englishmen emerge from the blackness.

"Where is Harold?!" Godiva muttered for the third time as she strained to see around her.

Hildreth was nervous. Finally back in England, she wanted just to go home. "Why has Gunthnot not come back, my lady? He was to seek out our countrymen...perhaps he was discovered by the invaders instead?"

"No," Godiva said, "he will be back soon to meet us here at the appointed time. Do not worry for Gunthnot, the man is cautious and resourceful. He will be here."

"He will be here soon," Godiva said again, partly to soothe her own growing discontent.

No one knew whether it was the parading of the holy relics of Saint Valery before the town and the gifts of gold coins with which the crusaders inundated the shrine that miraculously altered the course of the wind, or if it was just damnable good luck as many of the Duke's closest companions thought. Whatever the reason, the wind had finally changed to southerly on Tuesday, the twenty-sixth of September, and it held steady quite long enough for Duke William of Normandy to launch his invasion the following night. After the false start two weeks before, Duke William had known that this would be his last chance.

The Lady Godiva also knew that she would have to try again to make the crossing back to England. Many, grand men and groomsmen alike, had fled after the Duke's first failed attempt to make it to England. Those soldiers that remained welcomed any who stayed to lend a hand with the horses and supplies. Godiva and her servants found no difficulty carrying on their masquerade once more. After what seemed like an easy Channel crossing this time, the army of the Duke of Normandy had spotted the coast of England and made their landing.

Quite a surprise to all was that the invasion force landed without any resistance. While the foreigners scrambled to organize their forces, erect defensive barricades and scout the coastal areas, the Englishwoman and her two servants slipped away into the dark woods.

A recognizable noise came from the trees to the women's left. It was Gunthnot's signal.

"Ah, Gunthnot," cried Hildreth.

Raising her hand to quiet the maidservant, Godiva spoke softly, "My good Gunthnot, what have you found? Where is the English army?"

"My lady," Gunthnot answered, "there is no army."

Godiva scowled. "Explain."

"My lady, I have spoken with a coast watcher, one of the King's men. Lord Harold did release the fyrd a short time ago."

"Released them?" Godiva cocked her head, then nodded. "Of course, it is harvest time. The men would have been itching to get back to their homes." Godiva stepped closer to her servant. "But, where is Harold?"

"My lady, there is more to the story," Gunthnot continued. "Lord Harold has apparently traveled far away to repel invaders in Northumberland. Or so the thanes of Sussex seem to understand."

"Northumberland?"

Gunthnot nodded. "Harold must have been needed to run off a raiding band of Northmen."

"Then there is no one to fight the Normans," Godiva said. "Gunthnot, you said you spoke to a coast watcher? Then the news of events here in Sussex has been sent to Harold?"

"I believe so, my lady," Gunthnot replied.

Godiva knew that Harold would head back south as soon as possible once he heard the latest news.

"We will spread the word that all able-bodied men should be prepared to join their King when Harold arrives." Godiva explained.

Hildreth dropped her head to her chest with a sob. "I am not cut out for this kind of life, my lady!"

The Lady grasped her maidservant's shoulder reassuringly. "I know, and I am sorry, Hildreth. But we must be off again. We will travel home to Mercia. I can gather the fyrd there and send them to meet Harold here in Sussex in days."

Gunthnot grunted. "Dare I say it, my lady, but that might be too many days."

"What choice have we? We must try, Gunthnot!"

"Yes, my lady, I agree we should organize the army. But remember, Harold would have only traveled north with his housecarls. The fyrd of Sussex and Wessex are closer than Mercia and can be called back from their fields to fight."

Godiva shook her head. "Mercia is our home. My people know me and will follow me."

"My lady, the people here are already learning there are invaders afoot on the Sussex coast," Gunthnot said. "You need only travel from shire to shire to give the people someone to rally around.

"Believe me, my lady, you are well known throughout all of England.," Gunthnot added. "The people will follow you."

Godiva paused only a moment. "You are right, of course. It is too far to Mercia. Let us also hope you are right about our ability to muster the fyrd here in Godwin lands."

Entry XVI

▼

In which Harold meets William near Hastings

King Harold and his housecarls made the long trip from Northumberland to the southern coast in record time. Still, it had taken time, and for two weeks there was only silence in the English woods. The invaders did not know what this meant. Duke William had known that Harold would be waiting for him. The Normans, with no supply lines and only hastily built defenses, expected the worst at any time.

Then suddenly, so it appeared to the invaders, a huge army of Englishmen materialized out of the dark Forest of Andredsweald. Heeding the call of Lady Godiva of Mercia, the fyrd had assembled in such great numbers that many of the local farmers had retired to their homes for lack of a place to stand amidst the English army massed at Caldbec Hill.

The invaders had moved at once to engage the enemy. Now, the foreign horde lay sprawled out below the ridge just south of Caldbec Hill. There were Flemish and Frenchman, Bretons and brigands, minstrels and marauders, cavaliers and crusaders. The weak hearted ones had already dispersed at St. Valery after the invasion force was pummeled by the contrary channel winds. Those that remained were intent upon plunder, slaughter, and defeating the evil English in the name of the Lord.

The lull before the fight could not last forever, and battle was joined well before mid-day on that late September morning. A stray arrow shot by a Burgundian crossbowman tested the range up to the waiting English army. English housecarls cheered on their fellow countrymen, all laughing at the bow shot from below that fell short. The invaders were strangely quiet themselves, even as the Englishmen shouted taunts and waved suggestive gestures towards the Norman army assembled before them.

Aldbald stood next to the King of the English, in the middle of the English line, holding the Golden Dragon Banner of Wessex that fluttered in the breeze overhead. Aldbald watched Harold look about him, as he had done so many times that morning already, and he wondered what the king saw. Faces of friends, strangers, nobleman and farmers all looked toward King Harold expectantly. For his part, Aldbald saw not a strong English army ready to fight for their king, but a mass of his fellow Englishmen assembled and ready to die for their country.

In their lines ahead of Aldbald, the ranks of English fyrd and soldiers stood eight men thick. There were far too many for King Harold to deliver battlefield orders with any hope of their being heard by all. The King had passed the word through his captains before the battle began that they would be defending the path. After the battle with the Norwegians and the forced march from the north, a defense of the hill was the best strategy. Let the invaders try and break through if they could.

With the Norman army organized not two hundred yards away, Aldbald would have felt more secure if the look in Harold's face was more relaxed. "My lord, King Harold," Aldbald whispered. "What is it? Are you worried about the upcoming battle?"

Robert FitzWimark overheard Aldbald's question as he approached the two men. He clapped Aldbald on the shoulder and laughed. "There is nothing to fear, friend. Your king has chosen well the point at which we should make the defense of our land!"

Aldbald turned to the newcomer with a questioning look. "I do not have an eye for battlefield tactics my lord. Are we then assured a victory today?"

FitzWimark spread his arms out in the direction of the invaders. "The enemy forces are assembled before us as you see, but placed as we are along this ridge perpendicular to the road heading north, our army stands guarding the only path the invaders can take inland. The Normans, for all of their cavalry and organization, can not simply outflank us in this difficult terrain. And they know it, too! You can see that they hold back."

Harold nodded. "Yes, and we must remain here to defend the high ground. Our men are battle-weary enough. We must not lose the advantage or we could lose the day."

Harold then turned to his young companion. "Aldbald. What do you make of it all."

"My lord?"

"First it was Haraald of Norway and Tostig. Now it is William of Normandy. What has gone so wrong that England would find itself so beset by aggression? You were with my brother and the Norwegians, I thought you might have some insight I seem to lack."

Aldbald hung his head. He did not want to be reminded of that fateful day at Stamford Bridge when he was forced to stand with foreigners against an army of Englishmen. When he did not answer, Harold continued.

"All I had wanted was to keep Englishmen safe and secure in their villages. Allow them to sow their crops and reap their rewards without the worry of raiders upon their homes, their families. Even the Lord himself seems to be against England! Why?!" Robert FitzWimark gave Harold a disapproving look; but, before he or Aldbald could say anything, Harold continued. "I refuse to believe, as the late King Edward would have, that these may be trials set upon us by the Lord because of the internal corruption within the English church and nobility. England is no different from the rest of Europe."

"Now Harold," FitzWimark began, "you know that William of Normandy used his contacts in Rome to gain the Pope's favor."

"Still, can I take it lightly that the Bastard of Normandy attacks England under the Papal Banner? How did I, a son of the great Godwin, get myself into this mess anyway? I never meant to be king. As sub-king under Edward, I had power and ability to keep England at peace. I had my health, and Edyth beside me. Whatever went wrong, the fire in the April sky may have been a portent of doom for England after all. Or—" Harold looked away from his friends, into some vaguely defined time and place. "Doom for me alone."

Robert FitzWimark was exasperated. "Do not even think it, my lord."

Aldbald wanted to say something, to agree with FitzWimark, but a call from the front ranks of the English line brought the three of them back to the battlefield.

"My lord," Aldbald said, "I do believe the invaders are attacking."

Harold shook himself. "Then let us show these foreigners what a mistake their invasion was!"

The English had no experience in fighting a foe on horseback. Even the standing army of housecarls who relied on the animals to deliver them across the miles of English paths and roads left their mounts behind when it was time to fight. The English had learned to fight from their Germanic and Scandinavian ancestors. It was not a matter of a preference for having the earth beneath their feet; but rather a simple lack of ever contemplating the use of a small English pony to carry them into the thick of battle. Standing on their own, English housecarls had gained quite a reputation for being the most fearless of fighters. Even now, in the face of an oncoming cavalry charge, something very alien to their experience, the housecarls stood their ground, holding the fyrd together with their own resolute stance.

That is not to say that the men of the fyrd were not scared. The chivalric army that threatened them was almost a demon, something brought out of Hell to ravish their lands. If not for the courage of the housecarls and their king, Harold Godwinsson, the farmers and craftsmen would have fled the field after the first onslaught. However, the English ranks held together and the Norman army found itself faced with something almost as horrifying to them as the cavalry charge was to the fyrd: the English battle-ax. Handled by the tenacious housecarls in the front of the English line, the huge battle-ax proved to be a deadlier weapon than were the swords, or even the spears which could be disastrous to a cavalry charge. The soldiers stepped free from the English shield wall, swinging their battle-axes freely to clear a path through the charging enemy line.

The invading army's initial attack ended in chaos. There were so many Englishmen that the initial barrage of arrows from below did little damage to the English shield wall. The foreign foot soldiers advanced, only to find a solid line of English still eight men thick throughout, and their assault did little to weaken the defenders any further. When the cavalry charged what they had hoped would be a weakened and demoralized line, Duke William and his cavaliers found they were unable to break the English ranks.

Aldbald held the Golden Dragon Banner aloft, and the English army drew up tight around their leader, awaiting the next assault on their position. Harold bent his head down, closed his eyes. Aldbald looked for encouragement from the King. "My lord! We have repulsed their attack. I cannot see well from our position amidst the ranks, but it looks like the invaders are in full retreat!"

"No, Aldbald," Harold shook his head. "I am sure we have not seen the end to the battle this day. Only a moment of respite while the invaders reorganize."

Aldbald watched as Robert FitzWimark walked among the Englishmen in front of them, clapping backs and keeping moral high. A cry of warning near Aldbald showed the standard bearer that the King had been right.

The invaders had reorganized quickly and another barrage of arrows came down from overhead.

The men in the English ranks felt strengthened by the knowledge that they had easily repulsed the first attack. The aggressors' next charge broke on the English right flank where the Earl of East Anglia stood in command. The invaders' left division, mainly Bretons from Maine, Anjou and Brittany, retreated through their own infantry and archers, escaped into the marshy valley below Caldbec Hill. The retreat spread to the Norman cavalry in the center of the attack, and then to the French horsemen of the invaders' right flank. The foot soldiers turned on their heels as well.

"King Harold was right," a housecarl of East Anglia called to Gyrth Godwinsson. "The horsemen need more room to maneuver! They cannot break through our shield wall in this terrain the King chose for our defensive line."

Gyrth glanced at his captain, then back to the invaders running back down the hill. "Harold was partly right, yes. But, see how they run from us? We should attack now!"

The captain pursed his lips. "My lord, I do not think that would be wise. King Harold ordered a defensive battle. We cannot expect to pass the word through the entire army that we are switching to the attack!"

Gyrth grunted. "I agreed to my brother the King's defensive plan and let him lead as he did desire; but perhaps I should not have. Harold and the housecarls of Wessex are tired. And rightly so, after such a great battle in Northumberland. But I am not so sure we should play this battle so conservatively.

"We have the Norman peasants on the run! I believe it is time to give these invaders a taste of English retribution. See there," Gyrth pointed, "the horsemen have become mired in the mud of the ditch. We might easily turn this retreat into a rout! Call out the charge, my friend. Let us pursue these villains while we have the upper hand. Harold will see and follow!"

A mob of Englishmen followed Gyrth, inflicting heavy casualties upon the foreign soldiers. Gyrth bellowed a cry of triumph. He spun around in shock when he realized the bulk of the English army still held their ground about their king. In a panic, Gyrth called for a retreat. Although the Earl of East Anglia and his followers had destroyed many of the Breton soldiers that had made the last assault, Duke William rallied his retreating army and brought a contingent of Norman cavalry to bear down on Gyrth. The horsemen rode down the motley crew of English trying to make their way back up the slope of the ravine.

Gyrth turned to face the horsemen coming at them. Recognizing the Duke of Normandy at the front of the counter-attack, the Earl screamed an oath as he dropped his sword and picked up a spear stuck in the ground near him. With all his skill and strength, Gyrth hurled the javelin at the leader of the invaders. The light lance traveled true; but as the Duke's horse reared up to jump over a mound of fallen men, the spear met the unprotected flesh of the animal just below the withers. William jumped free as the beast went down. Still holding his sword, the Duke of Normandy ran to cut Gyrth down before the Englishman could rearm himself.

Without needing a direct order, Englishmen moved from the ranks behind to strengthen the weakened right flank. The handful of Gyrth's men that survived regrouped with the main body of the English line, looking for some outward sign from their King to help rally them. In the pause that followed the attack, the word spread through the ranks that Gyrth had died, and a great cry went up from the mob, challenging the attackers to try again.

Aldbald heard the news passed from the front of the line. "My lord King," Aldbald cried. "Your brother Lord Gyrth is dead!"

Harold clasped his left hand over his right forearm, letting the point of the sword he held drop to the ground. "Damn. What was he thinking? Of all days to decide not to listen to me—"

"My lord?" Aldbald's question was answered as Robert FitzWimark came up breathless to stand beside Harold.

"Harold, your brother broke ranks! He knew you had ordered a defensive battle. It is the only way to hold our own until we can recuperate our full strength. I know Gyrth wanted to attack, but why did he not listen to your orders?"

Harold looked down at his right arm, tried to raise the sword that seemed immovable. "That is a good question, my friend. Why?"

Aldbald was quiet for a moment, then whispered to his king, "My lord, the enemy comes again."

Harold glanced up and over the English line to see Duke William's army approaching with what looked like the exact same maneuver as they had tried in the previous assault.

"My friends," the King said, "I do believe the invaders think the English line has been thinned enough to be weakened. They are in for a surprise!"

"Indeed they are!" With that, FitzWimark was off to make sure the King's right flank was reorganized.

The English shield wall again stood firm, and the attackers were repulsed. It was the French on the invaders' right flank that broke first this time, and Leofwine Godwinsson, the commander of the English left, called out for vengeance for his brother. He led a band to follow the retreating enemy. With no order from Harold, the bulk of the English army stayed fixed in their place, leaving the Earl of Kent in the same precarious position his brother had been only a short time before. This time, however, a band of Norman cavalry had been held in reserve to meet such a circumstance. Duke William again led the charge as the horsemen slaughtered the unprotected Englishmen to the man.

The word was passed through the English throng, this time that Leofwine Godwinsson was gone. The ranks of the fyrd began to falter. Robert FitzWimark again made his way through the English line to Harold.

"My God, Harold! Leofwine is gone now!"

"Yes! Rob, I know," Harold spoke quickly. He felt as if both of his arms had been amputated, his heart pulled straight out of his chest. But there was little time for remorse. The Englishmen around Harold lacked the insight to take on the battle themselves, lacked the courage without their leaders' strong presence. With his brothers gone, it was completely up to Harold and FitzWimark now.

Harold grasped his friend's shoulder. "And we have already lost more men than I had hoped to, Rob. Still, our lines are thick, our shield wall strong. Aldbald, bring my banner behind me! I will stand beside Rob at the front of the line so that all our people can see me!"

As Harold moved forward, the Norman army made another offensive move. Some of the English fyrdmen had let their weapons drop, were beginning to scatter. Harold moved into the midst of them. He did not need to say anything, his mere presence in their sight offered the encouragement they needed. Those who could not see their king directly saw the Golden Dragon of Wessex roaring defiantly overhead. Men retrieved their weapons, dashed them against their shields to meet the oncoming enemy with a horrendous racket. The Norman cavalry drew reign, and the English became all the louder in their excitement.

The English were not the only ones that had gotten a glimpse of their leader. Duke William spotted Harold in the middle of the remaining Englishmen, and brought his Norman cavalry together around him.

"Men," the Duke pointed to the Dragon Banner on the hill, "that is where we will concentrate the strength of our next charge. Osbern, have the bowmen all aim in the vicinity of that banner in the middle. We must break their line this time, or we will be forced to retire. It is already getting dangerously dark for riding our steeds up that hill!"

Norman bowmen that had moved up ahead of the horse soldiers let loose a barrage to sail in a high trajectory over the English line and into the ranks behind, then the foot soldiers moved up the hill once again and the cavalry prepared to charge. The day was getting late, and the invaders had lost more men and horses than they cared to notice.

If not for a stray projectile, the English may have won the day. In the face of the enemy, Harold looked to heaven with a prayer, and an arrow dropped out of the sky and into his eye.

In the dusk, the attackers did not recognize that Harold was hit, but the English around their King knew immediately. The fyrd in the back lines began a disorganized retreat to the woods behind them. Aldbald let out a cry when he saw Harold go down, let the Dragon Banner he held start to drop. Robert FitzWimark who had moved off to the left, reached their position as quickly as he could. He grabbed the pole from Aldbald's hands.

"Do not let the royal banner drop! Our countrymen must see it waving above them."

"But Harold is down!" With that, Aldbald left the banner to the half-Breton and knelt beside Harold, was surprised to find Harold lived still. The arrow had come down at such an angle that Harold's right eye alone was destroyed. Aldbald broke the shaft of the arrow, but left the point to be removed by someone who knew more about medicine. Harold moaned, held his hands to his head to try and squeeze the pain out. With one eye damaged, the King could not see out of his unharmed eye either, could not speak through the pain.

"He lives," Aldbald said, as he looked back to Robert FitzWimark. "But he cannot fight anymore this day. He must be taken to safety."

FitzWimark glanced quickly at the English line breaking up around him. He grabbed a fyrdman who still stood his ground. "You there, let us offer a great service to the King. Hold this banner aloft. The remaining housecarls and I will defend this position for as long as possible." He turned quickly to Aldbald.

"Go, Aldbald! Take Harold to the woods where some of the camp followers can help you get him away. If we can hold this position just a little longer, the oncoming nightfall will save us, and Harold. Go now!"

Aldbald did not hesitate. He took a deep breath and hoisted Harold up. The position of the wounded man's hands made it difficult for Aldbald, but the younger man maneuvered slightly so that the king's weight was on his back. Moving as quickly as he could among other escaping fyrdmen, he reached the trees and was met by Lady Godiva herself. Aldbald was too intent on the King to be surprised at that.

"What has happened to Harold?!"

"King Harold is injured. I fear the day is lost." Finally noticing just which camp follower he was addressing, Aldbald grabbed the lady's wrist. "My lady, Godiva—" Aldbald lost his train of thought, lost even his sense of urgency. He stood motionless for a moment, but suddenly felt the weight of Harold. He dropped to one knee and laid the wounded man down. Harold groaned.

"My lady, you are in peril here! I must get you and the King away."

Lady Godiva bent over Harold, used the bottom of her mantle to wipe away some of the smeared blood oozing from between the man's fingers as he held his damaged eye. "Harold! My dear Harold!"

The groaning stopped for a moment, and Harold reached out one hand. "Edyth? Edyth?" he whispered.

Lady Edyth and a few others joined them. There was panic in her face as she watched the fleeing fyrd. "What has happened? Is Harold retreating?" Edyth asked, not recognizing the man in Aldbald's arms.

"The King is wounded!" Aldbald cried, his sense of urgency restored.

"Edyth!" Harold yelled through his pain.

"Harold!" Edyth Svanneshals pushed past Lady Godiva and fell to her knees with a cry, taking Harold's head in her lap.

Just then Gunthnot broke away from a group of fyrdmen and came up to Godiva. "My lady, the enemy has the field. My duty is to you now."

Aldbald recognized the man he had met in Normandy. "Gunthnot," Aldbald spoke quickly, "we must get the King and Lady Godiva safely away before the enemy breaks through the remnant of our lines."

As he spoke, Aldbald looked back to Robert FitzWimark's position. In the gathering darkness, Aldbald found he could still see FitzWimark, looked on in horror as he watched the Norman cavalry just then break through to Harold's half-Breton friend. Duke William and three other horsemen rode him down and literally cut him to pieces. The fyrdman standing next to FitzWimark was trampled by the Norman steeds. The Golden Dragon of Wessex fell to the mud, buried under the bodies of the last of the English housecarls.

Edyth could not take her eyes away from her love, but Lady Godiva's eyes followed Aldbald's gaze. "Oh, no!" she whispered. "It is over."

A contingent of Bretons were already making their way toward their position by the woods. Fyrdmen ran past them seeking protection in the darkness of the trees.

Gunthnot grabbed Godiva's wrist. "My lady, we must away." He reached with his other hand to grasp Aldbald's shoulder. "Aldbald, we must all get to safety."

Aldbald looked away from the battlefield, glanced back at Harold and Edyth, met the Lady Godiva's eyes. Godiva reached forward and touched Aldbald's hand in earnest.

"Yes, my friend, we must get the King away. Help us."

For a moment the battlefield receded and all of Aldbald's dreams suddenly materialized before him. He grasped Godiva's hand and sighed, remembering his first poem to the lady: Far above me, but before me.

"Yes, of course. I will help you get away...help the King get away." He lifted Harold once again, but hesitated, did not make a move to leave. Edyth stayed close to Harold in Aldbald's arms, but the other two had already taken a few steps away. They turned around as one, with the same question in their eyes.

Gunthnot scrambled back to Aldbald's side. "It is over, my friend. We must get away!"

"No, it is not yet over!" Aldbald leaned over to Gunthnot. "Take the King. Take King Harold to safety my friend!" He turned to Lady Godiva, caught a hint of his own reflection in her wide eyes.

"God's gift…perchance to meet under better pretense…Get yourself away from here, my lady!"

With that, Aldbald stepped away from Gunthnot and his King, looked away from the Lady Edyth, turned away from the Lady Godiva. Godiva could only stare wide-eyed at the young cottar. She too suddenly remembered a poem she had once received, a poem she thought had been written by the minstrel Davydd of Wales. She opened her mouth to speak, but Aldbald was gone and Gunthnot pushed her to move toward the cover of the trees.

Aldbald became intent upon the Bretons heading toward him. He picked up a discarded battle-ax. He would not normally have had the strength to heft the weapon, but just then his condition was not normal. He would realize later that he had drawn his strength from a battle madness. He did not go berserk with a lust for blood, however. Aldbald's madness was one borne of intense fear, not for himself but fear for the life of his King and the Lady Godiva. The young man swung the ax in a desperate attempt to offer a last protection to King Harold. Fleeing fyrdmen, strengthened by the sight of Aldbald's display and slightly shamed for their own actions, joined in a final struggle with the invaders. In the shadows of dusk, the charging Breton horsemen steered their animals into a ditch. Aldbald, with his battle-ax held high, led the group of Englishmen down into the ravine, where they slaughtered the Bretons as they struggled with their mounts.

Duke William dismounted his tired destrier after attacking the command point of the English line. The man they had mutilated was not Harold. William began a frantic look around him at the bodies heaped about. Count Eustace of Boulogne was already back on his own horse.

"My lord Duke, I do not believe Harold was here after all!"

"He must have been!"

"Perhaps through most of the battle. But now he may be off with the rest of the English retreating into the woods. There," and the Count pointed. "Some English are attacking the Breton cavalry! That may be Harold himself leading the counterattack, but I daresay we cannot do anything about it now. The night has come. I cannot see but a few feet in front of me."

"We need no light! The Almighty above will guide us!"

With that, William was back on his horse. "I want everyone in that counter-attack captured! Do you all hear me? After waiting two weeks for this battle, I will not have it end in a stalemate. I want Harold!"

Entry XVII

▼

In which William fails to find the Lady Godiva and Aldbald escapes

"And how are you feeling, my friend?"

"Fine." Aldbald's voice was almost too soft to be heard. The young man was actually far from fine. In a little under a fortnight in mid-September, Aldbald had stood in the middle of two of the most devastating battles England had yet known, and he on the losing side at each one.

The first had been bad enough, surrounded by men who's faces and ways were mostly unfamiliar to him. But, standing amongst the ranks of the English fyrd at the Battle of Hastings, watching their numbers dwindle by the minute, their line draw in shorter and shorter; this had been the hardest thing the Mercian had ever done. There had been so many men pressed in along the ridge, Aldbald knew not a one near to him save for King Harold. Yet, every man around him was an Englishman. They were his clan, his people. And he saw far too many of them die on Caldbec Hill.

In the many weeks that followed, Aldbald had found time to think long about how it had all come to pass. He could not help but feel he had somehow been the ill wind that brought the great Godwinssons to their downfall. Perhaps, he thought, the Devil had placed him beside both Tostig and then Harold. Why he should be the cause of harm to either of them, Aldbald did not know. But, he could not run away from the result: Tostig was dead, and Harold cruelly maimed, the other two of Godwin's sons destroyed. Aldbald wondered why the Duke of Normandy kept him alive and a prisoner, when he often wished that he himself were dead. Though all this was on his mind, he did not see how he might even begin to describe his feelings to his friend.

"It is good to see a friendly face, Caedwig. How is it that you gained permission to see me?"

Caedwig stepped through the doorway to the dirty prison cell. Despite Aldbald's mood and the sorry state of his surroundings, the monk smiled at the other man, squinting to focus on Duke William's prisoner. "You have an influential friend."

That got Aldbald's attention. "Harold? Have you come to me from King Harold?!"

At once the cleric's smile vanished. "No, my friend. Have you not heard after all these weeks as a prisoner of the Normans?"

Aldbald furrowed his brow. "Heard what?"

"Harold is dead."

"No!" The prisoner grabbed the monk's arms.

"I am sorry, Aldbald, but it is true."

"But, Edyth Swanneck—"

"Yes, she identified the body the very day after the disaster near Hastings."

"But, I saw him. I left him alive! His wound—"

Aldbald had only known one other man to have been blinded. Thom the tailor of Coventry did not survive either.

"No!"

Hearing of Harold's death was that which overspilled his cup. Aldbald
fell to the ground and wept. Caedwig knelt beside him and patted his
shoulders, let the man's tears run their all too short course. Aldbald sat
back up and looked intently at the monk.

"Tell me what other news I should know."

Caedwig sighed, "Where should I begin? So much has happened in the
past three months."

"If Harold is dead, is there no one to stand up and face the foreigners?"

"It does not appear so, I am afraid. The Duke of Normandy and his
army have been ravishing the countryside around London, but the man
has yet to take the city. Stigand the Archbishop of Canterbury has just this
week pledged his support to William. I am afraid that is just the beginning. The rumors I have heard are that the Archbishop of York, the young
northern earls, and with them Edgar the Aetheling, will capitulate as well,
if for nothing else than in the hopes the Normans will then stop their
plundering of the countryside. November has been truly the blood-
month, only the food for the winter was not up for the slaughter. Instead
it has been the English country folk this year."

Aldbald's face went white. "Caedwig, do you remember the new manuscript you let me see before I left England with Tostig Godwinsson? The
story of Beowulf, the great King of the Geats?"

"Of course, my friend."

"Beowulf did lose his life trying to slay a merciless dragon, and the
whole encounter was brought on by the simplest of actions. The dragon
was aroused by the stealing of an insignificant amount of the dragon's gold
by an impoverished man. Sometimes over the past few weeks, I have
thought of that story, and likened Harold to the King of the Geats. Now
that I know Harold is dead, I think of it again. I wonder if Harold was
fated to die, just as Beowulf believed he was." Aldbald was silent a
moment. "Do you think King Harold will be remembered as favorably as
is the great Beowulf?"

"I cannot answer that, my friend, but certainly none now in power in England will endow the writing of Harold's story."

Aldbald was quiet for a moment. "And what of Queen Edith, Harold's sister?"

Caedwig's intense look faded into a glazed, distant gaze into the dirt of the floor on which they sat. "Queen Edith was the first to submit to William, surrendering her Wessex properties at Winchester."

"No!"

"It is so, and it was I who guided Lady Edith to that end."

"Why, Caedwig? The loss of the ancient seat of the king's of Wessex would certainly come as a shock to the English people as well as help to build the confidence of the invaders! Is that not true?"

Caedwig hung his head low. "I daresay I was not thinking about England when I offered my guidance to the Queen. I was thinking only of Edith."

When the monk looked up and saw the confusion evident on Aldbald's face, Caedwig spoke softly. "Aldbald, think on it from Queen Edith's perspective. Within fourteen nights she had lost her four strong brothers: Tostig at York and then Harold, Gyrth and Leofwine at Hastings. And all this on top of Edward's death less than a year before, from which the woman still has not fully recovered! I suggested she capitulate to William in an effort to put it all behind, allow her to recover as best she could without the added cares of a drawn out struggle with the invaders. Perhaps it was not the best advice, but it was all I could think of at the time to ease her pain a little, and she did heed my advice. I delivered her myself to relative safety within the walls of a nunnery." Caedwig paused a moment, remembering the first time he conveyed the queen to the same nunnery many years earlier. This time, he expected, the woman he still loved would never leave her safe confines.

"What you have said about the loss of Winchester might surely have worked in William of Normandy's favor," Caedwig continued. "But, it seems passing strange that The Duke has not used that victory to his benefit as you might have guessed. He has moved in on London so cautiously, scouring the countryside in a roundabout way to the gates of the city. Since Hastings, no one has offered much resistance. Yet, it is as if Duke William is afraid of something."

"Or looking for something."

"What do you mean?"

"Since I was taken prisoner, I have seen men from the Duke on numerous occasions. The Duke of Normandy seems to think that I have information that he could use. Duke William appears to be interested in finding the Lady Godiva of Mercia. Because I spoke of her once in Normandy, I guess the Duke believes I can help him find her. I think he has gotten frustrated by my lack of offering anything of substance. No one has come to question me for a quite a few days now. Why he is looking for Lady Godiva, that I do not know."

"Perhaps it is because she is the one who organized the fyrd of Sussex, so that Harold had an army waiting for him when he arrived at Hastings. William may have learned this, and he may fear her as a threat to him. So indeed, his cautious approach may then be explained, because he is looking to silence something that he fears."

"That may be. I admit, I do not know of the Lady Godiva's whereabouts. But I will tell you, Caedwig, if I had the power to fulfill but one wish, I would choose to see my Lady Godiva one last time."

The light came back into Caedwig's eyes. "Your Godiva?" The monk teased Aldbald. Color came into Aldbald's face then as the young man blushed, and the monk smiled wide when he saw the other's pale complexion redden with embarrassment.

"I did not mean—" Aldbald stammered.

"Oh, do not apologize. I told you that I was sent here by a friend of yours. An influential friend."

"Yes?"

Caedwig leaned close and whispered, "It is the Lady Godiva of Mercia who has sent me to you."

"The Lady Godiva?"

"Yes, and—" the cleric jumped up and looked out into the hallway outside the small cell. "Oh my, I was supposed to give Gunthnot a little time, but I have sat here and talked far too long. Come with me. We may have only a short time now."

Aldbald did not move. "Come where? What is going on? The Lady Godiva sent you...to me?"

"Yes. Gunthnot, the Lady, and I have shared stories of secret letters and such. But, that is no matter now. If we are successful, you can discuss it at great length with the Lady herself this evening. Right now, we must away."

When the other man still did not move, the monk continued. "The Lady Godiva found a Breton soldier she had met in Brittany who was less than satisfied with how much plunder he had received from Duke William so far. She offered him a goodly portion of gold. In exchange, he agreed to take the guard duty over you and the other prisoners this day. For a little more gold, he agreed to let me in to see you. For yet a bit more booty, the guard promised to not notice the fact that, although only one monk arrived, there will be two who will leave these catacombs."

Aldbald hardly heard Caedwig's description.

"The Lady Godiva is here?"

"Yes," the cleric fought the desire to scream, "and she awaits!" Caedwig threw some cloth to the other man. "Hurry, take this extra habit and drape it around you as I wear mine. I have been talking too much, and we have not much more time."

"But, where will we go? What will we do?"

"Your first stop will be Waltham Abbey outside of London; but, I suggest you worry about that when the time comes. You may have to hide for awhile. But, then, I think all of England will need to hide from the Norman onslaught to come."

*   *   *   *

Hugh of Avranches stood proudly before the arrival of Duke William of Normandy. The young man, through his inordinately violent fighting against the English, had been knighted by Duke William on the battlefield amongst the piles of the dead. In the weeks that followed the Battle of Hastings, Hugh's new reputation had preceded him. Already his companions had dropped his title of the Fat in favor of the Wolf.

"My lord Duke William! It is good to see you today. It has been two weeks since you left us, and the men of your garrison here were beginning to get tired of the waiting! You have brought good news from London?"

William FitzOsbern dismounted alongside the Duke, spoke up first. "Good news indeed! The English have no taste for fighting us. I believe that, before the year is out, all the remaining men of influence in England will offer their submission to William."

Hugh the Wolf fell into step beside the Duke and William's seneschal FitzOsbern. Duke William was strangely quiet, and Hugh thought he knew why. "My lord Duke, what of this Edgar of whom I have heard? The one the English call the Aetheling. As a descendent of Aethelred, he will surely contest your right to authority in England, papal banner or no. Will he not?"

Again, the Duke made no effort to respond, and FitzOsbern replied to the question. "Edgar is nothing. If he proves to be troublesome and is foolish enough to hold out while the rest of the English in positions of power submit, then we will deal with him just as we dealt in the end with Conan of Brittany. Remember Edgar's own father Aedward who had been in exile in Hungary? How easy it was to slip a man into the confidence of the English gentry; how easy to swap a bottle of wine with the Duke's own bitter brew. William's influence does reach far, Hugh; but should any one man threaten William, then poison can once again be the first friend in the Duke's diplomacy."

As the three left the Duke's retinue behind, they entered a little room empty save for a wooden table and a small number of chairs, Duke William turned to glare at Hugh and spoke at last.

"Have you still learned nothing? Must I order a census of the entire country just to find one woman?"

"My lord Duke, I have found out precious little, or I would have sent word to you before now. I fear the language barrier makes it difficult to glean everything we might, but I truly do not think the prisoner knows much more than we do about the woman's whereabouts. There seems to be a confusion over where she comes from. At one point I was sure it was a town called Coventry, but then it seemed it must be Chester. I believe that the Lady Godiva must hold lands in both parts of the Midlands of England. From something the English man has said, I would wager that the main residence of the Earl of Mercia is located in Chester. Since you have told me this Godiva had been the wife of an earl, perhaps it is to Chester that the lady has fled."

"Perhaps." The Duke turned and slammed his fist into the wall. "Why? Why would the Lord grant me such a great victory, and then keep me from gaining full capitulation?"

Hugh asked, "Duke William, is it not true those that hold out in London will most likely offer you the crown of England?"

"That may be," William answered, "which means we may not have much time. Hugh, I may need to dispatch you to Chester."

"But, my lord," the seneschal FitzOsbern interrupted, "you may have beaten Harold, and London may be ready to submit, and soon you may even wear the crown of England. But, the English countryside has yet to be conquered. The land is full of hostile people, and no safe place through which to send young Hugh. Moving a force to Chester might take a little time."

"And I have no time to lose, Osbern! For now, the winter is upon us, and our army has been drastically reduced by death as well as with the garrisons I have had to leave throughout the southern part of the isle. We are in need of more men and many more supplies if we are to survive.

"But, if I were to be crowned King with someone such as this Lady Godiva by my side, then the English people might be mollified. Without that, how can I conquer this land? It might take many years! No, I will not believe my destiny is to rule an embittered people.

"Remember the flaming sword in the sky! We felt cheated in Normandy when the wind kept us from attacking England. Yet, see what we did learn? That same north wind brought the Norwegians down upon Harold's north country. He was forced to leave the shores he had guarded all year, just as we then were granted the south wind we needed. These things point to divine intervention, Osbern.

"Let us go and speak with the prisoner one more time." The Duke turned from the others and moved toward the door. "If we cannot learn what we need from this Englishman, then we'll kill him and be done with him."

Barging out of the room, Duke William collided with two monks walking quietly down the hall. The clerics were knocked off guard as well as off their balance. One caught himself against the other wall of the corridor, but his companion fell to the floor. The Duke himself, with momentum on his side, was practically unaffected. In a swift motion he reached down and gruffly lifted the fallen monk back onto his feet. As he did so, the hood of the cleric's habit fell back to reveal a young face framed by hair that was short, although still far from the usual tonsure of a monk. Duke William did not notice the clergyman across the corridor reach under his own habit to a weapon hidden within. With a look from the exposed cleric, the other man dressed up as a monk hesitated, leaving his small hand ax undrawn. Gunthnot wanted with all his heart to strike this foreign usurper; but at that moment, the safety of his mistress was even more important than the possible death of Duke William of Normandy. There was a silence that lasted but a moment, yet felt like an hour as the Duke gazed into the big blue eyes of Godiva. With the Duke's eyes still fixed on Godiva, he finally spoke over his shoulder to his seneschal.

"This is why I came to England!" The Duke exclaimed. No one moved, and the silence hung for another long moment.

"Osbern," the Duke laughed, "look at this young man of God! Tell me, would you ever find such a scandalous appearance on any monk of Normandy?" It was not a question that needed answering, and Duke William continued to talk. "Indeed not! I will admit to you now, I had thought that we stretched the truth quite a bit when we did proclaim to Pope Alexander that the English church needed cleansing. Now I do see that we may have well been right on the mark. I tell you, the Almighty God will be pleased with the work we do here in this land!"

"Yes, Duke William!" Hugh the Wolf laughed then, but the Duke was already moving past the clerics and further down the hall. William FitzOsbern was by his side, and Hugh pushed past Godiva and Gunthnot to catch up with the Duke.

The Lady's housecarl drew his hand away from his ax and wiped a bead of sweat from his upper lip. "My lady, that was close. I thought for sure we were found out!"

The Lady Godiva smiled as she too relaxed. "I too thought it might be the end of our sham! Good thing for us you have always heeded my signals, always listened to my commands! If you had drawn your weapon, we would have both been killed, and all of this might have been for nothing. I thank you once again for your loyalty, Gunthnot."

"My lady, dare I say we were lucky this time. It is clearly too dangerous for you here. I should have come alone!"

"Stop," Godiva snapped. "I alone know these corridors well, and we have not a moment to lose in this charade. If the true cleric in this conspiracy has done his job, Caedwig and Aldbald should be out of the cellars and heading to the bailey. We must meet them there or they will hesitate, perhaps come looking for us. We cannot let that happen. We cannot trust the guard we have bribed."

"My lady, I slipped the Breton you bribed some strong ale to celebrate his windfall. I daresay that guard will not have had the time for any second thoughts about his decision this night."

"Still, we must be gone as soon as we can! I will not be content until we are away."

"Nor I, my lady! The horses await in the trees outside. All we need is to pass through the gate."

Godiva put the hood over her head once again. "Then let us resume our playacting. We must meet the other two in monks' garb, and then we can be gone."

Epilogue

▼

"Will you hear my confession?"

Baldric kneeling at the altar, glanced around when he heard the voice in the room. He had come to the chapel to make his annual pre-Christmastide visit to the house of God to offer a prayer for those gone from the earth. He would not have been surprised to have seen someone else at the holy site, but he found he was shocked to see that he was addressed by the hermit.

Twenty years had passed since Duke William of Normandy was crowned King of England on the Eve of Christmas in the year AD 1066. Whatever was the exact time, many remembered that it was a year and a day after the death of King Edward when hardship and woe began to spread from war-ravaged southern England to the rest of the kingdom. In part to justify his search for the Lady Godiva of Mercia, William ordered that records be taken that would assess all the lands of England, notes that would in time become the Domesday Book, a judgment of the worth of all the lands in England. By 1070, William had nominally conquered even the north of England. It was soon clear that the arrival of the Normans was nothing like that of the Angles and Saxons many years before them. Where the Germanic peoples migrated, colonized, intermingled and expanded throughout England, the Normans invaded and stole the land. People throughout the country who had always thought of themselves as

-437-

simple villagers above anything else, soon learned what it meant to be English first, as the Normans and other foreigners moved in to take the lands William had given away as grants.

By 1086, William's census was compiled, and the lands of England given away completely, except for those areas which were laid waste and not fit for any to inhabit or worth anything to control. If the English people retained anything after the Norman invasion, it was their Germanic stubbornness that did not allow them to give in completely to the conquering race from the continent. The rulers of the island would be thought of as foreigners for some time to come; but the new generation of English were born to a people that recognized times had changed for the land. Even so, there were still left many places on the island where some English men and women could retire, could remove themselves from the trials besetting the land, and live in general seclusion. Some still watched the woods with a hopeful eye; but even so long after the invasion, no tree cut half-way up its trunk in the summer of 1066 had reconnected, much less budded and borne fruit.

The man known to the local villagers as Baldric had chosen two decades earlier to make a home for himself in the Welsh borderlands outside of Cheshire. Chester was the last city to surrender to the invaders from across the Channel. It was shortly thereafter that the Frenchman named Hugh the Wolf came, a man who had formerly been known as Hugh of Avranches, but who now used the title of First Earl of Chester. On the other hand, the hermit who had taken up residence in the small chapel at the cemetery outside of Chester was relatively new to the area. No one knew anything about the man, where he came from, or why he chose to wear the scarf about his head at all times. Baldric restrained an urge to pretend to be a priest, although he wondered at what kind of confession he might have heard.

"My good man," Baldric said, "I cannot hear your confession. I am not a man of God."

The hermit walked slowly down the short aisle to the altar. His robe was worn with age, Baldric could tell, but looked to be clean, which surprised the villager. The man behind the scarf must be old, Baldric guessed. Though his features were hidden, his walk was that of one who has seen many roads, many years. The hermit paused at the altar, made the sign of the cross and knelt with great difficulty beside Baldric, favoring his left knee as he bent down.

"Are we not all men of God?" The hermit's voice was strong, made Baldric believe his assessment of the man's age might be incorrect.

"Yes, of course. I meant only that I am no priest. I cannot forgive your sins."

"I am not so sure a cleric could forgive me my sins, either." The hermit sighed deeply, the scarf about his mouth rustled with his exhaled breath.

Baldric turned back to face the altar, still watching the other man out of the corner of his eye, trying hard to catch a glimpse of the man beneath the wrap. "We have lost much here in England over the past years, but let us not also lose our faith in God and his ministers on earth. Surely your sins are not so dastardly as to warrant such fear on your part. A truly penitent man is beloved of Jesus."

The reclusive one laughed so strongly, so suddenly, that Baldric jumped up from his perch.

"You surely sound like a priest, my friend," the hermit teased, but made no move to get up. Feeling foolish for having reacted in fear, Baldric knelt back down next to the other man.

"Perhaps it is due to my years spent in the company of monks."

"Indeed. Make no mistake, my friend, I did not mean any disrespect for the clergy. I only meant that it is from you I would seek forgiveness. Most all others I have known are gone."

"Why would you need my forgiveness? Do I know you?"

The hermit did not answer right away. He left Baldric searching again among the folds of the face scarf.

"When war and woe passed through our land, I fled. I fled with a woman whom I did love, with a woman I did marry. While England was overrun by foreign armies, I traveled abroad and did enjoy as much as possible all the days I had with my wife. Sometimes I feel a pain of regret that I did abandon England in its time of greatest need." The hermit turned to look through the slits in the scarf at the other man. "More often, I feel like I abandoned the people of England! I feel like I abandoned you, my friend."

Baldric stood up, stepped back from the altar, cautiously keeping his eyes on the hermit. "When did you abandon me? I think you mistake me for someone else, sir."

"Do I? Are you not Baldric of Cheshire, once known as Aldbald of Coventry?"

Aldbald's heart skipped a beat. No one had called him by that name since he had escaped from the prisons of William of Normandy so long ago. For almost twenty years he had lived with his wife in seclusion and anonymity. Who was this man to address him by his long dead persona? Though he had backed away, Aldbald realized there was no menace in the man. He stood over the hermit, asking the question that had been on the mind of everyone in the village for the past year since the strange man had arrived.

"Who are you?"

The hermit stood up, but his knee gave out under his weight and he fell backward to sit on the floor. Aldbald reached to help the man up, but the hermit waved him off with a laugh.

"Do not worry about me, my friend. I will just sit here a moment."

Aldbald crouched down on the cold earthen floor of the chapel beside the other man. Looking now straight into the hermit's face, he wondered how the man could see with the scarf wrapped so about his eyes. Aldbald waited, but the other man made no effort to speak.

"Who are you?" he asked again, softly.

Although his voice was his strongest outward feature, the hermit seemed now unable to speak. Aldbald was about to ask his question a third time, when the man reached up his right hand, untied the scarf on his head and slowly unwrapped the cloth. As the last of the wrap fell away, Aldbald gasped and stood up. It was not the wound on the hermit's face that startled him, nor was it that he thought he was seeing a ghost; rather it was the simple fact that Aldbald realized he did know the man after all. His shock quickly turned to sheer joy, but his excitement did not allow him to say anything but the man's name.

"Lord Harold!"

The hermit smiled at Aldbald. "Just Harold, and even that is more than I am known by now."

All Aldbald remembered of his last sight of Harold was blood all over his king's face. The arrow wound had healed better than Aldbald might have guessed it ever would at the time, leaving a scar from above Harold's eyebrow down to his cheek bone. If not for the horizontal lines of age across the man's forehead, the vertical scar would not be as pronounced as it was. The older man was clean shaven, and it was this lack of the man's ever-present mustache that most surprised Aldbald about Harold's appearance. Aldbald was transfixed, did not move until Harold laughed at the expression on his face.

"But, lord Harold...you are alive! You have been alive all this time?"

Harold was still laughing. "I daresay I must have been alive all this time to still be alive today."

"It is a miracle!"

"No, not a miracle. Merely the truth."

Aldbald crouched close to Harold. "Everyone thought you were dead. Where have you been all these years? For mercy's sake, Harold, tell me what happened to you!"

Harold's laughter had quieted. "There is not much to tell; and too much as well. Suffice it to say that I did survive the Battle of Hastings, thanks to you. My elegant Swan-neck told me it was you who delivered me from the field."

"Yes, but…Edyth? The monk Caedwig said that she had told the Normans you were dead. Even that she had identified your body among the fallen Englishmen!"

Harold sighed. "Indeed, and that allowed us to make our escape from England. As soon as winds were favorable enough, my children helped Edyth get me to Denmark. We stayed there long enough for my head wound to heal. Then Edyth and I traveled the continent, spent many wonderful years together, just she and I."

"And where is the Lady Edyth?" Aldbald glanced over his shoulder to the door as if he expected to see Edyth standing there.

Harold sighed. "Edyth is with the Lord above."

Aldbald bowed his head. "I am sorry, my lord."

"The Lord God took her as she slept one night, painlessly I believe, which was a mercy. I have come to recognize that old King Edward was more right than I had believed at the time. There are a lot of things beyond our control as human beings on this earth."

"So I believe as well, my lord." Aldbald nodded in agreement, watched the other man's good eye relive events the younger man could not imagine.

Harold's eye came back to focus on the other man. "Aldbald, I knew as soon as I was conscious after the battle against William, that I could never lead an army again. My eye was gone; and more. So too were my brothers. And I admit, gone also was my will to fight. Even so, I felt guilty. Then I was angry." Harold's fist clenched.

"Angry with God for everything that had happened."

"But lord Harold, surely you do not believe the Norman invasion was God's will?"

Harold's fist relaxed, and he sighed again. "No. Gildas had described our ancestors' invasion of Albion as the divine judgment upon the Britons for their sins. But I do not believe, as Edward probably would have, that the coming of the Normans was His punishment for the English. No. It was just the inevitable change that time does bring."

Aldbald reached out a hand to Harold's shoulder. "Then why come here seeking forgiveness, my lord?"

Through his one good eye, Harold could see the other man's look of confusion. "My friend, I came to find you, came to seek your forgiveness. I often felt like I left you alone on the battlefield. I did not want to leave this earth without thanking you for my life."

"You need not thank me, Lord Harold!"

The older man smiled. It must look comical, Harold thought, to have the villager calling the blind English hermit lord.

Aldbald continued, "Tell me more about your travels! How did you get away from England?"

"Let us leave that for another day, perhaps. For now, tell me something of your own life in these years since the invaders from Normandy landed. You mentioned our friend Caedwig! I found him still a simple monk, now staying with those at Waltham Abbey where I did visit first upon my arrival back in England. It was he that told me where I might find you."

"Yes, Caedwig has always been a good friend. We spent a year hiding at Waltham ourselves, letting settle some of the uproar following the Norman invasion before we ventured out into the countryside. My lord, it was not a pleasant sight to see. The land laid waste, the earthenwork ramparts and wooden fortresses dotting the countryside—"

Aldbald caught himself, stopped his description of the ravaged kingdom. "We made our way up to Chester, one of the last places to hold out against the Duke. My wife and I have been here ever since."

Harold leaned forward and grabbed Aldbald's wrist. "Do I know your wife?"

Seeing the look of keen interest on the older man's battle-scarred face, all at once it was twenty years ago, and Aldbald stood next to his King on the battlefield before the invading army. The younger man looked intently into Harold's one good eye, but was interrupted before he could speak by a woman's voice from the doorway to the chapel.

"Yes, Harold."

Both men turned to face Godiva at the door. She still did not look her age, the extra years only having thinned her somewhat from how Harold remembered her. He knew that there were a few wrinkles, and her overcoat did not cover the same youthful body he had known the woman to have. Still, her eyes were the same, and her hair, with wisps of gray, was just as dramatic as he remembered. The woman smiled and walked over to kneel beside Aldbald.

The younger man was suddenly embarrassed for his momentary resurgence of jealousy toward Harold, and it was Aldbald's turn to laugh. "Of course. You do remember the Lady Godiva of Mercia? We were married at Waltham, Lord Harold."

"Then we came to Chester where I still held lands and had some money," Godiva continued. "The land was soon given away to foreigners, but we were able to hide some gold away. Not much, mind you, but enough that we could see ourselves through the tough times after the invasion. We had to take on new identities to stay out of the Norman's dungeons. It seemed that all Englishmen needed to become lost in their own country to survive."

"I took up the trade of a tailor to have something to barter at the infrequent markets," Aldbald said. "We have prospered as well as might be hoped under the circumstances."

Harold only then released his grip on Aldbald, sat back and smiled. "Caedwig did suggest as much, and I hoped it would be true. And, you," Harold looked into Godiva's eyes, "are well?"

When Godiva did not answer right away, Aldbald spoke. "Lord Harold, my wife Godiva and I are fine."

Godiva leaned close to Harold. "I left you with Edyth so I could try and gather the fyrd together the day after the battle. But there was no band of housecarls to rally around. The fyrd could not fight the Normans alone. When the word was out that you were dead—", Godiva's statement trailed off. Neither of the others spoke, and the woman continued after a moment. "On many occasions I have wished that I had told you I carried no enmity for you in my heart. Getting you off the Hastings battlefield left no time to discuss such matters. Then you were dead."

A smile shattered Godiva's intensity then. "I had suspected something amiss with the Lady Edyth's proclamation that you were dead." She laughed. "It is good to know you did not die twenty years ago, Harold. I am at peace. Mayhap you are as well."

Harold's wounded face lit up. "And I am, then." Harold struggled to get up, finally making it with Aldbald's assistance.

"My lord, you will come home with us. Godiva and I have plenty of room. Please, come share our Yule log."

"No, my friend. Let us each go back to our lives. You to being Baldric, tailor of the Cheshire countryside, and me to being the nameless hermit who lives on the hill."

Godiva laid her hand lightly on the man's back. "Then you will stay here at the chapel awhile longer?"

Harold looked around him at the sparse furnishings in the small room. "Yes, it has been a reasonable place to be for the past year. I think it will be sufficient for the little time I have remaining on this earth."

Aldbald almost exploded. "No, lord Harold. Do not come back to life, then talk of dying once again, all within a few minutes of time!"

Harold bellowed his strong laugh. "All right, I will not speak of it. But neither should you speak of who it is that lives in this cemetery chapel." Aldbald started to protest, but Harold cut him off. "It will be better for all of us that way."

"Yes, I suppose so," the younger man spoke slowly.

Godiva and Aldbald watched the man fumble with his scarf. The great Harold Godwinsson, once Earl of Wessex and King of England, making ready to become the unnamed, untitled hermit. Aldbald felt a slight pain of pity, not for the older man, but for England and what his country lost at the Battle of Hastings. As Harold turned to go, Aldbald could not stay quiet.

"Lord Harold, know now that you are not forgotten in this land! I will write of your life and one day all will look favorably upon your reign as King of England."

The older man faced Aldbald again. "That is kind of you to say; but I daresay it will not be healthy to speak of Harold of Wessex in a Norman England. I do know, though, that no Norman king, no matter how long he might reign, will ever be as happy as I was as King of England for a year. Aldbald, my friend, I am content, whatever the histories will show."

"But, let me do something for you!"

"I need nothing, but I thank you for the thought all the same."

Harold's stiff hands hesitated. He looked back at Aldbald. "Perhaps you could do me one favor."

"Name it, Lord Harold, and it is done."

"Help me wrap this cloth about my head once again."